Fiddlehead

Tor Books by Cherie Priest

Fiddlehead

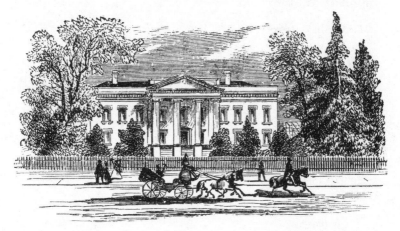

Cherie Priest

A Tom Doherty Associates Book *New York*

This is a work of fiction. All of the characters, organizations, and events portrayed in this novel are either products of the author's imagination or are used fictitiously.

FIDDLEHEAD

Copyright © 2013 by Cherie Priest

Edited by Liz Gorinsky

A Tor Book
Published by Tom Doherty Associates, LLC
175 Fifth Avenue
New York, NY 10010

www.tor-forge.com

Tor® is a registered trademark of Tom Doherty Associates, LLC.

Library of Congress Cataloging-in-Publication Data

Priest, Cherie.
   Fiddlehead / Cherie Priest. — First Edition.
       p. cm.
   "A Tom Doherty Associates Book."
   ISBN 978-0-7653-3407-7 (trade paperback)
   ISBN 978-1-4668-0789-1 (e-book)
   1. Inventors—Fiction. I. Title.
   PS3616.R537P75 2013
   813'.6—dc23
                                    2013018477

Tor books may be purchased for educational, business, or promotional use. For information on bulk purchases, please contact Macmillan Corporate and Premium Sales Department at 1-800-221-7945, extension 5442, or write specialmarkets@macmillan.com.

First Edition: November 2013

Printed in the United States of America

0 9 8 7 6 5 4 3 2 1

Acknowledgments

So here goes *Fiddlehead,* which is not exactly the end of the series—
but it brings us to the end of the war, at least, and perhaps it may be
the last full-length project in the Clockwork Century. For a while.

I am both a little sad and a little relieved at the prospect,
really; I love this series from the bottom of my heart, and I have
been terribly flattered, honored, and delighted by the response it
has garnered from the genre community. But at the same time,
twenty years of civil conflict is a very long time, even in a fictional
universe. I have always said, from the very beginning, that this
series should be the story of two nations on the cusp of what they
could withstand. This was always meant to be the story of how
the fictionalized war ends, and why.

And now . . . here it is.

But first and foremost, I must detail my undying thanks to
everyone at Tor—in particular my editor, Liz Gorinsky, who
first talked me into taking a chance on *Boneshaker* . . . and then
threw herself behind it with everything she had. None of this
would have happened without her. She believed in these books
when I believed they were maybe a little too wacky, a little too
unconventional; she encouraged and guided me through neuro-
ses, crises of faith, and other assorted potholes in the process,
and I cannot say enough to commend the persistence of her
awesomeness.

Next up, the inimitable Jennifer Jackson, my agent extra-ordinaire—my bottle rocket of fiery justice. From whip cracking to hand-holding, she's 100 percent weapons-grade awesome, and I seriously could not navigate the frothy waters of this industry without her.

And then there are the other usual suspects—so usual, in fact, that I fear I begin to repeat myself in these acknowledgments . . . because I pull open the last couple of books to take a peek (and remind myself of all those who've let me lean on them, all this time) . . . and I realize that I am hella-lucky to have found myself in such outstanding company.

Therefore, broadly and in brief (this time): a million and one thanks to Team Seattle and the Cap Hill Crew, Uncle Warren's Secret Service, all the lovely people (and visitors) at Woodthrush and Robin's Roost, the Nashville Brigade, the Consortium, Team Capybara and all its affiliates, and my spouse.

And of course, all the steampunks, alternate-history geeks, and other assorted amazing readers who've been kind enough to spend time with me on this bizarre and beautiful journey.

Thanks again, to all of you. Everywhere. Always.

Now this is not the end. It is not even the beginning of the end. But it is, perhaps, the end of the beginning.

—WINSTON CHURCHILL
November 10, 1942

Fiddlehead

Sally Louisa Tomkins stood her ground. She jerked her elbow free from the congressman's hand and refused to take even one small step toward the door. Instead, she planted her feet on the speaker's stand and turned on him, pointing a finger between his eyes. "I came here at your behest, Mr. Caperton, but I will not stand for your disrespect."

"Captain Sally," he tried, reaching for her elbow again, but missing, as the tiny dark-haired woman ducked out of his reach.

"Nor your condescension, thank you very much. I came to say my piece. I was *invited* to say my piece—"

From the second row on the left, Herschel Cobb interjected. "You were invited to discuss your hospital."

"And so I *am*," she fired back. "If you don't like my report, that's well and good. It's a terrible report, one that I hate to make— but my facts and figures are true! Gentlemen, we have an *epidemic* on our hands. One that the Robertson Hospital is neither equipped nor prepared to fight."

"Don't sell yourself short, Captain. We have great faith in you," assured Francis Pugh, in the third row on the right. He smiled indulgently, his muttonchops stretching across the wide expanse of his fleshy pink cheeks. "Your rank is testament to that."

She sneered, and took one measured step away from Boyd Caperton, who opened his arms as if he might ask her to dance.

"Apparently my rank is meaningless here." And before the gentle hems and haws of protest could rise loud enough to drown her out, she declared, "For nineteen years I've served the Confederacy. Nineteen years, I've made this work my life—taking no husband, bearing no children, and bankrupting myself in the bargain. I'd do it again in a moment, because it's *good* work. I've saved thousands of men. Tens of thousands, and still counting. I keep them clean; I feed them and bathe them and stitch their wounds, hold their heads while they bleed and cry. And most relevant to this testimony, *I watch them.* And I know what I've seen! You can't make this go away by pretending I'm a madwoman!"

Senator Landon Barksdale rose from his seat. "Miss Tompkins, no one is accusing you of being a madwoman."

"Yet you treat me like a liar or a scoundrel. And a fine irony that is, as I stand here before your *Congress.*" She spit out the word, and eyed Mr. Caperton, who hovered about her now as if he wasn't entirely sure how to proceed.

Praying that he wouldn't make another, more aggressive grab, Captain Sally turned her back and addressed the assembled men. "You sit there behind your little desks in your fine suits and act like you understand this war and these soldiers more fully than I do . . . but every last one of you knows better than that. Josiah Snead, I see you creeping toward the door like you're trying to escape me—*you,* sir. It was your son who picked up three bullets in Henegar; and everyone said he'd die, didn't they? But they got him to me, and where is he now? Home with your new grandson, unless I'm mistaken. And Wellers Chrisman, don't you hide your head. Your brother would've died without the attention he received at the Robertson. Morgan Cluskey, your father wouldn't be here without me. Charlie Hartridge, your nephew. Robert Batson, your sons—both of them!—still walk this earth because of *me.*"

She glowered at them, her gaze darting from face to face.

She knew them all, in some fashion or another. She'd received letters from many of them, begging, accompanied by money, all of them essentially the same: "They say this man is done for, but at the Robertson he may have a chance."

When they prayed to God, they prayed for *her.*

And still they treated her like a fondly regarded pet, a reliable watchdog, or a steadfast mule.

While she still had them stunned into uncomfortable silence, she lowered her voice, steadied it, and continued. "Out on the western coast, in the Washington Territory, a substance seeps from the ground—a toxic gas, which kills anyone who breathes it. But the people it kills don't lie down and rot. They walk, they hunt, and they feed. The gas is largely confined to a walled, partially abandoned city called Seattle, but its ill effects have scaled the walls and headed east in the form of a drug—sometimes called *sap,* sometimes *saffron*—which has become terribly popular with fighting men on both sides of the Mason-Dixon."

"Conjecture!" cried Morgan Cluskey, who sat back in his chair with an impatient sigh.

His sigh gave Boyd Caperton the nudge he needed. Caperton caught Sally's arm again, and this time, she could not shake him loose.

As he determinedly, carefully ushered her off the speaker's stand, she called out over her shoulder, "Men are dying—more men than I ever saved at the Robertson! And if you think"—she tripped over Caperton's foot, and recovered—"if you think it'll stop with the soldiers, with the poor men from the Southern fields and the Northern factories, you're idiots, every last one of you! The problem grows bigger every day."

"We're aware of this drug, Captain Sally," said Wellers Chrisman. "But it's a *Union* problem. Who cares if the illiterate Italians blast themselves senseless?"

Frantic now, she grabbed the edge of a table. That bought her another few seconds while her escort tried to figure out how to more forcibly accost a lady without being too ungallant in front of God and everybody.

"Exactly how many *Union* soldiers do you think I treat at the Robertson, Mr. Chrisman? It's *our boys, too,* and we've got fewer of them to lose. Take off your blinders and take action while there's still time. Gentlemen, the world will judge us by the steps we take right now. The whole globe is in danger!"

Her grasp on the table edge failed. She lost a few steps, then caught herself on the door frame. But before Caperton pushed her out with absolute finality, he bowed his head so that his lips came close to her ear, and his breath lightly tousled the stray curl that dangled there. "Captain Sally, you put us in a difficult position."

She turned her head so fast that it cracked his face. "More difficult than mine?"

He let go of her, then, so he could hold his nose, waiting for it to start bleeding. It didn't, so he removed his hand. "This isn't a problem of war. It's a social issue."

"It's a disease!" She tried another angle, pleading now. "A disease spread by soldiers, not so different from cholera or typhoid. That makes it an issue of war, does it not?"

"Not on the word of one nurse."

"One nurse, fine. What about two? What about a dozen? A thousand? How many nurses will it take, Mr. Caperton?"

"You're missing the point. Bring me a doctor, and let him testify. In the meantime, the Confederacy thanks you for your service, but you must return to your duties and let the men run the war."

"Which you've done a bang-up job of thus far."

He didn't answer. He only shepherded her through the last great door and shut her out of the proceedings with heavy, slow calmness.

He leaned against the door then, holding it shut even though she no longer pushed or knocked. All eyes were on him. He wiped at his nose once more, in case it'd begun to bleed after all. But no. He was not injured, just unsettled. He cleared his throat. "Gentlemen. Now that the matter is resolved, let us return to business."

The room sighed its relief with a rustle of papers and the creaks of men shifting in their seats, suddenly more at ease. The fifteenth Congress of the Confederacy was in session still, in its enormous hall with gilt ceiling, leaded and colored glass windows, and polished wood trim—all designed to advertise and reassure that Danville was not finished, and certainly not broke.

In the far corner, a young man still in his teens wrote feverishly, recording the minutes in his cleanest Pitman shorthand. He captured every word faithfully, scrawling like a phonography racehorse, noting the last bits of the tense exchange between Captain Sally and Congressman Caperton. He even dutifully included the muttered gripe of Robert Welch, who'd complained, "Shouldn't have let a woman address the floor in the first place, rank or no rank. Let her take her pride in it, but give her no privileges apart from cashing checks."

Above and behind the stenographer, on the second-story balcony that ran around the congressional hall, a board creaked under a finely heeled boot, and a spindly white cobweb was swept aside by the long hem of a cotton skirt.

This woman did not approach the floor, but withdrew from it, leaning back among the shadows that had hidden her thus far. She did not want to talk to the men. She'd come to see Captain Sally, though the captain did not know it. Now that the fireworks were finished, this woman took her leave exactly as she'd arrived: in silence and darkness, with a widow's veil to hide the smile that spread coldly across her face.

But she had not gone unnoticed or unrecognized.

In the back row, seated beside the stenographer, a man collected his belongings, sorting his papers and straightening them before slipping them into a satchel, as if he were any other clerk wrapping up his business.

He was no clerk. Nor was he a congressman, senator, or any other party to the CSA.

As he retreated from the seat he'd borrowed from an absent legislator, he mentally composed the telegram he'd send within the hour.

KATHARINE HAYMES IN DANVILLE STOP PLEASE
ADVISE

One

Gideon Bardsley was working in the basement of the former Jefferson Hospital, which had been converted into the science center that housed his laboratory, when the first window broke. He heard the brittle sound of glass being strategically shattered, but he did not turn off the machine. Instead, he glanced at the dial beside his hand. Its tiny needle leaned hard past the yellow warning threshold, and tapped against the red zone.

A second window broke upstairs.

He rejected the reflex to look up at the basement door. Looking at the basement door would not tell him anything he did not already know—nothing he could not discern from the sounds of motion upstairs. Two intruders, at least. Entering from the western side of the building. Not close yet; not even in the correct wing of the disused hospital space. But coming.

He had time, but not much.

Gideon reached for a large glass knob and turned it carefully, but as quickly as he dared. He checked the dial again. Its needle careened farther to the right, fully in the red, but fairly stable. The lever on the left would activate the printing apparatus upstairs. He pulled it.

He needed an answer, and he needed it *now*.

The mighty computational engine strained and hummed, its gears and chains struggling against the request. At the rear a fuse

fizzled and popped, but did not blow; a circuit objected with a fit
of sparks, but held steady; a row of lights flickered, but did not
go out.

Now Gideon looked up at the basement door. He stared at
it. Hard. And he willed the system to work the way he told it to—
please, just this once, if never again.

Three seconds passed. He knew because he counted.

Click.

Whir.

A blue-green glow sparked to life on the machine as a thin
line of watery light pooled through the crack where the bottom
of the door met the top stair.

"*Yes,*" Gideon breathed, but he did not smile. Turning on the
apparatus was not the hard part. It was the first hard part.

The printer was far too large to share the basement with its
companion device, which occupied two-thirds of the downstairs
floor space. Ordinarily this was a source of great irritation for
Gideon, who would've been much happier to have everything in
one room, or at least on one level, preferably at a quarter of the
present size. But just this once, it was a good thing.

So long as everything worked. And sometimes, it didn't.

The lines, wires, tubes, and lumpily soldered joints that connected the two machines were strung through holes in the ceiling
and floor, carrying more information at a greater speed than any
such wires were ever expected to bear. They twitched, sparked,
and jerked as electricity surged from the master device, deposit-
ing Gideon's answer into the printer's circuits, where the information sorted and arranged itself.

And then the printing apparatus began to translate the electric
and magnetic impulses from the mechanical brain in the basement
onto paper.

The nimble, spindly lead keys clacked slowly at first as rows
upon rows of them rallied for the task, pressed themselves against

ribbons of ink, and banged down on the paper receipt with sticky gravitas. Then the rhythm rose in volume, the noise soaring into something loud and rumbling, like the gravelly grunt of a diesel engine.

A tremendous roll of paper, bought from the *Washington Star-News,* unspooled within the printer's belly. The apparatus dutifully pressed its message on the newsprint, and through a slot that emptied into a basket it spit out paper covered with whatever the brain downstairs commanded.

He grabbed his grandfather's coat off the back of a chair he never had time to sit in, and donned it with a fast hitch of his shoulders. He also seized a cast bronze plaque created as a gift by former president Abraham Lincoln—not for sentimental reasons or because the plaque was as valuable as the coat, but because it praised and identified Gideon's greatest creation.

A series of heavy blows battered the door to the laboratory upstairs, but Gideon was finally smiling. He already had a plan— plans were never the problem. Time to execute them was more often the difficulty.

He dashed up the stairs in a hurried tiptoe that muffled his steps, opening the basement door with care to keep it from squeaking.

Whoever was trying to get inside through the reinforced main door had discovered his folly, or so the scientist assumed. That particular portal was lined with lead, and fastened to the wall with hinges made to hold a firehouse door.

Gideon checked the paper basket and said, "Excellent!" Before his eyes, the basket filled and then overflowed with a billowing flutter as the paper kept coming, covered with facts and figures of such outstanding volume that it surprised even the man who'd demanded them, knowing the answer would not be brief. And knowing it would not be good.

Apart from the printer's clatter, he heard only silence.

The intruders had given up on the door, but it wouldn't take them long to come around the side and realize there was another way into the office.

Crash.

Not long at all.

The breaking glass of his office window was followed by the scrape of an arm, cleaning out the frame and pushing the shards to the floor. After this came the crush of feet on the scattered fragments, and the grinding sound of heels turning the glass to dust.

Gideon picked up an armful of paper and scanned it. His eyes widened.

A man called out, "This way! I see him!"

Without lifting his attention from the printout, Gideon kicked the office door shut, then twisted the lock. It wouldn't hold forever—not nearly as long as the main entrance. But he needed more time. The printing apparatus wasn't finished. It spewed its contents without pause, flinging more and more and more still into the basket, faster than Gideon could empty it.

The heavy thump of a big man's body shoved hard against the side door. Then three shots—something high-caliber, something that could punch holes in a body or blow away a lock. The fastener held through the fourth round. Gideon was not dealing with the world's greatest sharpshooter.

A booted foot kicked the door open with a bang.

The printing apparatus wasn't finished yet, but Gideon told himself that this much would suffice—it was enough to give him his answer, and, if he was very lucky, it might even be enough to make his case.

The stacks of numbers were so fresh they smeared ink across his palms as he hurriedly seized them and bundled them together. In the office doorway, a man with a red bandana over his face and a gun in his hand shouted, "Get away from that machine!"

Irritated at the interruption, Gideon tore off the printed paper and gave its dangling, still-growing edge a rueful look before hefting the bulk of the printout. He crushed it in his arms, holding it between himself and the gunman.

In the brief pause that followed, he let Lincoln's plaque slip quietly from his grasp, hidden by the crinkled, fluffy mass of wadded paper.

It fell.

And at the moment the plaque landed atop the printer's console, Gideon flung himself behind a table and used his hip to knock it over. He dropped down for cover as the gunman opened fire. Two shots plunked into the heavy oak, which banged against the scientist's elbows as he twisted, rolled, and folded the paper into a more manageable mass. Meanwhile, someone fired another shot, maybe more. It was hard to tell them apart over the rattling industrial clank of the printer's keystrokes.

A second set of footsteps joined the gunman, and two more bullets went wild. Maybe both of them were terrible shots. Something to keep in mind, but it didn't mean he could disregard them. They only needed one lucky shot between them.

"Back there!" The first man pointed. The upended table rocked again as another volley dug a row of deep, splintering holes.

Behind the incessant clatter of the still-pounding printer keys, he thought he could hear the intruders reloading. Even if it was his imagination, it was only a matter of time before they fired again. He needed a way out.

Several plans presented themselves from his vantage point. He sorted and prioritized them according to likely cost versus success rates.

The men stood between him and the stairwell door, but that was fine. He didn't want to lead them down there anyway.

No. Behind him. The trapdoor to a storage cellar. That'd be a better option. It had once been part of the basement, before the basement had been finished out for Gideon's work. The old hospital was a rabbit warren of such places, and he knew them all, having studied the blueprints before establishing his professional headquarters.

Of course, the cellar's exterior door may or may not have been barred from outside, closed up fast against storms or burglars. There was always the chance that choosing this escape route would render him a fish in a barrel, but he ran the odds in his head and was reassured. Despite the risk, this was his best chance, both for preserving his equipment and for escaping the facility unseen.

Gideon jammed the unwieldy bundle of paper under his arm and glanced about for something to tie it with. Nothing obvious presented itself, so he dropped that idea. He'd have to carry it unsecured. A little noisy, and a little inconvenient, but not impossible.

"Is this the Fiddlehead?" one of the men shouted to the other over the cacophony of pounding keys.

"I don't know! What does it look like?" came the uncertain reply, meaning they hadn't yet seen the strategically relocated plaque.

Behind a counter over to his right, Gideon spied a jar of aluminum powder. His eyes narrowed, swiftly scanning the room until he remembered that the potassium chlorate was in the cabinet behind it.

"Science to the rescue," he mumbled as he scooted on his knees and one hand—the other clasping the wadded sheaf of paper against his chest—across the floor and toward the aluminum.

The intruders must have heard him . . . maybe only a rustle of his old coat and the fast scrape of his boots as he scrambled out of the way, but they fired in that direction anyway, aiming wherever they guessed he might be heading.

They didn't hit too close. The noise from the printing apparatus disoriented them. Sometimes Gideon forgot how unsettling it could be to people who weren't accustomed to it.

He ignored it, fully and happily embracing the sound as cover as he knocked over a chemistry set on a repurposed tea tray. More confusion. More gunshots. But here was the aluminum. He'd have to stand for just a second to get the chlorate.

He put the printout down by his leg. He'd need both hands for this.

He closed his eyes and mentally checked the layout of the cabinet; he knew everything in it, every bottle on every row. Positioning himself as close to the right spot as possible, he counted back from three . . . two . . . one . . . and reached up to pop open the small door, hoping like hell that the morons with the guns wouldn't shoot up the contents and blow them all to Maryland.

He nicked the bottom edge with a fingernail and the metal door flipped open. With a turn of his wrist, he seized the potassium chlorate without looking, simply trusting his memory.

To his casual delight, his palm was not aerated by bullets.

Over by the printer, his visitors had finally stumbled upon the plaque he'd left behind, which stole their attention at a convenient moment.

"Look at this!"

"What is it?"

"It's a sign, see? This goddamn piece of junk . . . it *is* the Fiddlehead!"

Gideon objected to the "junk" part, but not *too* strongly, given that these people couldn't tell a sophisticated calculating device from a relatively mundane printing apparatus. "Idiots," he mumbled softly as he unscrewed the powder's lid.

"It's huge," one gunman correctly observed.

"Sure is making a lot of noise."

While they talked over the printer's racket, Gideon found an empty measuring glass and filled it with the aluminum powder. Then, with exceptional care, he added the chlorate.

"Don't worry about it: It's only noise, not a weapon or nothing. Now where'd that nigger get off to?"

Gideon paused, lifting an eyebrow. "Just for *that* . . ." He reached over his head, jabbing his fingers into the cabinet again, this time nabbing a vial of sulfur. With a gentle tap, he dumped the yellow substance into his mix, jostled it oh-so-gently, and turned once more to the map in his mind.

Now he needed a spark.

He considered the printing apparatus. He mentally examined the console and dismissed it, knowing it was too well sealed. The most obvious target was across the room where the wires emerged from the basement. They were hot now, their uninsulated ends casting small fizzes of light all along the switch box.

The printer slowed. Its keys pounded down with less regularity, coming to the end of its instructions, to the very end of the answer Gideon needed . . . and the room fell quiet.

Even Gideon's ears were ringing, so he knew how strange the silence must feel to the men who weren't accustomed to the outstanding drone of the metal keys. Still, he'd have only a few seconds while they shook their heads and found their bearings and a few seconds more than that before their ears calmed down enough to hear the hum of the big machine downstairs.

He couldn't let them notice.

"You got the dynamite?"

Gideon's back straightened when he heard that word. He didn't like it. Should've expected it. But would have to work around it now, and analyze the meaning of it later. His brain needed to stay on track, just the *one* track, which he'd narrowed down from many.

He retrieved the paper, bundling it up under his arm and clamping it against his ribs. He tore off a blank strip from the edge, wadded it into a ball, and used it to stopper the small glass cup.

The sound of tearing paper got the gunmen's attention again. One of them shouted, "He's over there!"

But before the words were out of the man's mouth, Gideon was on his feet. He flung the glass across the room and immediately turned his back, dropping back down behind the table.

His aim was better than the gunmen's, and his concoction was true. The glass shattered against the fuse panel and the powdered mixture exploded—and the room went blank with fire, a blinding chemical light, and a terrible smell.

It threw a shadow so strong that Gideon squinted, even though he was crouched down on the floor and facing the other direction.

"My eyes! Jesus Christ, my eyes!"

"He had a bomb!"

"Give me your dynamite!"

"I can't see! I can't see anything!"

"I can, a little bit—give me your sticks!"

The idea of two half-blind fools playing with dynamite was not the sort of thing to make a man dally, so while the gunmen struggled with their explosives, Gideon seized the trapdoor ladder and withdrew into the unfinished cellar. At the bottom he kicked the final rung, bringing the ladder down with him. If the gunmen wanted to follow him, they could jump and break a leg.

He climbed the steps to the exterior door and unlocked it, shoving it with his upper back. It was heavy, but it wasn't barricaded from the other side. He knocked it open and stepped out into the crisp November night.

His breath clotted in the air, and the stars looked like ice. He was free, and his unwelcome guests didn't know it yet.

But had the unwelcome guests brought company?

Gideon gently let the door fall shut behind him.

He stayed close to the building for now, sticking to the shadow of the eaves and hustling toward the front of the old facility, ducking down away from the windows and putting as much distance between himself and the laboratory as possible.

The men had brought dynamite. Their mission was sabotage—and possibly espionage as well, but he didn't think so. Only seven people had ever seen the Fiddlehead, and none of them could've used it if their lives depended on it. Only Gideon could coax it into its calculations. Only Gideon understood it, and there were days when even he was stunned by what it could do. No, even if someone, somewhere knew precisely what the device was for . . . there wasn't another scientist in the world who could operate it. He would've bet his life on it.

Therefore, whoever sent the men didn't want to use the Fiddlehead. They wanted to destroy it.

Behind him, a blast shook the night—a terrible percussion that rocked the building and made the earth beneath his feet rumble unsteadily, like the ground might open up and swallow him. He staggered forward, adjusting for the quake and hunkering as he moved, bracing himself against the shingles and other bits of small debris that followed him.

When the last of it had settled, he heard nothing. Not the two men talking, not anyone chasing after him. Not even his own feet as he started to run.

Eventually his hearing caught up to him, and his head echoed with a high-pitched hum. He shook it, trying to cast the buzz out of his ears like so much water after a swim. The hum wavered but stayed, keeping him company as he cut across the lawn, past an old fountain that had been dry for decades. He turned through an overgrown gate, pushing past the vines that knitted the old garden exit shut, stumbling briefly as his boots tangled in a brittle patch of rose briars.

Past the garden and into the woods he went, though the woods were almost too swampy to call them that. His feet splashed through puddles left by the recent rains, and the half-frozen water soaked between his toes. He held the papers up high, sometimes over his head if he was afraid of falling.

The woods thinned quickly and gave way to a road with two wide lanes and intermittent traffic. Some of the carriages and carts boasted those new combustion engines that were all the rage. Gideon liked the noise of engines more than he liked the chatter of people or the whinnies of horses, even though it all meant the same thing: civilization. Some element of safety, he supposed, assuming that no one intended to murder him in front of witnesses. And how likely was that? He couldn't say.

He crossed the road, letting the traffic flow between him and the hospital. Here and there, over the dull ringing in his ears, he heard people asking one another what that loud sound might have been—Was it an explosion, do you think? Was it artillery?—for the D.C. population always had a good reason to be nervous. Now more than ever, he supposed, when Southern spies with dynamite were running about, blowing up advanced technology willy-nilly.

With a bit of distance from the hospital, Gideon played the scene over in his head one second at a time, examining every detail as he walked a road he usually traversed in a horseless carriage belonging to Mary Todd Lincoln and driven by his old friend Harrison.

As he hiked, he reviewed his information. He assessed the details and considered the motives.

The intruders had absolutely planned to kill him. Why destroy the Fiddlehead only to let its creator survive to build another one? Men who didn't know what such a machine could do probably wouldn't know how preposterous the idea was: Gideon could build another Fiddlehead, yes, but not without a vast sum of money and several years at his disposal. His life's work could not be conjured back into existence with the blink of an eye, but it could be conjured eventually.

So, yes, his life was in danger—that much was certain. But in danger from whom? He had assumed that the saboteurs were Southerners, but upon reflection that may not be correct. Regional accents were dead giveaways, in Gideon's experience, and although one of the men might have come from the South, the other one was definitely a northeastern coastal resident.

Mind you, a Northerner still could've been hired by the CSA. Allegiances shifted across state lines every day, and mercenary loyalties came with price tags, not regional fidelity.

He couldn't be sure. This made him unhappy, because he liked to be sure at all times, of as many things as possible. It made for better plans.

That having been said, he *was* sure that it was well over two miles back to the Lincoln house. His feet were cold and wet and he didn't want to walk, but there wasn't much choice. He had no immediate means of contacting anyone, and he carried no money for the purposes of flagging down a carriage and buying a ride.

He disliked money on general principle. It had its uses, but it seemed insubstantial—entirely too false. Little more than a promise on a piece of paper, written by dead men, miles and years away. Paper could burn, and paper could lie.

But the paper under his arm did not lie. It crinkled and crackled, urging him onward. Reminding him of what was at stake.

One foot in front of the other, he trudged along the road's edge, every step leaving his toes a bit more numb. It wasn't late, and the night still had room to get much colder; everything might freeze, he thought. If there was one single, solitary thing he missed about southern Alabama, it was the unimpressive winter weather.

(He missed it only fleetingly, and with some private disgust.)

There was never any question of where he might go now.

Home? Certainly not. It was even farther away than the Lincolns' house at the edge of Capitol Hill. Besides, what would he do there? Sleep? Wait for morning, for a more reasonable hour to demand an audience?

He wished he had a bag or a satchel to hold the papers. Every few yards he adjusted them, squishing the unspooled document tighter and making sure nothing trailed on the ground behind him. He didn't know how much he'd lost to the intruders' interruption. Every surviving line was more precious than diamonds, but the cumbersome bundle drew stares from drivers and passengers, and from the men and women on their own trips home from a factory shift or an evening's meal on the town.

A line of shiny black vehicles came roaring up toward him, brightly lit from within and spewing odd-smelling diesel fumes. All of them built with technology stolen—or, more likely, purchased—from the Texians, and spreading across the continent with speed that couldn't bode well for the Confederacy. Texas tech was one of their last remaining advantages, and it, too, was slipping from their grasp.

This thought made him smile glumly as he plodded forward. His feet had become blocks of ice, and his hands gone likewise numb. His gloves were back at the old hospital in the basement somewhere, lying atop the Fiddlehead. Had the roof held, or had the dynamite brought the whole wing crashing down upon the calculation engine?

Gideon's pace slowed, then picked up again. Worrying wouldn't change whatever facts awaited him back there, and he couldn't return to find out. Not until morning, he suspected, and maybe not even then.

If the Fiddlehead survived, then it must survive as a secret.

He squinted against brilliant pairs of front-facing lamps. As one of the cars passed him, he heard laughter within. And music. Someone had brought a violin, and someone else was playing a fife. Despite the cold, some of the carriages had left their windows down, and as they rolled past, Gideon smelled expensive food and perfume, and alcohol and tobacco.

Somewhere in the city, a ball or some other gala event had just ended, and a beautiful room filled with finely presented tables was emptying, which meant that Mrs. Lincoln might not be home yet. She often lingered at these things, partly by her own preference and partly because she served as her husband's social eyes and ears, for the former president rarely left the house since his near-fatal injury at Ford's Theatre. It was too trying, he said; too much trouble for other people to accommodate him. So he kept to his own home and his own grounds, which had been altered to better suit his needs.

Gideon kept his eyes open on the off chance Mrs. Lincoln's buggy might pass by and he could flag her down, but it was not his lucky night. He walked the full distance, and by the time he reached the Lincoln estate his legs were heavier than lead.

So far as estates went, it was a surprisingly modest one—at least from the exterior; the inside was filled with expensive gifts collected over the years from dignitaries near and far. The house itself was a simple two-story home with two wings, and a lift inside, for the president could not ascend stairs without immense assistance. Also due to Lincoln's mechanized chair, all the outdoor paths were paved.

Gideon almost tripped over the first walkway he passed. He might have cursed except that he was so relieved to have arrived. Lights burned up the hill at the homestead, giving him more than the nighttime sky or traffic to navigate by. He homed in on these electric torches, drawn like the moths and mosquitoes that hovered around the devices in a buzzing cloud. Up the half-dozen stairs he climbed, bypassing the ramp because it was less direct. Even after his long, cold hike, he was more impatient than tired.

The front door opened before he could knock, and there stood a confused-looking Nelson Wellers.

Mr. Lincoln's personal physician was a gaunt young man with a cadaverous complexion. He was quick and capable, but he always wore the expression of someone carrying the weight of the world. Friendly enough despite his nervous disposition, he was well liked and trusted, even by Gideon, who had worked with him before. Together they had designed and perfected the ex-president's wheeled chair, as well as some of the other tools that made life easier for the badly crippled politician.

"Gideon!" Nelson cried. "There you are—thank God!"

"Not a greeting I get every day."

The doctor reached out and grabbed the scientist by the coat lapels, drawing him bodily inside and shutting the door behind them both. "We just heard about the explosion, and Ephraim said there was no sign of you out at the Jefferson building. I was on my way to . . . to . . . to see if I could find you, I suppose. Did you *walk* all the way back?"

"Yes."

"Dear God, it's *freezing* out there."

"No, not quite."

From the parlor doorway, a woman gasped. "Oh, Mr. Bardsley!"

Gideon threw her a nod, but did not make eye contact. "Polly," he greeted the household lady-in-waiting, as Mrs. Lincoln often called her. One part maid, one part nurse, Polly Lockhart was a girl of mixed and indeterminate race—more white than otherwise. She was stout and small, much like the former first lady herself. She wrung her hands together, so they'd have something to do besides flutter.

"Dr. Wellers was just about to go looking for you."

"So he says."

The doctor went to the nearby liquor cabinet and poured himself a stiff draught of very good bourbon, then offered one to Gideon, too. He shifted his bundle of paper and accepted the glass, knowing better than to hope it'd warm his feet, but appreciating the gesture. The beverage and the crystal service set beside it were a gift from a French ambassador, and easily worth more than his niece. He knew, because ten years ago he'd bought her freedom when he couldn't steal it. The cost of the furnishings could have brought many more families across the line. The math filled his head but did not make it spin. Very few things could accomplish such a feat, least of all numbers.

Gideon downed the drink and watched the new electric lights sparkle through the damp crystal.

One of Polly's fluttering, fretful hands touched his arm. "What happened out there?" she asked. "Can I help you with your . . . with this . . . package?"

"No, Polly. I've got it under control. Two men broke in," he answered her first question, handing the glass back to Nelson and glancing at his feet. He still couldn't feel them, but he watched as they dripped and oozed a large damp spot on a very expensive rug from somewhere in the Ottoman empire.

"Are you sure you aren't hurt?" the doctor tried again, scrutinizing Gideon with a professional appraisal that was already telling him that all was well. "Can Polly take your coat?" he asked, his dubious tone suggesting he already knew the answer to that, too.

"No," Gideon replied, a little too quickly. "No, I'll just sit a minute by the fire, if you don't mind. I need to see Mr. Lincoln." He squeezed the printout. It felt strange, like it had shrunk on the way from the hospital. But it'd only become crushed as he'd kneaded it down, over and over again, making sure he didn't drop it. "He needs to see this. *This* is what they came for."

He barely heard the faint motor hum of the president's chair approaching, but he did hear it because he expected it, and he listened for it.

Nelson Wellers stood aside, and Polly withdrew to the edge of the room. Gideon stayed where he was, and the sixteenth president of the United States rolled into their midst.

His chair was a marvel of science, the only one of its kind. Propelled by an electric motor, it was manipulated with small levers and buttons, customized for the old man's long, slender hands. Those fingers, which had once signed laws into being, were crumpled now, bending and unbending only with great effort; but they were firm on the steering paddle as he brought himself forward.

This was the man who would've freed Gideon's family, if he'd had the chance. If the bullet hadn't blown his head almost in two, leaving him a stiff, twisted figure made of scars and odd angles. He was a hero. That made Gideon a hero by proxy, so far as his mother and brothers were concerned. His mother told everyone about it: how her boy worked hand in hand with the great leader, coming into his house through the front door like a proper gentleman. Her gushing pride embarrassed him for complicated reasons—reasons he never shared, because they would've only confused her.

Abraham Lincoln gazed levelly at the scientist with his one good eye. "Gideon, you did it."

Not a question, but a statement of certainty. Abraham Lincoln liked to be certain, almost as much as Gideon did.

"Yes sir, but this is all I could save. I needed more time."

"We always do." The former president nodded solemnly, his thin frame bobbing softly in the narrow black suit he so often wore. "It will have to be enough." He gestured toward the library, and turned the chair to face it. "Polly," he called over his shoulder. "Could you bring Dr. Bardsley a pair of slippers? Something from my closet, to wear until his boots are dry."

"Yes, sir. I will, sir."

To Gideon, he said, "You can take those off, and we'll put them by the fire. Your feet must be miserable."

"Yes, they are. Thank you, sir." He followed the chair he'd helped build, and Nelson Wellers fell into step beside him.

Speaking over his shoulder again, for he could not easily turn his head, Mr. Lincoln said, "I'm glad to see you escaped unscathed, Gideon. When we got word of the blast, I feared the worst. But Ephraim said he didn't see any sign of you, not in the rubble— or in the basement either, when he dropped a lantern down there. You barely missed one another. He rode out on horseback and only just returned. You made awfully good time on those frozen feet of yours."

Gideon didn't hear any of it after the part about the lantern. "The basement? So the floor held? Is the Fiddlehead intact?"

"The floor held. Your printing apparatus is so much scrap metal, I'm afraid, but as for the Fiddlehead, I do not know. Ephraim couldn't say. There was a great deal of debris, and dust, and smoke too, I think. There was a small fire, but it was quickly brought under control."

"But there's a chance . . . ?"

"There's always a chance." He reached the library and maneuvered the chair through its doorway. "But we won't know anything until morning, so let's not worry about what we cannot change. For now, I want you to show me what you were able to save. And then, of course, you must tell me what it *means*."

 *Two*

President Ulysses S. Grant shook his head and watched his watery reflection quiver in the glass of Kentucky whiskey. He had better beverages on hand—more expensive beverages, at least—but he picked one of his finer bourbons for the other man, who barely sipped it. What a waste. He should've kept it for himself.

"I don't like it when you talk in absolutes. It usually bodes ill." He kept his eyes trained on the glass while he waited for a response, because the glass was more likely to tell the truth.

Desmond Fowler leaned in close, trying to force the president's eye contact and failing. He gave up and withdrew into his narrow seat. It wasn't intended to be comfortable. Grant didn't want him to stay.

"Freedom and slavery are absolutes. War and peace."

"You're wrong about all four." Grant swallowed the last of his drink, but neither put the glass aside nor filled it again. He held it firmly, lest his hands shake. They often shook these days. He called it nerves or exhaustion. "But these two things are true, Fowler: They can't hold on much longer, and neither can we."

"You're wrong about both, if I may be so bold."

"I've never stopped you yet, even when I should have."

Grant looked up in time to see him frown. "Sir, the program is vital to—"

"The survival of the nation, yes, as you've said. But we're fooling ourselves if that's what we're out to save. The nation has been lost for years. Maybe even since the war began. You could make a case for that."

"And you've done so. But now we're arguing semantics."

"So we'll argue, then. We can't *save* the United States; we can only reconstruct it. And we can't do that until we wrap up this damn war."

"Which is why I—"

The president slammed down his glass. "I don't like the program," he said bluntly.

"And I don't like the war," Fowler replied. "I thought you didn't, either."

It took all Grant's strength to keep from calling him a liar. If he'd been a bit more sober, or a bit younger, or a bit less alone in a quiet room with a man he could not trust, he might've done so. Instead he calmed down and forced himself to breathe.

He rubbed at his eyes until they were red, then folded his arms and matched Fowler's stare. "I hate it. But this is what it comes down to: Do we hate the war more than we love our country?"

Desmond Fowler did not quite squirm, but was clearly uncomfortable. "I'm not sure I understand."

"The war can't go on forever, but if a Union victory costs all hope of reconciliation, then what have we truly won? Shall we govern a conquered, resentful people by force—until they rally to rebel again? Or shall we welcome our fellow citizens back into the fold?"

"Obviously one hopes to welcome one's fellow citizens," Fowler tried carefully. "But Alabama and Mississippi still cannot agree with Lincoln—or yourself—regarding who is a citizen, and who constitutes property. Reconstructing the Union will be an uphill battle regardless of how the war is concluded. The question is not one of tactics, but of expediency."

"And there you go again—now you've turned the matter into a

binary. Another absolute. We can end the war expediently, tactically, without . . . without . . ."

"My program is the fastest, most efficient option."

"The most brutal, you mean. Killing Americans, civilian and soldier alike."

"Killing Confederates, and thereby ending the conflict."

"And killing our own men, too. God knows how many of them. You've said it yourself, there's no safe means to deploy such weaponry. Not without tremendous casualties to both sides. We'd have to lie to our soldiers, assure them we aren't leading them to their deaths."

"All soldiers assume, or at least suspect, that they're being led to their deaths. And as for the deployment, we're working on that," Fowler assured him. "And sir, we must be pragmatic. The simple fact is that we have more men to lose than they do. If it costs us a handful to kill thousands of the enemy, then we—"

"The *enemy*? Our fellow Americans, you mean."

"No, sir. Not anymore. By their own choice, and their own hand. Some days, I don't understand why we fight so hard to keep them, when they fight so hard to get away."

It was true, and Grant knew it. True, anyway, that Desmond Fowler didn't understand why the Union should be preserved, or that the men and women on the other side of that line were not all godless foreigners. They were not dogs to be killed or tamed, any more than the Union armies were fodder to be sacrificed in pursuit of . . . what, precisely?

The Great Experiment.

Leaving a nation in the hands of its people, to govern itself. A terrible risk barely a hundred years old, and it could not fail so soon, so completely. Grant believed that with all his heart, because if a successful democracy was not possible, then what alternative was there? Chaos or kings, he supposed. And he regarded both with equal dismay.

"Sir, you want to end the war," Fowler started afresh.

"Doesn't everyone?" The president asked it too flippantly, given the company.

"My program is our best option. Not the prettiest, not the easiest political decision—no one's trying to make that case. But it's for the best, and we need your authority to proceed. We need your signature to release the funds from the War Department. Otherwise the program will languish, and we will miss our window of opportunity."

"I'm sure another one will open. I just . . . I can't. Not yet. Come back when you have more information, better numbers, or a better idea of how, exactly, this weapon would work. At present, you can't even guess the extent of the damage. There's no research to say that it won't poison the land for a thousand years."

"You're asking for guarantees."

"I'm asking for absolutes. I thought you liked those."

"But that could take weeks! Months!"

"Then you'd better get started," Grant said, as he flicked a glance toward the door. He heard a familiar noise approaching from down the hall, and was relieved to realize that he'd discovered a way out of this interminable, wheedling conversation. "Right now, I think. I have another visitor, and I need a word with him in private."

Before Desmond Fowler could muster a response, the incoming hum grew louder and a mechanical chair appeared in the doorway. Fowler sprang to his feet, and made a small, formal bow. "Mr. Lincoln, sir."

President Grant got to his feet somewhat more slowly, but he was balancing his weight against the alcohol in his blood. He leaned on the arm of his sturdy chair and smiled a greeting. "Abe, it's good to see you. Come on in. Pull up to the fire. Fowler was just on his way out."

For a moment, Grant thought Fowler might fight him on it—

that he might scramble for some excuse to stay, some flattery he might apply or some social pressure he might leverage. Thankfully, he decided against the effort in time to politely bow again.

"Yes, I was just leaving. But it's been a pleasure as always, Mr. President. And Mr. Lincoln." He retrieved his overcoat from a rack by the door and took his leave.

When Grant and Lincoln were confident that Fowler was well out of hearing range, Lincoln adjusted his chair, backing up and pulling forward again so he could shut the office door. While he did this, Grant moved his normal guest chair aside to make room at the hearth.

Abraham Lincoln said, "I was afraid you'd be in the yellow oval. It's a fine office, but I find it hard to reach, these days."

"Nah. I don't like that office. Too big, too much to look at. I can't get a damn thing done in there. Can I get you a drink?"

"No, thank you. But don't let my temperance stop you from having another."

"I never do." President Grant refreshed the whiskey before dropping back into the big armchair. Its leather had become so fire-warmed that it stung, but he liked the sharp heat seeping through his clothes.

Lincoln removed the blanket that covered his knees, folding it over the arm of his chair. His long, knobby legs leaned slightly to the right, and his shoulders stooped to the left, but the chair had been created with his height in mind and he looked more or less comfortable. Minus the eye patch, and with the addition of his infamous hat, he might have looked like he was just sitting down and not confined there.

"What did Fowler want you to sign this time?"

"Something for the War Department. I told him no."

"Then he'll be back," Lincoln said quietly.

"Well, he *is* the Secretary of State. If he didn't come back, I'd have a problem. Another problem, I mean. There are always plenty to go around." He changed the subject, fishing for a more casual tone or topic. "So, why are you out and about tonight? I'm always happy to see you, but I thought Mary had some kind of party she was using to hold you hostage."

"That was last night, and I didn't attend. I'm not much of a dancer anymore." He smiled, and the top of his scarred cheek disappeared under the edge of his eye patch. "I never liked parties much, anyway."

"Me either. But I hope it went well."

"I expect that it did. Now, let me ask you something: Have you heard about what happened to the Jefferson?"

A memory flickered at the back of Grant's mind. He'd heard something that morning, part of a briefing that had piqued his interest. "The science center? They told me there was an explosion last night during the party."

"Correct."

"And you have people working out there, don't you? That scientist from Alabama?" They'd met once or twice in passing at the Lincolns' house. Grant recalled a quick, impatient colored man, with eyes too old for a man still in his thirties.

"Gideon, yes. That's him. He was there when it happened."

"Dear God . . . did he survive?"

"Oh yes, yes indeed. Some of his work was lost, but he saved as much as he could. Quite a lot of information, considering."

"That fellow's research . . . what was it about, again . . . ?" Grant rooted around in his memory. "He's teaching a machine to count, or something like that?"

"Something like that."

"Oh, wait, I remember: He was building a machine to solve all the problems that mankind can't. Once upon a time, you would've argued that there were no such problems. You were such an optimist, Abe. You believed we could do anything."

"I still do," he insisted softly. "Mankind remains a marvel; and this machine was built by a man, after all."

"True, true. Did it work? Can it count? Or was it destroyed in the explosion?"

"It worked."

Grant shifted forward, his elbows on the tops of his knees, the glass still perched in his hand. "Did you ask it . . . did you ask . . . ?"

"We gave it all the known parameters, variables, and information points we could find—everything from disease figures to population density, weather patterns and industry, money, trade, and commercial interests. And then I asked your question—*our* question. The only question worth asking a machine of its caliber. I asked the Fiddlehead who would win this conflict, and how long it would take, assuming no new variables are introduced."

Lincoln hesitated, and a brief spell of silence settled between them.

Grant did not break it. He was afraid of the answer, knowing it wouldn't be a good one—and feeling as if he'd asked a gypsy's magic ball for military advice.

What would a machine know, anyway? How could nuts and bolts, levers and buttons, tell him how to fight a war, much less how to end one? The president was a man of instincts and suspicions, and he understood the flow of battle like a riverboat captain understood the surge of the Mississippi. He could take the pulse of an altercation and listen to the rise and fall of artillery, coming and going like thunder. He had known war firsthand, many times over—and that knowledge had brought him to the nation's highest office and kept him there for three terms, because men believed in his instincts.

This time, Ulysses S. Grant was terrified that his instincts were right.

He cleared his throat to chase the tremor out of it. "Well?"

Abraham Lincoln withdrew a carefully trimmed packet of papers from a satchel on the side of his chair. He sorted through them, picking out two or three sheets and tidying them before handing them to his friend. "As far as the machine can tell, the United States of America will end. But it won't be the war that breaks it."

"I beg your pardon?" Confused, Grant took the pages. They'd been cut by scissors, as if pared down to size from a longer piece of paper. It felt like the onionskin of newsprint, smeared with inky fingerprints and smelling faintly like wet pulp.

"The North won't win, Ulysses. And the South won't win, either."

"You're not getting all philosophical on me, are you?"

"No, I'm not. There's another threat, an indiscriminate one. One that maybe . . ."

Grant lifted an eyebrow and peered over the paper. "Maybe? Maybe what?"

"That maybe can't be stopped."

The president quit trying to decipher the papers and returned them to his friend. He didn't understand any of the abbreviations, or the columns of numbers that covered the sheets from margin to margin. If this was a record of war, it wasn't one he could read.

"What are you talking about, Abe?"

"We've long known that disease can turn the tide of a war more easily than strategy. Cholera, typhoid, smallpox—name the plague of your choosing, and it can devastate an army more effectively than any mere man-made weapon."

"Hold on, now . . . are we talking about the stumblebums?"

He lifted one long finger aloft. "Yes, well done. The stumblebums. That's one word for them."

"Guttersnipe lepers, I've heard that too."

"Leprosy isn't the worst possible comparison."

Grant waved his hand, dispelling the idea, and splashing his drink in the process. "Goddammit," he grumbled. While he blotted at his pants with his handkerchief, he said, "But it can't be. We have doctors working on that problem, even as we speak. Entire hospital wings dedicated to the investigation and treatment of the issue."

"Entire wings, yes. Filled with violent, dying men. Eating up resources, even as the situation worsens."

"We'll get it under control."

"Do you think so?" Lincoln asked. "These numbers tell us otherwise. The epidemic is spreading exponentially, turning a small vice of war into something big enough to bend the arc of history. You could call it a self-inflicted and self-defeating problem, except that when these lepers get hungry, they bite; and their bites become necrotic with deadly speed. One lone leper can kill dozens of healthy men. Perhaps hundreds. God only knows."

God wasn't the only one who knew, Grant thought bitterly. Desmond Fowler's clandestine program probably knew it, too.

"It is thought," Lincoln continued, "that there may be a secondary cause of affliction—something unrelated to the drug itself." He paused to watch Grant's reaction, but Grant didn't give him one. "But there's still so much we don't know."

"Then tell me what we *do* know. Or tell me what your Fiddlehead knows, at least."

Lincoln looked down at the pages again, then withdrew a pencil from his satchel. He pressed a button to activate his wheeled chair and brought himself closer to the president, pulling up alongside his seat. The firelight warmed and brightened them both and made the brittle paper look brighter than a lampshade.

Lincoln circled one column's worth of information. "You see this part, here? These are casualty figures from three skirmishes two months ago. None of the field doctors reported any lepers, or any drug use among the men."

"I see," Grant said. But he didn't.

"The numbers are precisely what you'd expect: Half of the men died from their wounds. Of those who remained, approximately half succumbed to known diseases or infection. These other men"—he pointed at a secondary line—"were too badly hurt to return to battle, but they *did* survive. Now, look at these figures, over here." He drew another circle. "These are numbers from four other skirmishes around the same time. Two in northern Tennessee, one on Sand Mountain in Alabama, and one outside of Richmond."

Grant took a slow, deep breath and let it out again as he read the Tennessee casualty figures. Fifty percent dead from injuries. Two percent injured beyond further combat. Forty-eight percent . . .

"Forty-eight percent dead . . . from what?"

"From necrotic injuries, inflicted largely by their fellow soldiers."

"What on earth have those Southerners done?"

"It's not just the Southerners."

"These are all Southern battlefields!"

"*Most* of the battlefields are Southern battlefields," Lincoln reminded him, using the gentle tone of someone who is dealing with a drunk. Grant didn't care for that tone, but he ignored it. He'd heard it from everyone, for years. "And the Southern soldiers aren't the ones chewing up our boys after the fact; these are *our* figures. *Our* men. That said, the Confederacy's having problems too—the same problems, almost exactly. In fact, the only time the Fiddlehead balked was when we asked where the drug came from, North or South."

"It didn't know?"

"It didn't say. Gideon says the question shouldn't have been phrased that way, since it might have come from someplace else. Something about contradictory absolutes, he said."

"So where did it come from, do you think?"

Lincoln shrugged, a gesture that made him look like a funeral suit sliding off a hanger. "The Western territories? The Mexican Empire? The islands? The machine couldn't tell us the drug's origin—only that the lepers will win the war."

"Balderdash," Grant spit. "It's utter balderdash, and you know I mean no disrespect."

"It's science."

"The war won't be won by the walking dead, Abe."

"And why not? Before long, we'll have more soldiers dead than living—and when the dead outnumber us, the advantage is *theirs*."

After a frustrated, uncertain pause, Grant said, "Your machine offers up more questions than answers."

"Its vocabulary is limited. It can only work with what we give it."

"It must be wrong."

"It's frightening, but I don't believe it's wrong. We can't win, and neither can the CSA."

The president laughed sadly. This was almost precisely what he'd told Desmond Fowler not ten minutes before. "Then what do you suggest we do?"

"The only thing we can do is stop fighting. Declare a cease-fire, call a summit. Explain the situation to Bragg and Stephens—they're reasonable men, *old* men. And they're tired of fighting too." He sat forward with some difficulty, and the firelight played across the sharp-cut angles of his cheeks. "You can tell them that we do not ask their surrender, and do not offer our own. Explain the greater threat and extend a hand of brotherhood. Not North against South, but living against dead."

Grant shook his head. "It would never work. They'll never believe us."

"They might. When we asked the Fiddlehead to tell us how the war would end, we had to estimate figures on the Southern side—we didn't have the precise numbers of living, dead, sick, or wounded. It was funny, really—or, rather, Gideon thought it funny: The machine accused us of lying to it."

"How's that?"

"It rejected our estimates as implausible, and supplied its own calculations. But we have every indication that the South suffers from the leper problem too, perhaps even worse than we do. We may get lucky: They may want a way out of the war as badly as we do, and if they're aware of the threat in their own land, they might be open to a conversation."

Grant harrumphed and scowled into the fire, as if he were asking it for a second opinion. "What if we could get Southern casualty reports? Send some spies out in search of accurate figures to feed into your machine. That'd give us a better idea of what we're up against, wouldn't it? It'd give us a hint about how open they'd be to . . . a conversation, as you put it."

Lincoln's good eye glittered warmly. "It might. But, as you'll recall, there was an explosion last night—speaking of spies."

"I'm sorry, come again?"

"Two men," he told him. "If not spies, then mercenaries—sent to destroy the Fiddlehead, and kill the man who'd created it. From Gideon's report, I doubt either one of them would've thought to make the attack alone. Someone paid them to make the effort."

"Any idea who?"

A slow, knowing smile spread across Lincoln's crooked face. "*Who?* Not precisely. But I appreciate that we both understand the *why,* and that we choose not to insult one another by pretending."

"You want to blame warhawks like Desmond, or his brethren on the other side of the line. But why would they go after your calculation machine? How many people even know it exists? How many people would put stock in the conclusions of a . . . a . . . a fortune-telling heap of nuts and bolts, assembled by a colored man? No one."

"I may be permanently seated and long out of office, but I'm not exactly *no one,*" Lincoln replied stiffly. "Gideon's work is sound. The machine is unprecedented, a marvel of science—and you just wait"—he waved one warning finger—"history will bear this out. The war has to end. We have to turn our attention to the leper threat. We must bury all the dead and see to it that they remain buried."

"I can't push a button and end hostilities," Grant fussed . . . but again he thought of Desmond Fowler, whose clandestine program might do just that. "You can't ask for such a thing based on a pile of paper that no one understands but you. And your team of tinkers," he amended quickly. "I can't go in front of Congress with the message that Abe Lincoln says we should all find some hobby other than war because dead men walk and we should do something about *that,* instead. You *have* to bring me more than this."

Lincoln slumped back in his chair, his good eye narrowed. "I don't have more. Not yet. And someone—perhaps a Southerner, perhaps someone in your own administration—is working hard to make sure I don't come up with any additional evidence."

"How so?"

"Because they went after Gideon, and when they couldn't catch him, they went for his family. They've taken his mother and nephew—kidnapped the pair of them without so much as a note. Dragged them back to Alabama, I suppose. But I've called in a good man to recover them, one of the old Liberation Rangers. You'd know the name if I said it, but then you'd have to do something about him, so I'll leave it there."

"Ah. Then I can make my guess. I remember the old case well—nasty business, that. I appreciate your discretion. But as for the scientist's family . . . you think it was a lure? Something to take him away from his work?"

"As likely as not. Gideon is the only man on earth who could rebuild or re-create the machine. Someone, somewhere, already knows what the Fiddlehead will tell us—and without that machine, it's our suspicions versus their profit. Our word against theirs."

"The word of a former slave—a political fugitive. It won't carry much weight."

"Then add the word of a former president. A political figure, instead. It will carry more weight than you think, and they know it. They're afraid I'll say something, but they're unwilling or unable to come for me. So they reach instead for Gideon, thinking that I have nothing without him, and thinking that he's vulnerable."

"And I expect they'll learn the hard way that he's not." Grant mustered a friendly grin.

Lincoln closed his eye. When he opened it again, it was to plead with him. "Yes, they will. But I need your help while I hold them at bay."

"What can I give you? Money? Men? I know you don't think much of the Secret Service, and neither do I sometimes . . . but they're at our disposal."

"Oh, no. I can't trust them any more than you can. I'll stick with the Pinks, if you don't mind—they've kept me alive this long. Mr. President, my old friend . . . what I need is *information*."

Three

Maria Boyd, sometimes called Belle and sometimes Isabella, stamped her feet and wished she was sitting closer to the big iron furnace in the corner of the room. She drew her shawl around her shoulders and eyed the empty desk beside the big iron hearth, where Andrew Kelly usually sat. He was away on assignment, and wouldn't be back for a week.

One long, cold week.

"To hell with it," she muttered. After all, no one was present to object: Rose Anderson was out of the office chasing down a murderer in Minnesota; Fred Williams was eyeballs deep in legal paperwork following that affair in New York last Tuesday; and Timothy Hall had been sent down to the jailhouse to bail out Percy Jones—who had gone and done it again, and might get fired this time, depending on the boss's mood.

Only James Elders was left on the main floor of the Pinkerton National Detective Agency office. And yes, he'd probably notice if she moved seats, because he noticed every time she moved anything, and was not precisely subtle about it.

Maria wasn't worried that he'd tattle to Mr. Pinkerton, who probably cared less than anyone in the whole of Chicago, but she didn't want to look weak. She hated looking weak like men hated looking foolish, and she worked studiously to prove that she was up to the same tasks as everyone else.

In fact, no one really doubted it. No one dared doubt it, because Allan Pinkerton himself had brought her on board last spring, politics and precedent be damned. If the old Union spy believed that the former Confederate spy was worth her salt, then everyone else who wanted a paycheck had best believe it, too. But that didn't mean they had to be nice to her, so every day she worked to prove that she belonged.

But she didn't belong.

Not in that office, typing up notes and filing signed papers, stamping the backs of checks and sorting telegrams like a secretary. Not in Chicago, either, where the heat-flash of summer suddenly gave way to a winter like nothing she'd ever known in Virginia. And Virginia got plenty cold, thank you very much . . . as she found herself reminding coworkers who teased her about her fingerless gloves and layers of scarves.

Not as cold as this, though. November on Lake Michigan, and the whole world might be frozen, so far as she knew.

On the rare occasions when she felt like defending herself, she insisted that there hadn't been time to do any shopping when she'd accepted the job offer. She'd packed her things and caught the first train to Illinois, desperate to escape an increasingly unhappy situation south of the Mason-Dixon, where she'd come under scrutiny that stopped just shy of an allegation of treason. She'd married against advice, been widowed against her will, and, if it weren't for the once-celebrated spy's continued friendship with General Jackson, she might've met a court-martial in her mourning dress.

Adding insult to injury, she hadn't been able to redeem herself yet, as she'd become altogether too famous for further espionage work.

Or any other work, as it turned out.

The CSA no longer trusted her, and the newspapers accused her of terrible things. What meager fortune her family possessed was lost in the war, her father's hotel burned, rebuilt, and then seized for taxes under flimsy circumstances. He'd died shortly thereafter, and her brothers were dead, too, lost to the war effort. One sister had succumbed to cholera while working as a nurse in a field hospital. One served as caregiver to her husband, badly wounded at the second battle of Shiloh.

There was no money, and what was left of her family was starving.

Maria Boyd wrote a book and gave tours, speaking about her time in Union prisoner-of-war camps and retelling her adventures as a spy, but it wasn't enough to keep anyone fed. She turned to acting, and the reviews were good but the pay was poor. She worked as a cab driver—one of the only women driving in Georgia, if not the whole continent. A seamstress. A cook. A governess. A messenger.

And still they went hungry.

So when the invitation came from Pinkerton—so unexpected and so unlikely—Maria was just desperate enough to take it, for here was a chance at an honest, interesting job that would earn her enough to eat, and to share.

In truth, her options were narrowing by the day. She could turn detective, or she could stoop to the prostitution of which she'd so often been accused—a prospect that might've been brighter in her youth. But so late in her thirties? She'd surely still starve, only more ignobly.

So she leaped, all the way from Front Royal, Virginia, to Chicago, Illinois.

She leaped with all her worldly belongings, which fit in a single steamer trunk and carpetbag. These worldly belongings had in fact included a coat, but the coat was insufficient for even a Virginia winter, never mind one in Illinois, and she wasn't dishonest enough to write off a new one as an expense.

Not quite yet.

She gathered her bag and the case notes she was writing up and moved. Andrew Kelly's desk was warmer by far. Maria sighed, loosened one of her scarves, and smiled to feel the furnace-warmed typewriter keys beneath her fingertips. Only three more invoices to record and file and she'd be finished for the day.

Allan Pinkerton's office door opened with a crash.

The aging Scotsman stormed through it just like he stormed everyplace, as if he could function at no other speed. His eyes landed on Maria's now-empty desk, then found her over at her borrowed spot, her fingers hovering guiltily over the typewriter keys.

"Maria!" he barked. He'd dispensed with any naming formalities months ago.

"Yes, sir?"

"In my office. I've got one for you."

She exhaled with relief. She belonged in the field. Even when the field was cold and miserable and she needed a better coat, she'd rather wander the streets of Chicago in the snow than sit there and type beside the furnace.

She left the warm spot with only a little rue. Her employer held the frosted glass door open as she passed him and took the seat across from his enormous oak desk. A simple name plaque announced that he was the owner of this desk, and the finely stenciled name and all-seeing eye logo on the door's glass announced he was the owner of this office, and that he never slept. Everything here belonged to him, and he liked to make sure everyone knew it.

"All right, Mr. Pinkerton. Brief me."

"Listen to you there, picking up the lingo like you're one of the boys. Never thought I'd see the day," he said, as he parked himself behind the desk, facing her. The wheels on his chair bottom rolled back and forth as he fidgeted. He put his elbows atop a pile of ledgers, reached for a cigar, and lit it. Then he used his knuckles to drag a big glass ashtray within easier reach.

"Rose uses the lingo, too."

"Rose is a special case."

"And I'm not?"

The old man grinned. His white-bearded cheeks inflated and puffed as he sucked the cigar to life. "All my employees are special. Is that what you want to hear?"

"Not really."

"Good, because it isn't true. How was that art job in Philly? You turned that one over pretty quick."

"It was easy," she said, which meant it hadn't been very interesting. "Sometimes the most obvious answer is the right one. Alastair Duggard's wife destroyed the painting."

"Why?"

"Because her husband liked it. And because she found out about his mistress, who she didn't like at all."

"Most obvious answer, indeed," he said, tapping a scrap of ash into the tray. "Too bad we couldn't get it back for him, but I suppose it's his own fault it's gone. He paid up?"

"He paid up. I was recording the last of the invoices when—"

"In Kelly's chair, I saw."

"I was cold. I am cold. *It's cold.*"

"You're in Chicago, dear." He said it "Shi-kah-go" like the locals, despite his native (if fading) Glaswegian patter. "It's cold here more often than not. You need warmer clothes, or thicker blood. Living down there in the jungles . . . it'll make you soft."

She didn't bother to correct him anymore when he talked about Virginia's jungles. He'd never seen Virginia—or a jungle, for that matter—but she had better things to do than waste her breath convincing him of it. "I need to move around more, that's all. And I believe you can help me with that—you said you've got a case for me?"

"I do indeed. And it's a big one, too." He hesitated, leaving something unsaid.

"Sir?"

"I'm not going to lie to you, Maria: I can't tell if you're the best candidate for this one, or the worst possible choice."

"Another job working for the Union, I take it? I managed the last assignment to everyone's satisfaction."

"That you did, but this one is . . . closer to the heart."

She was confused. "My heart? Your heart?"

"To President Lincoln's heart. Literally and figuratively."

"You . . . you want me to work for Abraham Lincoln?"

"The situation is unusual—but not the same kind of unusual as usual."

"You've always had a way with words, sir."

He looked past her shoulder. "Do me a favor, dear—reach behind you and shut that door."

She did as he asked, and he continued, but in a quieter, more serious tone. "Mr. Lincoln and I have remained friends for many years, despite the incident at the Ford. Depending on who you ask, my son either saved his life or ruined it, and Mrs. Lincoln held the whole thing against us for a while. Abe's recovery came so slowly, and so incompletely. . . . Still, the president has continued to accept our service in good faith. He presently employs one of our D.C. operatives—a young man named Nelson Wellers, who happens to be a physician."

"These days, I guess Mr. Lincoln needs a doctor more than a bodyguard." Maria cocked her head and frowned. "But this Dr. Wellers is no longer sufficient? I worked as a nurse, but quite briefly, I want you to know; I wasn't cut out for it. If you're only looking to send me because I'm a woman—"

"No, no, no." He dismissed her concerns with a wave of his cigar, leaving a trail of smoke to underline his impatience. "Wellers is fine. Nothing wrong with him. Mr. Lincoln doesn't need a nursemaid or another security agent for himself. He wants to hire someone to investigate a crime against somebody *else*."

"Oh."

"*Really,* Maria. If I wanted to insult you, I'd do it more directly." He lifted one elbow and retrieved a file, then set his cigar in the glass tray's groove. "So here are the brass tacks. The man in question is Gideon Armistead Bardsley, a doctor from Alabama. Not the kind of doctor who fixes you—this one's an inventor. A scientist."

"Another negro," she noted from the picture, a good daguerreotype that showed a long-waisted, broad-shouldered man in a suit that fit him well. He must be a little younger than she was, but she detected some lightness at his temples, the premature gray of someone who works too hard. "I'm sensing a theme."

"Twice isn't a theme, it's a coincidence. Will it be a problem?"

"Wasn't a problem last time. Won't be a problem this time."

"Good." He slid some paperwork across the desk. As Maria started to read, he pitched her the highlights. "Dr. Bardsley was a slave in Alabama until a dozen years ago, when he escaped. He got as far as Tennessee."

"No one sent him back?" The Bloodhound Laws were still on the books in the South, and anyone who'd returned the runaway would've been richly compensated.

"The University of Tennessee at Fort Chattanooga paid for his freedom, on the condition that he stayed there and made them look good. Brilliant man, this Bardsley fellow. A real-life genius, if his diplomas can be believed. In four years he earned a master's degree in some kind of advanced math, *and* a doctorate in electromechanical engineering—a brand-new field. I don't think any other school in the South even offers such a degree. The next year, he bought freedom for the rest of his family still living: a couple of brothers, his mother, and a nephew."

"What was he working on in Chattanooga?" she asked, still absorbing the information on the pages before her. "It must've been profitable. That kind of buyout takes more than chump change."

"Civic planning, if the public information can be believed. He felt there was no good reason you couldn't generate power for entire cities with old-fashioned technology like water. He was developing schematics for water turbines that could convert the flow of rivers into electricity with the right kind of dams and wires. It's a bit over my head, to be honest, even if it *is* true."

"You think it's not?"

"I think he was working on military projects. I can't imagine any other reason the school would've paid for his life and his education."

"A negro designing weapons for use against the North? I don't know about *that*."

"Maybe not weapons. Armies and navies need a million and one things to operate smoothly. He could've been working on any of 'em. When you meet him, you can ask him."

"Is he still in Washington?" The document in her hand was a courthouse copy, identifying him as a free man of color with an address in the capital.

"In 1876 he defected to the Union, taking his mother and nephew with him. He started out in Philadelphia, but moved to D.C. when Mr. Lincoln took a personal interest in one of his projects."

Maria flipped through another page or two of biography. She stopped at an engraving of a machine emblazoned across a patent application. " 'The Bardsley Automatic Computational and Calculational Device,' " she read, eyeballing the diagram and marveling at its implied dimensions. "Good heavens, it must be enormous."

"A whole roomful of a machine, I'm led to understand."

"A whole mouthful, too. Why do inventors do that? Name their inventions such ridiculous things?"

"Any number of reasons, I'm sure, but the Lincolns agree with you, at least. When Mrs. Lincoln explained the project to Dr. Wellers, she called it a giant mechanical brain—a brain that could think faster, better, and more accurately than any man ever could.

Wellers said that such a thing could really fiddle with a fellow's head, and she laughed . . . so now the thing is called Fiddlehead for short. Think of it as a code name, if you like that better."

"Got it. So the Lincolns are . . . what? Dr. Bardsley's patrons? Sponsors?"

"Yes. And at the moment, they're his lifeline." He passed her a newspaper article, then continued. "Three nights ago, armed men broke into the doctor's laboratory at the Jefferson Science Center, destroying a great deal of expensive equipment, and doing their best to kill Bardsley in the process."

She didn't lift her gaze. "Was the Fiddlehead itself destroyed in the incident?"

"Damaged, yes. Destroyed, no. Apparently the doctor tricked the intruders into vandalizing less interesting equipment."

She set the newsprint article aside. "So he's not just a brilliant man, but a clever one, too. Tell me, then: What was this Fiddlehead designed to do? A giant brain, you said, but everyone everywhere has a brain. What makes this one so special? What was it told to think about?"

"The war," he said simply. "They asked it to analyze the war."

"And the results were . . . ?"

"Nothing I'm at liberty to discuss right now. You'll get that information from Lincoln, as well as further details on your assignment. He knows more about the machine than I do, and I'm sure he'd be happy to fill you in."

"Your certainty on that point exceeds mine, sir. Does he know you're sending *me*?"

"Yes, he knows. And I've assured him that you're a consummate professional who will do the job you're given, with no qualms, concerns, lingering political loyalties, or complaints. Do I make myself a liar, or do I make myself clear?"

"Abundantly clear, as always. But while I appreciate the vote of confidence—"

"I don't need your appreciation; I just need your follow-through. Listen, Miss Boyd: Abraham Lincoln might not have been *your* president, and I understand. However, he is nobody's president anymore, and right now he is *my* client."

"But he's still active politically, isn't he? I've heard that he's a vigorous advocate for ending the conflict, presumably with a restored Union," she replied carefully.

Allan Pinkerton paused, settling back in his chair and peering thoughtfully across the desk at her. "Presumably," he said at last. "I've never asked before, but perhaps this is the time, before I send you jaunting down to D.C. on a delicate mission—"

It was Maria's turn to interrupt. "You want to know how I feel about the war." She folded her hands atop the paperwork. She took a moment to organize her thoughts, then she told him. "It's a hard thing to explain, you know. I earned my fame as a child, Mr. Pinkerton. I thought—and operated—with the fearlessness of a child, accepting what I was told by my nearest elders. I still believe some of it—or, it might be more accurate to say that I still *feel* some of it. The South was my home, and I do not believe it was fairly treated in the years leading up to Fort Sumter. When war broke out, the whole thing felt like a grand adventure."

Pinkerton snorted. Maria smiled tightly, unhappily. "Oh, I know. A stupid thing to feel. But, again, I was still in my teens, and the war was young too. It hadn't taken so much yet." Her voice trailed off, then recovered. "So I sit here now, two decades and thousands of miles away from my youthful adventures, with tens of thousands of lives lost to a cause I didn't understand very well and I understand even less now. And you want to know how I feel about the war."

"Well," he pointed out, "you still haven't told me."

She swallowed. "I still believe in the rights of states to self-govern, and some of the points the Rebels have fallen back on as they've lost slavery as a political option. But the older I get and the farther I travel, the less I think of slavery itself—and I won't pretend the war would've happened without it. It's complicated, that's all. I understand why some people thought the subject was worth fighting over . . . but at this point, is it worth fighting further? I . . . I don't think so. The South isn't fighting for slavery anymore, but for survival. The North isn't fighting for abolition anymore, but for reunification. And there are days when I feel . . . when I feel like the whole world is burning to the ground around us."

Burned like her father's hotel, and her brothers' bodies. Like her family homestead. She fought to keep the bitterness out of her voice, but failed. The words tumbled out, landing in a pile between her and the man who'd saved her. "It's taken enough already, from both sides, that any victory may be Pyrrhic. Give it another few years, and we'll all be scrabbling around in the dirt, fighting for scraps and starving, regardless of who wins."

"A sad summary, Miss Boyd."

"A sad state of affairs, Mr. Pinkerton. In my more cynical hours I don't know who to resent more: the slave owners for the peculiar institution, or the slaves themselves for what it's cost to end it."

"That's hardly fair."

"I know, and I hate myself for it, particularly since I've come to know and respect . . . some former slaves." Her voice petered out again. There were things her employer was welcome to suspect, but needn't know for certain. "But you're decent enough to insult me directly, so I'm decent enough to tell you the truth. I'm only being honest."

"As if that excuses anything."

She sighed, and met his stare blink for unhappy blink. "You asked me how I felt and I told you. I wish I were more noble than this, but I'm not. I wish there had never been slaves. I wish there had never been a war. But if wishes were . . ." She hunted for some expression she hadn't heard a thousand times before. Failing to find one, she tried again. "I am capable of controlling my behavior, if not the sentiments I learned in the cradle. I would like to believe that actions are more meaningful."

"There might be something noble in *that*. Or maybe only hypocritical; I can't decide."

"Decide whatever you like. You've already told me that my performance is satisfactory. I have grown accustomed to compromise, sir."

"And do you think compromise is enough?"

"Not particularly. But it's worked for the last twenty years, and it'll work for the next month in D.C., if you're still game to send me."

His chair popped and creaked as he leaned forward. He tossed another envelope onto the pile of paperwork and said, "Oh, I've already booked your ticket. I just wanted to make sure you were still game to *go*."

Four

Mary Todd Lincoln brandished a gun. She was small in stature and getting along in years, and guns made her feel better, stronger, and more prepared.

Gideon understood. He had one, too, tucked into the back of his pants, underneath his grandfather's coat. It wasn't within easy reach, but he needed both hands free in order to rummage through the wreckage of the Jefferson. Night was falling, and it was already dark enough in the basement where the Fiddlehead lurked, even with the lantern Gideon held aloft, aiming its watery white light into every corner.

Some curiously hopeful part of his brain thought some of the missing printout might have fallen into the basement with the rest of the debris, but he wasn't stupid enough to bank on it. That was good, because he could barely find the monstrously sized machine, much less anything lighter or more ephemeral.

Dynamite had blown the laboratory windows outward in a spray of fine glass shards, and it'd taken down two of the walls, too. The ceiling dipped and teetered ominously, held aloft by the work of some architectural wizard whose load-bearing walls were bearing more than they were expected to. For the time being, the roof remained where it ought to be, though it creaked unhappily and leaned at a frightening angle.

It all felt very much like being in the hold of a ship, surrounded by damp and danger, listening to the environment moan and grumble like a hungry stomach.

He could see the roof through a crack in the basement floor. He could see the sky, too, and Mrs. Lincoln pacing back and forth above him, gun in hand and a grim, fierce look that stopped just short of being comical.

She paused her pacing and peered down through the rubble. "Gideon, is everything all right down there?"

"Yes, ma'am," he assured her. It was only somewhat true.

"How's the . . . the machine?"

"I won't know for certain until I can see the whole thing, and right now—" A grating scrape announced the imminent fall of something from above; Gideon pinpointed its location with his ears and sidestepped in time to avoid being hit by a clump of bricks held together by old masonry and force of habit. "Right now that's not an option," he finished.

"Oh dear. I was hoping it might not be so bad as all that," Mrs. Lincoln sighed. "I heard Abe say 'intact,' and I hoped for the best."

Gideon murmured, "Never a good idea, really."

"I'm sorry, come again?"

Louder, he replied with a fib. "I said, I wonder if the generator's still good."

"Why does that matter?"

He sighed, and was glad she couldn't see his face. "Because the Fiddlehead can't run without it, even if everything else is whole and undamaged." He shoved a beam up out of his way, clearing a short path that took him a few feet closer to his goal. "Without power, it's useless." It wouldn't be easy to rig up a fresh supply. The generator had been a cobbled-together affair, more powerful than anything in the District except perhaps the big machine that ran the plates and presses at the mint.

A series of thoughts flickered faster than lightning through his head. The mint: *Its* generators would be hearty enough. The Fiddlehead was too badly damaged to move, even if it weren't too bulky. The mint's generators . . . would also be difficult to move. How difficult? He'd need a look at them to know for certain. Impossible at this time of night, but maybe he could get in tomorrow. Or maybe he'd have a better plan by then.

He sure as hell hoped so. This one had too many holes.

"Where's the generator?" Mary Lincoln had a lantern, too. Gideon could tell from the shifting light and the tone of her voice that she was walking around the basement's edge, following him or trying to find him.

But before he could reply that it was in the next room over, she barked out to someone else: "You, stop there! Put your hands up!"

Gideon froze, listening to see if this was a problem or merely another watchman startled to find the former first lady patrolling the grounds with a gun.

"Hello there, Mrs. Lincoln," came the response. A Southern voice, from somewhere deep in the CSA. Gideon tensed and slipped his hand around his back, reaching for his own firearm; but then the speaker said, "My name is Henry Epperson. Your husband told me I could find you here. He . . . he didn't mention you'd be carrying . . ."

"If my husband sent you—"

"He didn't send me," Henry interrupted. "He invited me. I'm sorry, and I sure don't mean to cause you any alarm. I work for the United States Marshals Service. Here's my identification papers—Mr. Lincoln said you'd want to see them. I was born in Mobile, and I never managed to shake the vowels; but my parents were scalawags, not fire-eaters, and now we're all living in Baltimore. Please, ma'am. I'm here to help." And then he added quickly,

"Oh, Mr. Lincoln said that if you still didn't buy it, I should say that there's a Pinkerton agent on the way to your home right now, arriving from Chicago."

Gideon unfroze, and returned his gun to its place against his back.

Mary also relented. "Chicago," she repeated. "That was the code word we picked between us. Hello, Mr. . . . . Epperson? Am I reading this right?"

"Yes, ma'am," he said. "It's a pleasure and an honor to meet you."

Gideon found his way to the basement steps and climbed them, emerging into a late afternoon that wasn't fully dark yet, but would be in another twenty minutes. "You're the man from the Marshals Service?" he said, not because he doubted it, but because he didn't want to sneak up on anyone with a gun. Mary was worrisome enough all by herself, never mind the armed federal agent.

Henry turned around, holding a wallet of folded papers. He was somewhat taller than Mary, and somewhat shorter than Gideon, with light hair and round, wire-rimmed glasses. He was casually but warmly dressed, though he wore no gloves. "Yes, that's me. You must be Dr. Bardsley. Just the man I'm here to see." He held out his hand. It was chapped and pink, but his nails were clean.

Gideon shook it. "Yes. And if you're here to clean up the Jefferson, I hope you've brought heavy machinery, construction equipment . . . something big enough to move this mess." He almost suggested a miracle, but restrained himself.

"Well now. I'm happy to lend a hand if a hand is needed, but I didn't bring anything big enough to make a dent. Those fellows really did a number on the place. But I hear they didn't get what they came for."

"No. Not that the machine does us any good, down there in that crater. I still can't tell if its power source is operational. It's a rabbit warren under there, and dark as a grave. So if you're not here to dig, and you're not here to open fire, what brings you to . . . to what's left of my laboratory?"

"My dirigible got a good tail wind, I guess, which is how I arrived at your home so early," he said to Mary. Then, to Gideon: "And since I landed ahead of schedule, Mr. Lincoln sent me here with word about your mother and nephew."

For one white-hot moment, a flare of pure, distilled rage seared Gideon's vision. It was a familiar, hateful thing—a thing he usually kept in a box in the back of his brain, labeled "do not open" and stashed under the plans for the Fiddlehead and other inventions. He'd boxed up that fury on the road from Washington to Tennessee one night, under cover of darkness with the family members who'd agreed to join him.

He blinked until he could see again, and the only white-hot anything was the lantern in Mary's hand.

"Did they find them, Mr. Epperson? Are they all right?"

"Yes to both questions, doctor. The Pinks were able to extract them. They were taken to a plantation in northern Alabama, not far from Fort Chattanooga. Right now they're at a railroad stop at Lookout Mountain. Mr. Lincoln thought you'd want to know."

"Thank you," he said. Gideon did feel some relief, but not enough to wipe away the last of the lava-bright anger. He clenched his jaw, then unfastened it to say, "And I'll thank him, too, when I see him. Will the Pinks bring them back to D.C.?"

"I don't know. Mr. Pinkerton thought they'd be safer . . . well, if they were farther away from you, if you don't mind me saying so. But he's called in Kirby Troost, in case an escort to the North is called for."

"Troost? How in God's name did he find him?"

"No idea, Dr. Bardsley. But I hope that meets with your satisfaction."

"Very much, yes. If we *do* need to move my family, he's the man to do it."

Rationally, Gideon knew the Pinkertons were right: Leaving them in place was probably the best strategy for now, though having Troost as a backup plan made him feel better about the whole thing. Let them stay close to their point of liberation while the pressure was on. Anyone in pursuit would assume they were running as far and as fast as possible, right back to the District of Columbia. Right back to Gideon, who'd always looked after them, hell, high water, or hunger.

But he knew his mother well—a simple woman who sometimes amazed him with her lack of curiosity, and sometimes annoyed him with her nervous nature. He knew of the safehouse in question, a quiet and hidden place at the edge of Lookout; he'd been there before, when he worked at the university. But all its quietness and all its hiddenness would never assuage her fears. She'd wear them like a blanket, and share them with her young charge. He thought unhappily of Caleb, a calm, quiet boy who'd been a toddler when they'd first come to the East Coast, and had grown into a solemn, silent thing that reached his uncle's hips in height. The poor child would absorb his grandma's fears, and hold them inside, and say nothing because that was how he'd made it this far.

Gideon sighed.

The best he could hope for was to protect them from each other. It was both the least he could do, and the most he could expect to accomplish. But these were not the best of times, and so far, he had not protected them from anything.

When there was nothing left to be done at the ruins of the Jefferson's laboratory wing, Mary, Henry, and Gideon Bardsley climbed into Mary's carriage and made the quick ride back to the Lincoln home. Once there, Mary left the two men in the library, where her husband was ensconced in his favorite chair with a blanket over his legs and a cup of coffee in his hand.

Thin, sallow Nelson Wellers sat in a chair across from the fire, and Polly stood by with the steaming pot, ready to dole out a warm beverage to the night-chilled newcomers.

"Gideon, Henry. Please come in. Take a seat," the president urged. "Coffee, anyone?"

Henry politely waited while Polly served. When the maid finally pushed her little cart out of the room, he asked Lincoln, "So, the Pinkerton agent—she hasn't arrived yet?"

Abraham Lincoln shook his head. "No, but any minute now, I should think."

Gideon lifted an eyebrow as he dropped into a large leather chair. *"She?"*

"Oh, yes. One of their finest investigators, or so I am assured. An eminently capable woman," he said. "But Henry's told you of your mother, I hope? She and Caleb are safe and sound, and Troost is en route to them as we speak."

"Yes, the marshal told me. They're in Tennessee."

"It's less than ideal." Lincoln spoke aloud what Gideon had privately concluded. "But it's the best possible arrangement at this time. If they run, the bloodhounds will chase them, so I think we can all agree that they're better off hiding until we know precisely what we're up against. Now, Henry"—he shifted topics so smoothly, Gideon didn't have time to offer some gentle agreement—"that telegram you sent was *most* alarming. I was hoping you could give us the particulars, and perhaps fill in some of the gaps between what we heard last week and your present understanding of the situation."

"It might be best to wait for the Pinkerton agent. He'll need— I mean, *she'll* need—to be briefed, and she might have questions."

A deep gong rang through the first floor, and Lincoln smiled. "A good suggestion, and good timing, too. I believe that's her."

Nelson Wellers reached one hand into his coat as if he did not share the former president's confidence that this visitor was a fellow agent, not something more sinister; and Henry Epperson tensed as well. But within moments Polly returned. She was flushed, and glanced nervously between the newcomer and the men in the room.

"Gentlemen," she said. "I . . . um. This is . . . this is Maria Boyd. She says she's with the Pinkertons, and she showed me her badge . . . but . . ."

"But nothing," Lincoln nodded reassuringly. "All's well, Polly, thank you. Could you bring us another pot of coffee, please? Our guest might care for a cup. And, Miss Boyd—that's your preferred address, isn't it? Thank you for coming on such short notice."

Stunned out of their usual manners, Nelson Wellers and Henry Epperson stayed in their seats for another awkward beat, then fumbled their coffee cups aside and rose as they recalled that standing was the usual protocol when a woman arrived. But Gideon Bardsley stayed where he was. He, too, was dumbfounded, but even once his shock passed, he had no intention of rising.

Maria Boyd, better known in the papers as "Belle Boyd," was of average height, with posture that indicated good breeding. True to rumor, hers was the sort of body to launch a thousand ships: voluminous, shapely breasts and a narrow waist, graceful shoulders and a long, lean neck, but only the very kind or terribly near-sighted had ever described her plain, horselike face as "beautiful."

She was no longer the hoopskirted coquette from the gossip pages. Now the notorious spy of yore wore something simple but more modern, a gray dress that was full only at the rear. Gideon was idly surprised to note that the Cleopatra of the Confederacy must have fallen on hard times—for he knew an oft-worn, insufficient article of clothing when he saw one; and her black cotton coat could not have been enough to keep her warm, even when augmented with a blue wool scarf that did nothing to mask the outstanding swell of her figure.

Calmly, deliberately, she unwound the scarf and unbuttoned her overcoat. "Gentlemen," she greeted the lot of them, even catch-

ing Gideon's eye in a pointed display of acknowledgment. "And
Mr. President, of course," she said to Lincoln. "'Miss Boyd' will
be fine."

But when she dipped her head to remove her scarf entirely,
Gideon saw a large black comb. A mourning piece. *Oh, yes,* he
thought. *That's right. Divorced, then later widowed.* By a Navy boy,
wasn't that the story? But that had been years ago now. Considering that she'd offered them no married name, maybe she wore it
out of habit, or for lack of other baubles.

Henry Epperson gave her a little bow and began to babble.
"Miss Boyd, yes, Miss Boyd. I suppose that'll keep things simple,
won't it? And I am sorry, ma'am—I don't mean to be rude or
strange, it's just that I'm very surprised, you understand. I didn't
realize you were the agent they'd sent, that's all. I just didn't know."

"There's nothing wrong with being surprised," she assured
him. She held her scarf in her hands like Henry would've held a
hat, if he'd still been wearing one. She held it between herself and
everyone else in the room. "I was more than a little surprised when
I was given this case, I don't mind telling you."

The marshal held out his hand as if to take her elbow and
guide her into the room, but she was out of reach. She followed
the gesture anyway, when he said, "Please, won't you pull up a chair
and join us?"

"Thank you, I believe I will. I've read the files and I think my
information is up to date, but I expect there's quite a lot we can
learn from one another, mister . . . ?" she prompted him.

"Epperson. Henry Epperson. Just Henry, really, if you don't
mind. Over there is Dr. Wellers—I mean, Nelson Wellers," he said.

She nodded. "Another agent, Mr. Pinkerton told me."

He nodded back and slowly reclaimed his seat. "That's correct. It's . . . a pleasure to meet you. I'd heard you joined the
company a few months ago. Excellent work on that *Clementine*
case, or so they tell me."

"You're too kind." She accepted the chair Henry brought her and drew herself forward into the circle. Once settled there, with her scarf now draped over the armrest, she addressed Gideon directly. "And I suppose that makes you Dr. Bardsley, the inventor. I've read quite a lot about you. They say you're a genius."

Gideon rubbed his thumb against the rim of his coffee cup. "Of course they do." Then he said to the former president, "Mr. Lincoln, I don't care what kind of badge this woman carries these days; she was a *Confederate* agent—I mean really, for God's sake, it's the only thing anyone knows her for. That and a mediocre production of *Macbeth.*"

Henry Epperson squeezed his coffee cup a little too tightly. "There's no need to be rude, Dr. Bardsley."

Lincoln said to the room at large, and to Maria in particular, "He's often direct like that. It's best not to take it personally."

"She's more than welcome to take it personally," Gideon countered. "I *intend* it personally. She campaigned for my people's enslavement—she was even a hero of the cause. I don't want her help or need it. I'd never be able to trust it, if I took it."

"Hero of the cause?" she repeated. "Dr. Bardsley, I was *evicted* from the cause because I loved the wrong man. So I lost my country and then I lost the man, too—on a Union submarine, might I point out."

"All the more reason to doubt your sentiments," he said flatly. "You have something to prove. *Everything* to prove, if you want your country back."

"And what makes you think I *do* want my country back?" she snapped. "I left that whole 'my country right or wrong' business back in my first marriage, right along with 'my husband right or wrong,' and you can rest assured that the CSA wants no further dealings with me. Let me help you, Dr. Bardsley—let me help solve this problem your machine is so worried about."

Nelson Wellers set his cup on the table beside the chair and put up his hands in a call for peace. "*Please,* Gideon . . . the woman is here at Mr. Lincoln's request, sent by Mr. Pinkerton himself. If they can trust her expertise, you may as well trust it, too."

Henry pleaded, "Really, Doc. Give her a chance."

"Dr. Wellers. Mr. Epperson," Maria said firmly. "I am grateful for your confidence, but I understand Dr. Bardsley's reluctance to have me here."

"Somehow I doubt that."

She jabbed back, "Do I understand it firsthand? No, obviously I don't. And no one says you have to cooperate. You aren't the first man to play rough because you can't stand the sight of me, and you won't be the last. But this is my job, and I'll do it—with or without you. If you want to stand in the way of your own advocates, I suppose that's your prerogative. If you'd like to find out what's really going on here, then get on board and play nice."

"Miss Boyd, I don't take orders from Mr. Lincoln. You can safely bet I won't take them from *you.*"

Maria Boyd appeared on the verge of losing her temper, but manners prevailed and she forced her composure to override her aggravation. "Again, doctor, that's your decision. I don't work for you, and I don't have to make you happy. I work for Mr. Pinkerton, as do you—Dr. Wellers? And Mr. Epperson, you're with the Marshals Service, is that correct?" It sounded like a too-desperate attempt to steer the conversation elsewhere, and to Gideon's intense irritation, it worked.

The marshal relaxed, happy to have a more neutral topic in play. "Henry—just call me Henry, please. And, yes, that's right. I suppose it was in your dossier from the agency?"

"Yes, because my employer knew you'd be present. Not much love lost between the Pinks and the service, is there?"

"No, ma'am, but this is a special case, and I trust we can all work together like civilized professionals," he said, casting a quick look at Gideon, who neither melted nor argued. "The U.S. Marshals

Service is prepared to cooperate with the Pinkertons, or any other organization which Mr. Lincoln sees fit to involve."

Something about the strict formality nagged at Gideon's attention, undermining his words. "I don't believe you," he blurted, before he'd really had time to work out *why*. "I think you're here on your own time, or at least on your own recognizance."

Nelson Wellers said, "Now, Gideon, that's not called for . . ."

But Henry fidgeted in his seat, flicking glances between Lincoln and Maria Boyd, so Gideon pushed. "Marshals don't play nice with Pinks. The Pinks only care about Mr. Lincoln here because he pays them—and maybe because the man on top still feels a little guilty about his son's failings as a security agent; I don't know. You're not here on behalf of the service, and I want to hear you admit it."

"All right, then: No, I'm not. Not exactly," Henry admitted. "But I believe in ending the war, and Mr. Lincoln has become the foremost face of that effort. If anyone can do it, he can. And I want to help."

Maria Boyd frowned. "And the Marshal Service doesn't?"

It was Henry's turn to shrug. "Yes, of *course* the service wants to help. As a point of particular interest, the marshals are increasingly interested in the disease threat out on the fronts. Evidence is mounting that we're looking at something that could cost the Union its impending victory, something worse than illness."

"Much worse," Gideon interjected.

"Yes, thank you—and Mr. Lincoln tells me that your research and my suspicions dovetail nicely. The thing is, I'm confident there's a money connection between the walking plague and certain warhawks in positions of power on *both* sides of the Mason-Dixon, and the service is not ready to commit to an investigation of people who are allegedly fighting on our side . . . people who would resent the implications of our interest, and are powerful enough to cause us problems."

Maria's frown became more thoughtful. "Warhawks sowing a plague. . . . That's a dark theory, Mr. Epperson."

"But you don't doubt it, do you? That there are men—and women—capable of manipulating tragedy to their own benefit?"

"I'm too good a gambler to bet against the bottomless depths of human depravity," she replied. For once, Gideon agreed with her.

Henry continued. "So it's true that I'm here on my personal time. But even so, I'm here with my badge and my authority, and I mean to make myself useful."

Abraham Lincoln made use of the opening. "And you're here with information, too. Possibly something of tremendous importance. Go on, tell them who you saw in Danville last week."

"You were in Danville?" Gideon interrupted. Not alarmed, but intrigued, and tired of other people steering the discussion. Here was something that interested him, so he seized on it. "At last week's Congress?"

Henry nodded. "Yes, I was there—again, on my own time, and at my own risk—and I saw two people of note. To be more precise, two Southern women of infamy and repute: Sally Tompkins and Katharine Haymes."

Nelson Wellers let out a low whistle and sat back in his chair, folding his arms across his belly. "Katharine Haymes. God Almighty."

"Haymes . . ." Gideon repeated. "I know the surname. Does she have any connection to Haymes and Sons Industries?"

Abraham Lincoln said, "Oh, yes. She is the 'sons' in Haymes and Sons. Whether it's a joke or a matter of practicality in a world of businessmen, I have no idea; but it was her father's company, and when he passed away, when there were no actual sons to take the reins, she assumed control. Under her command, it's become a million-dollar weapons factory."

The pieces clicked together in Gideon's head, tap-tap-tap, like the printing device's keys pounding ink onto paper. "She financed a good portion of the research back at Fort Chattanooga. Her money was generally welcome there, but not entirely. There were *stories.*"

"What kind of stories?" Maria asked. "I ask at the risk of boring these other gentlemen, but I seem to be the only one here who hasn't heard of her."

Lincoln supplied the missing unpleasantness. "She tested chemical weapons on Union prisoners of war. As far as the North is concerned, she's a war criminal."

"And she's not much more popular in the South," Henry added. "Even the CSA wasn't happy about that particular incident. There was a general outcry, and it even made the papers in a few places."

Gideon had been present in Tennessee at the time of the incident, and he remembered it well. He didn't remember much of an outcry, but maybe he hadn't been listening for one. "About the death of—what, a few hundred Union men? The CSA couldn't afford to feed them anyway. They probably thought she was doing them a favor."

But Nelson Wellers shook his head. "No, not at all. Too many Southerners have family of their own stuck in Union camps. Even if you think they lack all milk of human kindness, you have to grant them a fear of retribution. Should word get around that Southerners were casually gassing war prisoners, maybe the North would start doing something equally awful to the men in their charge."

"All right," he relented. "I *will* grant them that."

"While you're at it," Maria Boyd added, "you may as well grant them a sense of fair play. War has rules, and let's all be as direct as Dr. Bardsley prefers: The South will lose this conflict. Sooner rather than later, I expect. And when that day finally comes, they'll want to bow out with some shred of grace—and a decent surrender treaty is difficult enough to negotiate without the shadow of war crimes looming over the proceedings."

"You're asking me to grant them pragmatism, but tell me—have they learned any, in the last twenty years? Because last time I looked, they instigated a war with a larger, better fortified neighbor . . . while policing a slave class that vastly outnumbered them in its strongest enclaves. If I sit here and think about it for a few minutes, I *might* be able to come up with a worse idea."

"Well, *you're* the genius," she said, not bothering to hide her displeasure with the veneer of civility.

He laughed. "If it weren't true, you wouldn't be angry."

"I'd demur and say that you're right, but you know that already. So instead I'll remind you that there's nothing I can do about the past, and that we have work to do here, now. Someone tell me about Katharine Haymes."

Henry answered quickly. "She's become an unpleasant secret. No one brought any charges against her for the incident with the war prisoners, which was ridiculous, and everyone knows it. It looked like all she got was a slap on the wrist and a scolding, but she was also asked to keep her head down. The CSA wants her money, but they want it quietly. Too many people in their ranks think she ought to be in prison, even though they protect her operations in Missouri, and are more than happy to make use of her information and technology."

"So what was she doing in Danville?" Wellers asked.

"Just . . . watching," he said. "Watching Sally Tompkins say her piece, and then watching her get dragged off the congressional floor."

Maria Boyd gasped. "They did *what*? To Captain Sally?"

Henry explained. "She was there to speak on the subject of the Robertson Hospital and its expenses; but when she got up to speak, she was mostly concerned about a disease, some illness striking the Southern troops. It sounded very much like the walking plague we already know here in the North—in fact, if it was anything else, I'd be astonished. But she was shouted down and physically removed from the premises. It was one of the most astonishing things I've ever seen, and I'm almost *certain* that Katharine Haymes was the one who orchestrated it."

 *Five*

The War Department meetings were not technically secret, but Grant could never quite shake the impression that they were clandestine nonetheless: always held in the evening, always at some private location, and without his personal guard staff—even the men who protected the nation's leaders were left outside to eavesdrop and wait.

More than once, Grant had idly wondered if he'd ever missed any of these meetings, simply by virtue of not having been invited. He was only the president, after all. President of the United States, or what was left of them.

Tonight's meeting was held in the dreaded yellow oval, an elaborate office he would've never picked for himself—and certainly wouldn't have decorated as it stood, not if his life depended on it. But there was something *fixed* about the place, or that was how it felt; even Julia agreed, and she was more than willing to tweak anything else in the presidential homestead. It was her right as first lady—she'd told him so more than once—but at night when they'd lie close together and talk about the day, she would admit that this particular room felt strangely untouchable.

He stood behind "his" enormous desk, pretending to look out over the gardens. It had rained that day, and the humidity had lingered, then frozen. The roses and other assorted bushes glimmered oddly as the electric lanterns sparked, casting chilled condensation into the night in soft wisps.

But he was not looking at the gardens.

He was watching the window glass, tracking the reflections of the other men in the room as they milled about, helping themselves to brandy and chattering just quietly enough to sound like they were discussing important things, matters of state. It was more likely that they gossiped like old hens.

But it felt like something important would happen any minute now.

He sensed it in the rising tension of the department members who had showed up on this occasion—which was most of them this time. As often as not, fully half would skip the formalities and ask for someone to send them word, as if Grant's secretary had nothing better to do than sit around and print up the minutes of these tedious meetings.

Perhaps John *didn't* have anything better to do, but Grant still disliked asking him to for this.

He didn't like asking John to perform any task, really. Didn't understand the need for a secretary. It felt silly. And he liked John well enough, but could never shake the feeling that John was always watching, taking notes—even if only in his head—in order to write the inevitable biography that would surely follow him out of office.

Whenever that turned out to be. Three terms already, and another one on the way—if the polls could be believed, the impending election was his to lose. No one wanted to change leaders in the middle of the war, not again. No matter how badly he wanted them to.

Sometimes he wondered glumly if the only way out of the White House was a bullet to the head, and then he'd think of Lincoln and feel like a jackass.

Finally the double doors opened and Desmond Fowler joined

the meeting, which looked increasingly like a party at a gentlemen's club, as three or four cigars were already alight, and almost
no one was seated. There weren't really enough chairs for a meeting. Why was it being held here again? Someone had surely told
him, but he'd be damned if he could remember.

He glanced down at his hand. He was still holding half a drink.
His fourth since he'd arrived, so he was pacing himself. Julia would
be proud, or maybe not. He wouldn't mention it to her, and if she
asked, he'd lie.

He swallowed what remained and set the glass down precariously close to the edge of the desk.

Turning around, he mustered a smile for Fowler, who wasn't
looking at him yet.

The smile melted into confusion. The Secretary of State was
not alone. On his arm walked a tall, terribly slender woman in an
expensive dress that Grant hoped his wife never saw, or else he'd
be buying one very much like it . . . and there was already enough
irritating public interest in his finances.

The woman in question was brunette. Very brunette. Her hair
looked like a pile of carefully coiffed raven wings, and surely he
wasn't the first to think of that, because her navy blue hat was
decorated with just such a taxidermied wing, set with a large,
presumably fake, square-cut ruby.

She was pretty. No denying that. He guessed her for forty, but
would've said thirty-five out of politeness, were he forced to make
any sort of public assessment of the matter. Sharp cheekbones, cool
green eyes. A thin mouth, but nicely shaped. A poet might have
described her as "willowy," but the word that sprang to Grant's
mind was "brittle."

Her presence caused a minor hullaballoo: This was a gentlemen's club, after all. Or, no, it wasn't. It only felt like it to a man with
(how many?) drinks in him. But men were smoking and speaking
of war, so it was a manly gathering, if nothing else. Invitation

only, and he was quite confident that this woman hadn't been invited.

The office lights wobbled, and for one awful second, he wasn't sure about any of this—where he was, what he was doing here, why Desmond Fowler had brought a date—should Grant have brought Julia?—but he composed himself in time to remember that, really, he was the goddamn president.

"Fowler," he said, just a little too loudly. He checked himself and started again. "Fowler, there you are. We've been waiting."

"My apologies, Mr. President, but there was a problem with our coach," he said smoothly. Grant would've bet his life that it wasn't true. The Secretary of State swanned forward to meet him, and the woman on his arm glided as if she moved on rails. "Please, allow me to introduce my . . . guest. This is Miss Katharine Haymes."

"This isn't a dinner party." He didn't quite mean to be rude, but there it was. "You might've mentioned you planned to bring someone. I'm not entirely sure this is appropriate." He tried not to meet this woman's gaze; those chilly green eyes unsettled him. Such a funny color, like cut limes, or a very strong julep. He couldn't recall the last time he'd had a julep. These days, it'd practically be treason.

Desmond Fowler opened his mouth to reply, but took a moment too long to formulate his response. Katharine Haymes took a step toward the president and offered him her hand, and now he was on the receiving end of those unearthly eyes, whether he liked it or not. "Mr. President, it's a privilege and an honor to meet you, I must say."

Reptilian sprang to mind. Or maybe he was drunker than he thought. He had no idea what color the eyes of any given reptile were.

But he took her hand, because it'd go well beyond the casual appearance of rudeness to refuse, and gave it a perfunctory kiss before saying, "I'm sorry, I've been an ass." Someone in the back of the room choked on a mouthful of something expensive, but Grant didn't care, so he continued. "But there *is* a protocol to this sort of thing. Isn't there, Fowler?"

With a fixed, unpleasant smile, Fowler replied, "Protocols were made to be tested, and occasionally revised."

"If you say so. But what occasion do we have tonight?" Behind him, Grant heard mutterings that were halfway meant to be heard by all. He hated that kind of muttering. Speak up and make yourself heard, and take responsibility for having said it, that was his philosophy. Not that he strictly disagreed with the room's general timbre, or its complaint that it *would not do* to have a lady present for such proceedings. He just didn't care for cowards, that was all.

But Desmond rose to the occasion, or at least described it with enough gravitas and aplomb that he got everyone's attention. "Because tonight we learn how we're going to end the war."

"Once and for all?" asked Emmet Wigfall, a man from someplace small and unmentionable in New York with an unfortunate name but a great fortune.

Fowler said peevishly, "Yes, once and for all. Or else why even take a stab at it? I mean *really,* Emmet. But we *are* going to end the war—and, more to the point, we're going to *win* it—with the help of Miss Haymes and her remarkable weaponry."

"Ah," Grant said. It meant nothing, except that Desmond's declaration seemed to require some answering syllable, so he provided it. And he followed it up with, "I see," for suddenly he *did* see—they were talking about Desmond's program. This was the woman who'd done the dirty work. Or she'd done *some* portion of the dirty work, that was for damn sure. Desmond Fowler never did much of anything that wasn't dirty.

It had taken Grant entirely too long to figure this out about his Secretary of State. If he'd only paid attention sooner, he might've been able to do something about this man . . . a brilliant man, of course, and no one would say otherwise. But he was not a man you wanted to keep very close.

No, that was wrong.

Friends close. Enemies closer.

Grant thought—and very nearly said aloud—that he ought to keep Fowler in a box under his bed for safekeeping. Only a glimmer of sobriety pulled the emergency brake in time to keep him from airing the idea to the room at large.

He shook his head, which only made the room wobble. By the time it settled, Desmond Fowler had led Katharine Haymes to a seat, and she was sitting decorously with a fancy beaded bag in her lap and her legs crossed at the ankle, offering a peek at a pair of boots that might've cost more than a horse.

"So this is where you tell us about your program to end the war. Or how you got the money for it, behind my back, if I can infer a few things from your grand announcement," the president said, just loudly enough to dampen the room's uncomfortable murmur. When surprised silence was achieved, he added, "Because I sure as hell didn't sign off on this."

Fowler stood up straighter and placed a hand on Katharine's shoulder. Grant couldn't shake the impression that he didn't mean to calm her, but to draw on her strength—and it unnerved him, though he couldn't find a clear enough place in his head to sort out precisely *why.*

"Mr. President," the Secretary of State began, with a defensive note in his voice. "Allocation of funds occurs at your discretion, yes—in this instance, at any rate. But I believed in Miss Haymes's program, and I was able to strike a deal that wouldn't dip into the Union's coffers."

Grant pulled up a chair. It was a big, heavy chair, and he moved it easily, leaving a trail as he drew it roughly across the knotted rug, which he found perversely satisfying. He dropped himself into that chair, facing both Desmond and Katharine. Fixing them with a gaze that demanded answers, even if he was afraid to hear them. "This must be one hell of a deal, then. It must be so good, you'll hardly have to sell it. I'm sure we'll all be on board the very minute the explanation leaves your mouth."

The room's other occupants—nine men of various allegiances, motives, calibers, and competencies—congealed around the scene, lurking at the sideboard and the liquor cabinet, or milling about at the edges of their bright, unhappy circle.

Fowler didn't waver or find a chair of his own. Katharine patted his hand, and then she answered for him. "Gentlemen, Mr. President, thank you for granting me an audience this evening. I am well aware that my presence here means this isn't a typical war meeting, but I want to assure you all that war is the matter at hand. I am here to offer you the keys to victory."

Jemison Simms, an old-timer from Pennsylvania, was almost as difficult to impress as the president. And, apparently, he was better briefed. "That's a peculiar proposition, ma'am, seeing as you're a Southerner yourself. You've tamed your accent well, but your reputation precedes you."

Her reputation hadn't gotten anywhere near Grant yet, a fact which he was prepared to place squarely in the deliberate, conniving hands of Desmond Fowler. He covered for his ignorance with a guess. "Yes, Miss Haymes—*do* explain why a Confederate woman of means has such an interest in seeing her nation defeated."

"Southern, yes. Confederate, no. They have nasty words for people like me south of the line, Mr. President."

Oh, but he had no doubt. And it took true physical effort on his part to keep from saying so. "Surely *not*," he mustered successfully, if without sincerity. Maybe it wasn't fair, the way he disliked her already—but if she wanted to make a better first impression on people, she could keep better company.

"If there's another name they'd like to give you, I'd expect it might be 'criminal,' " Simms pushed, his fluffy white facial hair hiding most of his uncertain frown, but not all of it.

Grant wasn't sure what Simms was talking about, but Wigfall chimed in. Usually the way Wigfall liked to state and repeat the obvious annoyed him. This time, he was glad for any shred of context he could glean.

"The Rossville incident," Wigfall said. "The Rebs may not have held you accountable, but you may rest assured that Washington *will*."

Desmond Fowler cleared his throat. "On the contrary."

"She's a war criminal," Jemison Simms asserted. "And an enemy sympathizer, at that—though considering how much she's contributed to the war effort down South, we may as well call her a treasonous enemy. She shouldn't be allowed in the District at all, and you've brought her into a closed meeting."

A dim recollection started to take shape in the back of Grant's mind. All these little pieces were adding up to a memory, some bit of trivia overheard and ignored. A Southern woman, making weapons and testing them . . . testing them inappropriately. Did she do it at a prison camp? Was that right? It felt right, as he turned the idea over, testing its familiarity. The more he thought about it, the more certain he was that yes, this was that same woman. Haymes. Not the sort of name that stuck out in a conversation. Not his fault that he hadn't recognized it immediately.

Wigfall joined in with Simms. "Perhaps we should contact the authorities, have her arrested on the spot."

Wryly, and not at all nervously, she replied, "I'm sitting in a room with the president. If you have a higher authority than that in mind, I'd like to hear about it."

This rebuttal caused all eyes to turn to Grant. Now he *really* hated her. But Desmond Fowler had cleared his throat and said . . . he'd said . . . oh, yes, now he remembered. The president asked,

"What did you mean by 'on the contrary,' Fowler? Why isn't she accountable here? Do you know something I don't?"

The question was so huge and ridiculous that he smiled in its wake. Fowler smiled back, and for one narrow, unreproducible instant, they might've shared a moment of camaraderie, had the subject been anything else in the world.

The moment passed. Fowler's grin condensed into something harder and differently cruel. "Miss Haymes and I have come to an agreement. A formal, legal agreement which has been signed off upon by Salmon P. Chase."

"Signed . . . signed off upon? That's not even English," Grant complained, but that wasn't what really made him mad. "You think you can go running to the Supreme Court every time you want to take steps I don't approve of?"

"You'll approve of this one when you hear it. But I didn't have time to convince you outright, so I've taken a shortcut. And before you say so, *yes,* I know you can fight the Chief Justice on this. I have only his word to back it up. The rest of the court is not yet involved, though it certainly *could* become part of the game if it has to."

"Don't threaten me, Fowler."

"No one's threatening anyone!" he protested. "I'm only explaining why I've taken the path of least time investment and resistance. And if you'll only let the lady speak, I think you'll agree that I've come to the right conclusion."

"If you're so sure I'd come around, why didn't you just ask me in the first place?" Grant demanded. He walked over to the liquor cabinet despite only halfway noticing that he needed another drink, so accustomed were his hands to finding refills before he'd even detected the glass was empty.

Fowler snuck a glance down at Katharine, who sat calmly and still. "Because Miss Haymes makes her case better than I do, but

I was compelled to guarantee her safety during her visit. I did not have time to risk the possibility of your disapproval. Now, I'm asking you, Mr. President, if you'll kindly hear her out. She might surprise you."

"Fine. Talk," he commanded, and when he was finished pouring, he found his seat again. He leaned back, feeling stronger with the drink in his hand. "You've gone to all this trouble, after all. It'd be a shame to waste a judge's signature. But I don't care if you surprise me. I want you to impress me—and it had better be good, or I might well be sending a carriage around to Justice Chase's house. The impolite hour be *damned*."

"Very well, and thank you," she said, and the other men in the room hovered closer, huddling nearer to the tense little axis of drama.

She began: "First, I'd like to thank you for giving me your time and your attention. And second, I must thank Mr. Fowler for being kind enough to make the arrangements which have made my visit possible."

Grant, out of patience and full of drink, interjected, "I hope 'third' brings us to the point."

"Third," she continued, as if she hadn't heard the naked irritation in his voice, "I am here because the CSA is losing the war, and I don't want to go down with it. I'm not altruistic, and by your definition I absolutely *am* a criminal. I have nothing to hide, because all I want is to protect myself. I want to survive the fall of the Confederacy, and whatever comes after it."

"And how do you plan to do that?" Jemison Simms asked, his usual grumpiness tempered by curiosity.

"I enjoy bargaining, and I do it well; indeed, this is something that Mr. Fowler and I have in common—a deep-seated belief that in the midst of any difficulty, there is a compromise to be found that will benefit all parties."

"So what do you bring to the table, Miss Haymes?" Grant

asked, because he knew better than anyone that political bargaining was just another way of saying "gambling."

"I bring the end of the South's rebellion. I bring the end of your war—thanks to a weapon the likes of which the world has not yet seen."

"We've already got one of those—a submarine we've fished out of New Orleans. Our engineers are having a devil of a time with it, but they say exactly what you're saying: It could end the war, reestablish the Anaconda plan, choke off their supplies at last."

A flicker of annoyance shadowed Haymes's brow. "I've heard of this machine. The papers say it's a modern marvel, and I have no reason to disbelieve them. But if I understand correctly, you can barely pilot the craft at all, and there's only the one prototype. If you're very lucky, you'll 'choke them off,' as you put it, within another year or two at best. More likely three or four, if you ask me."

She wasn't entirely wrong, and that was the only reason Grant didn't interrupt.

Since no one else interrupted, either, she went on. "I can bring you something better. Something faster, and more powerful. Something tested, proven, and catastrophic—something that could end the war in a single battle, if the battle is chosen wisely. Or a single target, depending on your personal commitment to the war's conclusion.

"I will provide you with this weapon, and it will cost you nothing."

"Oh, it'll cost us *something*," Simms growled.

"Nothing you value," she clarified. "I ask for amnesty and immunity with regards to any charges resulting from the Rossville incident in 1878, so that when the Union is ultimately restored, I can rejoin it with a clean slate. No charges, no threats—just the chance to begin again."

"Without a cloud hanging over you?" Simms asked, almost as rude sober as Grant could be while drinking. "That's what it was, am I correct? Or that's how I've heard it described."

Grant didn't have time to hide his confusion. "A cloud?"

"Of gas. Poisonous gas, used on our soldiers. One witness said it looked like an enormous yellow cloud, heavy enough to settle across the compound and kill everyone who breathed it."

Without so much as a penitent lowering of her eyes, Katharine Haymes replied, "Not a bad assessment. That *is* what it looks like to the uninformed observer, yes—a yellow cloud. But whatever it looks like, Fort Chattanooga demanded a field test, and you can't seriously think that they would allow me to test it on Confederate soldiers. They were the ones who decided to use prisoners, not me. And once the results hit the papers and telegraph wires, they needed someone to blame for the breach in wartime protocol, so they picked me. The weapon was designed with my money, in my factory, with my scientists and developers. My name was attached from start to finish. I was an easy scapegoat."

The president found it very difficult to believe that this woman had been anyone's scapegoat; she struck him as the kind of person who used other people, not the reverse. But she was a woman, it was true; and she was a woman with money, and he'd known plenty of men who didn't like that combination. He mustered a small sliver of doubt, only to feel it wither and crumble.

She continued: "I know all too well what the Union thinks of me now, but none of it was my call. I want to make clear that I'm an ally, and I was an American before I was ever declared a Confederate. That's why I'm requesting formal amnesty."

She sighed, and made a visible effort to soften herself. "As you must know, it can be difficult for an unmarried woman to survive in this world, in this *war.* While my father was alive, I could rely on him—never my mother, who passed away when I was a child. So you see? I've been alone, without guidance or protection for all of my life. And I'll be the first to admit I've made mistakes. Plenty of them, if you want the truth. But I refuse to allow this one to haunt me through the reconstruction of my nation. I am a patriot, Mr. President, but I have fought for my own survival long enough. It's time for me to fight for my country: the United States of America."

"That's a pretty way of saying you don't want to go to prison." He looked down at his glass. It was empty. He couldn't remember having taken a single swallow.

"Take it as you like. But I'd like to throw my weight behind the Union, if the Union will have me. I'll end your war in a fortnight if you'll let me take charge of the project, or if you'll allow Mr. Fowler to pursue it on my behalf, with my assistance."

"That's a bold claim." The way Grant said it was just short of an accusation. She couldn't possibly do any such thing. Could she?

"It's a bold program." She patted Desmond Fowler's hand. "And it's a bold man you have on your team, to take such a risk. As for the weapons we're developing—I could arrange for a demonstration, perhaps. Not soldiers, of course," she specified. "Maybe dogs, or horses, or—"

Grant was too drunk to keep the horror to himself. "Dear *God,* woman. If the weapon is half what you claim it is, it ought to be tested in battle—not on dogs, and certainly not horses!"

She smirked at him, and he wanted to punch her—a desire which shamed him even as the thought of it delighted him. The prospect of running a fist into her smug, pretty face. A face that Desmond Fowler could scarcely stop looking at. A lying face. He was as confident of that as the drink in his hand. Except the drink was gone, his glass empty.

Fine, then. He wasn't sure of anything.

"Very well then, Mr. President. I understand your reluctance, and I'm flattered by it. You give me credit for having created something terrible, and I thank you."

He shuddered. "What an awful thing to say."

"More awful than war itself?" she asked. "Terrible things are necessary sometimes. One might argue that any means to the end of hostilities might call itself a virtue, no matter how frightful the initial cost. If we kill a few thousand people in the South and they tremble before the Union's military might . . . then we might save the lives of tens of thousands more. How many have died already, Mr. President?"

"More than tens of thousands. Hundreds."

"Hundreds from battle alone, or hundreds more from the disease, terror, and famine that comes in a war's wake?"

"I could not say." He did not know.

"But you've seen it yourself. You know the war better than anyone, and I do not think that you love it. I believe you want to see it concluded, in order to begin the long work of reconstructing the nation."

She had him there. "I hate the war. If I could end it tomorrow, I would do so."

Her smile was both sharper and more frightening than a line of bayonets, and Grant had walked right into it. "Then we do agree after all. I do think we can work together, Mr. President. I'll end your war if you let me. I'll give you back your country, in exchange for a clean reputation."

He shook his head, not to argue with her but because she was asking for more than he could offer. Immunity from prosecution? That was easy enough to come by; he could hand it over with a signature. But should he? He did not believe her when she'd called herself a scapegoat. He did not believe that she's unknowingly been party to a war crime, and he did not believe that she wanted nothing else from him—nothing at all. But if he asked her now, she'd only lie some more, and he was too drunk to sort out the particulars.

There was nothing else he could say. He could either play along and pretend he was running the show, or he could fight and lose, and then everyone would know how weak he'd truly become.

And to think, these men wanted him to run for another term. But he hadn't fought that, either. He'd missed his chance. And now, he was on a ballot, in a yellow oval, in a white house, in a cage of his own making.

Could he survive a fourth term? Would he *want* to?

He stood up without another word, set his glass down on the sideboard by the door, and walked out.

He did not stumble until he was around the corner, so no one saw it, thank God; except then Jemison Simms stuck his head out to ask, "Mr. President?"

Grant did not turn around, only waved and said, "I'm fine. Leave me alone. I need to think."

Simms, having known the president since they'd served in the war together, on the ground and on horseback, in uniforms instead of suits . . . decided (wisely, in Grant's estimation) to leave the matter alone and go back inside.

The president assumed that Simms would settle things and send the cabinet home from what had to be one of the worst War Department meetings in the history of such meetings. Was it even an official meeting? No. Not with that woman there. Not with that cat among pigeons.

And Desmond Fowler—the fattest, worst pigeon of them all— was standing right behind her. His hand on her shoulder, not to control her but to take direction from her. Grant did not like that. Not in the slightest. Because Fowler was right about several things, including a few he hadn't said, but only implied, like the fact that Grant would lose if he fought him. And that was the crux of it, wasn't it? He'd brought Fowler in to be the Secretary of State because Fowler understood the way Washington worked. He understood politics, and politicking, as a duck knows water. That's why he'd needed him eight years before, and that's why he'd become so powerful: because Grant was a soldier, not a statesman. He did not know—and had never understood, not for five sober seconds—how things worked between men of state.

Maybe war *wasn't* the most terrible thing of all. It was easy to understand, for all the carnage and misery. Here is one side. Here is another. You try to kill each other, and the best army with the best strategists wins, barring unexpected interference.

As his thoughts tumbled and clattered together, he found his way to a small library, one he'd only ever entered once or twice. It had a door, one he could shut behind himself. It even had a lock, which he used, then turned a switch to raise the dimmed electric lights. Then he turned them down again, because they made his head hurt.

"A patriot," he mumbled.

That's what Katharine Haymes had called herself. And he was certain Desmond Fowler thought the same of himself, as did the rest of those men in the War Department—scheduling war without setting foot inside it, or not anymore.

"To hell with the patriots," he said, scanning the room for a liquor cabinet and not seeing one. He rubbed his eyes and sat down on the floor before his legs gave out underneath him.

"To hell with us *all*."

 *Six*

It took so little time to reach Richmond from Washington, D.C., that Maria wondered how the two cities managed to fight on opposite sides of the same war. It wasn't even terribly difficult to travel between them; all it took was a false set of paperwork (provided by Mr. Pinkerton) claiming that she was a Red Cross nurse, a train ticket, and finally a carriage that took her to the doorstep of the Robertson Hospital.

The hospital was once a very large house, owned by a judge who'd fled the premises when the Yankees were coming, back in 1861. As the Confederacy stabilized into a state of war, the house's original owner had made several attempts to return and reclaim the property; but Captain Sally had countersued, on grounds that possession is nine-tenths of the law . . . and besides, she was performing a service for the nation, a service she successfully argued was more important than the cowardly relocation effort that left the house abandoned in the first place. Since then, the house had been augmented extensively in order to accommodate the thousand or so men who found their way to Robertson from the fronts each year. Now it sat in the center of a small compound of tents, outbuildings, storage lean-tos, and a carriage house for the single ambulance that operated on the hospital's behalf.

Maria Boyd stood on the steps in front of the main entryway and took it all in.

She'd heard stories about the Robertson for years, even as a teenager, long before it became the sprawling institution she saw before her. Renowned around the world, it was a first-class facility with a shocking 90 percent survival rate—unheard of for civilian hospitals, much less for a ward that almost exclusively treated battlefield injuries. Doctors visited from distant nations and scholars wrote papers on the exceptional cleanliness of the premises, drawing parallels between the unexpected medical success and routines of boiled laundry, washed floors, and frequent patient baths.

Maybe the cleanliness *did* have something to do with it. Maria didn't imagine that a filthy hospital was ideal, but as odors billowed forcefully from the open windows, she couldn't help but wonder precisely what a dirty hospital must smell like, because this was positively *awful.*

The air was permeated with a frozen fog of blood and medicine, burned hair, charred skin, body odor, rotting flesh, and some sharp, unidentifiable note. Maria put one gloved hand over her nose and mouth, but it didn't do anything, so she reached for the door's latch instead.

It vibrated under her hand, and a humming noise buzzed through her glove. Steeling herself, she pulled down the lever. The door snapped outward with such ferocity that it nearly knocked her back into the yard, but she held on, and planted her feet against the ensuing gust.

Three enormous turbines on rollers stood against the far wall, aimed at the open windows on either side of the door, overlooking the driveway and the carriage house. These giant wind-screws were powered by a diesel generator; they blasted air from the back of the main foyer to the windows on either side of the door, and now they caught Maria in their horizontal tornado.

Her hatpins struggled against the wind; her hair flapped and blew; her skirt whipped around her legs. She squinted against the bitterly cold onslaught and saw no beds, equipment, or people. Then a voice cried out, "Time! Go ahead and turn them off!" And, indeed, the generator clacked to a halt. Within a few seconds the giant blades slowed to a stop, pivoting with a soft creaking sound but making no further commotion.

Shortly thereafter, the room flooded with nurses and retained men in improvised hospital uniforms. They swarmed Maria, rushing past her to close the windows and open the interior doors. And then she saw that yes, the beds were in those *other* rooms. Rows and rows of them, perhaps a couple dozen in each of the clusters she could see from her vantage point right inside the foyer. Each bed had a warmly bundled body upon it, and each small ward had a series of attendants, as well.

Maria realized she hadn't shut the door behind herself. She hadn't been able to. She reached back to do so now, and finally someone approached to acknowledge her.

He was tall and heavyset, missing part of his left hand and the whole of his right eye. His voice was all Alabama vowels when he asked her, "Excuse me, ma'am . . . can I help you with something?"

"Yes, I . . . I . . ." But she couldn't gather her thoughts, not while she was testing the integrity of her hat and hoping the feeling would come back into her frozen cheeks sooner rather than later. She also remembered her accent. Chicago had been filing off its edges, so she sharpened them afresh to make sure she sounded like a local. "I'm sorry, could I ask you—those fans . . . ?"

He nodded and gestured at them with his good arm. "Just installed 'em a month ago. And I do apologize for the temperature in here; they chill the place up good. We only run them for a quarter-hour, twice a day. It circulates the air, keeps the smell down, and dries the laundry good." He pointed up at the ceiling, where hundreds of dangling sheets were strung across a jungle of tightly stretched cords. "Don't worry, we warm 'em up before we put 'em back on the beds."

"But isn't it hard . . . on the patients, I mean? It's colder in here than it is outside!"

"No, ma'am, it only feels that way. And as you can see"—he cocked a thumb at the newly opened doors—"the patients are all tucked away. There aren't any fans in the wards—just ductwork and ventilation to draw the bad air, so we can shoot it out the windows. The furnaces will kick on in a minute, and the whole place will come up toasty, quick as can be. Now, what can I do for you, Miss . . . ?" he tried uncertainly.

"Boyd," she supplied. She sniffled, and her nose stung. "Miss Boyd. And if you could direct me to Captain Sally, I would dearly appreciate it. Is she in? And might I have a word with her?"

The greeter's demeanor shifted very slightly. His remaining eye darkened, and he sized her up again. "Could I ask what business you have with the captain?"

She reached into her bag, pulled out the paperwork Mr. Pinkerton had arranged from Chicago, and offered it to him. "I'm with the Red Cross," she said. She hadn't expected to need a more indepth story than this, perhaps with the addition of "I'm a nurse," but she didn't say that. Her instincts suggested another direction, so she ran with them. "I want to speak with her about what happened when she testified before Congress. We want to hear what she tried to say. What she wasn't *allowed* to say."

Now the man relaxed, even brightened. "Well, thank God!" he exclaimed. "Come on, now. I'll bring you up to her office. I'd offer to take your coat, but I expect you still want it."

As if on cue, the diesel generator rumbled to life once more—but this time it wasn't for the fans. A lower sound, coming from deeper in the basement, suggested that the circuit had now been shifted to serve the heating system. "Yes, thank you. I'd prefer to wear it, if that's all the same to you."

Through one of the sickrooms he led her, past men who slept, men who groaned, men who stared at the wall. They were all tucked in beneath quilts. A good idea, Maria thought, since it seemed they couldn't work both the fans and the furnace at the same time.

He took her through a corridor, around a bend, and up a set of stairs. At the top of the stairs they were stopped by a man who was larger still than her guide. He did not look injured, so perhaps he wasn't one of the retained men, too badly wounded to return to the war. In fact, he looked physically fit, and prepared to hit somebody.

He asked her companion, "Who's this?"

"Red Cross woman. Wants a word with the captain about the wheezers," he said, unable to keep a note of excitement out of the explanation.

"Red Cross? Do you have the papers to prove it? Miss Barton and Captain Sally are friendly, you know. They have more in common than in difference, never mind the lines. I didn't hear word that she'd sent anyone . . . and I wonder why she didn't come herself. The captain's been trying to reach her for weeks."

"Of course I have papers," she said, and handed them over, hoping they were good.

The man at the top of the stairs perused them, his frown never melting. Finally he said, "Fine. I'll take you to see my sister. Thanks for bringing her up, Richard."

Richard took the hint, bowed, and left Maria there.

"Your . . . your sister?" she asked her new escort.

"Sister-in-law, if you like that better." He put one arm behind her shoulders, not quite touching her, but urging her forward. "And I hope you don't mind, but I'll be coming with you, to have whatever word it is you want."

"There have been threats?" Maria surmised. "Problems, in the wake of what occurred in Congress?"

He didn't answer, but he didn't need to. When she glanced at his chest, she saw the large six-shooter he kept tucked in a holster—it peeked out from the underside of his jacket, and she had an idea that he probably had a matching weapon under the other arm, too.

"This way," was all he said. He knocked on a closed door. It was a calculated knock, two strikes with a pause, and then a third.

A muffled voice called from inside. "Adam?" It was a cautious voice, but not a frightened one.

"There's a woman from the Red Cross here to see you," he said through the door. "Her papers look good, but it's not Miss Barton. Shall I bring her in?"

Ten seconds later, a bolt slid back and the office door opened wide to reveal a slim, smallish woman with tidy, sensible hair and a crisp brown dress. Her eyes were large and intelligent, and they scanned Maria coolly, with interest, and then . . . with recognition.

Maria swallowed. "Captain Sally," she began, but the captain cut her off.

"Adam," she said, her eyes never leaving Maria. "Thank you for bringing this woman to my office. I know you intend to stay for the sake of security . . . but I think we can have this particular chat without you."

"You and I *agreed,*" he said firmly. "I'm not leaving you alone with anyone who's not on the list."

"I'm adding her to the list. I know her business here, and everything will be fine. But I thank you for your vigilance, and I would ask that you remain nearby, if that's all right."

He bobbed his head, still not pleased, but prepared to defer. He withdrew, and Sally stepped aside to let Maria join her. "Please, come inside," she said . . . and when her brother-in-law was gone, she added, "*Belle.*"

Maria held her head up and did not cringe as she entered the office and the other woman closed the door.

"Won't you have a seat?"

Maria did. She resisted the urge to pat at her tousled hair—not because she cared, but because she wasn't sure what to do with her hands. Instead, she put them in her lap and folded them. "Thank you for taking the time to speak with me," she tried as an opener. When in doubt, lead with manners.

Sally Louisa Tompkins shook her head. She said, "Skip the formalities, dear. I know who you are, and I want to know what you really want."

"That's an abrupt way to begin a conversation."

"I could've begun it with a lie, as you began your visit. Richard and Adam believed you, I expect. Both of them good men, but easily distracted, in their way. They expect a different kind of treachery from women, and aren't on guard against the worst of it."

"Very well, but if you value a woman's treachery so highly, then why did you let me in?"

She smiled. A proper smile, one backed up by a laugh that she wouldn't release. "As I said, I know who you are. Or I know who you *were.*"

Maria wanted to ask what she meant by that, but it wasn't necessary, much as it annoyed her. "I'm not here as a Yankee. Not as a Confederate. I'm here as a human being, in pursuit of the truth."

"If that's what you want to tell yourself."

"Right now the continent has bigger problems than Northern and Southern ones, wouldn't you say? Or, more to the point—isn't that what you *tried* to say? At the congressional session. When you were so ungraciously silenced."

Sally cocked her head to the right. "Word made it over the line? All the way to . . . where are the Pinkertons headquartered these days, Chicago?"

"Chicago," Maria confirmed. "And yes—word went fast, and went far, though that's not where I first heard of it."

Sally leaned back in her chair and tapped her fingers on the arm-rests. "How embarrassing," she mused. "Not my most dignified moment."

"You weren't the one doing anything undignified. Did they really drag you off the floor, rather than hear you speak?"

"Oh, yes." She shook her head at the memory. "And afterward, everyone pretended that I didn't exist. It was as if I'd died and had a funeral, and no one had told me. Old contacts, old friends. Old colleagues . . . people I'd worked with for years. They behave as if they've never known me, except for Clara. She responded to a telegram on Monday, saying she'd heard about the hullabaloo and wanted to talk. When they said I had a caller, I thought it might be her messenger—I know she's as busy as I am, these days. But then I saw *you*."

"Sorry to disappoint."

"Not sure if I'm disappointed or not, but I'm definitely intri-gued. Since you didn't correct me, shall I assume I've heard right? You're working as a Pinkerton agent, these days?"

Maria smiled nervously. "I didn't realize it was such common knowledge."

"It's not a secret, if that's what you mean. It made the papers here and there, usually in the gossip lines. I'll admit to a weak-ness for them, at the end of the day—sometimes I sit in bed with whatever dreadfuls or magazines I can find, so long as the stories have nothing at all to do with the war. And I'll read them cover to cover, even if they aren't very good or very inter-esting. Just . . . spare me from the casualty reports, troop move-ments, and mentions of the Mason-Dixon." She sighed. "A few months ago I saw a paragraph or two, that's all—no more than that, surely—saying that you'd moved up north and taken up detecting."

"I wonder who wrote it. I wonder why anyone knew, or cared."

Sally shrugged and said, "People are nosy; it isn't any more complicated than that. You were a celebrity—a golden child, weren't you? And then . . . you *weren't*. Actually"—she smiled— "I thought it was interesting. I read about your exploits when I was younger—when we both were. You were such a character, like someone lifted from one of my dreadfuls."

Maria eyed the diminutive officer, and estimated that she was likely in her mid-forties. A bit older than herself, but not much. "It's been a long war," she said.

"That is has." The captain was eyeing Maria back. For a moment, she didn't say anything. Then she came to some conclusion, and pulled her chair forward so they could speak more closely. "It seems unlikely, but . . ." she began quietly.

"But?" Maria leaned in closer.

"But you might be just what I need right now. So improbable . . . but sometimes that's the way the world works. Maybe the unexpected is all we can count on, given the state of things. But tell me the truth: Why did the Pinkertons send you to me? Answer that first—and depending on your answer, perhaps I'll give you the keys to the kingdom." Then she cast a brief glance at the door, and added in a mumble, "I can't keep them much longer. Not here, and not like this. I have to give them to *someone*."

Almost too eagerly, Maria replied. "I'm here because a scientist in Washington, D.C., made a machine designed to think like a man, but much faster and much more efficiently. The machine can't lie; it can only report its calculations, and it says that neither the North nor South will win the war—but both sides will lose to a coming plague."

"The wheezers . . ." Sally breathed, her lips scarcely moving to form the word.

"Up North they call them stumblebums, or sometimes lepers— or some variation. I've heard guttersnipe lepers and goldenrod lepers; and I've heard them called pollen-heads too, though I don't know where that designation comes from."

"I do. And if you like, I'll show you—but it isn't pretty: Around the nostrils, ears, lips, and other orifices . . . the wheezers collect a yellowish, grainy substance that accumulates uncomfortably unless it's washed away."

"Dear *God*."

"I said it wasn't pretty. But tell me more about this machine."

"Well, it was saying we should end the war, and turn the full attention of both governments toward addressing this mutual threat—at least, until someone tried to kill the man who made it. Someone, somewhere, does not want the Union or the CSA to hear its analysis."

Sally nodded unhappily. "Must be someone who makes quite a lot of money off the conflict."

"You might as well assume; no matter how hard I try, I can't imagine any other excuse big enough. One of the first things I learned as an operative was to chase the money. See where it flows, see where it pools. See who's pouring it out, and who's collecting it."

Conspiratorially, the captain asked, "And what have you learned so far? About the money behind the attempted murder, I mean."

"Precious little," she confessed. "I only just arrived in D.C. last night, in time for an awkward briefing and a change of clothes."

"Why was it awkward?" Sally asked.

Maria mentally weighed the truth against the potential cost. But she'd gotten this far by being straightforward, so she stayed the course. She kept her voice as soft as possible, while still making herself heard. "Because Abraham Lincoln is the man who hired me. It was a real shock, let me tell you."

Sally's eyes went wide. "No doubt!"

"But this is what I believe, Captain: Lincoln is working to end the war; he's struggling to protect this innocent scientist, whose family was kidnapped—though the Pinks are working on that, and I'm told that the missing people have been recovered. The former president is investing a great deal of his personal fortune

in a peaceful future, and he's leveraging every ounce of his remaining reputation to bring this war to a halt. He believes in the
machine and the man who built it, but his resources are limited.
He no longer commands the federal army, so now he can only
buy agents like myself—unless he wants to rely on the Secret Service, which he apparently *doesn't.*"

"But he asked for you?"

"To no one's greater surprise than my own."

Sally put her elbows down on the desktop and frowned
thoughtfully. "Now that I've had a moment to consider it, I'm not
sure I'm surprised at all. You're perfect for his purposes, just like
you're perfect for mine."

Genuinely confused, she asked, "How so?"

"Southern in sympathy, from sheer habit if nothing else, but
carrying the clout and the badge of a Northern authority. I think
Lincoln gambled on you, hoping that you still care enough about
the South to help him defeat it, just in time to save it. And save
the rest of the world, too."

"That's a grim thing to say. Particularly grim coming from *you,*
Captain. How much of your own fortune have you lost to prolong-
ing the war—cycling these boys back out to the front?"

"All of it, and then some. At present, the hospital operates on
research grants and foreign investment funds, mostly doctors and
universities overseas who want to know the secret of our survival
rate. I have nothing left of my own, and when the war ends, I do
not know what will become of me. But the war *does* need to
end. And you know as well as I do that the CSA is a sinking ship.
The only question left is how far it will fall, and how many can be
saved before it's lost altogether."

They sat in silence, neither of them happy, yet somehow relieved to have that frightening sentiment out in the open.

Eventually, Maria spoke—still quite softly, in case anyone listened on the other side of the door. "What can we do?"

Sally stood up. "For starters, you can come with me. Keys to the kingdom, remember?"

"Hard to forget an offer like that. So you've made up your mind?"

"I'm running out of time—and if Lincoln will gamble on you, then I will, too."

Maria rose to her feet, uncertain but strangely hopeful. She had no idea what these "keys" might be, but this was progress— and she couldn't shake the feeling that she was on the cusp of something *big.* She only hoped she'd prove worthy of the captain's trust. And the former president's. And the U.S. Marshal's. And the head Pinkerton's.

The captain opened the door, and yes, her brother-in-law was beside it. Whether or not he'd been listening was anybody's guess, but it didn't matter. Sally told him, "Everything's fine, Adam, but follow along and watch our backs, if you don't mind. I'm taking Miss Boyd downstairs, so I can show her Mercy."

"Show me . . . ? What?" Maria asked, but Sally didn't answer that question, not yet.

She said instead, "We're going to the basement, dear. And if you think the main floors smell miserably ripe, then I apologize in advance for the state of our laundry room. It's an appalling place, something out of Dante's stories, or so it seems at times. Come, this way. We'll go down the back stairway, the one the old judge's servants used."

"As you like," Maria answered, her hopefulness wilting into uncertainty.

She followed in the captain's wake. Farther behind came Adam, who pretended he simply had business in this general direction, in case anyone was watching. Down the back corridor they proceeded, all in a line; they descended stairs past nurses in fluttering aprons, they stepped aside for colored women carrying sacks of grain and bales of laundry, and they ducked quickly past a pair of men who were moving a bed from ward to ward, and at the end of the hall they rounded a corner.

Sally opened another door and a wave of steam gusted forth, shocking both for how pleasant the sudden warmth was, and for how bad it smelled—even there, in a land of terrible smells.

Maria winced. Sally said, "I would've grabbed you a vial of perfume, if I'd thought about it. Most of us become accustomed to the air here, eventually. You can always tell the newer workers, men and women both, because they're the ones still carrying such things."

"No, it's fine. I can take it," she insisted, even as she wished she'd taken a smaller breakfast so there'd be less to throw up later.

"I believe you. Now come along, it's not much farther."

"I still don't understand why . . . why the laundry room?"

"Because," Sally said, taking her arm and whispering the rest into her ear. "We hide our secrets where no one will ever wish to look for them."

The laundry room had overtaken the entire basement, and if there was nothing else to be said for it, the temperature was a welcome change. Great furnaces boiled water nonstop, and enormous tubs collected it, brimming with the foam of industrial soaps and bleaching powders; vats simmered and bubbled with the tart, faint tang of peroxide. The room bustled with strong-armed, stern-faced women both colored and white, women who heaved and dragged sacks of wet laundry along tracks above their heads— drawing it forward and then yanking the cord to open the bags, dumping the contents into carts for sorting and drying. Some of the women wore nurse's uniforms, some did not. They all wore sturdy boots made for workmen, unless Maria missed her guess; and when she slipped almost badly enough to fall, she understood why.

"The floors are wet. Always," Sally told her. "Be extra careful past these tubs; yes, that's right. It's soapy over here, too. Good morning, Edna," she added to a tall woman whose arms were blotchy and red up to the elbows. "Everything running smoothly today?"

"Yes, ma'am, though furnace number three is being fussy. Might want to send David along to take a look at it."

"Yes, I'll do that. Thank you for the suggestion."

Edna paused and dragged the back of her wrist across her sweaty brow. "The incoming room is fresh, I hate to tell you. If that's where you're headed."

Without breaking her stride, Sally said over her shoulder, "It won't be the end of us."

Maria tried not to worry about how bad it must be, if this hardened laundress felt the need to hand out warnings. She asked, "The incoming room? Is that . . . ?"

"It's where the dirty laundry dumps down the main chute. It's sorted according to type. Pillowcases, sheets, blankets. Clothing. Bandages that are good enough to reuse. I don't like putting the bandages back into circulation—it feels . . . dirty, somehow, and I can't abide dirt. I believe in the bottom of my heart that this hospital's lack of dirt is its saving grace. Literally, perhaps. But we get the wraps as white as we can before we give them back to the doctors and put them back into service. Cotton isn't the disposable commodity it once was, and we must conserve every scrap."

She stopped at a basket hanging on a wall beside a set of double doors. She reached into the basket and retrieved a pair of masks—one for her, and one for Maria. Presumably, Adam would wait out this particular leg of the adventure; he lingered back at the end of the corridor, looking out of place and distinctly uncomfortable.

Maria took the mask, a cotton one with straps to tie behind her ears. The mask was scented with lavender oil and a hint of eucalyptus.

Sally said, "We all wear them, down here. Put it on, or you'll wish you hadn't."

Maria gratefully donned the mask, and when Sally opened the double doors enough to let them both inside, she was glad for the distraction of the fragranced cloth across her face. The incoming room truly *was* hell on earth.

One large metal chute dumped an intermittent tumble of filthy laundry into a terrifying heap, confined by a bin so large it could've comfortably held a pair of horses. Each new bundle was announced by the muffled clatter of its descent from the floors above, falling wetly, gruesomely into a heap like a blood-and-vomit-soaked pyramid of human misery.

Maria gagged.

Sally sniffed and cleared her throat. "Only a little farther. Back behind the mountain of things you don't want to touch."

Sally was right. Maria didn't want to touch it. She didn't want to see it, either. She didn't want to know it existed at all, and if she could retrace her steps for a minute or two and smudge out the memory with a piece of India rubber, she would've given her soul to do so.

Stumbling behind Sally, Maria followed—almost blindly, her eyes watering from the vapors of stomach bile and pus, the old-penny scent of drying blood, the slick yellow stink of feverish sweat, the porklike odor of burned flesh, and a hundred other things too horrible to tease out from the whole. And the laundry fell and fell, bundle after bundle, dropping down the tin chute and sometimes landing with a thump, sometimes with a squish, sometimes with a splash. The laundry mountain grew and shrank, fed and whittled down at a similar tempo as masked women with elbow-length gloves and leather aprons removed it, one nasty arm-load at a time, for sorting in the bins along the wall. Almost as if it were alive and breathing—but that was a thought so impossibly awful that Maria choked on it, and swallowed it down lest she throw it up.

Sally pressed onward until she reached a small cupboard door behind the massive pyramid of disgusting cloth. "Here," the captain said. Her voice was thick but satisfied as she drew out a leather satchel that was stuffed quite full. "This is what they want. Take it with you. Keep it safe. Give it to Mr. Lincoln and his scientist, and see if it can help them. Because if it can't, then God help us *all*."

Seven

"What do you mean, they won't let me on the floor?" Gideon came very close to shouting. Only the near proximity of Abraham Lincoln's face prevented him, and even so, this measure of restraint took a great deal of self-control.

"Not at this time," he replied carefully. "Sessions are closed this week, and they aren't admitting any new testimony until Wednesday. But *Wednesday*," he emphasized, "you're first on the list. Eight o'clock in the morning, you can say whatever you like. It's a good thing, I think. This way, we have time to plan. Time to decide and prepare."

Gideon crossed his arms and leaned up against the cold, hard wall of the Capitol building.

For twenty-four hours he'd been ready to storm Congress with facts, figures, and numbers. He was ready to present proof of what had befallen him, his machine, and his family; he was prepared to offer evidence about the coming plague that would end the nation more surely than the war could ever do. He'd swallowed all the outrage he could swallow, and he needed to unload it—and he'd been counting on doing so here and now.

"I don't *want* more time to plan. I already know what to say."

"Yes, but I think you and I can work together, with regards to how you might say it. Gideon," Lincoln said more gently. "You have a mind without equal, but a tongue that costs you listeners.

To be honest, I'm relieved that you won't go up on the podium today."

"Sir, I can't agree. The sooner we get the message out, the sooner the world will know, and . . ." He moved away from the wall now, leaning over the man in the mechanized chair. Not for menace, but for emphasis. "Nothing else will help us. If we make the information public, we take away the power of those who wish to conceal it."

"You and I agree on the fundamental principles; we only disagree in the execution. We won't get a second chance to introduce the world to the goings-on that your machine has brought to light. The presentation is almost as important as the message itself, and so is the presenter; if we alienate those we wish to sway, we will accomplish little, or nothing."

"Mr. Lincoln, if the facts aren't enough to sway them, then we're worse than doomed—we're surrounded by fools who don't *want* to be saved." He jammed his hands into his pockets, turned around, and walked away, trusting that Lincoln would know better than to call him back.

Gideon left the premises to the tune of Lincoln's chair puttering in the opposite direction, down a different marbled corridor, rolling deeper into the bowels of a building Gideon viewed with deep-seated loathing. This wasn't a place to be heard. It was a place for men of power to meet and conspire.

His long, old-fashioned coat dusted the back of his thighs as he barreled outside, into the blinding light that seared the city every time it snowed.

A thin crust of powder and ice coated every building, tree, and walkway with a sharp, chilly sheen. Not much had fallen, but everything that fell froze, and now the world was slick as well as frigid. Gideon didn't mind. If it was going to be this cold, the city might as well have something pretty to show for it.

Out on the street, horses stamped and shot clouds of steam

from their nostrils. Women drew their coats tighter and walked more quickly, prancing from step to step in fancy shoes; and the old men at the newsstands clapped their hands together, teeth biting hard on hand-rolled cigarettes and the stems of pipes.

Gideon adjusted his scarf and worked his hands open and closed, open and closed. His fingerless gloves were warm knitted wool, made for him by Polly as a Christmas present the year before. The gesture had touched him more than he'd admitted, and he made a point to wear them not only because he liked them, but because he wanted her to know that they were appreciated.

He buttoned his coat up to his neck and drew the scarf up over his face. It wasn't quite cold enough to warrant such measures, at least so far as the locals were concerned. But he wasn't a local, not in any original sense, and though he appreciated the freeze for its change of pace, he wasn't so accustomed to the weather as someone who'd lived with it for a lifetime.

Much as he hated to consider it, and his innate impatience bristled at the prospect . . . he suspected that Lincoln was right.

He found it virtually impossible to pretend to the niceties that served as social lubricant for the masses. He did not like all the runaround and flowery difficulty that accompanied even the simplest transactions. Why couldn't everyone just say what they meant? Why did they need to couch everything so cautiously? The truth should always be enough, regardless of its delivery.

He stamped his feet while he walked, as the chill worked its way through the soles of his shoes. His socks were thick and warm, but they were damp with mud and melted ice, and now he carried the slush of the streets along for the ride.

He considered catching a cab, but to where? Back to the Lincolns' home, where he lurked in unhappy hiding? How could he rest under the ostensible guard of Nelson Wellers, a man who looked too fragile to wind a watch? He needed to stretch his legs. He needed to stretch his brain.

Abraham Lincoln was not wrong. But at the moment, he wasn't interested in the president's help. It wasn't that he didn't value the assistance and patronage; far from it. But there was some gap, some disconnect between them that occasionally could not be traversed. It might've been as simple as money, except that Lincoln had grown up poor as well . . . though not enslaved. It could've been as complicated as power, but were those two things different? Money and power? Gideon thought so, but he would have been the first to admit that the line between the two was thinner than D.C.'s icy air, and the overlap between them could not be overstated.

In simple fact, they did not always understand each other. And while Lincoln was a great speaker, a great writer, a great orator, even . . . he wasn't the man whose audience Gideon craved right then.

And just like that, he knew where he wanted to go.

He hailed a cab after all, climbed inside, and gave directions to a townhome on the other side of the Capitol.

On the way, he stared out the window and watched the city churn, slipping across the ice and pushing through the weather to run the daily errands that would only become more difficult as winter established itself in earnest. He was glad that it wasn't any worse, not yet. Not while he needed to come and go, and while the carriages pulled by horses, or driven by diesel engines, had to chain up their wheels and trudge through the streets like everyone else.

The carriage took him all the way over the Anacostia River, through some wooded, then swampy acreage, and up to a house called Cedar Hill. It left him at a curb that had been swept clean of ice and snow. Up a spate of stacked stone stairs he climbed, stopping at a door painted a tasteful shade of red. He gave the brass knocker a couple of good gongs and shifted his weight from foot to foot while he waited for an answer.

It arrived momentarily, when the door was opened by a teen-age colored girl in the plain domestic outfit of a maid. "Can I help you?" she asked.

She was new. "I'm here to see Mr. Douglass."

"Do you have an appointment?"

"Tell him Dr. Bardsley is here to see him, and if he leaves me standing on the stoop for too much longer, I'm likely to be shot."

The girl's eyes widened in alarm. "Shot?"

"Stabbed. Poisoned. The possibilities are endless. This having been established, I need a word with your employer."

But she was stubborn, and perhaps not completely stupid. "I'm sorry if that's true, about someone wanting to shoot you, but you'll have to wait here. I'll try to ask quickly. I'd rather nobody shot you on the stoop," she confessed, and she closed the door.

It'd been an overstatement on Gideon's part, or so he'd assumed when he said it. But now, in the silence between asking admission and receiving it, he second-guessed himself. They'd come for him at the Jefferson building, hadn't they? Why wouldn't they follow him, hunt him to someplace less conspicuous than the Capitol, or the home of a beloved former president?

He eyed the passing pedestrians, wondering who was safe, and who might be watching him . . . closing in on him. It wasn't like him to be paranoid, but then again, it wasn't like him to have murderers on his trail. Not specialized murderers, anyway. Bloodhounds were a generic lot entirely, and he could scarcely bring himself to count them.

In another half-minute, the door opened again. The girl said, "You can come inside. Mr. Douglass will be with you shortly. Let me take your coat, and—"

"No," he said. "I'll keep the coat."

"As you like." She nodded. "But come this way, and I'll make you a cup of tea."

"I'd rather have coffee."

"I'll . . . I'll see what I can find."

The parlor was a warm, intelligent place, lined with shelves covered in books, most of which were well loved and well read. A fire burned in the hearth, and two pairs of shoes were drying before it, propped up with their soles facing the flames. Gideon pulled up a chair and aimed himself toward the heat.

From the columned entryway to the home's main wing, a voice asked, "So what's this about you getting shot, or stabbed, or poisoned?"

Gideon rose from the chair. "Anything's possible."

"But is it *likely*?" asked Frederick Douglass, a handsome, graying negro in his early sixties. His shirtsleeves were rolled up, and his waistcoat held a small notebook with a pencil strapped against it. He wore a nice pair of house slippers, and a set of reading spectacles pushed up over his forehead.

The men shook hands, and retreated to the warmest seats in the room. Gideon again cocked his feet toward the fire and finally answered, "It's hard to say. They started with guns and dynamite, and neither one worked out for them. I can only assume they'll move on to something more subtle next. Knives or potions."

"They could always go the opposite way, and reach for larger guns."

"Maybe," Gideon agreed. "But I suspect that I've been targeted by someone more cautious and cunning. Brute force isn't her style, unless she's playing political games."

"And that's not what you're caught up in? A political game?"

Now that someone else said it aloud, it was silly to insist otherwise. "All right, then it's a political game. There's always the chance that I'm wrong, so let's call it a hunch and hope for the best."

Douglass said, "I'd like to think that the 'best' would imply that you were destined for a long, happy life, with no interference from dynamite or politics. What's going on, Gideon? What can I do for you? It's been . . . oh, six months since I saw you last. Should I assume you've had your nose buried in that Fiddlehead project all this time?"

"Yes. And the Fiddlehead is why they want me dead."

"On that ominous note . . ." Douglass raised a finger to indicate that the maid had returned with coffee for Gideon, and tea for her employer. He told her to leave the tray behind, so that they could serve themselves at their leisure. When she was gone he selected two cubes of sugar, and took up the question he'd left dangling before her arrival. "Now, why don't you tell me who 'they' are. The mysterious 'they,' who you've used a feminine pronoun to describe—so I am terribly curious, if you don't mind me saying so."

Over the next half hour, Gideon told him everything, starting with Abraham Lincoln and the Confederate spy Belle Boyd working for the Pinkertons, and moving right along to the Fiddlehead's conclusions, Katharine Haymes, and the tenuous connection between her company's war crimes and the walking plague. It felt good to lay it out on the table, even if the table wasn't his own, and didn't belong to his usual benefactor. If anything, being forced to tell it all from start to finish, to someone who hadn't heard it yet and wasn't familiar with all the details, gave his brain room to sort through the particulars and see the connections better himself.

When he'd exhausted the subject from several angles, he held his still-full, now-cooled cup of coffee untouched in his right hand as he waited for a response.

"I must say," Douglass began slowly, "it sounds like a very fine mess."

"It's not the first time people have wanted to kill me," Gideon noted. "I refuse to be cowed."

But Douglass was less firm on the matter. "Perhaps you *should* be cowed by it, a little if not a lot. And I'm not perfectly confident that they'd prefer you dead. It'd be smarter to discredit you. If I were you, I'd be more worried about *that*."

Taken aback, Gideon set his coffee down too hard. It rattled, and all the small spoons quivered on the silver tray. "You think I should back down? Hide? Run back to Lincoln with my tail between my legs, until he gives me permission to speak?"

"No one can make that decision for you, but there's good reason to consider a more cautious stance than the one you're taking right now. When you left Tennessee, you risked no one but yourself and your family. If everything you've said about your machine and its calculations is true, then you're gambling much more these days when you put yourself at risk. Upon your message could rest the fate of two nations, millions of people—*including yourself and your family,* a fact I wish to underscore. Let it not be said that I fruitlessly urged you on a path toward altruism."

"I give the world the fruits of my labor. That's worth something, isn't it?"

"Yes, but you don't do so from a sense of duty. You do it because you prefer an audience, and because the more people respect your results, the more grant money you acquire in order to produce more results. You will change the world, Gideon Bardsley. Whether you give a damn about it or not."

"I'm *trying* to save it. They won't *let* me save it."

"They, they, *they.* Another 'they' for you to blame." Douglass shook his head. "You're so single-minded at times. Think broader. Think in another direction. That's your forte, isn't it?"

"Yes, but I don't know what I'm thinking toward, not anymore. And what does it matter right now? No one will deign to hear me until Wednesday."

"Deign to hear you, yes—you say that like it's the easiest thing on earth to waltz into Congress and make people listen. Lincoln pulled strings and called favors to put you on that podium next week, so it's a pity you begrudge him the delay. He's working for you, not against you. But since he can't help you the way you want, right this moment," Douglass continued, "you beat your head against the wall because you think your only path is blocked. But it *isn't*. Lincoln's right about taking time to craft your message, but he's wrong that you'll have to wait until Wednesday to have it heard."

Gideon's unhappy fugue flickered, but he did not straighten up from his position in the chair. "How so?"

Frederick Douglass sighed. "Son, Congress isn't the only stage in the nation. It's not even the largest, not by a far cry. You don't have to start there, and you don't have to stop there, either. You need the audience, as much as you want it. You need to shine a brilliant light into the shadows, and teach people that things are being hidden. The governors are buying things and paying for them with blood, without the knowledge—if not yet against the will—of the governed."

"Ah." He understood. "You think I should go to the papers."

"Not just ours, but up and down the coast—to Baltimore and Philadelphia, Chicago, New York, and Boston. For that matter . . ." he pulled out his notebook and began jotting things down. "If you have that Southern woman in your camp—infernal Cleopatra though she may be—she might be useful. Once we've written up your findings and made your case in a straightforward, compelling fashion, she might be able to place the editorial in the Richmond papers, or Atlanta. You never know, she might have contacts in Houston. The Texians are a tricky lot, but they don't like being exterminated any more than anyone else. You might find a more willing audience there than you'd expect."

It was a lot to consider, but Gideon considered it. "You're right. I should bring the message to the people who would be most affected by it. I thought I should appeal to the authorities, but the authorities are very likely causing the problems in the first place."

Douglass smiled like a proud tutor whose student has finally seen the light.

"Which is why you can't ignore them altogether. If you want to be heard, you can make yourself heard in the halls of government, it's true—and you'll have to take your case there eventually. But that case will be all the stronger when the masses stand behind it. Change happens two ways: from top to bottom, and the reverse. If one avenue is cut off, you *must* try the other."

 *Eight*

"But Captain, what *is* it?" Maria asked.

And as the laundry fell, the workwomen sorted, and the crank and grind of the generators and washers drowned out all but the very nearest noise, Captain Sally leaned in close. She said, "They're notes, from a half-abandoned backwater on the West Coast, in the Washington Territory. They were written by one of my nurses. She's been sending them every few weeks like clockwork— observations, suggestions, and prescriptions for dealing with a poisonous gas."

Maria could hardly believe her ears. Was this the connection they'd all been seeking?

Sally continued. "It occurs naturally out there, near a volcano called Rainier. This gas has destroyed one city already, and it's destroyed countless soldiers here on the fronts, because it converts to a substance that's sold as a narcotic. There are a hundred names for it, and a hundred names for the men who become addicted."

A loud shout pierced the workday commotion in the hot, disgusting incoming room, and Sally jerked to attention. Maria checked to make sure the satchel was fastened shut, and she slung it over her chest. "Was that Adam?" she asked. It was too loud to tell. Too many other things were going on around her.

But Sally didn't know. A second shout led to a third—and

soon the laundry commotion began to wane as the laundresses became curious about what was happening outside.

The captain took Maria by the shoulders. It felt like a funny gesture, coming from a smaller woman. "Now go to Washington, and raise some hell."

Then a gunshot shook the basement, and the laundry women screamed. "Go!" Sally said more urgently. "Not the way we came. Take that side door—over there!"

"But, Captain!"

"Leave us," she insisted. "Leave, and there's nothing here for them to take!"

Maria still had a thousand questions, but someone on the other side of the incoming door had a gun. She had one, too, but she also had something heavy to carry. She ran where Sally'd pointed her, dodging dirty laundry, sidestepping puddles, and almost forgetting the smell that surrounded her.

Out the door she fled, into a narrow corridor without any windows—but there was a door at one end, so she raced for it and paused long enough to withdraw her Colt. She jammed the gun into the satchel so its handle was easily grabbable, and she opened the door.

On the other side she found stairs going up, but also leading down. To some kind of subbasement or cellar, she assumed. Only a fool would go down farther, and probably wind up trapped there. No, she'd go up and take her chances.

First floor.

She pressed her ear to the door with the large number "1" painted on it. She heard hollering on the other side. Hollering for her? Hollering at her? No, it didn't sound like it. These were the shouts of doctors giving orders, and the sounds of wheeled gurneys squeaking hastily between the rows. Maria heard nurses answering the doctors, and asking for supplies; injured men moaning or vomiting, and explanations being cast back and forth across the turmoil. Was it truly loud enough that no one here had heard the gunshots below?

Maria took her chances with the door and opened it, revealing utter chaos: dozens of freshly arrived patients, rolled in on chairs or tables, being sorted and positioned and addressed with professional but imperfect haste.

"Oh, God," she said into her mask, then pulled it off because she hadn't realized until then that she still wore it. She dropped it on the floor and pushed her way forward, through the teeming crowd of the wounded and their caretakers, taking a gurney to the hip with such force that she cried out, bounced off it, and stumbled forward around an operating table that had been wheeled into place right beside it.

On the table was a man who was about to lose his leg; even a laywoman like herself could see that for a fact. A nurse held the man down as he writhed and cried, and a doctor struggled to put a molded glass mask over his face for ether, but the patient thrashed. Maria watched, fascinated, unable to tear herself away. The nurse lost her grip on the mangled leg and a jet of blood gushed several feet in the air, spraying Maria across the face.

She could hardly move for the horror of it, but she forced herself toward the rear of the room, where another door promised an exit, or so she hoped. She wiped at her face, tracking a streak of crimson across the back of her hand. Though she blinked and blinked, the vision in her right eye still swam with red. A bucket of clean rags in soapy water sat by the door, and although she remembered what Sally had said about every rag being sacred, she took one anyway. As she retreated, she wrung it out and wiped at her face, working the rag's corner into her eye even though the soap stung.

Her sight cleared, and she swabbed her décolletage, fretting over a splotch or two on her scarf and another on her bodice. But she'd have to wash them later, there was no time to take a trip to the washroom now. Not when she heard—*bang*—another gun-shot somewhere behind her.

It might've been anything, she told herself. Might've been some agitated, delirious soldier burning through ammunition, threaten-ing the very people who would bring him back from the brink if he'd give them but a chance.

But she wasn't prepared to wait around and find out.

As she reached the door that should take her into the main lobby, the stairwell door crashed open and another gunshot rang out.

The reaction was immediate and loud; nurses screamed, pa-tients howled, every able-bodied person ducked for cover. One of the doctors drew a weapon of his own to fire back at the man in the doorway.

Maria only got a glimpse of him and all she could tell was that he was a white man in a long brown coat. He ducked back into the stairs, only to return fire . . . right into the room where all the wounded were waiting for help.

"Despicable!" she gasped, and reached for her Colt's handle, but came to her senses before adding to the fray.

Besides, the doctor was returning fire with the skill and calm of a sharpshooter, and maybe he was one, or had been. This was a war hospital, after all, and surely most of the surgeons had seen the field at some point in their service. Maria said a prayer and wished him luck, concluding that the best way she could help defuse the situation would be to leave it behind and let the gunmen chase her to another place.

So she kept running, out the door and into the circular drive-way, where four ambulances of military make were jumbled to-gether, having just arrived from the front. Their rear doors hung open, bloody rags and clothing spilling out from within, as if the vehicles had been disemboweled. At least two of these mechanical carriages had been left with their engines still running, pumping

black smoke from their exhaust pipes, their idling motors gur-
gling.

Maria had never driven an ambulance before.

But when she looked inside the nearest cab and scanned the
controls, she recognized most of them. The machine wasn't wholly
different from the newfangled taxis she'd driven in Atlanta during
one summer's desperate effort to feed herself.

She came to a decision. She tossed the satchel onto the seat,
seized her Colt, and jumped back onto the lawn in front of the
house-turned-hospital . . . and fired her gun twice into the air.
"Hey!" she shouted at the top of her lungs. "Hey, I'm out here!
Follow me, boys—I've got what you want, so come and get it!"

Silence fell in the wake of her proclamation. For a moment, she
didn't know what to do. Try again? Wait a little longer? See what
happened? But the decision was made for her. One of the hospital's front windows broke as an elbow smashed through it and
the barrel of a gun emerged in the hole.

Before the attempted assassin could squeeze off more than a
shot, she dived back into the cab of the ambulance and shut the
door, hunkering down as low as she could while still operating
the controls. There was a clutch? Yes, a clutch. There, that pedal.
And the diesel injector, yes. That pedal there. Where was the gear-
shift? She fumbled around until she found it on the side of the
steering wheel—doing most of this by feel, since she couldn't see
much of anything. But she got the vehicle moving.

And immediately struck one of the other ambulances.

She didn't hit it hard, but the impact knocked her head against
the dash, and she swore like no lady ought to.

A bullet shattered the windscreen and she was showered
with shards of glass, but she shook her head and brushed them
away, then sat up just long enough to see where she was going—
and to shove her foot onto the accelerator as soon as she spied an
opening.

Over the grass the vehicle hopped, winging a low stone retaining wall as she skidded inexpertly over the driveway and then alongside a ditch, into which the ambulance leaned sharply, threatening to flip and fall. But she urged it up, up, and onto level ground. Now the shooters were far enough behind her that they couldn't hit her except by the most outrageous accident. Or so she was fairly certain, because she could still hear the shots cracking behind her, but nothing striking home.

She guided the unwieldy craft onto the road and did her best to avoid any horse-drawn carriages, dogs, men or women on foot, wagons, or other motored devices; but it was hard to see with the windshield gone and the sharp, cold air flying into her face without mercy. Maria squinted against the wind and wished for goggles like the airship flyers used . . . but if wishes were fishes they'd all cast nets. So she drove on, paying so much attention to her technique that she'd gone a mile before putting any thought into where she was headed.

Was she still being followed? Hard to say.

She was rolling toward downtown, and the traffic thickened as she neared the city center. If any assailant followed, he did so with a remarkable obedience to the rules of the road—undoubtedly a better one than Maria herself displayed, as the ambulance stalled out twice, leaped a curb, and ran past a policeman swinging a sign that urged CAUTION.

It was just as well that her career as a driver hadn't panned out, or so she told herself as she tried to recall what she knew of this city, and where its train station was located. She'd been there before, but it'd been a while, and she didn't wish to stop for directions while driving a somewhat stolen ambulance and running from armed gunmen.

But she did stop, once she recognized her surroundings and correctly extrapolated the way to the station. She abandoned the ambulance beside a saddle company, and then was off once more, making a beeline for the station. It wasn't far, and she almost felt better on foot, now that she was reasonably confident she'd lost whoever was chasing her.

Unless she'd become too comfortable too soon.

Over her shoulder she noted a pair of men keeping pace. It might have been anything, or nothing. It might've only been two perfectly ordinary gentlemen on an unrelated errand, likewise headed in the direction of the train station. They did not brandish any weapons, and they did not jog to catch up, but something about their carriage and posture reminded Maria entirely too much of Pinkerton agents. Men on missions, staying casually unremarkable for the sake of efficiency and invisibility.

But she was one of them now. She knew how they worked, and these two men were working on her—she was almost certain of it.

There was always the chance they were Pinks after all, sent as backup or as checkup. It'd happened before, that work was spread among agents, and they'd catch one another up in a more or less friendly fashion in their free time.

She angled her next turn to catch their reflections in a shop window advertising warm winter cloaks. Two white men. Both dark-haired and dressed for indoor work, but not expensively. If these were Pinks, they didn't come from the Chicago office—she would've recognized them—but there were four other offices, so she couldn't assume they didn't. She could, however, take note of their appearance and shoot a telegram back to her employer. If they *were* from her organization, she'd raise a stink. She didn't like being second-guessed.

In truth, Maria did not think they were Pinks. But if they weren't, they were hired hands from some other corner, and she wasn't ready to handle that prospect yet. What corner might it be? There were other agencies, to be certain—the biggest and best-known in the South was probably the Baldwin-Felts company. She hoped it wasn't them, as she didn't think much of that particular establishment.

Of course, depending on who you asked, the Pinks weren't much better. But she had a badge for the Pinks, and could reasonably expect to be safe from friendly fire. As for the other, God only knew.

She took a sharp turn, a fast one that she saved for the last second, and kept a brisk pace but did not run. No one runs unless they want to be chased. Better to let the sidewalk crowds buffer the distance between them than become a casualty to whatever might otherwise transpire.

She didn't dare look over her shoulder. She waited at an intersection because she had to, and when a glass-windowed cabriolet went lumbering by, she scanned its reflections for the men behind her and spotted one of them. Only one? Maybe the vehicle passed too quickly, and she'd missed the other. Or maybe the other man had broken off from the direct chase, and was circling around from a new direction.

While she waited for the traffic director to give her leave, her mind raced.

How much farther to the station? No more than a few blocks, surely. Any available shortcuts? She didn't know the city well enough to say for certain. She swallowed hard and, when the traffic director waved her across the road, she continued onward, still pretending that nothing was wrong, no one was behind her, and hers was an ordinary errand to the train station—no different from a thousand other ordinary errands performed every day.

Under pretense of stopping to adjust her shoe, she surreptitiously checked and confirmed that one fellow was still on her tail—the fact of this never more obvious than when he realized she'd paused . . . and he did likewise, investigating a news stand with sudden, intense interest.

"Maybe he's an amateur, or a Baldwin after all," Maria griped as she straightened up and resumed her path.

A sign posted beside the road pointed an arrow at the station, noting that she was still over a mile away; so, her recollection of how the city worked had been foggy indeed. She swore under her breath. A mile was a long way to run, and a long way to evade anybody. It gave the men plenty of time to close in on her, cut her off, and do whatever it was they planned to do.

And she still didn't see the second fellow. He could be anywhere.

However, she *did* see one of the new electric streetcars clattering toward her. It wasn't pointed in the right direction, except that right now the right direction amounted to "anywhere else but here."

Chicago did not yet have these electric street lines, so she had no experience with such things. She sized up the elongated, open-air car. It didn't look too complicated. When the painted trolley came close enough for her to touch it, she reached out and grabbed one of the vertical poles along its exterior, like she'd seen people do in other places during her travels.

It didn't move quickly, but it moved determinedly, yanking her off her feet with exactly the precision and insistence she'd hoped for. She grunted with surprise, then smiled as her feet found a step. Tightening her fingers around the bar, she shielded her eyes from the sun shimmering off the frosty city. She spied the first man at the curb behind her, visibly aggravated that he'd arrived too late to join her.

Moments later she saw the second man hunting down a side street. He did not see her hanging off the side of the streetcar like she did this every day, like any of the other passengers who took such a casual attitude toward their transportation and bodily safety.

When she felt confident that she was unaccompanied, at least temporarily, she waited for the next stop and asked the driver if he could help her reach the train station.

The driver delivered the gentle admonition that she'd gone the wrong way, and she pretended she hadn't known—because every man liked to be a hero, or at least enjoyed being of service to a lady in distress. And why deny the nice gentleman a warm feeling of helpfulness?

She finally made the right connection, and soon she reached the station, bought her ticket to Fort Chattanooga, and positioned herself comfortably on the last train of the day to the fort as the train prepared to depart.

Maria sat next to the window but turned her face away from it, in case anyone had caught up to her. She had no doubt that whoever'd sent the two men would learn her location soon enough, but there was no reason to make it easy for them.

The train lurched forward and found its rhythm.

And now she had hours before her with nothing else to do but familiarize herself with the nurse's missives.

The pages were difficult to skim, due largely to the questionable handwriting of the woman who'd composed them. At a glance Maria could see that the nurse had never enjoyed more than a few years of formal schooling, as the earnest, rounded letters showed the charming diligence of a child's hard-practiced lessons. But there was nothing charming or childlike about the message these shaky letters conveyed.

She checked the most recent letters and saw that the handwriting improved over the course of the correspondence, practice making something closer to perfect. Even so, the early pages were slow going, and the rollicking track of the train gave Maria a case of motion sickness that almost made her quit trying; surely it would be easier to finish the reading from a stationary location.

But a phrase leaped out at her. She drew the page in question up close to her face.

". . . if you could hold him still for long enough, a doctor would pronounce him dead."

Her attention now more fully engaged, she made the effort to peruse the entire section from whence the eye-catching line emerged.

I have now seen four cases here in the underground, and they all go the same: First, the victim breathes up some gas—usually because a mask springs a leak, or isn't fixed good on his face in the first place. But sometimes it happens because the mask gets knocked off, or one of the tunnels isn't sealed up as good as everybody thought. Doesn't matter how it gets inside, it always goes the same.

After a man breathes it, his nose starts running with yellow mucus, and the mucus is sometimes bloody. Sores break out around his eyes, ears, and mouth. It looks like the gas is eating him up from the inside out. Then the heart stops, the pulse quits. No more spit or tears, and the skin around his eyes turns yellow. He starts panting, and it sounds like his lungs are being chewed up into rags. You will never forget what it sounds like, when he breathes. For that matter, if it weren't for that breathing, you'd never know he was alive. Everything else about his body has done stopped, like he's been killed by a plague. If you could hold him still for long enough, a doctor would pronounce him dead.

But he won't stop moving like a polite dead man. Just when he ought to lie down and take a proper Christian burial, that's when he starts running around, trying to bite people.

Sometimes it happens quicker than other times, from start to finish. The people I talked to say it's because the gas is very heavy, and it collects thicker in some places than in

*others. It moves like a real thick liquid, like a syrup you can
hardly see.*

Maria sat up straight and frowned at the paper. As promised
by Captain Sally, the text described a poisonous gas, and it definitely *sounded* like the walking plague. In fact, the nurse had used
both of those words, fairly close together: "walking" and "plague."
She kept reading.

*Once a man's been bit by a rotter, treatment is pretty much
a race against the clock. Whatever gets bit has to get cut off.
The bite causes a festering that moves like blood poisoning
through a body, or like septic rot, but faster. If a finger gets
bit, you'd better cut off the hand. If a hand gets bit, you'd
better take the whole arm. If the amputations don't happen
in time, the patient will die within a day or two. I am told
that a patient who dies from a bite will not start walking
like a rotter, and so far this seems to be true. But I only seen
it on three occasions so far, and that is not enough for me
to say for certain.*

"Gruesome," Maria murmured with fascination. She flipped
to the next page.

*Nobody knows how long the rotters will keep moving,
but the oldest ones have been kicking around for about
fifteen years, by everybody's best guess. The real old ones
are raggedy now, and when you see them, you wonder
how they manage to move at all. Most of the skin has
rotted off, and the muscles are hardly more than strings.
I hear they take nourishment from what they eat, but
since their blood don't flow I'm not sure how that's
possible. And since there is not much to eat inside the*

*walls, it makes me wonder. I guess they have been eating
the Doornails or the Station men, but I am told that, these
days, it is unusual for more than half a dozen men to die
that way in a year. For the most part, people have figured
out how to live here without getting eaten. But those first
few years after the wall went up, a whole bunch of people
got killed by the gas and the rotters. Mostly I think people
were trying to get inside the city and either loot it or get
back the stuff they'd left behind. And I'd like to tell you
that it was a stupid thing for them to do, but until they
did it, nobody knew what would happen to them. Now
everybody knows.*

*I know what happens to the men who do the gas-drug,
too, but no one will listen to me. I've tried to tell people,
and to ask for help. I used letters and the taps as best
I could, but no one from the* Dreadnought *has answered—
though my friend Angeline says I should try the Texas
Ranger again. His name was Horatio Korman, and if you
can reach him, he may be of some help to you. You might
also ask after the captain on the train, a man by name of
MacGruder. I have got to say he conducted himself like a
hero, but I doubt you'll have any means of finding that one,
as he's someplace up north. I am told there's also an airman
named Croggon Hainey who might serve as witness, but
him being colored and being a pirate, he's not likely to be
believed.*

Maria was startled to see the air pirate's name. Croggon Hainey
was the captain of a ship named the *Free Crow* (though it was
briefly called *Clementine*). It had played a role in her first case as a
Pinkerton agent, the one she'd been reassured had been resolved
to everyone's satisfaction . . . including the pirate's.

"Small world," she said under her breath.

She flipped back to the top of the stack, scanning for a location or an address. Nestled between two stacks of notes tied with twine, Maria found a brown paper envelope with the information she hunted.

The name on the envelope was "Venita Lynch," at odds with the reports themselves, which were usually signed "Mercy." "Seattle," she read aloud from the return address, wondering if she was pronouncing it right. "The Washington Territories." She knew where Washington was, at any rate. It was as far west and north as you could go, without getting very, very wet . . . or wandering into Canada. Upon inspection of the postal mark, she saw that the envelope had not been mailed from Seattle at all, but from Tacoma. "Where the transcontinental line ends," she mused. The two cities must not be far apart.

But she was confused by some aspects of Mercy's reports. These rotters . . . they were obviously victims of the walking plague, or something very like it, but she'd implied that they got that way from breathing the air, not taking a drug. What on earth had happened in Seattle?

For that matter, if a catastrophe had occurred, how did people still live there? And furthermore, *why*?

The mention of gas masks gave her one clue, as did the reference to an "underground." But if there was more to be gleaned, she'd have to keep reading.

So she did. And by the time she reached Fort Chattanooga, she had drawn some terrible conclusions about the poisoned city of Seattle, the walking plague, and Katharine Haymes's diabolical weapon.

 *Nine*

"Leave me alone," he ordered the nameless, blank-faced agent who walked in his shadow. "Stay right here, and don't move until I return. I can look after myself for ten minutes in the washroom, for God's sake. No one's here today, anyway."

Secret Service indeed. Couldn't keep secrets. Didn't perform much in the way of service. He should've done as Abe suggested and sent them away. Better a paid force than a government agency. Better to have a receipt.

Besides, Grant had bigger guns and better reflexes, never mind more experience and a faster eye. In his entirely unbiased opinion, he could've outshot any of the young bucks they assigned to him—knowledge of which didn't make him feel safer in the slightest. He abandoned these silent, suited men every chance he got. They felt too much like crows on a laundry line. Vultures in a tree.

The agent knitted his brows and twisted his lips in a disapproving grimace, but he followed orders and held his position.

And with one or two fierce, insistent glances backwards to make sure the man stayed put . . . Grant was free to roam unobserved.

Desmond Fowler had an office in the Capitol Building. *Just like everyone else these days,* or so Grant thought as he walked the gleaming, echoing halls in search of the door with the right name stenciled on the glass in black paint and fancy lettering. This plan was ludicrous and he knew it—so ludicrous that he wanted to be sober for it, and had a headache for his pains. And he'd kept it from his wife, who didn't need to know anything about it.

He was the president. He could wander the building on a Sunday if he liked.

He was clearing his head, if anyone asked. Heading for the washroom, like he'd told his forced companion. Taking a little stroll.

Or he could even tell the truth, to a point: I'm looking for Fowler, and I thought he might be here.

On the contrary, he very much hoped that the Secretary of State was out, and planned to stay that way for the afternoon. He hoped it so much that he assumed it, partly because he'd made his secretary insist on a rare weekend meeting at Fowler's estate on the other side of town to sign and clear up some paperwork. Scheduled for this very time. Why on a Sunday? So the signatures and all their attendant useful seals could be filed first thing Monday morning. That's what Fowler wanted, wasn't it? Immediate approval and full cooperation? Well then, he could do a little work on a Sunday, and perhaps the Lord would forgive him.

Grant did not know if the Lord would forgive *him* for this particular trespass. But there were so many other things in the heavenly queue for which he was even less likely to be forgiven that he didn't worry about it too much.

If everything went as expected, he'd have at least three hours before Fowler could possibly return. His office should be deserted, locked up for the Lord's Day, with no potential spies or villains there to report to the Secretary that the president had been up to no good.

And inside that office, he expected to find . . . what, precisely?

Evidence? Information? Leverage?

He didn't know, but he was tired of being left in the dark by those he'd appointed to assist him; he was exhausted and ashamed for feeling useless in the great seat of power, with no power to speak of except what was granted to him by subordinates.

Well by God, he would *not* be left in the dark anymore.

Though, if he had a drink, he was reasonably certain he could do something about that headache.

No. Clearheaded was the only way to proceed, even if that clear head came with a cost. He couldn't seize control of his life and his administration as a sick old drunk, so he'd do it as an angry sober man with nerves of steel and shaking hands. The people had elected him. They'd hired him, and they depended on him, and he'd turned over the henhouse to the foxes because he hadn't known what else to do.

Here was a chance to redeem himself, through petty crime with an ethical underpinning. He could trust no one—at least, no one he felt comfortable endangering.

The buck stopped here, at Fowler's office, where he would break the law and save the nation . . . or maybe that was a grandiose delusion of an old drunk. But he liked the sound of it, so he rallied around it as he quietly stalked the hallways.

Yes, he could admit it to himself: His third presidential term had been weak. He'd overheard whispers about how he shouldn't have taken the post again—that he ought to have left office in favor of going on a speaking tour, or writing his memoirs, or some other entertainment to which he'd be equally ill-suited, in his opinion.

But no, he'd stuck with the job. Not for Fowler. Not for Congress. Not for the courts, nor the lawyers, nor the slick, strange men who made their money on the misery of others—on weapons, murder, and government contracts.

Not for them. But for everyone *else.*

For the abolitionists and the people of color who he refused to think of as slaves, even down in Mississippi and Alabama, where the Southerners still called them that. The Southerners were wrong, and he'd show them the hard way if he had to. But they'd insisted upon that, hadn't they?

He stayed in office for the soldiers, old and young—the ones who'd lost limbs and lost sleep, the ones who'd gone home only to die slowly of the sudden confusion of not having anything to fight for. He did it for the ones who'd rather end it quickly, even after they'd slipped through the corpse-catching sieve of the front and were given the chance to begin again.

He stayed for the ones who never got the chance. Who never came home. Tens of thousands of them, hundreds of thousands now. More like a million, when you factored in everything—the disease, the suicides, the civilians . . . and the walking plague.

His reverie was interrupted when he reached the door bearing Fowler's name. It was painted on the frosted glass door in the expected fancy letters, for a fancy man who thought he knew better than everyone else. Grant had once believed it, too, that Fowler was the smartest, the cleverest politician of them all.

And now? Goddamn, but he hoped he was wrong.

He reached for the knob, but its firm, reassuring lock suggested that a smith would be required to compromise it. The president didn't have a smith handy, and he didn't feel like calling one. Instead, he had the silence of this particular hall, confidence that the office's occupant was absent, and a hammer hidden inside his coat.

He wrapped the hammer in his scarf and shattered the door's glass with one heavy swing.

Before the last clattering, clinking shards had fallen to the office floor, Grant jammed his hand into the hole and unlocked the door from within.

Was this a crime? Perhaps.

Was anything a crime, if the president authorized it? An excellent question, and one he'd put to Lincoln the next time he saw him. A good philosophical starting point for a conversation over brandy—he could imagine it now, and he did so with great anticipation, particularly with regards to the brandy. He'd been dry for hours, and those hours were starting to tell.

The door scooted open, scraping the broken glass aside and clearing a rainbow-shaped path on the enormous rug that filled most of the room.

"Close the door behind you, if you don't mind."

He froze, one hand on the knob.

"Not that we can have a *private* chat at this point, given the state of the door, but I would appreciate the gesture all the same. Mr. President?"

He found his voice. "Yes?"

"The *door.*"

Slowly, he drew it shut until it clicked into the frame.

Katharine Haymes was seated behind Desmond Fowler's desk, more perfectly at home than if her own name had graced the glass before it was broken. She wore a pair of reading glasses, which she now took off and set on a dictionary that Fowler had probably never opened. "Please," she urged, gesturing with a pen in her hand. "Won't you sit down?"

The president's head swam with confusion and embarrassment, but a fresh infusion of anger steadied it. "I will, but not at your request. This isn't your office to occupy, Miss Haymes."

"Nor yours to vandalize, Mr. President. Let's have a civilized talk instead, shall we?" As he made his way to one of the chairs that faced the desk, she added, "Could I make you a drink?"

"You'd like that, wouldn't you? Get me off my toes and into my cups."

"I'm only being courteous. Why? Are you implying that I might do something untoward if I could compromise your faculties?"

"No such thing was implied," he responded, trying to keep the hint of defensiveness out of his voice. But he was off-kilter already, thrown by the situation. He wouldn't have admitted it, but the drink might well have sharpened him.

"Well, in my experience, people who break into offices rarely have polite intentions, so you'll have to pardon me. But you were going to do that anyway."

"It doesn't work like that."

"It doesn't?" She cocked her head. "Desmond tells me otherwise. But you and I both know that the world doesn't run on his word. He certainly likes to think so, though, doesn't he?"

Grant sniffed. "So what does that make you? The power behind the throne?"

"Oh no, don't be silly. I stand behind no throne, Mr. President. Not his. Not yours."

"But you came to *us*. You're the one who needed a deal."

She shook her head. "No, I didn't need one. I merely wanted one, and Mr. Fowler made it easy for me. I don't require your clemency any more than I require your affection or respect. My time and my money are my own, and I've never needed permission to make use of either. I won't start asking now."

"So why, then? What game are you playing at?" he asked, determined not to be led in circles.

"The same game I always play, and I always win." She leaned back in the Secretary of State's oversized chair. It made her look small, almost childlike.

Grant reminded himself that it was an illusion. "What are you so afraid of?" he asked her.

"Afraid?"

"Only the frightened are so hungry for power."

"Oh," she said, appearing to consider this. "I see. You think I'm compensating for some loss, or gathering up my coins against the coming storm. Not so at all, I'm afraid. I like games, and I like being in charge. The economics of warfare are a perfect fit."

"For a woman?"

Her eyebrows tensed into something very close to a frown. "For *me*. It's not my fault you fellows are so reluctant to let us play. Worried you'll be beaten by a lady, I expect."

"That's got nothing to do with it." The protest sounded a bit weak, even in his own head. "I'm not remotely concerned about being bested by you, or anyone else."

"You ought to be. You won't be president much longer, Mr. Grant. What power you have, you've squandered. You've passed it off to men who are weaker than you, but quicker and cleverer. And you're reaping the rewards already. Their crimes are your responsibility." She shrugged prettily, wickedly. "Perhaps you're comfortable with that. For all I know, it's the most useful truth you learned in the army—how the man on top is the one who takes the blame. Tell me, do you think that's why you were allowed to become president?"

"I wasn't 'allowed' the office. I was granted it by the voters."

"Whatever you prefer to tell yourself, sir. But if you think for a moment that the rest of us had nothing to do with your appointment, then you know less about how the world works than I thought."

Gruffly, he laughed. "The world is a battlefield, Miss Haymes. And I clawed my way to commander in chief because I am the best at what I do."

"You were shoved into the role by people who wished to manipulate you, and take advantage of your political ignorance."

"You don't know anything about me. Or why I took the nomination, or why I've stayed as long as I have."

She sighed, as if this whole conversation had gone beyond the tedious and he was missing her every point. "Very well. Then we know nothing about one another, and this is all one great mystery— like how we ended up in this room, together."

"Don't say that like you planned it, because we both know you didn't." He almost added that she was wrong, that he could guess or infer a great number of things about her; he knew her kind. But he didn't want to tip that hand, or give her anything else to refute.

"Of course I did. You sent your secretary after Desmond on that ridiculous Sunday errand. I laughed, but he's too greedy, too excited that you were offering him what he'd demanded. It didn't occur to him that you might be up to something."

He still didn't believe her. "But it occurred to *you*."

"It's a simple trick, which is why it worked, I suppose. An oldie but goodie, as they say. Magicians do it all the time: Distract the audience with one hand, so they miss what the other is doing."

"You like magic tricks, do you?"

"Very much." She nodded. "I wanted to be a magician when I was a child. My father told me there was no such thing as a woman magician. That was the first time I hated him."

"Because he was right?"

"Oh, no. He was entirely wrong. I hated him because I was too weak to prove it at the time. I think if he were still alive now, he might grant that I have indeed become a Mistress of Illusion, after a fashion."

Grant didn't like where this was going. "And what audience have you spellbound lately? What illusions did you perform while they were distracted?"

She pursed her shapely lips in a smile, showing no teeth, but something else instead . . . some unkind, happy trait that made his skin crawl. "All the world's a stage, Mr. President, not a battlefield. I believe the Bard would have my back on that one. And if I told you how the trick worked, I'd be a terrible magician, wouldn't I?"

"It's also a terrible magician who performs a trick that no one notices."

"Oh, all right then," she said crossly—but lightly, as if her irritation was feigned. She wanted to be asked. She wanted to answer. "By way of throwing you a bone . . . you agreed to my amnesty because you believed I needed it. Poppycock! Utter illusion, from start to finish."

"Is that so? Then what do you really need?"

"You'll find out soon enough," she said. Her promise was every bit as unsettling as her smile.

"That sounds rather like a threat."

"Oh, no. If I wanted to threaten you, I'd pull out the gun that's sitting in my lap. I'm reasonably certain it overrules your . . . hammer."

"And you think that's all I brought?" he asked.

"Whatever gun you're carrying, you can't reach it more quickly than I can reach mine. And since I win that particular little gambit, let's move on to the next one. I'll start: Tell me, what did you hope to find here, in Desmond's office?"

"Brandy."

"Oh, droll, sir. Very droll. Particularly since I offered you a drink, and you declined. So what else were you looking for? I'm game to play along."

"Nothing that's any concern of yours."

"I doubt that very much," she said. "At present, almost any affair of Desmond's is an affair of mine."

Grant found that prospect alarming, but unsurprising. He only let the latter sentiment show. "I'm certain that constitutes some breach of national security."

"Then arrest me."

"Apparently I can't."

"So why don't you ask me whatever burning questions you hoped to have answered? We both know you can't touch me, so I have no reason to lie. You never know—it might be easier than rifling through Desmond's drawers."

It would be easier, if he could believe anything she'd willingly tell him. Still, he might learn something from her falsehoods, if he asked for the right ones, in the right way. "All right," he tried. "What's the true nature of Desmond's project? The one I've signed off on, but know so precious little about."

"How much do you know already?" she replied—which wasn't an answer, but the basis for another trick. It was one Grant had used himself in the past, usually while trying to manage someone who outranked him.

"I know it's based on the technology you deployed against Union prisoners in Tennessee. Some kind of gas, wasn't it?"

She didn't rise to the bait. Maybe it wasn't bait. "Some kind of gas, yes. One hundred percent effective, both as a killing agent and as a psychological weapon."

"One hundred percent?" he exclaimed, knowing he'd picked the less interesting of the two things to ask about. But he'd get to the other one shortly.

"Yes. Better than that, really."

"How so?"

"One hundred percent of the soldiers were neutralized, and some of the neutralized soldiers killed those who had avoided the test weapon altogether. It was awful," she said, so flatly that Grant thought maybe she meant "awful" in the Biblical sense rather than any humane one. "Best of all, word traveled fast, through the survivors—and the guards, the administrators, nearby neighbors, and passers-through. The incident went from a scientific experiment to a legend in less than a week."

"Experiment?" He choked out the word, wondering how many helpless men had died at this woman's hand, only to be dismissed by such a clinical term.

"A tactic, then, if you prefer. You've killed more men in a casual afternoon strategy when you still manned the front. Though not so brutal as your cohort Sherman, I believe; I'll give you that much credit," she said, but her voice darkened, and Grant had a feeling he'd received no credit whatsoever. "You never scorched the earth. You never burned the homes of women and children who were already destitute and left them with less than nothing. And that, sir, is why I've left my gun in my lap and tolerated this conversation."

Privately, Grant had similar sentiments about his fellow general; but it wouldn't do to share them, and he refused to give her the idea that they might hold any feelings in common. It would only give her power, and he'd lost enough of that already.

"I suppose I should thank you for your patience," he said, not believing for a moment that it was patience that prompted her to give him an audience. It was something else, crueler and more calculating. She wasn't there to answer questions; she was there to ask them. So it was up to him to ask them first. "Now, let's see how long I can persuade you to indulge me. Tell me about the weapon. Tell me about the project. I don't even know its name, if Desmond ever gave it one."

"Project Maynard," she graciously supplied.

"Maynard? A rather . . . uninspiring title. Not very evocative of a plan to wipe out a nation."

"Of course not. That's the point of a code name, isn't it? It's fitting, though. Named for the first man to die of the gas."

Grant filed that bit of information away, suspecting it was minor enough to be true. "How does it work?" he pressed, wringing the conversation out, even if it only told him things he already knew, or half-truths to wonder about later. He wouldn't have her attention for too much longer—he could sense it—so his questions became more direct.

"The gas kills anyone who inhales it. But a significant portion of those who breathe it don't stop moving. Instead, it takes over their nervous system and makes them into mindless cannibals. They turn on their fellow men, spreading the contagion while seeding terror."

"I should think so," murmured Grant. "If I heard that dead men were coming to eat me, I'd be quite terrified."

She leaned forward, her thorny smile brightening. "Oh, but that's not even the worst of it. Everyone's afraid to die, yes, but everyone dies eventually—we all know it, even if we'd rather not think about it. But imagine all the horrors of dying, without the reward of *resting.* Imagine no longer being in control of your own faculties, at the mercy of a chemical flood, a brainless compulsion that turns you against the people you once knew and loved. *That,* Mr. President, is truly a fate worse than death. And our studies have shown that, indeed, men fear becoming one of the shambling plague-walkers more than they fear a bullet to the head."

It was such a precise comparison that Grant knew it must be based in experience, but he couldn't bring himself to ask. He couldn't bring himself to say anything, for a moment.

"So this is what it's come to."

She reclined, somewhat crossly. Apparently that wasn't what she'd wanted to hear. "Yes, this is what it's come to. You want the war to end? This is how you end it."

"It sounds . . . unethical. Unfair. It doesn't sound like war; it sounds like cheating."

"Call it what you like. But for all your talk of preserving and restoring the Union, I'm the only one doing anything about it. You've been sending boys to do the jobs of men. It hasn't worked out. Now it's time to give a woman a crack at it. And let me assure you: *I will do what needs to be done.* I'll do what none of you have been able to do so far, or what you haven't had the stomach for."

Grant shook his head, then sat forward to tap one finger on the edge of the desk for emphasis. "Now, Miss Haymes, it is my understanding that this weapon is only effective for a mile or so—

that's one of the only things I know about it for certain—and that it's too big and heavy to be deployed from a cannon, or even hurtled down a hill. That was my complaint to Desmond, when he brought it up: Your magnificent war-ending weapon needs a team of, what—two dozen men? At least?—to deploy it, and those men will almost certainly die in the delivery. Even if we could find men willing to sacrifice their lives on account of this stunt, it's highly unlikely that one of these gas bombs would be enough to end the war. I'm not certain it could even turn the tide, except to galvanize the South. Deploying a weapon of such . . . terror, that was the word you used? Deploying such a thing will frighten them more than it will harm them."

"And fear does no harm?"

"Sometimes fear is a source of strength. You're talking about a nation that has been at war for an entire generation—and, like what's left of the United States, their population has become almost complacent about it. Warfare has become the standard of existence, a miserable constant, but a predictable one, given this long-running stalemate."

"But it's *not* a stalemate," she argued. "The South is in decline."

He launched the tapping finger of emphasis once more. "Precisely. We have held on long enough that they're finally bending under the weight of this conflict. To change the rules now is to risk a resurgence in effort and planning on their part. Your weapon will give them something new to rally against—it will give them back the focus they've begun to lose."

"You're wrong," she told him. "And if a few dozen men are required to safely transport the Maynard, then a few dozen men are an acceptable sacrifice. Military men know the danger of assuming the uniform. They'll likely die with or without any treachery on their government's behalf."

Exasperated, he gave up on the finger and threw his hands in the air. "Precious few of the men who serve us now signed up to do so of their own accord!"

"Fine. So it's murder either way you look at it. The government conscripts them and sends them to war, and they die. The result is the same. I don't understand why you're taking such issue with the particulars."

"I don't understand how you write them off so easily," he complained. "And I do not believe that wasting good Union men on a square mile of devastation could possibly turn the tide of the war, except to turn it against us."

"You've made your case. We must agree to disagree."

A clattering outside in the hall made them both stop talking.

A maid appeared with her cart. She gasped at the glass and swore at the cleanup required . . . then spied two people chatting—amiably by all appearances—within the breached and broken office. She opened her mouth to say something—likely an admonition, or a reminder that these offices were closed.

Then she recognized Grant, and her expression shifted from irritation to surprise, then to concern that she'd interrupted something she shouldn't have. "Mr. . . . Mr. President," she stammered. "I . . . I didn't realize it was you."

He forced himself to smile at her. "Mr. Grant will work just fine, my dear. And I do apologize about the mess. It's my fault entirely."

Katharine rose from her spot behind Desmond Fowler's desk and smiled as well. Grant hated it when she did that. It was as if every upturn of her lips lowered the temperature in the room by a few degrees. But she was kind to the girl, saying only, "I hope you'll pardon us. Mr. Fowler sent me to retrieve some important documents, and Mr. Grant was kind enough to see me inside, but he must have closed the door too hard, and . . . Well, these things happen. I'll leave an extra tip on the desk for your trouble."

"Oh . . . thank you, ma'am. Miss. Ma'am." The girl finally settled on an address. "That'd be very kind of you. And if you'll just lock up behind yourselves. . . . Or . . . don't bother with that, I guess. I'll come back in a little bit."

Katharine shook her head. "No dear, that won't be necessary. The room's all yours. The president and I were just leaving."

Ten

"The war will end, and no one will be the victor. This is the assured outcome, provided that the menace that threatens both North and South is not addressed, and addressed immediately—with the full attention, commitment, and vigilance of the governments and people on both sides. This menace has many names, some regional, some colloquial.

"I am speaking, of course, with regards to that peculiar affliction that ruins men—and sometimes women—throughout the continent. You've seen the symptoms, or heard of them at least: A yellow tinge to the skin, particularly around the eyes and joints; difficulty breathing; a running nose with bloody mucus; receding gums and protruding teeth; an emaciated, cadaverous appearance; and, eventually, a mindless pursuit of human flesh. And although those who carry the affliction cannot spread it, their bites spread a gangrenous rot that is very often fatal. Among doctors and scientists it's commonly described as 'necrotic leprosy'—but this term is not well known outside those circles.

"This—not the war—is the crisis of our time.

"For quite some time, this plague progressed quietly, taking primarily soldiers in its grip, because soldiers were the primary consumers of the substance which is believed to cause the disease: a common, inexpensive drug sometimes called saffron, which is smoked or otherwise inhaled. But increasingly, unaccountably, the situation has worsened to such an extent that thousands are dying by the day—either by drug use and subsequent sickness, or through the cannibalistic assaults that follow. Our troops are being decimated, and the Confederate troops are similarly burdened.

"But this must not be considered a purely military matter. The walking plague is now escaping the uniformed ranks and spilling into civilian society, taking not merely those soldiers who contaminate their bodies with the drug, but also those who struggle to live in the midst of this never-ending war.

"The war must end, and it must end immediately. If it does not, this creeping horror will consume the continent beyond salvation by 1886. Figures in the rest of the world are more uncertain, but rest assured this is not merely a problem of North and South. This is a problem of which the planet must be made aware, and the U.S. must lead by example. The threat is a scientific fact, measurable by advanced calculating engines created by the nation's top scientists."

Gideon paused there, and looked up at Nelson Wellers. "I don't understand why I can't just name myself. *I'm* the top scientist. It's *my* machine." He fondly, almost wistfully imagined the Fiddlehead as it'd been before the sabotage—all bright keys and jaunty levers, chewing up numbers and possibilities, offering its direct, complex answers on a roll of paper. Cryptic only to others. Never to him.

"That you are, and that it is. But most people don't know your name, and those who do might be . . . disinclined to take your warnings as seriously as you'd like them to be received."

The wistfulness melted, and he glared across Lincoln's library in the doctor's direction. "Because I'm a negro."

The physician shrugged and shook his head. "It doesn't help, but that's not the whole of it. Don't look at me that way. You've taken great pains to remain more or less anonymous. Well, congratulations. No one knows who you are. Your campaign has been a *roaring* success."

Gideon glared some more, but didn't argue. He returned his attention to the handwritten draft before him, and continued reading aloud, his last review before heading off to the papers. "The Union is aware of these scientists and their devices, and President Grant has been advised on the matter." He looked up again. "Bit of an exaggeration, isn't it?"

Wellers shrugged again. "Lincoln said he talked to him. Even if he didn't, or even if their conversation skirted around the issue . . . the president will surely want an audience with you when your letter goes public. You can brief him then."

"To explain myself, yes. I expect you're right—and perhaps it's an underhanded means of gaining an audience, but it will almost certainly work. Very well. That part stays."

He picked up where he'd left off. "President Stephens has been informed of the dire situation as well. Though details are not available to the author of this letter, this devastation allegedly affects Southern troops at a rate twice that of Northern ones."

Wellers held up a finger to interrupt. "You made that part up, yes?"

"More or less. There's always a chance that the problem isn't any worse down South, but since virtually all problems *are,* it's a safe enough guess. I can't offer up the Fiddlehead's figures because the incoming stream was incomplete. The results are speculative, by the machine's own admission, but within a calculated margin of error."

Wellers chuckled softly. "You talk about that thing like it has a mind of its own."

"It does," Gideon assured him. "It has mine, only better. And besides, I see no good reason to tell the South that their problems aren't as bad as ours. Let them think they're taking the brunt of it, assuming we can get this message to go public down there."

He set his papers atop his knee. With more earnestness than he usually felt or showed, he asked, "Do you really think this sounds all right? It feels odd. It doesn't sound like me at all."

His companion smiled. "I thought that was the point."

"Don't be a jackass."

Wellers's smile grew even bigger. "Go on, keep reading. It's hard for me to judge the document as a whole when you keep stopping like this."

"You're judging it?"

"You asked for my opinion, so yes. I'm taking great relish in judging it, because you so rarely care what I think."

Gideon tried to frown, but couldn't muster it. "I don't *care* what you think. I want to *know* what you think. It's not the same thing."

"And Douglass and Lincoln are away right now, so you'll settle for me. I'm still flattered to be third place to such company."

"I'm not trying to put you in their company, Nelson. If—"

Now he laughed outright. "No! No, you can't take it back now— you've flattered me, and you're just going to have to live with it."

Gideon gave up and grinned back. "Fine. You've been complimented. Don't get so goddamn excited about it."

"I'll try to contain myself. But do go on—finish it up. Let's hear your closing. The paper offices will shut down in another hour or two, and if you want to get this into tomorrow's edition, we need to be on our way."

Gideon cleared his throat and picked up the papers again. He scanned the last few lines and began afresh. "In Washington, D.C., luminaries such as Abraham Lincoln and Frederick Douglass are calling for an immediate cease-fire in order to discuss the pressing threat which all of us face. In Richmond, the renowned hospital manager Captain Sally Louisa Tompkins is aware of the situation and has made efforts to rouse the CSA's own Congress, to limited success. For make no mistake: There are those who wish the war to continue.

"Though it may sound ridiculous, inhumane, or impossible, there is money to be made in a war—huge money, for people without ethics or sentiment. These people have always existed, and they will always stand in the way of peace, for they are powerful. But we are more powerful still.

"Now is the time to call for action. Rally your representatives, petition your governors, and refuse to stand by in the face of indifference. Silence is not our friend, and it will not protect us. Only through public inspection and open discourse can we combat this problem, and we must do it together—Northerner and Southerner, white and colored, Indian and Texian, blue and gray. We are all human, and all living, breathing men. We must act accordingly, lest our entire species be eradicated from the face of the earth."

After a pause, Wellers nodded and gave a round of formal, steady applause. "I like it. And that is a fierce climax indeed, at the end of an impassioned call to arms."

"I wouldn't call it impassioned."

"You don't have to, because I just did. You've written a fine piece of propaganda. Let us hope it works as well as it ought to, if only to get people talking."

Gideon sighed hard with frustration. "We need for people to do more than *talk*."

"Yes, but this is a start."

"It'll have to be a *quick* start," he grumbled. "The Fiddlehead suggests wrapping up the war immediately—preferably years ago. We're given a window of six months to instigate a complete turnaround in hostilities, and to engender absolute cooperation between the states."

"Six months? When you put it like that, it sounds impossible."

Neither of them spoke for a moment, but then Gideon agreed. "You're right. It sounds impossible. And it might *be* impossible, but if we don't try, we're doomed for certain. It's this or nothing, until and unless someone else comes up with a better plan."

Nelson Wellers rose from his seat and stretched, cracking his back and straightening his waistcoat. "I don't imagine any better plan forthcoming. You're our last, best hope. I pray that isn't too much pressure."

"Not at all. Do you think I should've mentioned Haymes and her project? I left her out because I couldn't tell if it would help or hurt."

"When in doubt, leave it out."

"Very funny," Gideon sighed, fiddling with the papers as if he couldn't yet bear to part with them.

"A little funny; surely no more than that. But I do mean it: You're right, and there are too many ways her interference could be viewed. The Southerners don't like her, but they think she's useful. The North might want to use her research for themselves. She's somewhere in the mix, but it's hard to say what she really wants, or means to do. It was the right decision, leaving her out for now."

"Then I suppose it's finished."

Nelson nodded. "Good. Then give it here, and I'll take it to the *Washington Star-News*."

Gideon stood up and shook his head, folding the missive and slipping it into his vest. "No. It's my editorial, and I'll run the errands to see it in print. But you're welcome to come with me. If anything, I expect you're duty-bound to do so."

Wellers made an unhappy little grunt, but admitted, "Yes. I promised I'd keep an eye on you."

"If you must," Gideon surrendered, and grabbed his grandfather's coat.

In truth, he didn't mind having Wellers assigned to his personal safety. Better the physician than the Confederate spy, after all—send that unreliable woman on some other errand. Wellers was preferable by far. For that matter, ever since Gideon's talk with Frederick Douglass, he'd been increasingly worried, though no new violence had occurred. He had a plan now, and that was the problem. It was just the one plan, and if someone were to interfere with it, there was no backup waiting in the queue.

All offhanded responses to Wellers aside, the pressure was getting to him.

Together they left the Lincoln homestead and climbed into one of the former president's personal carriages—a carriage with a ramp that lowered to the ground, so that his mechanical chair could be lifted aboard with minimal effort. Gideon liked these carriages; they were oversized to accommodate the bulky seat, and there was plenty of room to stretch out when its owner was not present.

The city was still brittle and bright with a sheen of ice, a half-present crust that made the world look damp and uncomfortable, too wet to be warm, and too warm to freeze.

Gideon sank into his coat and buried his chin in his scarf, watching small puffs of his own breath dampen the air and vanish. The streets scrolled past outside the window, and Nelson Wellers gazed out at his side of the avenue—both men watching for suspicious persons, or for any vehicles that might be following them. Nothing piqued their sense of alarm, but they still didn't relax. Being out in the open required too much of their attention, and their previous good moods shifted into something less friendly and free, and far more wary.

They did not speak the rest of the way to the *Star-News*.

The newspaper office was an impressive building—a monument to the freedom of the press, if you believed in such things, though Gideon tended not to. Regardless, he had to admit it was handsome, with Georgian columns over brick and wide stairs funneling visitors inside. Tasteful landscaping, and tidy walkways. It looked efficient and earnest.

Inside they found the office they needed, and an editor by the name of Sherwood Jones—a once-burly man whose impressive

shape was beginning to sag. He was bald, and one of his promi-
nent ears had a long-ago-healed tear in it; his nose looked like
it'd been broken once or twice, and maybe a third time, a long
time ago.

"To what do I owe this pleasure?" he asked, rising from his
seat behind his desk and shaking both Gideon's and Nelson's
hands. "A pair of doctors, ganging up on an old man. I hope I'm
not dying or in need of some . . . scientific treatment. I hope you'll
pardon me, Bardsley, but I've never been too clear on what it is
you do."

"A little of everything."

"Then my potential for peril is great indeed! Draw up a chair,
fellows. What can I do for you today?"

"You can help us spread the word on a matter of national importance," Gideon told him, and handed over the statement he'd
so meticulously prepared. "You can publish the most important
letter you'll read this year." Then he sat back with Nelson Wellers
and waited as the editor read it, watching for the man's eyes to
widen, or for a gasp to escape his lips.

They were disappointed on both fronts. Sherwood Jones maintained a stony silence and stillness as he read. When he finished, he
put the paper down on his desk, then folded his hands atop it.
"So you want me to run this as an editorial?"

Wellers, a little surprised by Jones's lack of surprise, made a
guess at what he wanted. "That's where you'll have to run it, unless you could be persuaded to accompany it with an investigative
piece."

Gideon instinctively balked at his friend's suggestion. "No, we
don't need . . . we shouldn't have . . . No."

"Why not?" asked the editor.

"Because the machine . . . There was an explosion," he said
vaguely. "The information is not reproducible at present, and the
original paperwork is in safekeeping at the Lincoln estate. Attempts

have already been made on my life, and there is some concern for the Lincolns', as well."

But the editor said, "If I understand what I'm reading, there's concern for the whole damn continent. I understand your desire to protect the Lincolns, but isn't getting the evidence out more important in this case? If you're serious about this—"

"What do you mean, *if*?" Gideon asked, annoyed, and now somewhat inexplicably anxious. Something about being in this office, on the verge of going so very public. Something about making a shout like this—a shout to the whole world—and knowing that the world might not listen.

Wellers also went on the defensive. "Are you trying to say you don't believe us?"

Sherwood Jones sighed and shook his head. "The awful thing is, I *do* believe you. Or, if nothing else, I think you're on to something. It might not be such a big something; perhaps this is just another one of those things like typhoid or cholera or consumption that is making the rounds through the ranks these days. But I'm hearing about it more and more. Everybody's hearing about it. We're already running a piece or two a month on the subject."

"I read the most recent one," Wellers said. "You talked to a colleague of mine—or, your reporter did, at any rate—wanting to know the medical details of the situation. Not all newspapers are so precise with their facts."

"Dr. Harper, yes. Might've known he was a friend of yours. See, we get letters and telegrams all the time from people asking what we know about it and if we'll do a more in-depth investigation. I'm aware of the scope and I'd love to do another exposé, but I lost a reporter to the project this past fall. He went to the front and didn't come back. The fellow I sent after him said everyone gave a different version of how he'd died, and he didn't know who to believe."

Gideon frowned. "Why would anyone lie about such a thing?

It's a public menace! I don't understand how people can just . . . bury their heads in the sand, and pray it'll all blow over."

But the editor shook his head. "It's not that simple. People are afraid, yes—and the people who are closest to the situation don't want to frighten anyone further."

"Leaving people unprepared and uninformed is better?" Gideon asked incredulously.

"How would they prepare for something like this? If we tell people that the walking dead are coming, and we don't know why but there's nothing we can do about it, it would only spread panic."

Nelson Wellers tried to see it both ways. "I understand what you're saying. It's true that there's no preventative or cure yet. But it's as Gideon said: Silence will not protect us. The plague is spread through a substance, and death also travels by direct contact with the victims. If nothing else, we can warn people to stay clear of the infected. At present, they're being treated like patients, often mixed in with a hospital's general population. We are reaching a time when we must consider them enemy adversaries, and segregate them instead."

"But this letter . . ." Jones gazed down at it nervously—but not despondently, or so Gideon thought. A gleam in the older man's eye said that he sensed some glimmer of possibility, but was torn. "You're brushing up against that truth, but don't state it outright. This letter could change everything. Or, if it is believed by enough people in enough places, it *could* lead to mass hysteria."

"Then let it," Gideon said coldly. "I'd rather see hysteria than ignorance. Hysteria, at least, has motive and agency."

"*Blind* motive. Blind agency," the editor corrected. "There are ethical guidelines about this sort of thing, for language that incites violence." Gideon leaned forward to interrupt, but Jones held up his hand, begging indulgence. "Which is why I will print this, but on one condition: Wellers, you must write me a companion piece. Write me a letter as a doctor, explaining what we know, little as it may be. We must give the people a plan, or else we are only seeding terror, and I won't have that."

"A plan? Jones, it's as I said—"

"Say it again. Write it down." He pushed a pen across his desk, and followed it with a few sheets of paper from his top desk drawer. "If all you can give are your qualifications and your suggestion to avoid the infected, then that's a start. Warn people against the bites. Give them some hope that this can be managed. To do otherwise would be cruel and unhelpful."

Gideon was not entirely happy, but he found it difficult to argue with that. "Cruelty can be effective. For the world's own good, we must frighten it awake."

"Then that's what we'll do. But we won't scare the city awake just to witness its own slaughter. Most people would rather die fighting than screaming."

"It's fine, Gideon. I'll do it," Wellers said, picking up the pen. "I'll write it, and he'll run it, and the word will get out. Just give me a few minutes. It won't take longer than that, for I have little to contribute to the effort."

As Wellers wrote, scratching the pen's quill across the page and pausing occasionally to refresh its ink, Sherwood Jones positively quivered, giving the lie to his former reserve. To Gideon, he said, "This is the break we've needed—an educated assessment that ties the facts together. For years we've heard rumors about what the saffron does to people, but its extent has been difficult to calculate. And here, in this office, when such things are discussed . . . well, the press is free, but some people think you get what you pay for."

"What do you mean?" Wellers murmured, without looking up from his letter.

"I'm saying that this needs to come from men of science, not men of words. A man of words can say anything, and mean nothing. But a doctor must do good, or at least do no harm. I'm ill qualified to do either one."

On their way out of the editor's office, Gideon felt something like optimism for the first time since the Fiddlehead had been attacked. It crept up on him, and he even smiled as Jones stomped happily off to the press.

"You think it'll work? You really think he'll run it?" Gideon asked Wellers.

"Is that a rhetorical question? I'm not sure I've ever heard you ask one of those. Didn't you once say that such queries were a pox upon serious conversation?"

"Do you ever forget anything?"

"About as often as you do," Wellers said with a cocky lift of his eyebrow. "But don't worry about Sherwood holding up his end of the bargain. He'll print it, and people will read it, and then they'll know. Of course, what they do with the information is up to them."

Gideon watched the editor disappear around the corner. "Douglass believes that educated people are powerful people. Let's hope he's right."

"And let's hope we're stopping a war, not starting a riot."

"Wellers? Is that you?" asked a voice from beside the front desk, where a receptionist in a prim uniform directed incoming visitors. A young man leaned over her, sorting through a stack of telegram slips. He grinned and waved. "And Dr. . . . Barksdale? Bardstown?"

"Bardsley," Gideon supplied.

"Bardsley, that's right. My apologies." He riffled through the papers, selected a couple, and approached them.

"Hello there, Timothy," Wellers greeted him. "Still running errands for Western Union?"

"That I am, doctor. That I am. And you two gentlemen can help shorten my workday, if you're feeling so disposed and the stars align correctly. Is there any chance you're headed over to the Lincoln estate?"

"As soon as we leave here," Wellers said. Gideon wanted to argue, but he didn't have a better destination in mind, so he didn't.

"Then I hope you could be persuaded to take a couple of messages along with you. I know the old president trusts you with his security, so I believe he'd trust you with his telegrams."

"I expect you're right about that," said Wellers, taking them. "We'll hand them over within the hour."

On the carriage ride back, the doctor and the scientist examined the messages. They were brief and not in envelopes, so it was difficult to avoid seeing the contents. Besides, if the messages were private, they would've come and gone via courier, not the junior runner at Western Union.

One was a note from a foreign ambassador, with thanks for a gift. The other was more interesting by far.

REACHED BIG RIVER YESTERDAY STOP ARRIVAL IN
TENNESSEE PREDICTED BY TOMORROW STOP WORD
FROM LOOKOUT ALL IS WELL STOP WILL BRING
CARGO TO DC STOP EXPECT FULL SHIPMENT BY
FRIDAY STOP

"Cargo. Shipment." Wellers turned the sheet over in his hand. "Railroad terms? If so, it sounds like the Pinks think it's safe to move your momma and Caleb."

"Safe as houses, if Kirby Troost is coming."

Wellers frowned down at the message. "Is that who sent this? It isn't signed."

"That's who sent it, I'd bet my life on it."

"Really? Your life?"

Gideon gave it a second thought. "Yours, anyway."

"Who is this guy?" Wellers asked. "I've heard Lincoln mention him in passing, but I'll be damned if I know more than his name."

A flash went through Gideon's head—a memory of a very dark night, chosen for its clouds. A hushed caravan, including a baby that'd been given ether to keep it asleep. A boat waiting at the river's edge, at Ross's Landing. A searchlight, shining across the tar-black water.

Gideon cleared his throat, and with it cleared away memories that had never quite faded. "You remember the Liberation Rangers? The Union's effort to meet the railroad in the middle, and lend a hand?"

"I remember it. Didn't last long."

"No, not long, but they freed a few hundred people when all was said and done, and it was work worth doing. But Grant, or someone in his administration, decided that the program was an inefficient allocation of funds," he said, quoting an article he'd read on the subject. "Resources were cut down to the bones, and most of the rangers were sent home. For a while they remained a very small special operations group—only the very best of them, you know—and by the end they were little more than mercenaries. But they did good things, Nelson."

"Were they the ones who brought you out of Tennessee?"

Gunfire and smoke. A baby who couldn't sleep through it, not even with the drugs. A drowning. A bomb. A mad dash that left no one behind, even for all of that.

"Yes. A small team, hired by Mr. Lincoln. Led by a captain named Kirby Troost." He let out a short laugh, right in time with a dip in the road that made the car lurch. His voice caught in his throat. "Funny little man. Not much to look at, but that's partly why he was so good at his job."

"Was? So he's left the business? Did Lincoln bring him out of retirement?"

"Oh, I have no idea what he does these days. He got drummed out of the service, and the service closed down behind him. It was a bad story—made the papers around here; you might've seen it. He got caught up with the wife of a congressman, until she turned up murdered. Her husband tried to hang it on Troost, and had just enough money and power to make it stick. Never mind that all the evidence said it hadn't been Troost at all."

"This is ringing a bell," Wellers said, scratching at a spot behind his ear. "Was this the Cartinhour scandal?"

"That's the one."

"The wife's own mother wouldn't have recognized her, or that was what I heard from the doctor who served as coroner at the time." Wellers scratched thoughtfully at his chin. "Yes, I remember it now. The subject was *quite* the rage, if you're the sort to watch for gossip."

"And you're not?"

"No." He shook his head. "I knew about it through Mary. You know how she keeps up with these things."

"Oh, yes. Mary. Well." Gideon reclined more comfortably, away from the rattling door and against a sturdy pillow. "Troost didn't kill the congressman's wife, and I'd bet *my* life on that. Cartinhour either did it himself or had it done. As for Troost, he took one last trip on the railroad, out of D.C. into God knows where. And about a year later Cartinhour himself turned up at a card table with his throat slit."

"Pure coincidence, I'm sure."

"Oh, absolutely. But apart from that one coincidence, I haven't heard so much as a rumor about Troost in half a dozen years."

"You two will have some catching up to do."

"Eh." Gideon gazed at the countryside zipping past out the window. "He's not much of a talker. But he's a quick one, and slicker than you'd ever expect. I never worried about him too much. He's the sort of man who always lands on his feet. It'll be good to see him." He surprised himself to realize that he meant it. "I wonder what he's been up to all this time."

Nelson Wellers shrugged. "Wait until Friday, and it sounds like you can ask him yourself."

 *Eleven*

Maria arrived at Fort Chattanooga the next morning, having slept on the train and dreamed of dead cannibals who wouldn't stop chewing. She awoke abruptly as the train shuddered to a halt. For a moment she was flooded with relief, then she remembered that her nightmares weren't really nightmares—not the usual, impossible kind—and the half-sleeping horror rushed back to take its place. She shook her head and wished for a spot to wash her face, have a drink of water, and flush away some of the disorientation left over from the restless night.

But here was her stop. She needed to gather her wits and the nurse's papers and get back to business.

Sleeping on trains was never something she enjoyed, and now, more than ever, she wished there'd been some alternative. She stumbled half awake down the steps and onto the platform, then went toward the station bleary-eyed, all the while watching to see if anyone had followed her here, or if anyone was waiting to pick up the chase. It felt like too many things to concentrate on at once. In the back of her mind she feared that an entire battalion of rogue agents could be on her tail and she might've slept right through them picking up her scent.

"Miss Boyd!" a familiar voice called.

It stopped her in her tracks. After a flash of panic, she saw the

speaker and recognized him as a friend rather than foe. It surprised her enough to jolt her more fully awake. "Mr. Epperson?"

"Henry, please!" he suggested for what must have been the
dozenth time. Jostling against the flow of the debarking passengers, he swam the short distance toward her—hand up, waving in
her general direction. Upon reaching her, he touched the front of
his hat and said, a little out of breath, "I'm glad I caught the right
train. There are two others coming in from Richmond today, and
I didn't know which one you'd taken. I heard there was an incident at the hospital. What happened?"

She sighed wearily. "I'll tell you over breakfast, if we can find
a spot that's quiet enough." She glanced around the station and
saw nothing promising, so she asked, "Do you know of a place
where we could get a bite to eat? Perhaps some coffee? I don't
know the city at all."

"I do know of a place, yes. It's just across the street."

As promised, across the street was a small café that specialized in tea and baked goods, but also offered a light breakfast.
Maria attempted to make note of the expense in order to bill the
Pinks later, but Henry wasn't having it, and he bought the morning meal for them both.

At a small table in the big front window, they warmed themselves with coffee and waited for their food. The street outside
was crowded with people, mostly train travelers and soldiers, for
this was a military garrison, after all. In fact, if Maria remembered
correctly, at least some portion of the city was walled.

Just like Seattle, the thought flickered through her head.

Since Henry was more familiar with the locale than Maria,
she asked him. "I understand this fort has a wall around it. Is that
right?"

"Most of it. The Tennessee River curves through the city, cutting it in half. There's a wall around the south side—the military

and industrial complex, where we are right now—that starts at one point on the river and ends at Moccasin Bend, near the foot of Lookout Mountain."

She struggled to picture it. "So, basically, the southern end of the city is ringed by the river on one side, and the wall around the rest?"

"Yes, ma'am, that's about right."

"And Lookout Mountain . . ." Her question trailed off as a serving girl put two plates in front of them. Maria had eggs and toast. Henry settled for biscuits with honey and a side of bacon. "Lookout Mountain," she began again, snapping her napkin open and placing it across her lap. "That's where our friend's family is taking vacation, correct?"

"Correct," he said discreetly. "Near there, at any rate."

"Within the wall?"

"Just outside it, I should think."

They kept the conversation chatty and open, lest anyone overhear and think they were whispering about something interesting. "Perhaps we should pay them a visit before we leave town," she suggested.

He spread a big pat of butter across the nearest biscuit. "That might be fun. In fact, I'm here on a mission from their favorite uncle because I need a word with their porter. I have paperwork they'll require, and expenses for the road."

"How kind of their uncle," she murmured around a sip of coffee, assuming they spoke of Lincoln.

"He's a kind man indeed." Henry let his gaze slip around the room, checking to see if anyone might be listening. No one showed any undue interest, but there were still several people within hearing range: two serving girls, another pair of customers, and the old woman who took orders at the counter.

Maria saw what Henry was doing, and came to the same conclusion. It wasn't safe to speak openly, not quite yet. So they chatted idly about nothing in particular until the room had cleared, leaving only the counter woman, who was engrossed in the daily paper on the other side of the shop.

Finally, Henry leaned in, the gesture charmingly, deliberately calibrated to look like flirtation. "The hospital," he prompted. "What happened there?"

It was Maria's rather well-informed opinion that Henry did "flirtatious" very nicely. She leaned forward to meet his intimately styled invitation, and replied in a similar tone. "The captain was most accommodating. She gave me a gift on my way out the door, but someone else wanted it. Badly. A firefight broke out in the surgical ward. I escaped."

In precisely the same purr he would've used to seduce her, he asked, "With an ambulance? I heard that one went missing, and turned up downtown."

She performed a girlish giggle, letting the ruse run wild. "It was faster than my feet, and I didn't see any horses handy. I made do."

"Were you followed?"

"Two men. Neither one worth describing. Lost them on an electric streetcar."

He set down his fork and reached one hand across the table to take her fingertips and kiss them. "Is there any chance anyone knew you were headed for the trains?"

"I couldn't say, though I did my best to remain ordinary and unremarkable. And I don't think anyone saw me buy my ticket or get on board. Speaking of which . . . how did *you* know I'd be in Tennessee?"

"I didn't," he admitted, releasing her fingers and retrieving his fork. "But based on some . . . increased media attention, our uncle recommended that I come here and help our incoming visitors with their packing and their papers."

Maria gathered the gist and nodded. "I see."

"And I thought you'd turn up here next, considering what I heard about the hospital." He lowered his voice. "You'd need a way out, and you wouldn't be ready to come home yet. They'd be expecting that, and watching the northbound trains."

"Excellent detective work, Mr. . . . Henry. If you ever tire of the marshals, you should try your luck with the Pinks."

"Thank you, ma'am, but I'm happy with the badge I wear already." He winked at her, and the front door opened, admitting three hungry soldiers into the warm little space.

The rest of their breakfast was spent in more idle chatter, and when they were finished Henry proposed they find a more private venue. "Under normal circumstances I'd never suggest such a thing, but I think you ought to join me in my hotel room over at the Saint George," he told her. She did not think it was her imagination that he said it with blushing cheeks.

She smiled at him, and when he held out his arm at an angle, she took it. She wasn't *so* much older that it looked strange—or she didn't think so, at any rate—and if he thought she'd be embarrassed by the suggestion or even the company, he had another thing coming. He was a polite, intelligent young man, strong and good-looking in an understated, easygoing kind of way, even with the glasses. His nervousness around her might've been due to his age—mid-twenties, she would've guessed—or her own notoriety, but either way it added to his charm. And anyway, sneaking up to an attractive lad's hotel room in the middle of the day? Bah. She'd been accused of worse things. This didn't even break the top ten.

His room was a clean but empty space, much like any inexpensive hotel room around the world. It was spacious and comfortably private, though it overlooked Broad Street, where the traffic was heavy and sometimes wild. Horses balked at motor vehicles and military men barked orders back and forth across the way; big engines moved big machines up and down the too-narrow thoroughfare, clipping the curbs, scraping stones, and frightening the city's dog population into a frenzy of howled complaints.

"It's not too . . . quiet," Henry apologized. "But it's tidy, and I can sleep through almost anything. Real close to the train station, too. So there's that."

"It's almost as big as my apartment in Chicago," she assured him, with only a slight degree of understatement. "And there's no need to make excuses for the background noise. The more the better, I say. Let it drown out any stray words that might drift through the walls. But, do you mind . . . could I bother you to turn up the heat? I'm a cold-natured thing, I'm afraid, and the window isn't keeping enough November outside."

He went to the radiator and adjusted its controls, sending pressurized, boiling water squealing through the pipes. "That's another nice thing about this place," he said, recoiling from the heater's valve and waving his hand at it. "Not as much smoke as a fireplace. I hear we'll have electric warmers in every home one of these days, and won't that be nice? And maybe they won't be so uncomfortable to set."

"Thank you, Henry. I appreciate it. I hope your hand isn't burned . . . ?"

"Just a smidge of pink, ma'am. If that's the worst I do to myself today, I'll be in real good shape. Now, at the risk of seeming ungallant, I believe we should sort out our information," he said stiffly.

She smiled, hoping he understood she was smiling for him, not at him. "At the risk of seeming unladylike, I'll take the bed. These papers will require some spreading out, and the desk in the corner won't do the job."

Henry drew a chair up to the bed and Maria sat on its edge, emptying the satchel of Captain Sally's notes and organizing them as best she could. Sometimes the dates were fuzzy or imprecise, and the nurse's grasp of numbers wasn't too much keener than her grasp of letters. Still, Maria marveled at the tenacious dedication of a near-illiterate woman writing so much, at such depth and length.

"There must be a whole novel's worth of material here!" Henry exclaimed.

"It's difficult to read at times, not merely for the content, but for the presentation," she said gently. And then she walked him through the letters, hitting the high points and marking some of the more interesting bits with a pencil.

It took two hours, and even then, Maria felt like the summing up had been too shallow.

Henry stood over the bed, festooned with its brittle sheets of damning paper, and put his hands on his hips. "We should send a telegram back to the Lincoln house and let everybody know what you found in Richmond . . . but we couldn't send off enough taps in a week of Sundays. Not even if we cut it down tighter than an obituary."

"No, not even then. Here's what I recommend: We'll write out the most important parts, digested down from this . . . this serialized journal. Then we'll express the important parts up to the Lincolns, and mail the original journals separately. But not to the Lincolns," she added suddenly.

"Why not?"

"Because they're being watched. Someone wants Gideon Bardsley, and he's staying there. Lincoln strikes me as a competent man, and with Nelson Wellers there to help, I'm not too worried about his personal safety, but we can't assume that packages won't be intercepted."

"We could send the originals to the Pinks," Henry suggested.

She grinned. "Precisely what I was thinking. I'll box it up and send it to Mr. Pinkerton for safekeeping. If it's not secure there with him, there's no hope for it at all. Is there a Western Union office nearby?"

"Back at the station, yes. I'll run around the corner and grab some wrapping paper and twine, and you start jotting down the important bits. I'll be right back."

Maria took out her pencil.

*Regarding the notes of Venita "Mercy" Lynch, nurse
formerly of the Robertson Hospital in Richmond, Virginia:
Approximately three hundred pages of letters about the
northwestern port city of Seattle, where a heavy, poisonous
gas has decimated the city, causing it to be largely
abandoned. . . .*

She kept writing until she'd revealed it all: the gas, the city in the Northwest, and the connection between the drug manufactured there . . . and the weapon proposed by Katharine Haymes.

In conclusion . . .

Maria heard Henry's feet on the stairs, returning with the promised paper and twine. She thought hard and fast, and gave up on formalities.

*In conclusion, gas weaponry is a dangerous, poorly
understood can of worms we can't afford to open.*

It took four sheets of paper. When Henry let himself inside, she folded them in half and stuffed them into an envelope, then began stacking the nurse's letters in a tidy pile before wrapping them up.

Henry took her pencil and reached for the envelope. "I don't suppose you know the address for the Lincoln estate off the top of your head, do you?"

"I know it well enough. But let's not write anything down until we get to the shipping office," she urged.

"You're right, you're right. I wasn't thinking."

The war had made mail problematic between the dueling nations, and although the Union still used the United States Postal Service, the Confederacy relied upon independent carriers. If you wanted to pass notes back and forth across the Mason-Dixon line, you either used Western Union or you smuggled the messages yourself. Since everyone knew Western Union was the most reliable way to communicate with the other side, it was watched, and tracked. If you had to use it, you didn't talk to anyone except the officer who took your money and stamped your package, and even he couldn't be trusted.

When both packages had been successfully—if surreptitiously—shipped, Maria and Henry left the Western Union office and stepped back into the chilly afternoon. It was crisp and clear, in the way of such places with brutally cold winters but not much snow. Maria's breath was cold in her chest and warm in the air, where it crystallized and hung in a satisfying fog that reminded her she was still alive.

She tucked her hands into her jacket pockets and wormed her chin deeper into her scarf, until only her eyes and nose poked out.

"And now," she said, the words warming her lips against the wool. "We need to find . . . a porter, you said?"

"Ah. Yes." Henry checked his pocket watch and nodded. "Down at the landing, in an hour. He'll meet us there, and perhaps we'll talk him into a late lunch. Have you ever had catfish fried right out of the river?"

"I don't think so . . . ?"

"That means 'no,' because if you'd ever tasted it, you'd never forget it. Come on now, this way. We'll have better luck finding a cab on the next street over, where the army vehicles don't block up all the roads. It's only a short walk to the landing, but you look like you're half frozen to death already, and we've only been outside a minute. I swear, you must be a little icicle all the time, up there in . . . in your new hometown," he caught himself. He ducked quickly aside as two soldiers carrying a steamer trunk between them begged his pardon.

He was right, so Maria played along. Keep the public chatter friendly. Let the city hear their accents and know they were local enough, and here on friendly business, and not anyone to be given a second glance. Maria attracted a second glance or two, but she'd become adept at hiding behind her hair, her hat, and now—conveniently enough—her scarf.

True to his guess, Henry found them a carriage to hasten the ride to Ross's Landing, a wide dock on the river that had developed into its own small neighborhood, serving the merchants who came and went in the steamboats, riverboats, paddlers, flat-bottom barges, and military freighters alike. It was a rougher part of the city—if roughness might be gauged by how few women were present, and how many men were out of uniform.

She saw boat workers and army boys on leave, dockhands and shipping magnates, laboring men, and white and colored men in big wool coats and boots caked with riverbank mud. She scanned the labels stenciled on crates as they were stacked and loaded by big-armed fellows on the curb, under the watchful eyes of an occasional officer or overseer. They seemed to hold mostly munitions and military necessities: tents, blankets, uniforms, horse tack, diesel fuel, motor parts, tools, engine grease, satchels, mess kits, bulk bags of flour and corn, and heaven only knew what else.

Down by the river's edge where the boats docked close, the piers were shiny and scrubbed, painted and repainted to rebuff the elements and rust. Street vendors offered newspapers, coffee, and fried fish wrapped in paper; they quietly hawked black-market passes for rations, and sold information by the scrap.

Maria and Henry stopped at a boat called the *Memphis Queen,* which was moored permanently at the edge of the landing and served as a saloon and meeting place on the water. The gangplank swayed under Maria's feet, bobbing with the slap and fall of short waves against the boat's sides, left over from the wakes of the big CSA crafts that puttered down the river's center. Once on board, the motion was minimal. She was glad—after spending the night on the rails, she wouldn't have ruled out a minor case of seasickness, even with the sea a thousand miles away.

"This was our contact's suggestion," Henry explained. "He likes this place."

Out of date and out of service, the *Memphis Queen* was none-theless a pretty thing, with gingerbread rails and a cheerful blue-and-white paint job that called to mind the Bonnie Blue Flag. An old-fashioned paddler, it had been retired in favor of the diesel models that had become more popular, courtesy of Texas. Best of all, the ship felt private. Full of nooks and crannies, doors that locked, and shades that were easily drawn.

So bright on the outside. So shadowed within.

Henry promised the barkeep a fee if he'd leave them alone, then he and Maria took a seat in a back corner without any windows, and only a low-slung coffee table between them.

The porter was right on time.

He didn't so much enter the darkened room as appear within it, standing beside Henry's seat as if he never walked anywhere, only manifested wherever he wished to be.

Maria managed to not look startled, but it took some effort. One minute he wasn't there, and the next minute . . . a smallish white man in a brown hat stood next to Henry, near enough that he might've stabbed him and walked away without anyone ever noticing. Probably an inch or two shorter than Maria herself, the porter wore woven tweed pants and boots so clean that they re-flected what little light came around the window shades. Every-thing fit him as if it'd been made for him, even the leather gloves and workmanlike gray coat. He was neither attractive nor unattractive, with brown hair and dark eyes. There was absolutely nothing remarkable about him in the slightest.

Just like the men who'd been following her.

For one nervous split second, she racked her brain trying to remember the two men in Richmond . . . but swiftly concluded that, no, he hadn't been one of them. It was just something about the breed, about a man who can be present without attracting attention. Maria had spent a lifetime trying to play up her appearance. This phenomenon, or trait, or knack for being invisible was something she'd only noticed—and attempted to cultivate—since starting to work for the Pinkertons.

If Henry was surprised to find himself suddenly accompanied, he didn't show it. Without looking, he put up one hand and punched the newcomer gently in the shoulder. "Ha!" he exclaimed, and then grinned up at the man who stood beside him. "Not even a minute late. A man could set his watch by you, Mr. Troost."

"And some men do," he smiled, cataloging Maria from the ground up as he responded to Henry. "Hello there, ma'am. My name's Kirby Troost. I'd give you a fake one, but that don't seem fair, since he knows mine already, and I know who you are." He reached behind himself and drew up a seat, then removed his gloves and rolled himself a cigarette from a pouch he kept in his left breast pocket. "It's a pleasure to make your acquaintance."

"Is it?"

He shrugged. "I meet a lot of shady customers. Not many are women of your stature. Or caliber."

"I'm not sure if I should take that as a compliment or not."

"Take it however you like; I meant only what I said. I've heard great things about you, from a surprising source or two."

"Oh, really? Care to name your sources?"

"A certain Captain Hainey sends his regards."

She was pleased, but did her best to keep from letting on.

Besides the fact that she didn't wish to admit he'd surprised her, she didn't feel like recounting her old adventures to Henry. It'd take too much explaining, and he'd have too many questions.

While she calculated a response, Troost continued, sparing her the trouble. "I must say, I never would've pegged you for a pirate queen . . . but if Hainey says you're all right, I'll take his word for it. Now, Henry," he changed the subject, then paused while he lit his tobacco. "I understand you've got something for me."

Henry looked back and forth between Kirby and Belle with no small measure of confusion, but when no one seemed ready to fill him in on the secret, he produced a thick envelope. "This is everything you ought to need. Next stop's . . . well, won't be Oak Grove, I don't expect."

Troost shook his head. "Not doing Indiana. Shooting for Middlesboro instead. It'll put us up closer to our favorite uncle."

"How long you think it'll take?"

Troost considered this while he took a long draw on the handmade cigarette. The paper crinkled, burned, and flicked away to ash. "To Middlesboro? No more than a night or two, assuming nothing goes wrong with the travel arrangements. The rest of the way? Another couple of days. Shouldn't be too bad, once we're past the bluegrass."

"Travel arrangements?" Maria was perplexed. "Middlesboro . . . Are you going by air?"

"Unless you know a better way to get there in less than a week. The train lines don't run that way, not since Sherman went barreling through the place in the seventies. But I've got a small rig set up on the Georgia side of Lookout. Would've rather come with my own crew, but the summons didn't give them time to make arrangements. So I'm here on my own."

Henry's left eyebrow lifted. "Your own crew? You're not an air captain these days, are you?"

"Captain? Who wants that kind of responsibility? Not me. I ride with a good bunch, though. The kind who don't mind if I keep my head down."

"Pirates," Maria said flatly.

"Unincorporated merchants," he corrected her. "Nobody worse than anyone you already know, *madam*. And the *Naamah Darling*'s gone about as straight as possible, these days. Her captain wants out of the nasty side of the business. Got a lady to impress, and she ain't impressed with what he was running before."

"So what's he running now?"

"Supplies," he said vaguely. "Now, Henry, where will we put our cargo when it arrives? Are we headed for the Land of Lincoln, or does the uncle have other ideas?"

Henry knew he meant D.C. Softly, he said, "Baltimore for now. Details are in the packet. So's the money and their free papers. Get 'em there safe, and there's another fifty percent waiting for you. Our good uncle knows you really bent over backwards to get here."

"I guess he knows how I feel about the District, too."

Henry cleared his throat. "You might-could talk an extra bonus out of him, considering."

"Nah. This is what we agreed, and it's enough. This one's important."

Maria asked, "Because of the scientist?"

Troost nodded. "That man's got a bigger brain than anybody I ever met, and if you knew the crew I run with, you'd know that's saying something. If it's true what he says about his toy, and what it's told him . . ." His voice trailed off like he was thinking of something else, and he wasn't very happy about it.

"You know about his machine?" Maria asked. "I thought it was of the *utmost* secrecy."

He laughed, and a puff of smoke flowed down his chin. "Secrets ain't a thing to me, Cleopatra. I collect them like some men collect butterflies, except I don't put 'em in a case for show. I *live* on them. They keep me alive."

"You must have some good ones."

"I do at that."

She pushed. "The kind that have kept you away from the District?"

"That kind, yes." For a moment he looked irritated, but it quickly passed. "And this kind, too. On the house, all right?" he said to Henry, in a voice dripping with conspiracy. "I understand you've got Miss Haymes involved in the situation."

Henry's eyes narrowed. "You understand correctly."

"She's trouble, that one. Worse trouble than this one." He cocked his thumb toward Maria, who very nearly took it personally. "Chatting up your Secretary of State in a real friendly way."

"She wants a pardon," Henry said. "That's what our uncle told me. And she's offering some new toys from her daddy's workshops in exchange."

Troost snorted, not quite a laugh but definitely a sound of derision. "That's not why she's sniffing around the District. It's just an excuse."

"Why, then?" Maria asked. "I thought she was wanted for murder."

"Murder, war crimes, what have you. She's got enough money to shake it off. No, that's not what she wants. She's gunning for a Union weapons contract. Give the war another five years, and she'll have more money than God."

"But the war won't last another five years," Henry argued. "Everybody knows it—and I thought that was the whole point of letting her come play up north: wrapping up this whole thing all the sooner."

"Oh, who knows how long it'll last," Troost said, coming to the end of his cigarette. He dropped the last coal to the floor and crushed it with his boot. "All she has to do is give the South something to get good and mad about, something they can take the moral high ground on, since they lost *that* the day they fired on Sumter. Then she can drag out the war indefinitely."

"And how do you think she's going to do that?" Maria asked. She thought of the hungry dead who never stop chewing, but she said nothing of it.

Troost rose from his seat and slipped his fingers back into his glove. "I don't know for certain," he said. A new stab of fear went jolting through Maria's heart. This was not a man accustomed to uncertainty. "But it will be big, it will be bad, and the whole world will see it. Right now the South is an international object of pity. God help the Union if Europe stops feeling sorry for the CSA, and becomes outraged on its behalf."

He turned to go, but Henry stopped him. "Wait. Don't go like that. What else have you got?"

He leaned down to whisper, just loud enough for Maria to hear him, too. "I'm told they're calling the project 'Maynard.' So keep your ears open. When you hear the big heads talking about it . . . that's when you really need to worry."

 *Twelve*

Grant sat alone in the yellow oval, a drink in his hand, but only his second of the afternoon. His second of the *late* afternoon. And he wouldn't allow himself another until sundown; that was the bargain he'd made with Julia. Espionage required clarity.

Again he considered if he were even capable of espionage within his own cabinet. Breach of privacy? Absolutely. Breaking and entering? You could make a case for it.

But the maid at the congressional office had a key.

And she had arrived.

Grant heard his elderly but reliable butler Andrews, who had been warned that the girl must be brought to the formal office whenever she appeared, and to lead her up through the back stairs. She'd come through the kitchen, he guessed. Even if the president didn't mind a more direct approach, the rest of the staff would never have tolerated the impertinence; and it likely wouldn't have occurred to the girl to wander up to the White House and knock anyway.

This teenage girl being ushered quietly in to see the commander in chief might've provoked gossip, if not for the fact that Julia was with him now, seated behind the oversized desk with her sewing and paying the needle and thread just enough attention to keep from sticking herself or ruining the piece.

Grant hadn't planned to involve Julia. No one would've dreamed that he'd bring her into the fray of secrets. But that was the point: should anyone look askance at the arrangement, this was a maid, being brought to interview with his wife.

An utter fabrication, of course. It wouldn't have withstood even a moment's scrutiny by anyone the ruse needed to fool. Katharine Haymes, for example, would've spotted it in an instant—that this was the girl who worked the halls of the Capitol building, who cleaned Desmond Fowler's office, who had accidentally interrupted her conversation with the president. Even Fowler himself might have taken a second look. But the president had a suspicion that, in general, girls like Betsey Frye were largely beneath the concern of men and women like Katharine and Desmond.

Girls like Betsey were the foot soldiers of the world, after a fashion. First to go in, last to leave, little respected, largely interchangeable, and virtually invisible . . . but indispensable if you needed someone with good eyes and ears and a willingness to follow orders. She kept her head down and did her job, unless you required something else of her. She was a lesser Andrews.

Ephraim Andrews himself was a stately, mannered colored man who must've been old enough to be Grant's father, and who'd worked at the White House since he'd been a boy barely big enough to hold a coin. If Andrews couldn't be trusted, then the whole damn world might as well burn.

It had been Andrews who learned the girl's name and address, and who had tracked her down that very same evening. He'd delivered the president's message and made the invitation without any telltale notes to haunt them later; and made the arrangements to see the girl and her mother moved to more comfortable quarters, in payment and gratitude for her service to the nation.

That was how Grant put it, anyway. He didn't know how, precisely, Andrews had phrased it. He hadn't been there. Maybe Andrews told her she'd answer to the president or be drawn up on charges; maybe he told her nothing except to appear, or else. Whatever the old man had said, it worked.

And here she was.

Still wearing her plain linen uniform, but covered with a winter cloak and a bag slung across her chest, Betsey stood before him. Eyes downcast, but flickering surreptitiously around the office. Back and forth between Julia and Grant, the rows of books, and the shimmering fixtures. Back and forth between the door and the windows, and at Andrews, until he left them there alone.

Julia, always the savior of such moments, set her sewing aside. "Betsey—that's your name, isn't it, dear?"

"Yes, ma'am," she said clearly, but quietly.

"We appreciate you coming, and we know that it's a risky thing you've done," Julia warmly assured her. "I understand that your employers might look askance at this, even with the president's permission."

"Insistence, really," he corrected his wife. "Do you have the folders I asked for?"

The girl nodded, pulled the bag's strap up over her head, and stepped forward to deliver it into his hands. "I picked up the two with that name on it—the one you told me, I mean. And another one I found nearby. I thought it might be important."

"Hmm." He opened the bag and saw the neatly bundled papers, only a little mussed from the covert trip. "Thank you," he said, even though he wasn't altogether pleased that she'd read the files. He hadn't even known she was literate, but she must be, if she'd realized any other material was pertinent. But there was nothing he could've done to stop her, and if he couldn't rely on her silence now, he was damned regardless.

He'd relied on plenty of politicians over the last decade and change, and it had never worked out very well. Now he'd try his luck with another class—a better class, if you asked him, though he might change his mind when he considered the sentiment sober. People were only people, and some were more easily compelled by power than others.

Fine, then. He'd use his power where it actually worked, instead of boardrooms and war rooms where he was treated as a friendly pawn, and see if that panned out any better.

When Betsey had been sent on her way, Ulysses Grant carried her clandestinely delivered package toward the liquor cabinet out of pure habit.

"It isn't dark yet," his wife noted.

"She was early. And if ever any reading on earth required a drink, I believe this might be it."

Fresh drink in hand, he dropped himself heavily into the chair Katharine Haymes had taken the week before. He retrieved the first file—MAYNARD—and opened it up, taking a hearty swallow from the beverage before he began to read.

"It can't be *that* bad, can it, dear?" Julia asked. She didn't pick up her sewing again, instead stuffing it into her kit and folding her hands.

"That bad and worse. There's nothing I'd put past this woman," he said, skimming for the important words. He saw mostly things he already knew on the first page. "She's a regular Lilith. Put her and Fowler together, and they'd end the world for giggles on a weekend."

"You don't really believe that."

"You haven't met her. It's like sitting across the table from a snake."

Julia frowned, very faintly. "Would you say she's any worse than any of the men you've dealt with?"

"Worse," he said firmly, eyes still fixed on the pages in his lap.

"Truly your greatest adversary yet? Or worst simply because she's a woman?"

"A little of both," he murmured.

She sighed. "You're making her sound like a monster."

"You haven't met her," he repeated.

"She's not a witch or a demon; she's a *person.* She's only differ-ent from what you commonly see, and the people you commonly fight."

"Dearest," he said, fluttering the pages in a pointed fashion, "now is not the time."

But Julia persisted. "You behave as if you can't *possibly* compre-hend her motives. When I asked last night what she wanted, you said it must be blood, souls, or a spot at the devil's right hand."

"Anything's possible."

"No." She shook her head. "Only the usual things are possible. She wants a long life, power and money, freedom and respect. Just like any man you ever met. She's only beyond your ken because you allow her to be."

"I believe we're finished here. I'll have Andrews bring the car-riage around. You should return to your mother's estate tonight."

"You can't dismiss me like I'm some naughty child."

"Then I'll dismiss you like I'm the president," he said, quicker than he meant to. Then, to soften it, he finished the last of his drink and set it aside. "I am sorry. But this is . . ."

Before he could offer some weak explanation or excuse, she rose. "I'll go find Andrews myself, and have Amanda pack me a trunk," she said on her way out the door.

"Dear, I didn't mean . . ."

"I know what you meant," she said, as she closed the door behind herself.

He sighed, refilled his glass, and continued reading.

At first, the folders mostly served to confirm what Haymes had told him. He was surprised to learn how much of what she'd said could be called true, though she had glossed over the details, and filed their edges to make them less sharp. According to a researcher for her company, the weapon's actual range was up to a mile and three quarters square, and it would require an estimated fifteen men to successfully move and deploy it, though twenty were recommended.

But in the next dossier, he found something that confused him: lists of parts and supply chains, budget estimates, and time requirements . . . to make another eight weapons. Why would they need another eight weapons? The whole of her sales pitch had been that *one* weapon would end the war. If another eight were in the pipeline, why should she earn a pardon? Why should she be granted amnesty or asylum?

The next folder answered his questions. In it, he found a series of contracts signed by Katharine Haymes, and receipts signed by Desmond Fowler.

Military contracts.

Vast ones, the kind that would make Haymes one of the wealthiest women—nay, the wealthiest *people*—in the world, if she wasn't already. A series of deals brokered by Fowler, behind Grant's back.

"Son of a bitch," he breathed. "They're betting against the Union." Or at least they were betting against a speedy victory. After all, it was entirely possible that she'd struck a similar deal with Stephens in Danville. For all he knew, she was playing both sides, selling the technology to the highest and blindest bidders.

But he wondered if the South had any money left to spend on her.

Maybe not, then. Maybe she was just throwing her lot in with the richer party, and plotting to bleed it dry.

He hated her. Deeply, vividly.

He gulped down the rest of his drink without even tasting it, without remembering what he'd filled the glass with in the first place.

One last folder. It was fastened shut with a little seal, the kind that meant it'd been classified at the highest level. Well, Grant *was* the highest level. "Commander in chief," he mumbled his title, in case it meant anything to the little wax mark that spread a green stain across the paper's seam. "It don't get too much higher than that." By then he was too drunk to notice that he was lying to himself again.

He briefly considered doing this the sneaky way, with a heated knife slipped carefully beneath the wax to preserve its shape. Then he thought, "To hell with it," and snapped the thing in two. Who cared if anyone knew he'd seen it? Everyone who kept this secret found him beneath contempt anyway.

The last folder, this sleeved set of documents, fluttered open in his lap.

The top sheet was stamped: POTENTIAL TARGETS

He read. And he read. And with every line, his heart climbed another few inches up his throat. He gathered the papers and jumped to his feet, clutching the bundle to his chest and gazing wildly around the room. "I was right," he said to no one. "Terribly right. Awfully right. She's going to . . . she's going to . . ."

Who could he tell? Who would believe him?

A glance at the grandfather clock said it was not late yet, only a little dark . . . but not too dark for the extra drinks he'd finished while he scoured his stolen files. He looked down at the papers, wishing he had something better to hold them. Then he folded the whole bundle in half and stuffed it inside his waistcoat. It looked ridiculous, but with his overcoat on, no one would notice.

Out the door he went, calling for Andrews all the way. "Andrews! Andrews, is my wife still here? Andrews?"

When the aging servant appeared, perplexed and wary, he asked, "Sir? Mrs. Grant has gone, yes. To her mother's estate, she said?" He let the question dangle, but when Grant didn't reply, he added, "Shall I fetch you another carriage?"

"Yes!" he said too quickly, jamming a wool hat atop his head. "As soon as possible. I have an errand to run, and it won't wait."

"I can drive you myself," Andrews said solemnly, obliquely telling Grant that between Betsey's transportation and his wife's, there was no one else on hand to perform the task.

"Ah, I see. Yes, thank you, Andrews. Under ordinary circumstances, I wouldn't ask it of you; but this is more important than I have time to explain. Please, if you don't mind?"

The miles were short to the Lincoln compound; the world streaked past as Andrews rushed the horses at Grant's insistence. Gas lamps and electric lights ribboned through the night, keeping to the roads along with everything else on the way out of the Capitol's center. Grant held on to his hat with one hand and the inside carriage handle with the other, sometimes switching out and stopping to pat the important stuffing he kept against his belly.

When they finally arrived, skidding up the driveway, Grant didn't give Andrews time to open the door. He flung himself out of the cab. Over his shoulder, as he ran for the main entrance, he cried, "Don't wait for me! Go home to Helen! I'll see you in the morning!"

Behind him, the stomping and panting of the recovering horses settled into something slower and more plodding as the carriage turned around under Andrews's expert handling and rolled back into the street.

Grant beat his fist against the door, knocking harder than decency would really allow. But these were indecent times, and, as he told the serving girl who answered his repeated poundings, "I need to speak with Lincoln, immediately!"

"I . . . I . . . please sir, come in." She fumbled with the door and then his coat and hat, arranging them on the rack and begging his leave awkwardly. "Just excuse me for a minute and I'll run and get him."

Moments later, the girl reappeared and said, "Mr. President? I'll take you to him, if you'll come with me. He's in the study."

Grant knew where the study was, but he let the girl lead. She gestured toward the open doorway and then vanished.

"Grant, what's the calamity?" asked Lincoln. He was reclined on a settee by the fire, his chair beside him and his long legs stretched out.

"Sorry to interrupt your nap . . . or your early bedtime," he tried.

Lincoln sighed. "I was reading, and then some lunatic came beating down my door, and here you are. So have out with it."

Grant stepped quickly to his old friend's side. Seeing no chair nearby, he seized a small stool and placed it close enough to share Fowler's secrets. He reached into his waistcoat and retrieved the documents, all of the sheets rumpled and warmed by his body, and made a show of spreading them out, half on Lincoln's furniture, and half across his knees.

"Good God, old man," Lincoln asked, adjusting his spectacles and noticing the Secretary of State's letterhead. "What is this? What have you done?"

"Only a few illegal things, and none of them immoral," Grant assured him.

"Well, that's a relief . . ."

"It's Fowler. Or rather, it's that woman Katharine Haymes. She's working him like a sock puppet, her hand right up his backside, making him talk her words, and sign her papers."

"Wait, wait, wait. Haymes? I knew of her involvement, and I knew she was in town; Mary saw her at the Senators' Ball and was all aflutter about it. But . . ."

"But nothing. I've seen her. *Spoken* to her. She's a viper in a dress, Abe. She's the end of the world in a bonnet, is what she is. Do you know what she's done? Have you heard?"

"Bits and pieces. She talked you into a pardon, I heard that much. You're really going to buy that weapon of hers after all? Please tell me that's not the case."

"It's *not* the case. Or it *is* the case, but it's not me doing the buying. It's . . . it's Fowler; he's the one. He's got the court in his pocket and her hand up his ass. *He's* the one who arranged it, structured it, and pulled the trigger. Or so I learned after the fact . . . *well* after the fact, and I'm . . . I'm lost, Abe. You were right about everything, and I tried to assume the best. Never again."

"Now, let's settle down just a moment. It can't be as bad as all that," Lincoln said mildly, but his good eye was racing across the pages before him.

"It's plenty bad enough. If we try to stop that weapon the official way, it'll go off before we can force the orders through the bureaucracy. Fowler will see to that."

"You're probably right," he murmured, still reading.

"Which bit are you looking at there?" Grant asked, leaning forward and seeing the requisitions report. "Yes, that right there. You see? She's making *more* of them, or planning to. It's not just one weapon—that was never the plan."

"I wish I could say I am surprised." Without looking up, Lincoln asked, "Do you know if she's approached the South? Do you think she'll sell to both sides? She was a Southerner by birth, after all. Then again . . ." He shook his head.

Grant picked up the thought and said, "I doubt they have the kind of cash she's chasing. She's a mercenary, through and through. She's here in D.C. because we're the only people on the continent who can afford her. But, look. It gets worse. This one was sealed."

"What is it?"

"A list of targets they're considering."

They fell silent as they skimmed through the pages together—Lincoln for the first time, and Grant for the second, still unable to believe what he was reading.

Lincoln swallowed, and turned to the next sheet. "None of these are military targets. Except maybe Danville, and that's only a capital."

"That probably won't be the first pick," Grant surmised. "She could do some damage in there, absolutely—but it might be too *much* damage. It might actually shut down their government and end the war in one shot, and she can't have that. Not when there are eight other moneymakers on deck. No, she'd more likely shoot for New Orleans. It's their most important port, and there are plenty of civilians to murder."

"Yes, but then she'd have to contend with Texas, and that's no small feat. If it's civilians she wants to kill, there must be . . . oh, half a million people in Atlanta, and it's closer. With no Texian military presence. That'd be a bigger mess, wouldn't it?"

"At *least* half a million. And did you read the part about how the gas cloud will travel? It could wipe out thousands . . . tens of thousands . . . beyond its initial targets."

"More than that if the wind, the water, the . . . God almighty. She can't possibly realize what she's unleashing."

"On the contrary," Grant argued. "No one else on earth knows as much about the gas weapon as she does. She's the one who developed it."

A quiet knock on the door frame announced an interruption. It was Mary, holding a package. She smiled and said, "Sorry to break up the chatter, boys, but this just arrived from Fort Chattanooga."

Lincoln frowned quizzically. "Chattanooga? That doesn't sound right. Miss Boyd was just in Richmond, getting into trouble at the Robertson Hospital." Then to Grant, he said, "There was an incident. I don't know the specifics yet."

"Miss Boyd?"

"A Pinkerton agent," he replied vaguely. "I thought she'd be on her way back to D.C. by now."

Mary handed him the package, a large envelope. "Perhaps not. This looks like a woman's script to me."

She left them to continue their conversation. Once she was gone, Lincoln said, "I think she's right. Let's find out for certain, then." He tore the envelope and extracted Maria's letter. On top was a cover sheet, from which he read aloud. "Dear Mr. Lincoln: Included, you will find a series of notes taken hastily by hand, condensed from a much larger set of documents. The original documents—a series of missives from a nurse on the Western shore—have been sent elsewhere for safekeeping, as I'm sure you will understand. Please forgive me for not including the particulars of the Robertson incident. I will save those for later, as this is far more important. I will remain in Chattanooga through Friday, visiting with our distant family and inquiring after the camp workers who were present during Miss Haymes's weapon testing. Depending on where this line of enquiry leads, I may either pursue the case elsewhere or return to D.C. at that time. Will keep you abreast of matters. Yours, Maria B."

Lincoln turned his attention to the remaining pages of the message, and Grant read over his shoulder.

They finished at approximately the same time.

Lincoln turned to Grant, and said quietly, "Perhaps there *is* someone who knows more about the gas and its workings than Miss Haymes, after all."

"This nurse . . . wherever she is," Grant agreed.

Lincoln shook his head, but he did so with a hopeful smile. "Yes, the nurse, but also Sally Louisa Tompkins, and now Miss Boyd, for they have read the nurse's letters. Likewise, if Henry is there with Miss Boyd, then he knows, too; and *we* also know, if only an abbreviated form. This is the way word spreads, my friend: hand by hand, reader by reader. This nurse from the Robertson . . . she might well have saved us all, if we can heed her warnings in time.

"Now," Lincoln said, shifting his tone and setting the papers on the armrest beside him. "I must ask your assistance. My chair is beside you there, you see? Help me into it, if you would. I need to get to my desk and write a telegram. You and I have a Union to save."

 *Thirteen*

Grant very much wished his wife was there, but he'd sent her away the night before.

At the time it'd been little more than a drunken dismissal, for all he'd insisted otherwise—to her, and to himself. Now he was torn because he wished fervently to have her present, yet he was glad that she was gone. She must be safer in Baltimore with her family. He took comfort from the thought, or tried to, at any rate.

The White House was cold again. The afternoon was growing late. That called for a drink, but he didn't make one. He wondered how Abe's telegrams had gone off. Had they been received? Answered? No one sent him any word, or if anyone had, the Secret Service agents must've intercepted it.

Or maybe he was becoming paranoid.

He stood in the yellow oval and watched the window behind the desk. The curtains were open, and beyond them a tree shook and scraped its limbs across the glass. A storm had rolled up, all bluster and blow but no ice.

Left unattended, the fire had burned low. The fractured, watery light of the coals did nothing to warm the place.

Julia was gone to her mother's. He'd sent here there, without even thinking.

Only that wasn't true, was it? Some instinct must have provoked it. Some leftover warning that muttered deep within his brain . . . some trigger from his youth on the battlefield, when he knew that a fight was coming even though the skies were calm and the taps were silent, and his fellow soldiers lounged in their tents, wearing their warmest wools and playing cards to temper the relentless boredom.

Ever since his evening with Abe, he'd felt it creeping along his bones.

And now he waited.

Not for long, he didn't think. No, the wearying tension had ratcheted tighter overnight, and all through the day, as the District churned onward without him. But this time, he'd withdrawn at his own behest, not as part of some gentling ploy by Fowler or another advisor to get him out of the way.

Today he wanted to be out of the way. He wanted a retreat, and needed one. He'd been too close to the situation, even as he'd been so unceremoniously cut out of it. Present, but not accounted for. Muzzled and leashed like an old dog who could watch, but not run.

No, he told himself. Like an old *lion.*

The carpet pattern beneath his feet called to mind crests, seals, and caves. It was meaningless. Julia would've said it was only a design, and he was silly. She would've been right, but he saw it all the same, and a Biblical phrase swept through his sober, unhappy mind.

A den of roaring lions, seeking whom they may devour.

They would not devour *him.*

In his right hand he held a loaded Remington, the sturdy 1858 he'd picked up in the war. In his left he held a second cylinder, all its chambers loaded and capped. He had six more stuffed into his pockets, ready to go.

He stood very still and listened, because yes, it was coming.

Or anyway, *someone* was coming.

Footsteps in the hall, faster than a servant would run if decorum ruled the day. He clenched the gun, and slipped the last cylinder into his pocket to join the rest. Instinct told him the runner would knock, because the runner was not sneaking up on him. An assassin would move more quietly, if with no less urgency.

No. This was a message. A friendly one, if not a good one.

A series of swift raps upon the office door.

He answered: "It's open."

And the door crept inward, letting in a long sliver of yellow light from the gas lamps in the hall. Were they lit already? It wasn't that dark, was it? Well, the sun would be down in another two hours, and the halls of the White House were dark enough even when the days weren't dreary.

His visitor was a young woman. She was familiar, but it took him a moment to place her. He finally recalled her as a member of the housekeeping staff, but couldn't think of her name.

"Mr. President," she gasped, her breath lost somewhere down on the first floor, on another wing. Had she run the whole way? He thought so, from her rumpled dress and loosened bonnet. "It's Andrews."

He was honestly taken aback. Of all the subjects he'd expected to hear breathlessly broached, the old man was not among them.

"Andrews? What of him? He's gone home to his wife by now. Or maybe not; have you checked the kitchen?"

She swallowed hard, shook her head, and only just then noticed the gun. She mustered a "Sir? It's not that," but didn't ask if everything was all right. She knew otherwise, every bit as well as Grant did.

"Then what is it?" he prompted her.

"Sir, it's a terrible thing—him and Helen both, sir. Murdered!"

He nearly dropped the gun on the floor. Only years of training prevented it. It was that training, rather than any conscious instructions he could muster, that guided him as he slipped the gun into his right pocket. "I'm sorry, you'll have to . . . what do you mean, *murdered*?"

Grant heard the prickling pinpoints of hysteria in her voice when she replied, "Oh, Mr. President, I mean murdered with guns and knives! In their home. Helen made it out to the street for help, but then collapsed." She stepped inside the office and stood there before the door—still backlit, and casting a witchy puddle of shadow on the floor.

It wasn't hysteria that he felt oozing through the surface of his thoughts, but something colder and more numb. Something familiar.

This is what happens when it begins, when the last domino is pushed. When the hammer has dropped. This is the sound when the fuse is lit.

"Andrews," he said the man's name, not really believing it. Not choosing to believe it. Why Andrews? What did he have to do with anything? And how could the White House function without him? The man was an institution. "And Helen, too," he added, only then realizing that the woman's name was all he knew about her. He'd seen her a handful of times, coming and going from the kitchen or laundry.

It hadn't always been like that. He hadn't always been the kind of man who knew nothing about the people who managed his life and home. Once he'd been a soldier, hadn't he? A good one. A *great* one. A serving man of a different sort.

When did it get away from him? Had it been bought with this distancing ease? Too many years riding on the shoulders of others?

"Sir? What should we do?" she asked him.

A pitiful question, yet one he couldn't answer. Send flowers? Console his family? Summon the authorities? A better suggestion, yes. "Have the appropriate authorities been called?"

Fiercely she nodded. "The police, sir. They're coming to talk to you, I think. Almost unseemly, one of 'em said, that they'd bother interviewing the president about a nigger, but it was *Andrews,* sir." The note of pleading nearly broke his heart. "You'll speak to them, won't you? You'll help them find out what happened?"

"Of course I will, and you mustn't hold any questions or ill will against the police. When a man's been murdered—any man— one must always investigate. Especially when he has such ties to . . . to government. To the president."

He wished for Julia again, and then unwished for her. He congratulated himself instead on sending her away. Then his warm confidence faded as he wondered: was Maryland far enough?

Still fidgeting and fretting, the girl added, "They say another colored man did it, sir."

He frowned. "I'm sorry, come again?"

"That scientist. I think you know him. Been living over with the Lincolns, I think."

"Bardsley . . . ? No, I don't think so. Not for a moment. They didn't even know one another, and if they did, there would be no reason . . . no reason at all for Bardsley to . . ."

But the story was already arranging itself in his head. No, there was no reason for the scientist to kill an old couple in a small house. But there might be an excellent reason for someone else to raise the question—to cast suspicion, and remove credibility.

Grant had seen the editorial. He'd read it himself, and his skin had crawled. He'd felt it then, too, the coming battle. Gideon Bardsley. The walking plague. Project Maynard. The Fiddlehead. All these things, bubbling together and finding their way into print, into the public. Into the light, for scrutiny.

Readers were talking. Editors were talking. Last he'd heard from Abe, the warning letter was about to run in New York. That'd drum up some real interest, wouldn't it? A thousand paperboys crying out, screaming the truth on the busiest streets in the world.

Unless.

Unless the truth was coming from a known murderer. Sometimes the answers *are* so simple.

"And sir? A message. I'm sorry, I almost forgot it." She came forward, holding a scrap of folded paper in trembling hands. "A lady gave it to me, and said I should give it to you. She said it was important, but I was so . . . I heard about Andrews, sir, that's all. I only just now remembered."

"It's fine," he lied. He took it from her hands and read.

> *Even the smallest actions of great men come with*
> *tremendous consequences. Now hold still and*
> *be careful not to touch anything else. I can take*
> *more from you than your pawns. Baltimore isn't*
> *so far off.*

"You can't threaten me," he said to the note, or to the woman who must have written it.

The serving girl gave him a puzzled look. "Sir?"

"Not you, dear," he replied without taking his eyes off the page. "Not *you*. But I want you to do something for me. I want you to tell the agent outside that I'm retiring for the night. Tell him to stay where he is, and his relief should remain downstairs, too, for I'm not feeling well. Then build me a stack of pillows in my bed, and don't say a word when I leave through the kitchen."

Fourteen

"How does it look?" Gideon called to Nelson Wellers from the ruined basement of the Jefferson. He could smell a storm brewing even down there, below the surface; the cold, shifting winds whistled through holes in the floor and spit through the remains of the scientist's printer upstairs. They rustled the ashes of paper, and scattered the broken press keys like so many pebbles.

The doctor cried back, "As bad as before, if less cluttered. They've been taking away the trash, at least. Getting the place cleaned up."

Gideon shuttered the lantern and stepped past a pile of cables, a stack of paper, and a splintered set of desk drawers. "Getting dark, isn't it?"

"Starting to. The weather isn't helping. Can you see all right?"

"Yes."

"How bad is it down *there*?"

"Bad." He looked up through the hole above, and imagined he felt a drop of very cold rain. A second spitting drop very nearly convinced him, but when he didn't feel a third, he began to hope it was a fluke. "How much waxed canvas did you get?"

"Enough, I hope."

"That's a miserable answer."

Wellers sighed. "Fine. It's . . . a stack of sheets about a foot thick. Each one is about . . . I don't know. Twenty by thirty. Lincoln said it was all Smithy could scare up on such short notice, so it'll have to do. I'm sure it'll cover the machine."

"The machine, yes. The floor above it . . . that remains to be seen." He performed some rough calculations in his head, and guessed the square footage he could cover. "We can deploy the sheets and weigh them down; might be able to save a few things that way. But we won't be able to waterproof this lower level. Rain will drain down and pool in the mechanisms. Ice or snow will be heavy, and melt. Then the water will freeze, and smash it apart from the inside."

"Always a ray of sunshine, aren't you, Gideon?"

"A very practical ray of sunshine, yes. We should start at the southwest corner," he directed.

"Is that where the worst of the damage is?"

"No, it's where the *machine* is. The worst of the damage is at the other end of the room, but we're running out of time."

"We'll do the best we can, and it'll be enough," Wellers said, insisting to himself—or maybe to Gideon, who couldn't see him and only halfway believed him. "I'll start unloading. Wait."

"What?"

"Wait," he said again, low and quiet, directed down the hole above Gideon's head. Then, to someone else: "Who goes there, eh? What can I do for you fine gentlemen this . . . afternoon, I suppose. Though it looks rather like evening, more so every minute."

"That it does," came the response. Gideon didn't recognize the speaker. "We're looking for Gideon Bardsley, and have reason to think he might be here."

Wellers hesitated, but only for the briefest of moments. "Gideon? No, he's not here right now. He's back at the Lincoln place, I believe."

"You believe wrong."

"Wouldn't be the first time," the doctor said coolly. "What do you officers want with him? If you don't mind my asking."

Officers? Policemen, Gideon assumed. Couldn't be good. Why were they here? Could they be charging him with libel, over the editorial he'd written? He smiled darkly, thinking of the piece's reception; he'd heard that countereditorials were being drawn up and printed up even as he stood there. He'd already read one or two. But more than rebuttals, he saw calls for action. Statements of concern. Demands for answers. And the demands were growing louder with every passing hour, much to his grim delight.

"He's wanted for murder."

Ah. Something else then. Something untrue. More untrue than libel, anyway. They weren't supposed to convict a man who spoke the truth, not that it necessarily stopped anyone. And as for murder? Innocent men were convicted every day.

So Douglass had been right. They were disgracing him, since they couldn't silence him any other way. He might've been flattered if he didn't feel so inconvenienced.

Nelson Wellers replied with a similar disbelief. "Murder? You can't be serious. Gideon never murdered anybody, and I'd very much like to see whatever evidence brings you out here to arrest him."

"Two witnesses have independently and confidently identified him, and the dead man himself wrote 'GB' in his own blood, right beside his body. Besides that, part of his laboratory coat was found at the scene—a pocket, torn off in the victim's struggles."

Laboratory coat? Gideon shook his head. He almost never wore a coat in the lab, only the occasional apron or belt for his tools. To call the charges trumped up was to give them more credit than they deserved.

"That's preposterous!" Wellers said with exasperation. "You have no way of knowing whose coat, whose pocket . . ."

But one of the policemen snapped, "The specifics are none of your concern, unless you're giving quarter to a known fugitive. In that case, it's absolutely your concern, because it's evidence against you, as well. Now, where is he?"

"I surely have no idea."

"According to our sources, he left the Lincoln household with you. To come here. To do . . . what *are* you doing, anyway?"

"You don't care, so what does it matter? You're looking for Gideon, and I haven't seen him. We parted company in town when we realized we didn't have enough supplies to perform our task. You might stop by C. T. Helman's shipping supplies."

"And why would we do that?"

"Because," Nelson said with an exaggerated note of impatience. "That's where we got the waxed canvas over there." He must have gestured at the cart. "And I'll answer your other question truly and on the house: We're trying to prevent damage to the basement level, where some very sensitive scientific equipment is presently exposed to the elements. If you take a look at the sky, you'll see we have some elements pending. Any minute now."

"You've got a point. Maybe *we* should take a look at all this . . . sensitive scientific equipment while we still can. It could be important to the case."

"I assure you, it *isn't*."

Gideon thought fast. Getting out of the basement, that was the first priority. On the one hand, he wanted to swear at Wellers for bringing up the machine, but he couldn't stay there anyway, so the sooner he was out, the better.

He glared at the Fiddlehead, source of and solution to so many problems. Could it survive the night without being covered? Maybe. It'd held on this long, hadn't it? A week, plus a couple of days. But there had been no rain, no ice. Water might be the end of it. Simple moisture destroying the most complex machine a man had ever made. He was certain that said something about Mother Nature, or God, or fate, but he didn't give a damn about any of them, so he seethed without remorse and didn't wonder after a deeper meaning.

But he couldn't save the machine if he was imprisoned or dead, now could he?

He seized a bit of waxed cotton canvas—the only bolt he'd brought down. He wrapped his hand in one corner and used it to snap his lantern in half, removing the simple circuitry from the bulb and examining it.

He frowned. The lantern was newfangled twenty years ago, before the electrical models hit the market; but now it felt like a Roman artifact in his hands. No matter. He'd work with what he had.

He popped off the bottom, removed the metal base, and then extracted the glass canister of fuel that rested within. There wasn't much, but it'd have to be enough.

Ducking under a fallen plank, he scooted into the next room over, where it was almost pitch black. That made it hard to see, but even harder to be seen.

He worked fast, using his teeth to tear off the cuff of his shirt-sleeve. He stuffed it down into the fuel, making a wick that he hoped was long enough. It had to be long enough, or he'd incinerate himself and the Fiddlehead alike.

There, crouched in the utmost darkness, he pulled a box of matches out of his pocket and struck one. He looked up at what used to be the ceiling, and targeted a pair of feet he could barely see, very near the edge of the basement pit. They weren't Wellers's feet—Gideon was pretty sure that Wellers was facing the other direction.

He listened to the voices for another moment. Yes, he was confident.

With a deep breath and a steady hand, he lit the scrap of cotton. It burned too bright, a beacon that would reveal him if he let it. The wick wouldn't last but a few precious seconds, and Wellers couldn't stall the men forever, so he chucked the tiny, sloshing bomb up through the floor as quickly as he could.

It shattered and the fuel ignited, spreading across the beams that remained. But it also spread out across the grass, a shallow pool of fire that chased the officers backwards while Wellers barked out something in surprise. A laugh? A cry?

Gideon wasn't listening. He was leaving.

Out he went, up the broken stairs and over the wall while the commotion blazed behind him. He hunkered down low, trusting the coagulating shadows and his grandfather's Revolutionary War coat to disguise him. He twisted his scarf around his neck, making it snug so it wouldn't flap or snag. And while Nelson Wellers and the officers stomped and tamped the flames against the damp grass, Gideon ran back out through the woods.

Yet again.

He was sick of it, but what else could he do? There were two kinds of help he could offer Wellers: one, he could physically assault the officers in question, thereby negating any murder defense; or, two, he could prove Wellers a truthful man by getting as far away from the premises as possible.

The last vestiges of Wellers's protest faded in the distance. Perhaps they'd arrest him, but it wouldn't be for murder—and there wasn't much Gideon could do about it either way. He had to trust the Pinkerton agent to manage the situation.

He hated trusting other people to take care of things without him. He'd much rather do everything himself.

But aside from absenting himself, the most helpful course of action he could take was to get to the Lincolns' homestead. Old Uncle Abe would probably know what was going on—he had ears all over the District, and Gideon had a feeling that these murders were already far from secret. Murder never stayed quiet for long.

As he dashed through the trees along the main road, he glanced at the sky. Was the air on his face wet, or merely cold? Was his nose running, or just freezing?

Whoever had thought of a murder charge was brilliant, really. When the facts align against you, loudly misdirect. Wonderful strategy. You could undermine anyone by calling them a lunatic or a murderer, especially a colored man whose respectability was precarious under the best of circumstances.

Even though the sentiments expressed in his editorial sounded outlandish, they were based on rock-solid, irrefutable facts. But all the proof in the world only mattered if it were known and accepted, which was rather unlikely if the proof came from a man accused of murder, especially what sounded like gruesome murders. Vicious, appalling, cruel, sick acts, undoubtedly—with the added lurid detail of a dead man's accusation, written in blood. How else would they call him a lunatic in the papers?

And on what other grounds might they take away his credibility? That he was colored? That he'd been a slave?

That was meaningless in the broad sense, but there were still fools who thought it mattered. Then again, such fools would dismiss him regardless of a murder accusation. No, this ploy was meant to sway the middle masses, the men and women who might otherwise be inclined to panic about this creeping leprosy that spread through the soldiers and into the cities.

This was a much easier panic, to be sure: a colored man on a murdering rampage. A bold headline! One that would push smaller, more dangerous headlines like "Evidence of Walking Plague's Association with Warfare Weaponry Mounts" down the page.

He'd become a point of gossip among the fancy set, just like the Charleston Caper or the Macon Madmen in his father's time. Oh, beware and behold the danger of letting negroes have their freedom! Ignore the facts, believe the manufactured story with its tidy villains and convenient foes. It's easier that way.

Gideon's chest hurt and his feet were going numb, but he kept running. It was only a couple of miles, not far at all. He could've walked it in an hour, but now was not the time for walking. Only when he thought his lungs would burst and his knees quaked from crashing through the underbrush beside the main thorough-fare did he slow.

He longed to reach out into the road and ask for a ride—he had money; he could buy one, certainly. But with the police on his heels, he couldn't bring himself to do it. If Nelson Wellers could convince them he was elsewhere, they'd look elsewhere. They'd already tried the Lincoln place, apparently . . . unless that was a lie and they weren't policemen at all, which was always a possibility.

A nasty possibility. But one he couldn't ignore.

He let his mind race when his feet couldn't do so anymore.

No. The safest thing would be to find Lincoln, and then . . . it depended.

He might have to pack up and leave. In which case, he could ask after Kirby Troost and his family, then meet them outside D.C. Troost could get anyone or anything out of anywhere, any-time.

Then again, if these were merely police, merely ordinary civil servants with a job to do, then they could be reasoned with. The very nature of their duties required them to assess evidence and weigh proof, did it not? Of course, that only applied to the up-standing ones—a policeman can be bribed as easily as anyone else. No, there was no one he could trust. No one but the men he'd already trusted this long, and if he couldn't count on *them,* then he was damned regardless.

While he caught his breath he watched the road, hunting for some sign of help, or, barring that, any suggestion that there might be a manhunt in progress. At one point he watched two official vehicles with side-mounted sirens wailing through the bitter evening wind, charging in the direction of downtown.

Of course, they might've been intended for someone else. There could be a fire, or lightning strike damage from the shifting sky throwing its weight around like a hurricane. It might not have been a response to murders, contrived to blame a blameless man in order to silence him. But he doubted it.

Gideon was grateful for the small things, that the rain and ice held off, and the wind worked with him. It shoved at his back and urged him onward despite heavy boots and hot, labored breathing. There was nowhere to go but forward.

Slowly, cautiously, a horse-drawn carriage rumbled close to the ditch at the road's shoulder. So close Gideon could almost make out the furtive driver—and, indeed, that'd been the point.

"Nelson!" Gideon barked as he flung himself through the trees.

Wellers grabbed his hand and yanked him up over the step and into the back. Gideon dropped down low and soon felt the weight of a canvas sheet down over his head. Wellers didn't say a word, and Gideon didn't ask any questions.

Within another five minutes they'd reached their destination, and by then, he'd almost caught his breath.

Mary was out on the front lawn, her dress billowing ominously in the whipping, driving wind. She held an electric lantern, its false white light beaming wildly as it swung in her hand, tossed about like everything else that wasn't nailed down. Polly stood beside her, another light in her own hand, equally out of control. Together, they flagged down Wellers.

He drew the cart up in a stop that left skid marks in the gravel. Polly grabbed the horses and said, "I'll take them, ma'am—you take the doctor!"

"Come back inside as soon as you're able," Mary commanded,

yelling at Polly over the wind. Then, to Wellers: "Doctor, have you heard? Where is he? Is he all right? Did they take him?"

"I've heard," was all he replied.

Gideon threw off the canvas covering and rolled over the cart's side, nearly spraining an ankle on the landing. He shouldn't have tried it—it was too high—but he was so tired from running that it was the only dismount he could manage. He leaned forward and put his hands on his knees, then straightened up and said, "They've accused me of murder."

"My, yes—they certainly have! Please, hurry inside! Before they come back!"

"I can't hide forever," he told Mary, even as he let her guide him inside, luring him forward with the unspoken promise of a fire and a friendly ear, of someone he could trust while the world burned down.

"No, and you won't have to."

"Where's Lincoln?"

"Inside, waiting for you. I'll . . . I'll make tea," she said as she shut the door behind all three of them. Gideon was quite sure that no one wanted tea, but it was the most normal, civilized thing she could think of, and these were uncivilized times.

"In the library?" Wellers asked, before she disappeared around a corner. She nodded without looking back.

"The coppers said two people had been killed," the doctor told Gideon as they paced swiftly down the hall. "An elderly colored couple. They worked in the White House. That's all I know." They rounded the corner and joined Abraham Lincoln in a library that was almost too toasty.

"Not just two," the old man said, overhearing. "Three."

"Three?" Gideon exclaimed. He untangled his scarf and let it hang limply around his neck.

"Indeed. A very kind old couple in Grant's employ, and a housekeeping girl."

"My God, I've been busy. How did I do it?"

"An ax in one case, and an excess of bullets in the other. My sources say that the girl had performed a bit of casual treason at the president's request—and at Katharine Haymes's peril."

"You drew that conclusion rather quickly," Wellers noted, settling onto the edge of a chair and leaning forward to warm his hands at the fire.

"I'm not an idiot," Lincoln said wryly. Then, to Gideon: "All this happened while you were out with Nelson, naturally enough. Or perhaps you're some kind of witch and you performed the first round of killings immediately before you brought the paper back from Smithy's."

"A witch?" Gideon chose not to sit. He was wound up too tightly, a watch that's been cranked but not set. Tired as he was, he could scarcely lean, much less be seated. "I've been accused of worse."

"Don't say that; there's far worse to come. The young woman was assaulted. Reports suggest she was ravished, though even if she wasn't, you can bet that's what they'll say."

A prickling sensation scaled the back of his neck. "A white girl?" he guessed.

"If she weren't, they might not care."

A quiet moment fell between them, filled only by the crackling sizzle from the fireplace logs and the hollow, whistling gale howling down the bricks and against the windows. Finally, Lincoln spoke. "It'll be in the papers. If not tomorrow, then the next day. How optimistic do we feel this evening, gentlemen?"

"Marginally," Wellers confessed.

"Less than that." Gideon sighed. "It's the same story over and over, like some nightmare I never awaken from. I begin underground and fight until I rise, only to find myself underground again. Slave quarters to university. A basement to the . . . the illustrious Lincoln estate. And tonight, out from the basement again, but headed to prison—or, more likely, for a tree or a bullet."

Lincoln replied, "Let's not forget: you're here, you're alive, and you're not in prison *yet*. There's room for improvement, but the situation could be considerably more dire."

"So what should we do?" Wellers asked, staring into the fire.

Gideon spoke firmly. "We keep the story out of the papers."

The doctor let out half a laugh. "And how do you propose we do *that*?"

"I haven't thought that far ahead. Give me a minute."

"I don't disagree, mind you."

"Good, because we *must* prevent the story from going public, and thereby prevent Haymes and her . . . her minions from discrediting me. We *must* get someone to defend my character, and remind the nation of the truth in my editorial. We need a credible person—you, perhaps, Mr. Lincoln—to write a follow-up to my editorial letter, underlining the key points and alluding to evidence that exists, and is confirmed, and will be revealed in good time."

Lincoln shook his head. "Gideon, you make it sound . . . well, not easy. But you make it sound doable, and it isn't. Not the way you present it."

"You won't write a letter?"

"I will, absolutely. I've supported you from the very start—from the very first plans you drew for the Fiddlehead. I believed in you then, and I believe in you now—not just because I know that you're incapable of having killed those people." He adjusted himself in his chair so he could face Gideon more fully, make absolute contact with his one good eye. He did not blink as he said, "If you were not right, and powerful, and dangerous, they would not have resorted to this. But because you *are* right, and powerful, and dangerous, they *have*. And they'll resort to worse before they're finished. I can feel it in my bones."

Nelson Wellers wrung his slim hands together and swallowed, then ran his fingers through his hair. "He was with *me* when the murders were committed. He has an alibi."

"Yes," Gideon said it fast, as the puzzle piece fell into place. "Yes, that's true. From a doctor and an agent of the law, after a fashion. We can prove I've done no wrong. I should've let them arrest me!"

"Gideon, *no.* You were right to slip away while you could. I sensed it the moment they arrived. They didn't want to interview me, or have me offer any statement on your behalf. And when they realize that I can vouch for you, they'll come for me. I . . ." He looked around, his gaze darting from corner to corner. "I shouldn't stay here. I'm a danger to you all."

"Wellers, settle down," Gideon groused. "No one's coming for you. I'm the problem here. if anyone should go, it ought to be me."

"But I'm willing and ready to plead your case and take the stand on your behalf. *That's* why they'll need to be rid of me. If they kill Gideon," Wellers said sharply to Lincoln, "they make him a martyr—they make his message louder. But if they kill me, he has no defense and he'll be shrieking his message from a jail cell, like a madman. I need to send a message to Chicago. I need to summon a replacement."

"You're abandoning us?" Gideon asked with disbelief.

"No. Absolutely not. But I can't speak on your behalf if I'm dead, and I won't stand for anyone else getting caught in the fray. Certainly not you, or Mary or Polly," he said firmly to the old man.

"Now don't say anything rash. Furthermore, don't *do* anything rash," Lincoln said in a calming voice. "They can't kill us all. They *won't* kill us all, even if they catch us. The police won't be back for another hour or two, I shouldn't think; and although Haymes has agents who are willing to break the law, they may not have arrived yet, and *surely* they won't come for you here. Not yet.

Not yet." He murmured the words like a mantra. "We have time to think. Time to plan for—"

He was interrupted by a knock on the door, hard and fast, a steady bang of the metal ring.

All three men froze in place, exchanging a violent lightning of glances.

The doctor said, "Gideon, hide."

And Gideon said, "*No.*"

"No one's hiding, not yet," Lincoln said, his timbre a plea for patience and order. It was a plea for time, but even that great man couldn't wring more from the moment than was already granted.

Down the hall a man came running, all heavy footsteps and rambling, long-legged pace; and behind him trailed the lighter, frantic footsteps of the serving girl. In the library, all three men drew guns, prompting Gideon to wonder where Lincoln had hidden one, and how he used one with those twisted fingers.

He analyzed the situation with his ears.

Polly's following behind him, whoever he is. He didn't break inside, he knocked. He is alone except for the girl, who can't catch up to him. This might not be what it sounds like.

"Abe!" the newcomer shouted before he reached the library. That one word blew the tension from the room like steam through a kettle whistle.

"Grant?" the old president asked, just in time to spy the leader flinging himself around the doorjamb.

"Abe, they've killed . . ." He stopped when he saw Gideon and Nelson, who lowered their guns but did not put them away.

"I know," Lincoln told him. "Your housemaster, and his wife, and the girl who stole those papers. I got your message half an hour ago, and I'm very sorry to hear of it. Is everything . . . otherwise all right?"

"No, it's not. Nothing's all right. This is about *you.*" He pointed at Gideon. "And me. They've done this to *us*, not just to those poor people they've killed out of hand."

"They wish to discredit me," Gideon said stiffly.

"Oh, that's not all they want. No, no, no. I'm afraid not." Grant walked to the far window. He held his hand against the glass to guard his eyes from the glare. Seeing nothing outside, he reached up to draw the heavy velvet curtains shut. He turned around. "They want to keep me cowed, as surely as they want to make you look like a murdering maniac. Maybe they want to make me look mad, too. I had to escape two Secret Service men in order to arrive here unseen. At least I *believe* I haven't been seen . . ."

Lincoln said, "Dr. Wellers is confident they want him dead, too. It's quite a party here tonight."

Gideon explained, "Wellers and I were together when the murders happened."

"Then he might have a point," Grant said. To Lincoln, he added, "You need to guard this man's life with . . . with *your* life. The four of us," he said, so out of breath from his trip, and from the revelations that had brought him there, that his speech caught in his throat, "are all that keeps them from milking the Union nearly to death, and slaughtering thousands for the profit."

Gideon put his gun back in his coat and clenched his fists. He measured his words against his fury and rising fear, and cast it all at the president. "God*damn,* but you're being shortsighted, sir! If the war runs on, it won't just be Atlanta that falls to the plague. Remember the Fiddlehead. Remember the numbers, and the predictions: the *continent* will fall within the decade if we cannot stop this madness and force a conclusion. Possibly the world!"

Nelson Wellers laughed ruefully. "It's not enough to save our own skins, or the entire nation." He sighed. "No, we must save the world as well. All from this library."

Lincoln gave a crooked shrug. "There are worse places from whence to mount a defense of civilization."

Grant seemed to agree, but he was flustered, and he rambled. "They threatened me, Abe. Not just me, but Julia—they've threatened her. That terrible woman, that dragon in a hat. *She's* the one who did this."

"Where is Julia now?" his old friend asked.

"Baltimore, but that's not far enough away to keep her safe from Haymes."

Gideon's nails dug into his palm. He fought to keep from hitting something for emphasis, but managed to restrain himself for only a few seconds before taking a swing at a bookcase. He knocked it so hard that it rocked precariously, then settled.

"For God's sake!" he shouted. "Have you not heard a thing? Baltimore won't be far enough. New York won't be far enough. Mexico won't, and Argentina won't. Canada won't. The Department of Alaska won't! There will be no place in this hemisphere far enough away to protect anyone from this walking plague!"

Nelson Wellers positioned his lean frame between Gideon and the other two men with his hands up. "You're right. We know you're right—we've already said as much. But in the short term, we must take what action we can."

"We don't have time for the short term!"

Wellers gave up, flung his upraised hands into the air, and finally hollered back. "*You're* the one who wants to stop a damn news story before morning! You're wanted for murder. That's a short-term problem, now, isn't it?"

"Oh, for Christ's sake!"

"Gentlemen!" Lincoln tried to roar, but it came out as a cough. Grant went to his side, and Nelson looked back to make sure that it wasn't any worse than that.

Gideon did not back down. He mimicked Wellers's tone when

he said, "They want you dead. That's a short-term problem, too, now, isn't it?"

"Short term for you—somewhat longer for me! But yes, fine. It serves my point," Wellers said, struggling to calm himself. "I would prefer to survive. You would prefer to stay out of prison. The Union must be preserved. The war must end. The weapon must be stopped. The walking plague must be addressed. We need stepping stones, Gideon. *Stepping stones.*"

Gideon argued, "How are we supposed to stop it? We don't even know where it's headed."

"Executive order!" cried Grant. "I do still wield *some* authority, you know. I'm only the president, as I've been reminded more than once in the last week."

"Then why not send an executive order *now*?" Wellers asked plaintively. "Recall the project, bring the weapon home."

Grant fidgeted like an angry man, pacing with a stomp. "Because no one will admit that it exists. I can't recall the project; I have to recall the mission itself. And *I can't find it.*"

A disquieting pause fell, and then the doctor said, "Someone will. Someone has to. Maybe . . . maybe Troost'll hear something."

Lincoln finished his coughing fit, then rallied himself to speak. "We've heard nothing from him since yesterday morning, and no mention of Maynard."

"If anyone can track it down, he can," Wellers said with desperate confidence.

Gideon didn't argue, but he worried all the same. Troost was one of a kind, but he already had one mission on deck: bringing the Bardsleys to safety on the northern side of the line. He could swing the impossible, yes, absolutely. But how many impossible things could he juggle at once?

Grimly, he warned, "We can count on Kirby Troost to do his job, and more. But right now, we need a plan. We need to get our story straight and our actions in order before Haymes makes her next move." He straightened the bookcase he'd knocked ajar in his moment of anger, nudging it back into place and setting two books aright. "We need to send word to our operatives before the police find their way back here, as they inevitably *shall*. And when Troost finishes evacuating my family, he'll be back. We must be certain that we are ready for *him*."

 *Fifteen*

On Monday morning, Maria awoke to a knock on her hotel room door. She threw her coat over her dressing gown and fished around on the cold wood floor for her slippers, but couldn't find them, so she gave up and tiptoed from rug to rug, turning up the heat as she passed the radiator. "I'm coming," she called sleepily. She wondered what time it was, but could see through the crack in the curtains that it must be an hour past dawn at least. She hadn't meant to sleep so late.

Henry Epperson was staying right across the hall, so she assumed that it must be him, but when she opened the door, she found an errand boy of perhaps ten or eleven years old with a stack of telegrams in his fist. "Are you Miss Boyd?" he asked. She nodded. He thrust the loose papers forward. "Here."

"Thank you," she said, rubbing her eyes. Seeing that the boy lingered, she added, "One moment, dear." Her bag was sitting next to the washbasin. She stuffed her fingers into the side pocket and pulled out some pennies. "Here you go."

She closed the door behind him and sorted the messages by the time they'd been sent—which was trickier than it should've been, as they were entirely out of order. But once she'd corrected the situation, she knew she needed to rouse Henry *immediately*.

She located her slippers, which had been kicked beneath the bed. She pulled on a pair of socks before donning them, not caring how silly it looked and doubting that anyone would notice. Across the hall she went, where she rapped her fist heartily, repeatedly on Henry's door. "Henry? Are you up yet?"

"Yes, ma'am," he said through the door, then opened it with a smile. "I've got some coffee in here. Can I talk you into sharing?"

"Coffee sounds wonderful." She stepped past him as he held the door ajar. "But there's no time to dillydally!"

He looked confused. "Not even for coffee?"

"An errand boy brought me these." She showed him the notes. "They've been piling up overnight, apparently. One in particular is marked for urgent, immediate delivery, but it would seem that the taps aren't manned as thoroughly as one might wish."

Henry shook his head. "The military missives get first handling. Civilian messages get processed whenever the intake officer feels like sorting them out."

"That's a bum deal if you need to send a note in a hurry," she complained.

"Far be it from me to argue with you. So what's the rush?"

She fed him the telegrams one by one.

SUMMARY OF NURSING NOTES RECEIVED STOP
AGREE ON ALL POINTS REGARDING GAS AND
WEAPONS PROJECT DESIGNATED MAYNARD STOP
WILL EXPECT REPORT ON ROBERTSON UPON YOUR
RETURN FRIDAY STOP UNCLE A

MAYNARD IS ON THE MOVE STOP AUTHORIZATION
GIVEN SANS UNCLE G STOP TARGETS CIVILIAN NOT
MILITARY STOP ALERT OUR COUSIN KT TO
WITHDRAW TO OTHER SIDE OF MD IMMEDIATELY
STOP YOURS DR W ON AUTHORITY AND APPROVAL
OF UNCLE A

"MD?" Henry frowned.

"Mason-Dixon, I should think," she replied. "But Project Maynard . . . if Troost was right, now's the time to *really* worry."

Oh, I'm already worried plenty," he said, and fiddled with the
small slip of paper. "*Civilian targets.* That's not good."

"It's not a surprise, either. Everything I've heard of Haymes
suggests she's utterly soulless. But it doesn't stop there. Look, here's
the next one."

DO NOT RETURN TO DC STOP FIND OUR COUSIN KT
FOR ASSISTANCE STOP MOST LIKELY TARGETS LARGE
CITIES STOP MAYNARD COULD CLEAR A SQUARE
MILE STOP RESULTING CLOUD MAY TRAVEL MILES
FURTHER STOP WILL SEND WHATEVER HELP WE
CAN MANAGE STOP

"I don't even know who sent this one," she said in a whisper.
"Dr. Wellers, I expect, though it might be Dr. Bardsley."

Henry didn't dwell on that part. "Oh, God," he said again.

"We need to find Kirby Troost, unless you think 'KT' stands
for anybody else. But it's his job to get Gideon's family out of the
South. I'm not sure how much assistance he can be to us until
he does."

He smiled weakly. "Only because you don't know Kirby. He
can handle more than one task at a time, and you can bet he'll
have some ideas and some connections. He always does. Come
on—get yourself dressed, and I'll get us a carriage. A clean
carriage," he emphasized, meaning one that wouldn't need a
driver.

"Five minutes, and I'll meet you downstairs."

In five minutes she dressed herself, threw on her boots, and lit
a tiny fire in the enamel basin to destroy the telegrams. When they
were reduced entirely to ashes, she grabbed her tapestry cloth bag

and dashed down the stairs to find Henry standing beside a tiny cabriolet with a puttering, sputtering engine that shook the whole frame as it idled.

"After you, ma'am," he said, holding the door open and offering his hand for her to climb up inside. She took it and ascended into the narrow cab, adjusting her skirts so he could shut the door. He crawled up into the other side, shut his own door, and adjusted the levers and wheel. He wrenched the vehicle into gear and it rambled forward, then he hit the brakes to avoid hitting a newspaper seller who'd dropped something in the road. "Sorry!" he shouted out the window. "Sorry," he said again, and set the car moving forward, more carefully this time.

"It's a shame there's no glass in these windows, don't you think?" Maria asked with a shudder. She tightened her coat and twisted her gloved hands up in her scarf, but that wasn't enough to make her comfortable, not with the wind rushing inside the cab.

"Not such a shame if you're keen to keep breathing. The exhaust creeps up from the engine—that's why the windows are fixed this way. It'll warm up a bit as we go, I promise. Heat also creeps inside, especially at your feet."

They drove a few blocks east, which was not at all in the direction of Lookout Mountain—a fact that Maria knew because she could see its craggy, winter-bald point off to the south. She was on the verge of asking why they were taking this path when Henry explained, "We have to get past the wall, and the nearest gate is over here. Under different circumstances, I'd take the long way around to cover our tracks . . . but we're short on time, and I don't know about you, but I haven't seen anyone following us."

"No, we've been fortunate so far," she said, with more confidence than she felt.

Before long, the wall loomed up close.

It was a sheer, flat, inscrutable thing—a vast construction designed with traditional military precision and lack of finer detail.

A massive half-moon over a hundred feet high, it was painted Confederate gray, partly as a patriotic statement, partly to protect it from the elements, and partly because gray paint was cheap. A wide double gate hung open, with one lane of traffic spilling slowly inward, and one lane of traffic proceeding outward at a somewhat faster pace.

Maria reached into her bag for the papers identifying her as a nurse, but Henry told her not to bother. "They check you coming in, not going out."

"They didn't check *me* coming in."

"You came in on the train."

"Ah." That was true—and her papers on the far end had been carefully scrutinized, now that she was awake enough to remember the process.

Henry waved to the guard, who waved back in a casual, unconcerned manner. Then they were outside, in the poorer suburbs that had been chopped off from the urban military center. Off in one direction, Maria saw Missionary Ridge curving gently around the valley; and to the right, she could barely see the leaning tip of the mountain peeking over the wall. It all felt very medieval to her, like a castle surrounded by serfs.

Henry guided the car to an overgrown side road, where they could watch travelers come and go through the gate without being easily observed. Several minutes passed without anything suspicious happening, so he and Maria concluded that they hadn't been followed, and were on their way with a somewhat greater sense of security.

Outside the wall, the roads were not made for horseless travel. They took it slowly because the engine was quieter in a lower gear, and because the brick-paved streets were rough on the hard-rubber wheels of the car, never mind its occupants. Horses came and went, sometimes ridden, and sometimes pulling loads; children dashed out into the slow-moving traffic, chasing dogs, toys, or one another. Potholes abounded, for bricks were sometimes pulled from the street and used to patch, repair, restore, and rebuild outhouses, sheds, and crumbling foundations. Intersections did not always meet at the correct angles, and no signs indicated which way traffic was expected to flow.

Big trees stood seasonally naked on corners and in yards, and their brittle branches reached high overhead, throwing scattered shadows around these outlying places. The houses were small and fiercely guarded, or else they were large and in uncertain repair. The people were overwhelmingly poor and not in the military—Maria did not spy a single uniform. And the closer they came to the mountain, the more colored families she saw.

"I feel . . . conspicuous," she whispered as softly as she could, while still making herself heard above the engine.

"We *are* conspicuous. But we are relatively safe."

"What if someone comes along behind us and asks if anyone has seen a carriage like ours?"

He shrugged. "The locals will say they've seen no such thing. No one who asks them questions has their best interests in mind. It's safer for them to see nothing, and say nothing. But they won't hand us over, because they know what we're doing."

"They can't possibly. *We* barely know what we're doing."

"They know we're going to the Church. Pretty much any white people who come out this way . . . that's where they're headed. And most of the people who live out here keep themselves blind and quiet, because it's the only way to help without putting themselves in danger."

Up to the long, narrow mountain's ridge they rode, rattling past the edge of the river's bend and along a packed dirt road that led under the railroad overpass that took all the trains around Lookout. The arch was overgrown with the dead trees left behind by winter—long branches, stripped roots, and a dangling lattice of Japanese weed, gone brown from the dry and chill. Along the

arch's top a train crept slowly, its wheels churning, its cars haul-
ing coal or timber from east to west, or farther down south.

Under the arch, a horse appeared, galloping quickly toward
them. Its rider almost lost his hat as he rode beneath the train, but
he held it fast—and he drew his horse up short when he reached
their car. Its hooves scattered bits of brick and pebbles, which
clanged against the car's metal plating, and the animal shifted
nervously from foot to foot.

"Henry, don't tell me that's you . . . ?" the rider called. He
firmly reined the horse up to Henry's window, and leaned his head
down low. "Well, I'll be damned. My luck ain't usually this good."

Maria leaned over, cocking her head to the side a bit so she
could look up at him. "Mr. Troost! Just the man we were coming
to see."

He spit a gob of tobacco to the side of the horse, away from
the car. "I should damn well hope so. Can't imagine why else
you'd be out this way. Anyway, I'm glad to see you've saved me a
trip downtown. We got problems."

"We got telegrams," Maria agreed.

"And I got another one just now," he said. His eyes were hard,
and his hands were tight on the reins of the unhappy horse.
"Follow me back to the Church and I'll give you what I know.
And jack that thing a little faster. We haven't got all day. Shit, we
might not have all *morning*."

He nudged the horse back the way he came, and kicked it into
a gallop once more.

Henry urged the car through first gear and into second, which
had Maria clinging to the door and wondering if she might be
sick. The vehicle tumbled over the lumpy roads, shuddering like
it might come apart at any moment, but it stayed intact as it trailed
Kirby Troost's horse through an overgrown neighborhood of small,
cheaply built bungalows with rickety porches and crooked steps.
They gave friendly chase down a narrow street, Maria praying at

every moment that they wouldn't meet anyone or anything coming the opposite direction.

They passed one church on the left, a tall, flat-faced wooden structure painted white, but apparently this wasn't the Station. They kept going until they found a sturdy stone African Methodist Episcopal church a few blocks farther down and partway up a steep embankment that disappeared into the mountain itself. Kirby Troost disappeared behind this church, down two scuffed ruts that passed for an alley. Henry followed him as far as he dared, until the winter-dead foliage threatened to bog down the car and stop it for good.

He pushed his foot down on the brake and hopped out.

Maria waited for him to open her door, then took his hand as she descended into the grass.

Kirby tied his horse to a post beside the church steps and then joined them. "Y'all'd better come inside."

Inside, everything was dark except for the colored light that trickled through the tinted glass windows. The place was wired for electricity and gas lamps, and she could see how old fixtures had been refitted for the newer technology. But nothing was turned on, and the place was cold. There was certainly a furnace, but no one had lit it. The church looked deserted. Maybe that was the intent.

They marched past straight-backed wooden pews in tidy rows with Bibles and the occasional dog-eared hymnal scattered here and there. Then they climbed straight down into the baptismal font. Maria felt strange about it, but she stood aside and smiled when a false bottom opened up and a secret staircase was revealed below.

"Ladies first," Kirby Troost said.

Henry elbowed him in the ribs. "Don't be an ass, Kirby. You have a light?"

"Right here." He pulled an electric torch out of his coat and offered it to Henry.

But Maria snatched it out of his hand and pulled the switch to turn it on. "Ladies *first,*" she reminded them, then sidled past them down the stairs. At the bottom she found a landing and a door, and Kirby Troost was beside her, though she'd never heard him join her. Only a superhuman effort kept her from flinching as he reached past her face and pressed a button once, twice, and three times . . . then paused and hit it once more.

"That's so nobody shoots when we walk inside," he told her as he retrieved the light. "This time, we'll have to set chivalry aside. They know me, and there's a chance they *might* know you, so stand back."

The door opened a crack. Around the corner peeked a colored woman about Maria's age with a lantern in her hand and a wary look in her eye. "Mr. Troost," she said levelly. "And you're not alone."

"No, ma'am, and the cat's not in the tree, either."

She nodded and withdrew, taking the lantern with her. Its glow illuminated the interior of a large, comfortable living area with three other people in it: an older woman and a boy of maybe eight or nine, both colored; and a white man with a gun who nodded at Troost and said, "Back so soon?"

"They were on their way to meet me, so I found them faster than expected," he said. "Everyone, this is Mary and Hank. They're here to help. Or, from another angle, they're here so I can help *them,* but that's how it goes. Mary, Hank, that's Dr. Bardsley's mum and nephew right there, Sally and Caleb."

"You know my son?" Sally asked quickly.

"I met him once," Maria said.

Henry added, "I know him; he's a great man. He might end the war and save the world, and we're trying to give him a hand."

This satisfied her, enough to release her death grip on her grandson. "All right then. Mr. Troost, if you say they're with you . . ."

"They are, so don't fret—not even for a moment. I'm going to take these nice folks back to the quiet taps. We've got some talking to do." He cast a sharp glance at the white man, who hadn't been identified.

"Go on back," he said. "I'll stick it out up here and see if the ship shows up."

"Good deal. Come on, you two, this way," Troost said to Maria and Henry. He led them back through the underground apartment with its hard wood chairs and two low beds, and out a door at the back end. As he went, he explained, "We have a telegraph line here. Runs underground, like the railroad, and it works just fine, so long as nobody messes with it. Not a whole lot of people know its signal, so don't go running off at the mouth. I probably don't have to warn you about such things, but don't take it personal. Caution is the grease that keeps this railroad running smooth."

"I understand," Maria said quietly, following him along a corridor and past a couple of doors.

"Maybe you do, and maybe you don't. If anybody gets a whiff of what goes on out here, dozens of people will get shot before word even makes it to the city. This whole block is floating on high treason, and everyone who knows about it is a suspect."

"I really *do* understand. Believe me, I was a spy for years."

"For *this* side, yes. You only know what the Grays will do to protect a body. You don't know what they'll do to destroy one. In here." He opened a door and guided them through. "I don't mean any disrespect, ma'am, but I'm thanking Christ Almighty that no one recognized you back there. Having you set foot in this place is sacrilege, so far as they would figure it."

"I never—"

He cut her off. "You want to tell me what you really think? How you really feel about slavery? Save your breath. If you want to help, and you don't want to make any trouble for these people, then you'll keep your past and everything else to yourself."

He stopped and faced her. Maria didn't flinch, but she didn't press forward, either, even though she had the extra height on him and—if she was honest with herself—a few pounds on him, to boot.

He said to her, a little more gently, "Your silence is the only thing that can prove you here. Hold your tongue, hide your name, and don't tell a soul about where you came from, or what brought you—unless you tell 'em it's the Pinks, because that's what I said already. Anything more than that and you start a panic and put us all in danger. You got it?"

"I . . . I got it."

"Now, here are the . . . facilities," he said, picking a word for the rigged-up taps system that filled the bulk of the room. Wires ran to and fro, and tap receivers were set up across a table, some of them quivering with a signal freshly sent or received. No one monitored them at the moment, though the white man from the living area showed up shortly to poke his head in the door.

"Holler if anything starts signaling through if it's longer than you want to read."

"Will do," Troost said, then returned his attention to his guests. "I can take the script, but I'm slower than *he* is." He cocked a thumb toward the door. "And, anyway, right now I've got other things to attend to. Most recent word from D.C. says we've got worse problems than we knew. How much have you heard?"

Henry said, "Maynard is apparently on the move. Could kill hundreds of thousands before it's finished. And it's pointed at civilian targets, not military ones, except maybe Danville."

"It's not headed for Danville," Troost said firmly. "Not enough of a population center. It would be more convenient to send it to a bigger city."

"Atlanta?" Maria guessed. It was the biggest city of all, outside New York.

"That's the word on the wires. At present, it ought to be

someplace south of Dalton, but north of Marietta. That's as close as anyone could pin it down. The taps are having trouble between here and there, but I don't know if it's a conspiracy, or just an inconvenience. You can rest assured I'll keep trying to rouse the Rebs, though. They'll sure as shit want to know about it, and might even be able to help. You never know."

"Anything's possible. And now Maynard is somewhere within . . ." Maria wracked her brain, trying to make an educated assessment. "Seventy or eighty miles of here? That's no pinpoint, but it's a narrower window than we had before."

"When we're finished up here and you're on your way, I'll drop Mr. Lincoln a line to keep him informed." Some flicker of uncertainty crossed Troost's face, but quickly passed.

But Maria saw it, and she asked, "What? Is something wrong?"

Troost laughed, short and harsh. "Other than the end of the world, you mean?" He pulled a map out of a drawer beneath the taps and spread it out beside them. "I can't be sure, but I think something funny's up in the District. I don't trust the wires there, not tonight. There's an interruption someplace, and I don't like it."

Henry stiffened, and he narrowed his eyes. "You think Mr. Lincoln's in danger?"

"I think everyone's in danger, more often than not. But yes, him in particular. And maybe the president, too."

"You think it'll go that far?" Maria asked.

"It's gone farther than him already. But there's nothing I can do about that right now. Not from here." Finished with the subject for the time being, he jabbed his finger at the map to guide them, and said, "All right. From where we're sitting now, the fastest way to Georgia is that road right outside, the little highway you came in on. But the more direct route is *this* road, which cuts through the south end of town and out past the ridge. The main road drops down that way, and it's a straight shot to Atlanta, then on to Macon, and so forth."

"Can we take that map?" Henry asked.

Troost rolled it up. "It's all yours."

"But will they be *sticking* to the main roads?" Maria asked. "They're on a covert military mission; wouldn't they take the side streets and back ways? They're less likely to be caught that way."

"I don't know what side streets you're talking about. Most of the way, it's the main road or nothing. And these men don't have much choice but to hide in plain sight. We're talking about two dozen soldiers, a half-dozen horses, and a couple of carts big enough to pass for a mobile hydrogen station. They'll be dressed in grays, with paperwork that'll fool anyone who'd stop them— especially since there's a big hydro facility in the middle of Atlanta. That may even be the truth, as that's probably where they intend to detonate the weapon. It's right at the edge of a real dense neighborhood, with plenty of easy victims."

"And if the cloud roams . . . ?"

"Can't tell you much about the weather, ma'am," Troost replied. "All I know is that word out of the city says it's fair and calm, but clouds are coming up from the southwest, so you never know. Might be a storm in the Gulf pushing up a breeze. Let's hope not, eh?"

She murmured, "You hope. I'll pray."

"Pray into one hand, shit in the other. You tell me which one fills up first."

"That's unnecessary." She frowned.

"It's a reminder, that's all. Get out there and do your jobs, and don't count on any help from above, unless it comes in the form of an airship."

Henry stuck the map into his coat, jamming it down into a pocket. "And it's *our* job to stop this caravan? The pair of us? Against a contingent of special Union forces?"

"A Pink and a Marshal against a squadron?" Troost grinned,

and it only looked a little forced. "I almost feel bad for them. Now, let's get you on the move so that *I* can get on the move."

Maria asked, "You're taking Sally and Caleb out? Tonight?"

"Yes, ma'am, I'm getting them as far from the blast zone as I can. Orders right from the top, from Uncle Grant this time."

Henry said, "I was under the impression he hadn't been too helpful so far."

Troost started to roam the room, packing up small items and throwing them into a satchel. "He's a sad old drunk who's sitting in a nest of vipers, but he's not a bad sort—and I don't know what convinced him, but I can make a guess or two. Uncle Abe implied that Miss Haymes showed up to give him a heart-to-heart in person. But you know how it is with telegrams. You have to guess at half the detail."

Maria tapped her fingernail on the table beside the telegraph key. "So, Henry, how fast can that carriage of yours run? It seemed a bit slow-going on the way here—not that I'm complaining, of course."

Troost announced, "I have a better idea."

Henry grinned. "I told her you might," he said, as Troost passed him a small packet of paper.

"Take this down to the dirigible docks on Missionary Ridge. Henry, you know the place?"

"I can find it."

"Got you a two-seater reserved. It'll be cold flying—and I expect that might be hard on a delicate magnolia like yourself, Miss Boyd, but—"

"Hush your ridiculous mouth."

"—but if you're living on the Chicago lake, I figure you'll survive the discomfort. Now, the craft's reserved under the name Henry Fisher, courtesy of the Texas Rangers. I ran it that way because your stars ain't too different, and if I'd put it under the

Marshals, they'd have put me under arrest. Sorry, but you'll have to fib it as a brown. How's your Republican accent?"

"Passing fair," he drawled.

Troost leaned on the table and gave him a critical eye. "Tell 'em you're from the islands. Say Galveston. The vowels aren't as long, and most Texians only halfway consider the Gulf part of their country anyway."

"Got it."

"Miss Boyd, you're traveling as Mary Wilson. I tried to think of something more bland than that, but I failed. I hope it'll do."

"It'll work just fine, thank you. How did you come up with all this so . . . so quickly?"

Henry flashed Troost a look that suggested he'd like to know, too, but Troost didn't feel like sharing. "Tricks of the trade," he said, and that was all. "Now get a move on. Every mile they go is another mile you have to chase them."

"God knows what we'll even do when we catch them," Henry sighed.

Maria said, "We'll tell them the truth. It's all we've got."

"Sadly, it's the *best* we've got. Troost, thanks for all your help."

"I'd say 'anytime,' except I wouldn't mean it. Stop those fellows before they do something we'll all regret—them most of all. When I get to the District, I'll try to arrange papers from Uncle Grant to make explanations for you. Until then, just make sure they don't shoot you if you get caught."

"That was part of the plan already," Maria assured him.

"You know what I mean. Now, make a run for it, make it good, and start practicing your story." Then he gazed hard at Maria, as if she'd given him an idea. Maria didn't like the feel of it, almost as if he was staring right through her . . . and perhaps he was. Then he snapped his fingers and said, "You remember your old friend Hainey, Miss Boyd?"

Calling the air captain an "old friend" was a little much, but she let it ride. "He's a difficult man to forget."

"I might be able to drag him into this. Might *need* to, in fact. I can't be everywhere at once—I'm good, but I'm not that good—so I'll need somebody . . ."

"Somebody as good as you?" she supplied.

He balked at answering. "As good as me? I don't know about *that*. But I'll fire up the taps and see if I can't flag him down. I'd love to have some help in the District, and I could do much worse than him." Before Henry could volunteer them, Kirby clarified, "Not *you two*. You're headed south. You won't have time to fly back and save the day if it needs saving. Neither will I, I don't expect. We can't spread ourselves that thin. So I'll see who I can press into service. If everything shakes out all right, I'll see you in the District in another few days. If it don't . . . I suppose I'll see you all in hell."

The steep slopes of Missionary Ridge were cold and treacherous—muddy from the rains of the past few days, and slowly freezing as the temperature dropped yet lower and a blustery wind kicked up from the west. Spitting hints of rain slapped against the windscreen as Henry drove, and flicked inside the open cab to sting Maria's cheeks. She huddled deeper in her coat and burrowed as far as she could back in her hard seat, despite the discomfort. She could feel the gears shift and yank, and the frame behind her shoulders rattled as the car tugged against the road's slick, unforgiving ruts.

The dock itself was perched high atop the tree-covered ridge overlooking the city, outside the wall and far enough away to provide a generous view.

"Tennessee likes to say their wall is one of the wonders of the modern world," Henry told her through chattering teeth. "I don't know if that's true, but"—he drew the vehicle to a halt and set its brake so it wouldn't roll—"it's a sight to behold all the same."

"Agreed," she said, through lips so numb she could scarcely form the word. Without the wind rushing in the windows, the world seemed somewhat warmer; but as soon as she opened her door and stepped to the ground, she found the currents were almost worse up there in the scenic elevations.

She wished for a good umbrella, something that would fend off ice and rain alike.

On second thought, it was just as well she didn't have one, as it would not survive the weather—or so she concluded when a fierce gust shoved up against her side, peppering her cheeks with needle-cold shards of sleet.

"Flying in this weather won't be any fun."

"Won't be very safe, either, but we don't have much choice." Henry tucked his own coat closer and made a beeline for the ticket house, a long, narrow building with four counter windows ready to do business.

While he handed over his papers and sorted out the arrangements, Maria eyed the dirigible offerings. She counted three big transport ships, far too large for their needs—and almost certainly too big for them to fly as a pair—but they had closed-in cabins with enormous glass shields, so she wished for one all the same. Two others were middling-sized, though one of those looked too bedraggled to fly. And she thought she spied several smaller crafts behind a tall wooden fence, the tops of their domes peeking above the barrier, bobbing against one another in the wind.

Henry returned with a pass and a set of keys in hand. "Let's go. The ticket girl says that the weather's supposed to get even worse. A storm's coming, spinning up out of the Gulf."

"Little late in the year for that," Maria grumbled. "You'd think the weather would be warmer, if that's where it's coming from."

"You would indeed, but such is not our lot in life. Not today, anyway."

They hiked against the wind until they reached a big gate, which opened with the turn of the largest key on Henry's ring. Once inside, they were protected from the worst of the chill, for the fence and the ships themselves served to break up the gale. "They tried to talk me out of it, actually," he told her, scanning the rows for the right slot. "They said we'd be crazy to fly today, and whatever we're doing could wait for morning."

"What did Mr. Troost tell them when he reserved the craft?"

"I'm not sure, but it had something to do with the war effort. I think he told them you're a nurse, and I'm a doctor, and we're running an emergency aid something-or-another to someplace. I'm sure the particulars were fascinating. He has a knack for detail."

"Strange little man, that."

"And *you* have a knack for understatement. Here, this is it: the *Black Dove.*" He used another key to unlatch the ship's anchor from a claw-style mooring, then pulled a lever inside the craft. The hook and chain retracted with a tinny grind, then disappeared into a side panel that closed behind them.

It didn't look so bad. Open to the elements, more than not. Engine-powered, but controlled by foot pedal, so their feet would dangle over an open chassis through which they could watch the land pass by below.

"It's sturdy enough," Henry surmised. "We'll freeze our noses off if we don't wrap up, but then again, we might freeze them off anyway. I don't know about you, but I can hardly feel mine anymore."

They climbed inside and drew the frame doors shut behind them. The seats featured a long strap of good hemp canvas to serve as a belt, but it fastened across them both, securing them to little but each other. Henry worked up a blush, but Maria refused—she was glad for the closeness.

"We'll both stay warmer this way," she told him as she settled herself as comfortably as possible, without a hint of an improper struggle. "Now, I've never flown one of these before, but I've ridden in one. What can I do to help?"

"Navigate," he said as he slipped a pair of goggles over his glasses and urged her to do the same. He used another key from the ring to remove a steel lock from around the ignition, then leaned out the window and deposited the keys and the lock into a basket provided for the purpose . . . and cranked the dirigible to life.

Its motor purred willingly, if with a faint clatter, while it warmed, then quivered, and then lifted them off the ground. Henry took an experimental turn or two with the thrusters, testing them for responsiveness. He fiddled with the steering mechanism and flipped switches and tugged levers.

Maria didn't think this looked very complicated, in the grand scheme of things. She resolved to learn how to fly a dirigible upon her eventual return to Chicago—assuming she didn't freeze to death in the sky above north Georgia. Well, assuming also that her mission was a success. And that the world was not overrun by necrotic leprosy.

Though, as the dirigible gained altitude, she considered that a plague might be all the more reason to learn how to fly. Victims of the ailment could run and eat, but they couldn't chase her off the ground, could they?

Henry valiantly fought the drafts and currents, forcing the *Black Dove* high enough to pass the ridge. His gloved fingers were tight on the controls, and his eyes dashed back and forth between the readouts, the levers, and the sky. Without looking at Maria, he asked her, "I gave you Troost's map, didn't I?"

"Got it right here," she said, withdrawing it from the satchel where she'd stashed it. Keeping a firm grip, she splayed it across her lap. "Do you see the southbound road?"

"No, but it can't be far."

He was right; it wasn't far. They found it fast, puttering and swaying against the intermittent rain and wind, dipping up and down above the trees, only to drop back down into the valley as they soared past the wall, so near that Maria could've stuck out her hand and touched it. Her stomach dropped and lurched, but luckily she hadn't eaten since the night before, so there was nothing present to cast out over Lookout Mountain as they careened off to the south.

The weather worked against them every mile of the way. It buffeted them head-on, and sometimes threatened to throw them off course. Henry wore himself out keeping the craft as steady as he could, and eventually found some violent rhythm to the trip. Maria couldn't see his eyes behind the lenses, but she had a feeling that they were hard and unblinking.

"There's a spyglass in my bag," he shouted to her over the rushing air and rumbling motor.

"I'll get it." She nodded, and fished around until she found it.

"I'm not seeing much traffic down there, are you?"

"No," she said loudly back, though her view through the spyglass was compromised by the lenses she wore to protect her eyes. "That'll change as we approach Atlanta. It's picking up even . . . even now." She gestured at the road, then off to the side, where a large factory compound coughed out soot from three tall towers. "That's Dalton, I believe."

"I'm sure you're right."

"So"—she squinted back down at the map, and pointed to a spot with one gloved finger— "we're about *here*. Still ninety miles from the city, I'd estimate, but I'll keep my eyes open. If we're lucky, they're still quite a ways outside town."

"If we were lucky, Troost would've gotten us a ride with a heater," Henry said. His icy cheeks were round and red, and he wasn't smiling.

"Just one more reason to hope we find them fast," she replied, though she couldn't feel her face at all, and her jaw must surely be freezing shut.

Talking was difficult, so they soon gave up and concentrated on their respective chores. Henry kept the craft aloft, and Maria watched the ground below, tracing the comings and goings of carts, horses, and diesel carriages as they chugged along the southbound route to the biggest city in the Confederacy.

She did not take her eyes off the road as she asked, "How much fuel does this thing hold?"

"Enough to get us to Atlanta, but not much farther. These little ones aren't made for the long haul, but we'll make it to the city," he assured her. "Even fighting the sky like this."

"Good," she said quietly. And then she closed her eyes, listening for something she heard very faintly, behind them and off to their left. "Even if we take a detour or two?"

"Detour?" He frowned hard enough that the goggles dipped on his forehead. "Why would we detour?"

"Not a detour, then. Call it evasive action."

Her ears pinpointed the noise and she turned her head far enough to catch it with her eyes. A ship was incoming, far enough away that she couldn't suss out the details, but it wasn't alone—and that was the main point of note. It had a friend, and that friend was approaching from the right.

"Two ships, Henry," she said evenly. "Coming up behind us."

"They could be merchants or military fellows," he tried, but he didn't sound convinced even as he said it. "This is a common enough trade route."

"Henry, we're being flanked."

"That . . . can't be by accident."

"I shouldn't think so, no."

"It might be nothing," he said, hands tight on the controls. "We haven't seen any other ships today because the flying conditions are nothing short of awful, but this section of sky is a regular roadway. They have no reason to confront us."

Maria turned the spyglass outward and caught the first ship in the round viewing area. It was small and nondescript, and still too far away to see with any great clarity. But the second ship was larger. She could just make out some lettering on the side, but not quite read what it spelled.

"What do you see?"

"I see . . ." she said, slowly, "a military ship, I think. It's big, but doesn't look well armed. Cargo, transport, something of that sort. It's CSA gray, at any rate. With . . . yes. The Bonnie Blue," she added, meaning a white star in a blue circle—to differentiate it from the Texian insignia, with a white star on brown. "It's one of theirs, or someone's made it look that way."

"You think it's one of the Union decoys?"

"Might be, but if the Maynard device wouldn't fit on something that size, it must be bigger than I'd assumed." She adjusted her grip on the spyglass and tried the other ship again. "The smaller ship . . . it's not marked for the military. I'm not sure it's marked at all." It was gaining on them faster than the CSA ship, but still she saw no identifying flag, insignia, name, or registration numbers.

"That isn't good."

"It might mean pirates. Pirates wouldn't bother a pair of adventurers in a tiny rented craft, not when there are travelers below and big city docks another hour or two out. I *do* hope it's pirates," she concluded.

"You're a peculiar woman."

"I've had good luck with pirates. I've been told I'm a bit of a pirate myself."

"Let's not talk of luck anymore, shall we? Or pirates, either," Henry pleaded through teeth clenched with chill or nerves. "We've already noticed that luck isn't with us. And as for pirates, you are no such thing. That having been said, you'll have to tell me that story sometime."

"Not much to tell," she lied, keeping one eye glued to the spyglass lens. "My first assignment as a Pinkerton agent had me working with a pirate crew. The captain was a runaway slave named Croggon Hainey. He's the friend of mine that Troost hopes to call in for backup in Washington."

"A *friend* of yours?" Even through the goggles, Maria could see Henry's eyes widen with incredulity. "All right, I'm not a man to judge. But if he's a pirate . . . do you think he'll help us, or the Lincolns, or anyone else? Even if Kirby Troost asks him to?"

Still peering through the glass, she told him, "Yes, I do. He's an adventurous sort, and no fan of Southern politics, as you might expect." She shifted her grip on the device, and directed the conversation back to more pressing matters. "And I wish to God that he was here with us right now."

"They're still on us?"

"Very much so."

"God*dammit*."

"Now, Henry, listen: the smaller craft is bigger than this one, but not so large as its brethren. Perhaps a crew of three. I don't really think it's pirates, but it could be anything—state, federal, or private."

"Do you see any weapons?"

"Not mounted to the exterior. Maybe it's an observation craft? Survey work?" She wasn't sure why she kept making guesses. The ships would either bother them, or not. "But here they come— another thirty seconds or so until contact. Look innocent, Henry."

"I'll do my level best."

The ships drew up on either side of the *Black Dove.* Now Maria could see their faces without the spyglass, so she put it aside. In the course of acting innocent, she waved cheerfully at the nearest ship—the CSA gray with blue and white markings. Without moving her lips, she said to Henry, "Wish I had a flag. I'd wave it."

"You'd look silly," he said back, smiling and joining her in the friendly greetings.

"Silly is usually innocent," she said, and blew the craft a kiss.

Inside the main cabin of the big craft she saw five men: three seated, two standing. All uniformed. None smiling or waving back; not at first. But then the captain gave her a small salute, and the others did as well, before deliberately turning their attention elsewhere. Shortly thereafter, the big ship peeled away from them and sped ahead, leaving just the smaller of the two hovering nearby.

"Can't quite see the little ship," Maria complained, straining to look around Henry's bulkily coated form.

"Shall I cut off my head?"

"Extremes aren't called for. Not just yet."

He forced a smile and released one side of the steering column to chance a quick wave. "Three men," he told her.

"Uniforms?"

"No. And I don't think smiling at them will be very helpful."

"It's usually more helpful than glowering."

"Glowering won't help us either. I think we have trouble."

"Do you see any guns?" she asked. "I didn't."

He sniffed hard, the sniff of a man who can't feel what's going on in his sinuses anymore. "They're inside."

The ship fell back, and then pulled around closer to Maria— who saw that, yes, the men within were heavily armed and did not look very happy to see them. She beamed at them regardless, and waved like she had for the military ship—which was now well ahead of them, keeping its course along the southbound road below.

No one waved back, but one man cranked open a side window, which jutted out from the craft like a fragile glass wing. He held a megaphone up to his mouth, and leaned out into the clouds.

"You there!" he shouted. "Land your craft immediately!"

Maria pretended she hadn't heard, or hadn't understood. "I'm sorry?" she mouthed, and pointed at her ears. "Too loud! So much wind!"

"Land this craft immediately!" he tried again.

"They want us to land," Henry said, staring straight ahead.

"Thank you, dear, I heard them," she muttered. Then to the

craft, as loudly as she could, "I'm very sorry, we can't hear you!" She trusted they'd get the gist.

They did, and it made them angry.

"Land the craft immediately! Right now!" And this time, he brandished a gun in a threatening fashion.

"I've seen bigger!" she yelled.

"Now you're just antagonizing them!" Henry complained.

"Oh, they can't hear a word I'm saying. Can we outrun them?"

He said, "I'm not sure. Maybe. Maybe not."

"Well, we can't just *land*. They'll kill us both, and that'll be the end of it."

"I thought you liked pirates."

"They aren't pirates," she said with more confidence than before. "They're mercenaries."

While the man at the window gestured with his megaphone and firearm, Maria lifted the spyglass again, to get a better look. Not at the man, but at the crates on the floor behind him. Something was stenciled thereon, and she could just discern the logo. "Baldwin-Felts." She said it like a curse.

"The detective agency? Something like the Pinks?"

"*Nothing* like the Pinks." She snapped the spyglass shut and stuffed it into her satchel, since that one was the closest. "Oh, all right, *something* like the Pinks—like a Southern version of the Pinks, with fewer morals, leaner pockets, and no problem with assassinating innocent bystanders."

"But people do say similar things about—"

She growled, "When the Pinkertons misbehave, they reflect badly on *Chicago*. The Baldwin-Felts reflect badly on *Virginia*."

"I see."

"How much ammunition do you have on you?"

"Look, there's a megaphone in the back. If you can reach it, maybe I can talk some sense into them. I'm a U.S. Marshal, after all. They may think twice about—"

"They won't." She held up one finger to the man in the other dirigible, asking him for just a moment while she rifled through her luggage in search of her gun. "They'll just bury you deeper, and figure no one'll find you 'til it doesn't matter anymore. They've threatened us, they're giving us orders, and they will shoot us down if we don't land ourselves. That's what the man's gun means, Henry. When he waves it around like that, he's telling us he's willing to use it."

"Thank you, ma'am," Henry said, jaw locked tight. "I'm clear on that. I just wonder if we shouldn't have some kind of plan, apart from shooting first."

"I'm a pretty good shot. Better with a ball turret. Pity we seem to be missing one." Using her shoulders to shield the other ship from what she was doing, she checked her chambers, grabbed a fistful of bullets for future use, and took a deep breath.

"I can't believe they're just . . . waiting on you. To see what you're doing."

"Men are trained from birth to wait on the whims of women. Even murderers expect it." She adjusted her goggles, looked back at the unnamed ship, and then at Henry. She leaned in close, so close that her breath warmed his ear. "All right, here's what I'm doing: Our ship is smaller than theirs, we're possibly slower than they are, and we're outnumbered. Our only advantage is surprise, and I intend to cash in that advantage before it's wasted. If you can fly as well as I can shoot, we might make it to our destination—and so far, you're doing a hell of a job. So don't stop now."

Before Henry could respond, she looked back over her shoulder. She saw that the man was getting impatient, but the window was still open, and he still hung halfway out of it—anchored by his feet somewhere beyond her view. She slipped her hand around the gun, put her finger on the trigger, and felt its gentle resistance against her glove.

She whipped out the gun.

Aimed in a fraction of a second.

And fired three times in a row, knowing that her shots might spin wild, given the motion of the ship and the air alike; and that she was a good shot, but not a great one, as she might have implied to Henry.

One bullet shattered the window, one bounced harmlessly off the metal casing, and one caught the man in the upper chest, just below his throat. He snapped backwards, clapped his head on the broken window edge, and flipped forward into the aether.

No time to savor the victory. She fired again, this time at their windscreen—hitting it and fracturing it, but not smashing it outright. The front glass was thicker; it had to be, to face the elements.

"Aim for their tanks!" Henry screeched, his elbows shaking with the effort of holding the craft in line.

"Not yet! We're too close! Any explosion will take us with it."

One of the other men leaned out the broken window while the captain kept flying—the grim set of his face implying that yes, they, too, were having a struggle of it. The wind was high and wet, and now he was flying with a broken window that snagged the currents and yanked the ship. She hadn't sent them down, but she'd given him more to fight, and that was good. It meant one less person shooting at them.

Four shots volleyed fast, fired by a man in an earflap hat and a very large coat.

Two of them didn't land anywhere important, so far as Maria could tell, but one winged a thruster, and a hard sound hissed against the motor. The last shot plunked into the bag at Maria's feet. She felt the shove of it, and for a moment assumed the worst— but no, something had stopped it. Hopefully not her extra stockings. She didn't own a third pair.

She aimed the gun his way, but he ducked inside, and then the

Black Dove ducked, too. With a hard, belly-bombing lurch it lost so much altitude that Maria thought something else had been hit, something more important than the fizzling thruster. "Henry!" she shouted.

"Hold on!"

"What are you doing?!"

"Getting away from them!"

"Let's not get away all the way to the ground, please?" she squeaked.

"Not to the ground . . ." he said, but whatever else he would've added was lost when his full attention was called for at the controls. He pulled up out of the dive in a veering sweep that brought them up again, higher than they'd flown before, to an altitude where breathing the air felt like chewing on ice.

"Oh God." Maria coughed, but she held the gun tight and pointed it back at the unmarked ship. She gauged the distance between them and hoped it was near enough to hit, but far enough to escape any fireball that might ensue.

She emptied the last of her chambers and hit the windscreen again, this time puncturing it with a short round of finger-sized holes. But the pilot was unharmed, and she'd come nowhere close to hitting the hydrogen.

Whoever that pilot was, he was good. As good as Henry. Maria could only pray he wasn't better.

The two ships soared around each other, circling and feinting in a deadly game of chicken, both sides aware that they were careening through portentous weather while strapped to tanks full of a gas so flammable they'd leave a second sun blazing in the sky if one of them lost the match.

Henry wrenched the steering column and kicked a lever by his foot. The ship zoomed upward again, so steeply that Maria's throat clenched shut and her eyes followed close behind. She couldn't look. "Henry, what are you doing!" she demanded, not really wanting to know, but needing to know—clutching the gun, but unable to reload it because then she'd have to take her other hand off the *Black Dove*'s frame. If she did, nothing would be holding her inside but the ridiculous hemp strap, which now struck her as so fragile as to be laughably useless. "They're right behind us! You can't outmaneuver them this way!"

"Not trying to! You have to reload!" he cried, leveling out and letting her catch her breath for a bit.

Her hands were shaking and she could scarcely feel them to guide the bullets. She picked them out of her pocket one by one like seeds from an apron. "What are you doing?" she asked again, fumbling and dropping one, losing sight of it as it tumbled downward.

"Are you loaded?"

"Only . . . only three!" She tried to keep the panic from her voice.

"Those tanks are pretty big. Can you hit them in three shots?"

"I think so, but . . ."

"From underneath?"

She paused. "I think so."

He grinned wildly at her. "The explosion will go up, so we'll go under. Hang on to your hat!" he roared, and dropped the *Black Dove* nose-down. The engine gurgled and fought, but didn't fail, despite the near free fall.

Maria laughed the unhinged cackle of a lunatic when she realized her hat was long gone, so all she had to clutch was her gun and this ship. So she didn't fall out as she leaned, squinted through her goggles, and aimed.

The unmarked ship loomed above her, its tanks dangling low and inviting on the sides. She only needed to hit one, but she had to hit it square, and she was falling, falling, falling . . . and had the engine cut out? She couldn't tell. There was nothing in her ears but the rush of the drop. The sky was huge above her, and the other ship was coming after them, but it was coming too slow as it turned to dive in their wake. Five more seconds and the angle would be wrong.

She fired.

The first shot missed, but the second hit home.

The craft did not shake or stutter, it simply exploded—the punctured tank first, and the other one an instant later. A ball of fire flared mightily above them and shot higher yet, and a warm wave of searing air snapped back against the *Black Dove.*

"Pull up, pull up!" Maria shrieked at Henry. He was already trying to level the craft, but the drag and the wind and the new push of heat were working hard to stop him. "Get us steady!" she added. She felt stupid for it immediately, but the ground was right there, and they were flinging themselves toward it, and the thruster—was it even working? It spit like a snake, and a thin, diluted jet of black smoke went streaming out behind it.

"Hang on," Henry told her. Maria hoped he felt as stupid about saying that as she'd felt about giving him orders.

She jammed the gun into her coat. No way she could get it in the satchel, which had only remained in the craft this long by virtue of being slung across her chest and smushed between her and Henry. Even through the wool of her pocket she could feel the gun's freshly fired warmth. It might singe the fabric, but what other option did she have? It was that or throw it away, and it was worth more than the coat and dress together.

Not that her clothing should be her biggest concern at such a time. Then again, what thoughts *should* she be having, in a moment like this? She wondered, faster than the speed of light, about what was appropriate to consider in one's last moments. A prayer? A wish? A bargain with whatever gods, saints, or angels might wait on the other side of the dark?

"Oh, God," she said. It meant nothing, but it was all she had.

The engine surged—so no, it hadn't stopped after all—and though a hard southwestern current shoved them into a lilting curve, the *Black Dove* righted itself. Maria's stomach dropped back into its usual position, and Henry's arms did not relax, but they quit fighting so hard.

The sky fell quiet, and Maria's ears popped from the shifting pressure of it all. But the thruster was definitely damaged, and the road stretched many miles before them. The CSA dirigible was nowhere in sight.

"Do you think," she began. It came out too hoarse and quiet, so she tried again—louder this time, and once more near Henry's ear. "Do you think we can still make Atlanta in this thing?"

He eyed the smoke dribbling from the thruster, and took a moment to listen to the ominous hiss. "I don't know. But we shouldn't have to make it all the way there, should we? We're bound to catch up to them sooner than that."

"Right." She nodded.

"If not, we . . . we set it down beside the road and hunt for a couple of very fast horses."

"You think we'll get the chance? To land, rather than crash?"

"Oh, yes." He nodded back at her. "Absolutely. It's a steering problem, not a propulsion problem. Might land us in a field, or on top of somebody's house, but I'll land us."

"Good to know." She patted his arm, breathing hard and trying to calm herself, with limited success. She scowled out across the skyline. "Now, where's the other damn dirigible?"

 *Seventeen*

"A *plan*?" Grant snorted. "She's already planned a thousand years ahead of us. She picked a fight, and we must answer it—and answer it with greater speed and power than she expects. Frankly, she expects so little in the way of return fire that it shouldn't be that hard to surprise her."

Gideon put his hands to his forehead as if it ached. "You're right," he admitted grudgingly. "But you're also wrong. She has orchestrated this, and orchestrated it well—but we're not so helpless as all that. After all, we've forced her to improvise."

"When? Where?" he asked, wracking his brain to think of a misstep the woman had made thus far.

"The *murders*," the colored man said, as if it were the most obvious thing in the world. Maybe it was, but he didn't need to be so insulting.

"Well, yes. *Those*." Grant felt a little silly for not having seen it, but he was still feeling the whole matter very keenly, very personally. Very guiltily, for the dead pawns—as she'd called them—had been captured on his behalf, and his fervor was fueled with an acute, painful awareness of it. He wrestled with the matter and came at it from another angle. "But maybe not: she's tried to silence and discredit you before."

"She did nothing but inconvenience me. She's very good, but she's wrong as often as she's right. If nothing else, her attempt to shut down my operation in the Jefferson drove me to proceed with a public undoing of her scheme."

Lincoln pondered this, and agreed. "She's smart and ruthless, but she's been sloppy with the details. She's very dangerous, but we are dangerous too. Though we are few in number, we are capable of mustering a response. Hell," he offered a rare curse, "we've done so already, as individuals. Banded together, we might successfully undo her."

"She's only one woman, after all," Nelson Wellers noted.

But Gideon Bardsley shook his head. "She must have an army of mercenaries at her disposal. How else could she manage so many things at once? And you don't believe for a second that she killed those people herself, do you?"

"No, of course not. But where would she get such an army?" the doctor asked.

Grant sighed. "Fowler could commandeer a few men for her, straight from the Union's forces. Or some of those dratted Secret Service agents who follow me about unless I threaten to shoot them."

But Lincoln didn't think so. "No, not our men. And not the Service, either. Not because they're above such things, but because the evidence might wend its way across your desk. I think Gideon's right: mercenaries, hired from elsewhere. Men like the Pinkertons, who've been accused of similar behavior—if you don't mind me saying so, Dr. Wellers."

"Hard to argue with you," he said graciously. "But these aren't Pinks in her pocket right now; the head man wouldn't play us opposite one another."

"Then that other firm, the one in Virginia. What's it called again?"

He might've speculated further, but Polly knocked nervously on the doorjamb to get their attention. Grant was startled to see the windblown girl wringing her hands, her cap and clothing askew and a dead leaf stuck to her hair. She appeared on the verge of tears. "My dear, whatever is the matter?"

"Some men are here," she whispered with just enough volume to be heard throughout the library.

Lincoln appeared puzzled. "I didn't hear anyone knock . . ."

"No, sir. I saw them coming up as I was outside closing the storm shutters. I asked them to wait on the stoop. I said I'd come and get you right away, but they must be patient because you're not in your chair, so I'd have to help you."

"Good girl, Polly. What do they want?"

Her eyes darted to Nelson Wellers. "Him," she said. "They're here to arrest him."

"Not me?" Gideon asked.

The girl said, "They've already been here looking for you. They did ask again, but I told them you still hadn't come back, and I didn't know if you ever would. They said that was all right, and that they were here to arrest Dr. Wellers, since they believed he was present at the killings."

"What did you say to that?" Lincoln asked.

"I said I couldn't say for sure if he was hanging about, because I'd been doing laundry, then closing up the barn and the shutters. I said that if he was here, I hadn't seen him."

"And these are police officers?" Grant asked, doubting it strongly.

She hesitated, and said, "They *said* they're officers, but . . . but I don't think I believe them, sir. Something's not right about them, and why would they want to arrest Dr. Wellers?"

"They don't," he said. He clenched his jaw so tight that his cheeks looked hollow. "They want to *kill* me."

Her eyes widened. She looked to Lincoln for a denial, rebuttal, or explanation, but none was forthcoming. Gently, he told her, "You've done very well, Polly. Don't worry about Dr. Wellers. I'll see to these men momentarily. Wellers? Please help me into my chair. I founded that force, and it will answer to *me*."

Grant watched his old friend shift from the seat by the fire and into his wheeled contraption. He did it laboriously and with apparent discomfort, but then he straightened himself, pulled his preferred blanket over his lap, and settled his hands around the controls. The chair clacked to life, some internal mechanism sparking and spinning, then humming like a very small engine. He aimed himself at the door.

But then the president stepped forward, blocking his way.

"No," Grant said firmly. "No, this is not yours to face alone. I won't hide in your books while you stare down that woman's wicked forces. Let me take this one. They won't be expect me; it'll throw them off. These are hired hands—and I bet they're not half so good as their mistress. I'm the goddamn president! I'll executive order them right back to where they came from."

Polly lingered in the hallway. She asked, "What if they're real policemen, not mercenaries?"

"Then I still outrank them. And unless they got the chief justice to sign off on the arrest, I outrank whoever authorized them, too." He wished he'd chosen his words better. They left a bad taste in his mouth. "Abe," he said firmly, still standing between the man and the corridor. "Let me handle this."

When neither Lincoln, the scientist, or the doctor responded, Grant stepped past Polly and strode forward. He took long, fast steps. It only occurred to him then—while navigating the halls of Lincoln's home—that his idea of comfort amounted to his old habits as a soldier.

But he hadn't loved the war.

He hadn't loved sending men to die, surrounded by nervous advisors and scouts, or risking his own skin in a too-hot or too-cold tent that could barely call itself shelter while he struggled to read hastily drawn maps as cannon fire shook the camp. But the *strategy*, the flow and sway of armies, the ebb of forces and might . . . the rise of victory, and the sickening slide into defeat . . . He understood that. It made sense to him, somewhere down at the bottom of his chest. He read war the way some men read music, and spoke it like a language.

Maybe he should've been thinking of this as a battle all along. Politics was not merely men in rooms telling lies and making deals, but a war of favors and foes, friends and promises, money and land and lines, and sometimes—he thought of the way Desmond Fowler looked fawningly at Katharine Haymes—matters of the heart as well. Well, of course it sometimes included the heart. If the heart never came into it, why would anyone ever play?

Polly trailed along behind him, close enough to see what happened, but far enough back to get out of the way if necessary. Another pawn, this one. Vulnerable, but knowing. Willing, but also forced, by virtue of circumstance and loyalties both bought and earned.

He said a little prayer for her, something fast without any words, because he didn't have time for anything fancy.

He reached the front door and whipped it open. The brand-new night and its terrific wind spilled inside the foyer, scattering leaves in a marvelous whirlwind that shook the fixtures and worried the nearest fire. He squinted against the bracing gust, planted his feet square, and locked his shoulders straight.

"What?" he barked sharply.

He stood face-to-face with only one man, rather than the two Polly had promised: a very tall, yellow-haired fellow in an ill-fitting policeman's uniform, purporting to be from the very station that Lincoln had established nearly two decades previously. Though he wouldn't have said it aloud in front of his friend, it was Grant's considered opinion that this *could* be a true and official policeman. It was no great secret that though the force contained some fine individuals, as a whole, they weren't up to the snuff of Lincoln's original vision.

"What?" the man asked back. Stunned, he stared at the president as if now he wasn't certain how he ought to proceed anymore. He tried again. "What, sir? I . . ."

Grant maintained the tone and projection of an old general. He'd carried more authority when he'd been promoted, not elected, so that's the truncheon he'd swing. Keep the tall bastard on his toes. "What do you want?"

To his very slight credit, the alleged officer rallied, straightening his posture to emphasize the size difference between himself and the older man. "Sergeant Delman at your service, Mr. President, sir. Didn't realize you came calling here. I don't mean to be rude, but I'm here on official business."

"That's what I heard," Grant growled. He disliked this showing off. If you're tall, be tall. But don't brandish your size like a bully. "You're looking for my friend Dr. Nelson Wellers," he said, exaggerating the relationship. He barely knew the man.

"That's right."

"What are the charges?" he demanded.

"Accessory to murder. That's the charge."

"Well, I'm uncharging him."

"You're . . . I'm sorry sir, what?"

"You heard me," he puffed up, responding to the extra inches in height with age and gravitas. "I'm *un*charging him. I'm the president. I can do that."

"I . . . I'm not sure that's true."

"Are you calling me a liar?"

"No, sir. Misinformed, perhaps."

"I'm not misinformed; I'm the commander in chief. Now, get off this stoop and get on with your business. Look at you, *policeman*. Some manners you've got. Coming to the front door of a great man's house and trying to arrest his physician. If you had a lick of sense you'd try the side, and be on your best manners! You don't waltz up and make demands!" The man was starting to shift and fidget, seeking some way out of the conversation or past it, but Grant was on a roll. "Is this how they teach you to approach your betters? Is that how the force is run these days? I will write letters! I will speak with your captain!"

The big fellow's eyes narrowed. "No, sir, you won't. And I don't have to walk away because you tell me to. I'm here for Nelson Wellers, and I will not be leaving without him."

Grant laughed cruelly. "Now *you're* the one who's misinformed. Get out of here before I send you off this property in a pine box."

"Are you threatening me, sir?"

"If you have to ask, I must've done a shit job of it. Let me try again." He pulled out his '58 and held it with the absolute steadiness of someone who's held a gun so long, and so often, that it comes as natural and pleasant as holding a woman's hand. "Get off this stoop or I'll blow you off of it."

The tall man leaned down, looming and scowling. Wind shrieked around him, cut into screams by the angles of the house and the hollow brick chimneys. "You're the president. You can't shoot me. And if you try," he snarled, "you'll regret it with your very last breath."

"You're not a real copper."

With a sneer, the tall man fired back: "And you're not a real president."

Without a second thought, and without a single drink left in his system, Grant pulled the trigger.

The shot was loud in his ears, even against the violent orchestra of the windstorm. They were close together—only a door frame away, maybe arm's length, and the space wasn't tight. Still, it was like he'd fired inside a closet. A simple gunshot—the most familiar

sound in the world—sucked all the air out of the space between
them.

For a moment nothing happened. The tall man didn't react
except to hold perfectly still. Grant held still as well, his gun still
raised. It flared warm in his hand, but the dry November storm
cooled the metal as he held it. A small coil of smoke rose, then
vanished as a particularly hard gust of wind shook the house.

The fireplaces moaned low and tunefully, like monks chant-
ing a prayer.

The tall man's uniform was dark, and it was now fully dark
outside, so Grant could barely see the damp hole in his belly.

With slow uncertainty, the wounded man took two steps back,
turned around, and reached for the handrail. He missed it, but
held out one foot to step onto the stair below the stoop. His knee
went crooked, and he fell forward onto the walkway that cut
through the yard.

And the moment he hit the ground, someone in the darkness
opened fire on the house.

Moving on instinct and years of training, Grant retreated and
slammed the door. He shoved his shoulders against it, and felt
that it was solid. It would withstand more than a handful of bullets before he needed to worry about its integrity.

His ears told him that there were three shooters.

No. Four.

The window to the right of the door shattered. Polly screamed.
Mary came stumbling down the stairs in her dressing gown, her
eyes huge and black.

Grant pointed at her. "Get back in your room!" Then he
shouted at Polly, "Get down—lower. *Crawl*, goddammit!"

She swallowed her next scream and dropped to all fours, then
scrambled upstairs after Mary.

Nelson and Gideon burst into the parlor, but they burst carefully, like men who knew better than to fling themselves into the

line of fire. Grant was pleased by their caution. It spoke well of them.

"Down!" he gestured, and both men crouched. Both men also held firearms. Once more Grant fired off a wordless prayer to the Powers That Be, this time one of thanks. He had two soldiers, which was better than nothing. He'd been in tighter spots before. This situation wasn't unfamiliar—it was only bad.

Bullets plunked against the exterior and whizzed through the window, crashing against fixtures and punching holes in the wallpaper.

"Wellers, how many doors lead in and out of this house?" he asked. More loudly than he would've liked, but now the storm had new ways to whistle, and the curtains flapped and shredded themselves on broken glass.

The doctor and the scientist crouched behind the staircase. "Three, including this one!"

"Is that all?"

He considered the house and its layout. "There's the cellar door, and one from the attic to the roof—but those aren't common knowledge, and I'm quite certain they're locked."

"I'll keep 'em in the back of my head for now. As for the more obvious points of entry, I've got this one under control—you two go secure the others."

Gideon scrambled across the floor and disappeared down one corridor. Wellers went back down the hall toward Lincoln, who surely had been secured and safeguarded in some fashion before they'd come running—Grant refused to think otherwise. In the meantime, he held his position behind the door. The gunfire slowed but did not stop altogether. It petered out and punctuated the weather. For one moment of light-headed battle hilarity, Grant thought of popcorn nearly finished in a pan.

He recognized this rush of energy and giddiness, shook it off, and ducked down low beneath the window, then up the other side, where he flipped the lever to turn off the gaslights. No one wanted bullets flying when the gas was working. Besides that, darkness was his friend.

The downstairs was pitched into a low murk, but nothing close to the wholesale midnight he preferred. Two electrical lamps shone on in the parlor.

He cursed the Lincolns for their embrace of technological progress, held his head low, and—keeping the front door between him and danger as best he could—scuttled back into the other room and yanked the switches on the lamps, noticing as he did so that the lights were off down the hall in Lincoln's library. Only the glow of the fire spilled out past the threshold, and that was good.

"Abe?" he called, with as much volume as he dared.

"I'm fine. I *dearly* want to know what's going on . . . but I'm fine."

"Abe, you trust me?"

Without a moment's pause: "I do."

"I shot a man on your stoop, and his friends didn't take it well: *that's* what's going on. Nelson and Gideon are securing the house. Mary and Polly are upstairs. Is there anyone else home?"

"No. There shouldn't be."

A volley of shots hailed from outside. When they paused, Grant kept as much cover as he could and smashed out the last of the glass at the bottom corner of the nearest window.

The outside lights still burned for the moment, but if the assailants had any sense, they'd rectify the situation momentarily. He couldn't believe they'd left them alight this long. It was an amateur move. Maybe he hadn't given the police force enough credit: Surely someone in an authentic uniform would know to meet darkness with darkness.

Keeping his head low, he peered past the curtains. The wind was cold and hard. It stung his eyes, but he didn't close them; he gazed long and hard across the lawn, back and forth across the boundaries. A row of trees to the east gave cover to at least one man—he saw motion, a shifting of position from this tree to the next one, hopscotching closer. He waited for the man to dash for the next tree, and when he did, Grant fired a shot at him.

Between the distance, the wind, and his own precarious angle, the odds were against hitting him. But he was good—damn good—and managed to hit a trunk close enough to make the man dive back for his original position.

One more shot for good measure. Make the bastard keep his head down.

Three more bullets answered him, but nothing hit close to home. One more windowpane broke. That was a shame, but he'd figure out how to repay the Lincolns later. Maybe he could sue Haymes for the damages. The thought put a smile on his face.

Now, where were the rest of them?

A small orchard began where the lawn ended to the west. One or two men might be hiding there, easily. To the north lay the road, and on the other side of the road a ditch. Beyond the ditch, nothing but woods—all of them too far away to provide shelter for anything but a supernaturally skilled sharpshooter. No, the onslaught came from nearer than that.

He kept a wary eye on the lawn, until one bright assailant finally thought to shoot out the carriage lamps that lit up the sides of the house. It took him a few tries each, but a climactic shot took down the little lantern that illuminated the stoop, and now the playing field was more or less even.

Another bullet pinged inside the house, striking a tall clock hard enough to rock it.

Not much to be done about the windows and their frailty, but what about those curtains . . . ? He wanted something heavier than the decorative cotton gauze. Something more like the blanket on the back of the couch in the parlor, come to think of it. Staying in a crouch, he went back to retrieve it, then used the door for cover as he hung it up over the window, blocking their view if not their ammunition.

But the window on the other side of the door was still a gaping hole in their defenses.

"Mister President!" Polly whispered. She'd snuck back down the stairs, her shape a doll-like shadow in the gloom. Only then did he realize how small she truly was.

"Polly, get back upstairs with Mrs. Lincoln!"

"Sir, I can't. Mrs. Lincoln came downstairs before me. She's in the library with Mr. Lincoln. I couldn't stop her. If you know her at all, you'll understand, sir, and you won't yell at me about it."

He grinned, though she undoubtedly couldn't see him. This one had a little spice in her. Good. He would've bet against it an hour ago. Maybe he had three soldiers, if you dared give a girl a gun. Well, that Boyd woman had a gun, didn't she? And that Haymes viper, too. Fine. He had three soldiers.

"Polly, have you ever shot a gun before?"

"No, sir, because I'm scared of them."

"Are you scared right now?"

"Deathly, sir. Very, very deathly, if you don't mind me saying. But I saw you cover the window with the blanket, and I had an idea about the other window."

"Excellent. Tell me."

"There's another quilt down here. Robert's old bedroom."

"Can you get it for me?"

"Yes, sir."

"Polly, be careful. But be quick."

"Yes, sir," she said, and she was off.

More shots. These worried him, for they came from the other side of the house. He couldn't leave his post, so he'd have to trust Gideon and Nelson. He had to believe that they'd regroup when they were able, but it was taking too long. They should've been back already.

In less than a minute, Polly returned with a quilt bundled under her arm. She collided gently with him in the darkness, partly because it was hard to see, and partly because things had gone quiet, and the poor girl had enough instinct for self-preservation to keep herself quiet, too.

"Here you go, sir," she whispered close to his ear. "It's not too heavy, but it'll make it good and dark."

"Excellent. Here, stand up right behind this door. It's thicker than a Bible, and it'll protect you. Hold up that side, and I'll hold up this side. We'll hang the ends over the curtain rods, all right?"

"Yes, sir. I think I can reach it."

She had to throw her end of the blanket, but with a foot on the windowsill to give her a moment's boost, she fulfilled her end of the assignment.

"Well done, dear," he said to her, though now he could scarcely see her at all.

The interior of the house was as black as a tomb, except for soft, warm glows where the fireplaces yet burned—though they did little to warm the space anymore, or light it, either. Not with the windows gone and the wind screaming outside, driving around the eaves and wailing down the gutters. The blankets flapped and let shadows and light flicker through, a second at a time. But the weak glow showed them almost nothing.

Gideon Bardsley manifested behind the stairs once more, warning, "It's me—don't shoot."

"Are the other two passages secure?"

"As secure as we can make them. But there's nothing we can do about the windows except to cover them up, and avoid letting them see how many of us are inside."

"Or how *few,*" Polly whispered.

"Now, you've been courageous so far. Keep your chin up. We have a handful of men with guns, manning a defensive position with which most of us are well acquainted—myself being the exception, of course. But I've been in worse spots than this one, trust me."

"I trust you."

"Gideon, you're right. We need to cover all the windows, at least on the first floor. That will be our next priority."

"I already did it. The back entrance locks up easily, and fastens with a full-length beam. They'd need a horse to knock it down, and even if they had one, they probably couldn't persuade it to help. So I took the long way back and drew all the curtains."

"Excellent. You've got a good head on your shoulders."

The scientist paused, and when he said, "Thank you" Grant thought he almost sounded insulted.

"How many guns do you have on your person?" Grant asked him.

"Only the one."

"What kind?"

"A Starr revolver."

"Ah, another '58 model. Good gun. How much ammunition?"

"A pocketful on me. More in my bag."

"You always travel armed to the teeth?"

"Only when I'm wanted for murder."

"Then today's our lucky day." Grant patted his own pockets to remind himself of his holdings. "I have a Remington and a fistful of cylinders."

Bardsley snorted. "What about you? Do you always travel so heavy, yourself?"

"Only when warhawks are trying to assassinate me."

Grant thought he saw Bardsley's eyes roll, but in the dark he couldn't be certain. "This isn't an assassination attempt. They didn't even know you'd be here."

"They're shooting at me all the same, and if they kill me, we both know what the history books will call it. Now, where the hell is Wellers?"

"He took the other wing, where Lincoln is. Might've stopped to look in on him."

"Polly, go check."

Polly dutifully crept away, relieved to be sent from the front of the fray.

"Mr. Grant," Gideon said quietly, and closer to him than Grant expected. The man moved like a cat, for God's sake. No wonder he'd stayed alive this long. "Lincoln has a gun as well. I don't know how much ammunition he's packed."

The president considered this, and said, "He should keep the gun for now, unless we get any other good ideas that require it. But I hope it doesn't come to that. If everything goes to hell, he might need a last defense, though I hope it doesn't come to that, either. It's a wonder he can even hold one. . . . Goddammit, what's taking so long down there?"

"I could go and find out."

"No, because if *you* don't come back, then I'm really up a creek. Stay here, and take shots at anything you see moving past the edge of that quilt, you got it?"

Grant shuffled low and fast back into the hall, even though it made his knees ache. All along the hall the other doors were shut. When he tried one he found it locked—and saw no key—so that was good. Maybe Wellers had done it, or maybe the Lincolns kept half the place closed up tight at any given time. Didn't matter. It was another line of defense.

He went ahead and ran the rest of the way, announcing his approach before flinging himself into the library. "It's me!" he declared as he darted inside. There, he found Lincoln in his chair with the gun across his lap and Polly at his side, while Mary and Nelson Wellers shifted books from the cases to the window.

"What are you . . . ?" he began to ask, but realized the answer before he finished the question.

Without stopping her task, Mary answered him anyway. "One of the windows broke from the shooting outside. The bullet went into that painting over there," she complained.

Wellers finished the explanation. "But I'd like to see a bullet break through a wall made of books."

Abe smiled, a smile you'd only recognize as such if you knew how hard it was for him to move his face. "It's a good thing I have so many."

"Hard to argue with that," Grant conceded. "Wellers, did you get the far entrance secured?"

"Yes, sir. Took me a minute, because I had to draw a sideboard across it, but I think the sideboard was made of lead."

Mary shook her head. "Oh dear, Aunt Agatha's sideboard? No, but it's rosewood, and filled with silver. You'll hurt your back, dragging around furniture like that!"

"My back is just fine, and they'll have a hell of a time opening the door past your Aunt Agatha's sideboard," he said, grunting as he stacked another armload of books—up over his head now. "Almost done with this," he promised.

Mary noted, "It doesn't need to go all the way to the top. Unless they're standing on stilts, they'll never get a bullet that high."

Lincoln's smile faded, and his good eye stared into space. "I need to get in touch with Allan Pinkerton. I have to send him a wire as soon as possible."

Wellers finished with the last of his books, and wiped his dusty palms on the top of his thighs. "If we can get a wire out to *anybody,* we need to send word to the District office. If we can get their attention, they can send agents to help us."

More shots erupted outside, and were answered by Gideon Bardsley from within.

"I'll get back there and help him," Grant said, giving up on the idea of signaling for aid. "Wellers, when you're done here, make a pass of the back of the house. Bardsley said he'd secured it, and I believe him, but they'll be circling so we need to circle, too."

"I can help," Polly said. "I can . . . I can sneak out through the cellar. Take a message to the District office, if you need me to."

"That's very brave of you, dear," Grant said kindly. But with the lights out and armed gunmen surrounding the place, it'd be a suicide mission at the very best, and he wouldn't have it on his watch. "But let's not resort to such drastic measures yet. The Lincolns need you here now. Abe, maybe you ought to give her your gun and let her stand guard."

"I'll give it to Mary, when she's satisfied with the blockade. She's an excellent shot, and I don't know about Polly's prowess with a weapon."

"I'm no good at all," Polly admitted.

Mary Lincoln said to Grant, "Polly's idea might be a good one. Draw her up a message, and let her run with it."

"No." He was thinking of Betsey Frye, who'd last run errands for him. He couldn't do that to this girl, too. "Not yet. They're getting the lay of the land, watching the house from every angle. They'll shoot her if they see her."

"They might shoot me even if they don't. They're tearing up the house right good, Mr. Grant," she said, some kind of terrible plea in her eyes.

She was afraid, and she wanted to run. Grant understood, but he also understood that if she ran, they'd chase her. "How about this," he started, but when another gunshot rang out from the front door where that colored scientist was valiantly holding down the fort, he spoke more quickly. "Let us figure out how many there are and where they've stationed themselves. At some point they'll dig in and call for assistance, but not quite yet. They're still trying to decide how many of us are in here, and how strong we are, and how determined we are to hold our ground. There'll come a window, Polly—a window when it'll be safer than it is right now. When that window comes, I'll give you the note and send you running, and trust you with all our lives, if you think you're up to it."

She nodded gravely.

He turned on his heels and dashed back down the hall, knowing he'd lied to her, but that it was necessary. The truth was, he'd only send her if it got so bad she was just as likely to die on the road as in the house. They'd see her in a heartbeat, even if she found a good dark cloak.

The Lincoln crew was already outnumbered—heavily so, he suspected—and he guessed they'd already sent for assistance; he knew it in his bones, like Abe sometimes said. In another few minutes—maybe more, maybe less—they'd be farther outnumbered and outgunned. But in an hour the situation would have settled into whatever form of havoc it would ultimately take, and then . . . then he'd either need Polly, or he wouldn't.

No. She was safer inside. They all were, for now. That could change in an instant. Then again, it might not.

He counted the variables.

Someone would've heard all the shooting, that was a virtual certainty. Who would they summon? The real police? Some local night watchman? Neighbors or friends? It was as likely as not that someone would rouse the nearest Pinkerton office. Everyone knew that Lincoln relied on them—his affiliation with them was the stuff of history books—and the District office was one of the largest outside of Chicago, second only to New York. They weren't the law, but they were lawful, so long as they were paid.

All right, then. Let it be mercenary against mercenary, and may the best army win.

But until reinforcements arrived by the gift of fortune or could be flagged down, Grant had a fortress to secure. And despite the peril to himself and to his friends, and the potential damage to his legacy for murdering a man on a stoop, and the fact that the fate of the nation—the fate of the *continent,* as Bardsley liked to remind him!—was on his shoulders . . . for the first time in months, he was sober. He was certain. He was ready.

He knew exactly what he was doing.

 *Eighteen*

"Can you see it anywhere?" Maria asked, scanning the horizon for the other dirigible.

"Along the road ahead of us, I think. We'll catch up to it soon; we're flying faster than that big old cargo cruiser, even with the thruster working funny." Henry adjusted his grip on the controls, his fingers moving stiffly with the chill and repetition. They should've been halfway to Atlanta by now, but the flight felt like it was just beginning.

They were both cold and uncomfortable, and still shaky from the firefight they'd left behind them and weather that simply wouldn't cut them a break. But the clock was ticking, and a weapon of unparalleled, poorly understood destruction was crawling toward the Confederacy's biggest metropolitan area.

Though Maria desperately wanted to beg Henry to land, for God's sake, and let her walk around for a minute—to get the feeling back into her feet, if nothing else—she said nothing except, "Then let's see how fast this poor little dove feels like flying."

He upped the pressure and changed a gear setting, and the craft lurched forward, listing to the left but keeping a straight course along the road that dragged out below them.

Traffic down there had dwindled to almost nothing. They were now a ways out of Chattanooga, and not close enough to Atlanta for anyone to be bustling along, save for a few farmers moving supplies to and from markets. As her eyes examined the path through the spyglass, she said, "If they're anywhere in front of us, they'll stick out like a sore thumb. There's nothing down there at all. Nothing interesting, anyway."

She turned her attention to the sky, scanning it until she spotted a dark pinprick several miles ahead. "That military craft, on the other hand . . ."

"What do you think it was up to?"

"Could be anything."

"Even Union agents with a Southern ship, looking out for their own," Henry suggested, wiping his nose with the back of his hand.

"Yes, a decoy ship, like we discussed. I wonder if that would do them any good."

"Having a cargo ship along for the mission? I can't imagine it'd hurt."

"No," she agreed. She removed the spyglass from her face, then jammed it down her scarf, into her bosom. She shuddered with the shock of cold metal against her naked skin. "In fact, if the gas bomb covers as much range as we've been told, they'd need a ship to take them far away, and fast. A cargo cruiser might cut it."

"I don't know. Maybe, but . . . what are you doing to my spyglass?"

"Warming it up. It's practically sticking to my eyebrow." She shivered at the press of the metal. "The simplest, most obvious answer might be the right one: It *could* be a CSA ship heading for Atlanta. There's a big military base there, yes?"

"Dobbins, yes. Specializing in aircraft."

"Well"—she retrieved the glass, rubbed the eyepiece shiny, and stuck it back up to her face—"if the simplest answer is the correct one, then we may have found ourselves a *fantastic* new ally."

"If we can get them to talk to us. Or listen to us. Hey, do you think Troost got through to the base?"

"If he did, the cargo ship's not evidence of it. That cruiser's going *toward* Atlanta, not flying out of it at top speed searching for a doomsday weapon."

"Good point."

"Thank you. I want to believe in your friend Troost, I really do; I find shady men to be the most effective, as often as not. But he's right about the wires. The lines between North and South are feeble enough when the weather is good and the troops are clear. We don't dare assume that Haymes's agents haven't performed some deliberate act of sabotage to keep the information out of military hands until it's too late. Besides, the taps are only as reliable as the people who man them. No"—she shook her head—"we have to assume that reinforcements aren't coming. If they do, we can be pleasantly surprised. By the way, I think the ship has stopped—we seem to be catching up to it."

Henry squinted hard against the sky, and against the wind that warped around the glass screen meant to keep it out. "Yes, you're right. Have they landed or dropped anchor yet? I can't tell if they're moving."

Past the spyglass, she observed, "No, but they're settling down now."

"Right on the road?"

"Get us closer and I'll be able to tell you."

She eyed the damaged thruster and wondered if they'd move faster if it worked better, but as far as she could tell, it mostly just caused the craft to pull to the left. Her impatience was matched only by the chill she felt—or could no longer feel, depending on which extremity she considered. If she had toes, she couldn't prove it by wiggling them, and it was a good thing that the shooting had happened before her fingers had lost all sensation through her gloves. Bending and unbending them was a Herculean exercise in the cold weather, and she had to be quite careful indeed with the spyglass, for the bare metal burned against her skin, even after her bosomly attempts to warm it.

The wind was unrelenting, and so was the spitting, driving rain that came from every direction at once as they tracked the cargo craft through the lowest clouds. "We'll overtake them in a few minutes," she said, through chattering teeth. "But what happens then? Do you think they saw us fight with the other craft?"

He was silent. "I don't know."

Maria mulled over the possibilities. "If they're Confederate soldiers, I *must* believe they would've turned around to assist us. We were a legally marked civilian craft, menaced by an unmarked crew that could've been piratical, as far as anyone knew. They would've turned around," she said again, more confidently this time.

"Because you waved at them? And they waved back?"

"Because it's their job to guard the skies over the South, and protect its travelers from harm during wartime," she protested— though privately she believed that, yes, good Southern boys would've hightailed it back to prove their chivalry, given half a chance to do so. "But they didn't. They didn't even stick around to watch. They just kept flying."

"So perhaps they didn't give a damn what became of us and went on their merry way, leaving the other ship behind to deal with a couple of maniacs out for a flight. You said they weren't armed."

"Didn't appear to be, no. But," she added quickly, "I might've been wrong. Do you think they'd gone far enough to miss the fireball?"

He shrugged. "Far enough that they wouldn't have heard it inside the cabin. If they weren't looking behind them, they might not've seen it. I don't know, and I still don't know what side they're on. But we're coming up on them fast, so tell me what you see."

"I see . . ." She held the spyglass a fraction away from her cheek. "There's something in the road. A . . . a caravan of some sort! Henry, this might be them!"

"If the cargo ship is hanging around it, then that's probably a good sign. Or a bad one," he said. If his lips weren't turning blue, they might've been set in a grim, uncertain line.

Under her breath she asked, "But are they stopping the caravan to investigate it, or help it?" Through the spyglass, she couldn't quite tell.

"Another five minutes and we'll be on top of them." Henry said it like a warning.

"Or . . ."

"Or what?"

The big ship stopped its slow descent and began to rise again. It pivoted to face them.

It was Maria's turn to issue a warning: "Or maybe they'll be on top of *us*."

"Shit."

While she still had a spare moment to do so, she turned the spyglass to the ground and did a hasty estimation of the caravan. As fast as she could count, she called it out. "Eight horses drawing four carts. Maybe thirty men, all uniformed. One rolling-crawler, the Texian kind, but bigger than the ones you usually see. They've stopped. They're hailing the cargo runner, like they aren't sure why it's rising again. The ship is there as friend, not foe. Henry, *set us down.*"

"Where?"

"Anywhere, but set us down now. Set us down!" she hollered at him, her throat too frozen to manage the shriek she would've liked to deliver.

"I'm . . . I'll try! What do you see?"

She saw a hatch ratcheting down from the ship's underside, a bulbous protrusion descending from the hull. She'd never seen a turret that could be retracted inside the belly of a ship before;

only the ones that were affixed and unmoving, that would leave anyone who sat inside them exposed to enemy fire.

"A ball turret," she breathed. "With one of the biggest guns I've ever—"

The cargo vessel's gun fired, kicking out a round of such power that the ship rocked gently as it sent the shell careening through the sky, covering the space between them in one, two, three seconds.

In one, two, three seconds Henry managed to swerve to the right. It was only a tiny, insufficient angle out of the way, except it meant that when the shell struck them head-on it didn't go straight through their windscreen and kill them both. Instead it crashed beneath their feet, cutting through the engine and out the top of the chassis.

The *Black Dove* balked violently, shaking almost in a full circle, sending them closer to upside down than Maria had ever been in her life. If she'd eaten anything at all that day she would've lost it in the clouds. But the hemp belt held her inside the small cabin, if not in the seat—she hovered above it, and then her backside slammed down again, jarring her whole body. Her head knocked against Henry's shoulder, and his knees crashed against the underside of the controls.

He fought to find the levers, wrestled with the engine, and lost.

Black, billowing smoke coughed upward and the motor went utterly silent.

The world froze.

The sky was cold, clear, and unmoving, and the ground below was sharp and distant, miles and miles away—or so it looked. And so it felt, until the end of that moment, when the *Black Dove* pitched forward, dragged by the weight of its dead motor, and began to fall.

Henry cranked viciously at the controls, jerking the clutch and receiving no response. Nothing. Not a cough or a sputter. Not a spark of electricity. Not even smoke. All of it was gone. The little craft sailed, gliding only at a tiny angle, aimed for the ground.

"Henry!" Maria screamed.

He reached over his shoulder and into the tiny back cargo space and pulled out a pack. "There's just the one!" he screamed back as he wrestled his arms into a pair of straps.

"One *what*?"

"Of these. Come here—I'm undoing the belt!"

"Henry!"

"Trust me or die!" he told her. With one hand he seized her by the waist. With the other he snapped the hemp belt free and stood up inside the shattered, uncovered cab, taking her with him. Dangling in the firmament, he grabbed her tightly—both arms now—and kicked free of the wreckage. And then they were still falling, but falling together . . . above the battered *Dove,* and then beside it.

Maria's clothes billowed violently and her hair tried to tear itself off her head. She wanted to fight Henry, in order to . . . what? Swim in the sky? Fall by herself? Take these last seconds in silence, to pray or to reminisce, regret or wonder, and prepare for whatever came next?

His grip was a vise around her ribs. He shouted into her ear, but still she barely heard him: "Hang on to me! Now!"

She gave up her struggle and did as he commanded, because why not? Let their bones break together, and let them dig a crater to be both of their graves.

But instead, Henry ripped at a cord that dangled from the pack on his back, and the fall jerked to a shattering stop—still well above the trees below. The terrific yank sucked all the air out of Maria's chest and nearly snapped her neck; but she thrust her face into Henry's throat and clung to him for dear life, now that she understood. Or, if she didn't understand, she *believed,* and that was close enough for now.

As long as they floated in the middle of the sky, held aloft by a great umbrella-like cloth that flapped noisily over their heads.

"Emergency harness!" he said loudly. "One's required in all these little passenger crafts!"

"Emergency," she muttered into his neck, refusing to open her eyes or look down. She damn well assumed it was an emergency piece, for surely no one in their right mind would don such a thing recreationally.

Her head ached, her ribs were bruised all the way around, and she could scarcely breathe. Her arms felt as if they'd been half pulled from their sockets, and her feet dangled until she wrapped them around Henry's legs, seeking whatever slight stability she could glean from the situation.

And still they fell.

They swayed back and forth, buffeted by the wind and without any protection at all, not even the pitiful guard of the tiny craft, which crashed somewhere below them. She heard it hit and crumple, and she thanked heaven and Henry that she was not inside it. Though being in midair was only marginally better, as she was still definitely alive—but for how long?

She could feel the wind dragging them in this direction, then that direction, and on top of everything else she was dizzy. "Can you control this at all?" she begged him, nearer to tears than she'd been in a decade.

"Not at all, I'm afraid," he replied, and he did in fact sound sorry. "Hold on tight, Maria! We're going down. We're going down *fast*."

Not as fast as they might have otherwise, but fast enough that when they fell through the tops of two trees it was like being beaten by a mob, and when the final tree caught them in its uppermost branches it was such a horrible way to stop that she almost envied the *Black Dove*—for at least its awful fall had ended already.

Their fall continued, though she clung to Henry until she was knocked free of him—and then she fell alone, down branches, through dead leaves and abandoned squirrel nests. Her body stripped a line of bark bare from the tree, and her gloves were no protection at all. Her skirts did a somewhat better job of shielding her legs, and her corset may or may not have guarded her organs like armor, but none of it helped very much. When she finally landed on her back, staring up at the hole she'd left in a tree, she watched the emergency sheet snag, tear, and wave forlornly above her.

And then she wondered where Henry was.

He told her: "Ow."

"Oh, dear—I'm . . . I'm sorry . . ."

She rolled off his arm, then kept rolling until she was on her back again, beside him. She hadn't left him after all.

She couldn't breathe. No, she *was* breathing. She put her hand to her chest and felt it rise and fall, but she was so winded that it meant very little. She could do nothing but lie there, as still as she could manage, and wait for her lungs to catch up to the rest of her.

Every inch of her body hurt. She scarcely knew where to begin to check for injuries, so instead she asked Henry, "Are you all right? Mostly? More all right than not?" The words came out in whispers, in time with her every exhalation. It was the only way she could speak at all.

"Yes," he said in a similar gasp. "No. Wait. Mostly, I think. My arm, though."

"The one I was lying on?"

"The one you landed on."

"Ah. Is it . . . ?"

He rolled over onto his side. "Broken. Not as bad as it could be," he said with a wince.

When she turned her head, she could see that yes, his hand was lying at an unhealthy angle. "Oh, no. We need to brace it."

She wiggled a bit and frowned. No longer lying on his arm, but she was somehow still lying upon *something.* Ah. Her satchel. Still slung around her chest. Would wonders never cease?

"There seem to be plenty of promising sticks lying about, thanks to us. As for you," he said, "we need to see about that pretty little head of yours."

"What about it?" she asked. But now that he mentioned it, a spot to the left of her forehead, just above her ear, felt hot. When she touched it, it stung, and it left the tattered remnants of her glove covered in blood. "Hmm." She wasn't sure how much of the blood was from her head, and how much was from her hands—the gloves themselves were in shreds, and scraped skin showed through them. She was quite confident that when she warmed up enough to feel her fingers again, every single one of them would be in agony.

"Let me see it," Henry suggested.

"First, let's see about that arm."

"Heads are more important than arms."

He had a point, so she let him probe the problem, but only briefly. "You see? It's all right. I'm fine," she assured him. "If that's the worst I get from the adventure, I'll be in excellent shape. Now. I can stand. Can you?"

"You can stand? Prove it."

"Fine, I will." She did, and though the effort was at first unsteady, she settled the matter by arriving upright. "Your turn."

She offered him her hand and he grasped it, clutching his broken arm to his chest and letting her pull him to his feet. "See? Me too."

"Apart from the arm, are you intact? How do you feel?"

"Like I just fell out of an airship and crashed through a tree. How about you?"

"The same. Now, let me bind up that arm, and I suppose we'll have to get on our way. Did I mention I used to work as a nurse?"

"Don't believe it came up."

"No? Well," she said, eyeing the ground for a promising splint. "I didn't last very long. I don't mind blood and bones, but I have trouble with vomiting and pus. Here. This will do nicely."

Before long, Henry was as patched up as he could expect to get, his injured arm fastened tight to a piece of wood, courtesy of the remains of the hemp belt, which had accompanied them to the ground. Maria had found it nearby and rejoiced. Henry's scarf served as a sling, tied up in a knot behind his neck.

Maria used her own scarf to staunch the bleeding above her ear. Her options were few, and it was dark enough that the stain scarcely showed. Maybe with a good laundering, it would vanish altogether. Or perhaps she'd pester Mr. Pinkerton for hazard pay, should she escape the mission alive. He could damn well buy her a new scarf for her pains. And maybe a good winter coat, too.

"Where are we?" she asked, hoping that perhaps he'd paid closer attention on the way down that she had. "What time is it? How far away do you think we are?"

He shielded his eyes against the sun, and checked the shadows filtering down through the brittle, naked branches around them. "Well, it's early afternoon," he said. "I think we landed a little to the east of the road. *West* should be that way."

"How certain are you, exactly?"

"Somewhat. That's the best I can do."

"It'll have to suffice. We need to find that road and . . . and stop that caravan."

"Single-handedly," he added, as he lurched forward in the general direction of west and south.

"Well, you'll be single-handed. But, between us, there are three hands." She mustered a smile. "And I'm sure we'll think of something."

Nineteen

Gideon crouched behind the front door, performing mental cal-culations and deciding that yes, it'd likely withstand a significant ballistic onslaught. It was oak, he believed—upon rapping it gently and feeling the sturdy density of it—and fully three inches thick, with some variation where it was carved for the sake of a paneled appearance. Regardless, unless someone was firing a canon at the thing, it'd hold just fine. The lock, on the other hand . . .

He examined it closely, since no one was firing at him right that moment.

It was nothing special. Brass, with typical, easily circumnavigated workings. A thief or a locksmith could breach it in seconds. Two men with stout shoulders or feet could've forced it. A bullet could do so faster, if it occurred to a shooter to come up close and take a crack at it.

He looked around for something to brace the door more firmly. Did it open inward? He checked the hinges. Yes, as all exterior doors ought to. But one couldn't assume.

Shortly down the hall was a standing clock of considerable heft. If he were to drag over and shove it diagonally across the door, it'd serve at least to slow down any efforts to come inside, through the door or the broken windows that flanked it at waist height.

He peeked under the edge of the quilt, being careful to block any firelight that might escape with the bulk of his torso. Staring across the darkened lawn, he saw nothing moving. No one sneak-stepping across the grass. Though, when he leaned over to peek at a different angle, he saw something on the stairs of the stoop. It looked like a leg.

On closer inspection, as his eyes adjusted to the dim, almost impenetrable murk, he determined that it was the body of whoever the president had shot.

Gideon had no particular love for the old general, no more than he held for most people he just knew in passing, but he respected the man's military prowess. He believed in his abilities as a soldier, if not as a politician—which probably put him in very good company, now that he thought about it. Not much of a president, but one hell of a shot and tactician.

So presumably the man on the stairs was dead.

But how many others lingered out there? Grant hadn't given his estimation, and Gideon hadn't yet heard enough gunfire to get a good idea of what was coming from where, so there was no way of knowing. Except . . . Grant was a master of these sorts of plans. He wouldn't tell them to board up the downstairs entrances for merely one or two men—so there must be three or four, if such measures were called for. Probably more than that.

Always the general, that one. He commanded like a general. Barked like one. Made assumptions like one.

Well, all right then—if he had to take orders from a general, let it be Grant. After all, the orders were professional, not personal. Grant would just as happily bark commands to Polly or Wellers, or to Lincoln himself. It was so ingrained in him from years of being in charge that it was difficult to hold it against him—and there was always the chance that he knew what he was doing.

So against his better judgment, and more than a little reluctantly . . . Gideon chose to believe in Grant.

He'd take responsibility for the Fiddlehead's evidence, and trust Grant to manage the armed intrusion. It was a trade-off he could accept, given the scheme of things, because he didn't know if any of them would survive the night, and he couldn't bear to be responsible for the deaths of the Lincolns.

Or Polly, for that matter.

Polly, who was not even important enough to kill, he realized, and which horrified him. It surely meant she'd die first, if it came to that, because that was how the world worked. She'd made him gloves, once, and he'd defend her with his life for those ridiculous gloves.

Gideon slowly lowered the edge of the quilt, lest the motion be enough to lure more bullets. He looked again at the clock, and wondered if he could move it alone. It was huge, and certainly heavy.

He scooted over to it and pushed it with his foot, testing the weight and balance of the thing. It didn't budge.

Out in the lawn—or at the edge of it—someone called out, hailing whoever might be inside.

"You there, at the door! We only want to talk!"

It was nonsense, of course. First of all, anyone out there would've seen Grant shoot their colleague. If they weren't total idiots, they would've *assumed* it was the president behind the door, and addressed him accordingly. They'd be wrong, yes, but it was the logical conclusion. By pretending they didn't know, they only made themselves look like they weren't paying attention.

Gideon returned to the window. Adjusting the edge of the blanket again, he took another look at the lawn, but saw nothing. He did not answer, of course, for his voice might betray him as an educated colored man from the South. But though they were hunting an educated colored man from the South, for the time being, they had no reason to think he might be in the house. He did not plan to disabuse them of that notion.

He held his tongue, but continued to watch. He saw nothing, but he kept his ears open, and the man called again. "Send out the doctor, Nelson Wellers! He's wanted for harboring a murderer!"

A ridiculous, made-up charge. Definitely not police officers; Polly had been right to distrust them. He wanted to tell her so, but she was at the other end of the house. And she already knew it, anyway.

Gideon still did not answer.

"Just send him out, and we'll call this a draw! There's no need for things to get any worse! No need for anyone else to get hurt!"

No need? No, he supposed not. But he didn't trust the speaker as far as he could throw a horse; and even if he did, he would never toss Wellers out onto the front yard and tell him he was on his own. In order to make that clear, Gideon poked the barrel of his Starr under the bottom of the blanket, through the corner window, and fired off two shots in the direction from which he'd guessed the voice had come.

Shots were fired in return. Several of them plunked against the door; he could feel them with his shoulder, but it was no more than a dull thud. He smiled. The door would definitely work as a shield. A good one, if he could do something about that weak point, the lock.

When the men outside ceased their response, Gideon returned to the clock. Positioning himself on the far side of it, he braced his back as best he could, and shoved it with his boots. Always the best leverage that way. Simple mechanics: levers, screws, pulleys. If more people were of a mechanical, scientific bent, the world would be an easier place—he was confident of it.

Then again, if more people were of a scientific bent, it might lead to a more vibrant criminal class.

The good would not necessarily outweigh the bad, but one could not pick and choose when it came to wishfully bestowing mythical aptitude on the masses . . . or so he concluded, as the clock moved by inches as he bent and unbent his knees. He kept his eyes on the clock's face. The large piece of furniture was top-heavy, and it wouldn't do for him to shove it too hard and wind up with the thing crashing across his lap.

A sharp hiss came from behind him. "What are you doing?"

He recognized it, and therefore did not startle. Instead, he said, "Mr. Grant, I am addressing a weak point in our defenses. The lock is a feeble thing. It could be resolved with one shot, at which point the door would open with a simple shove."

Gideon half expected the president to observe that the door stood between two broken windows, either one of which any fool could leap right through, as they were guarded only by blankets. But his good impression of the man's strategic mind was borne out when Grant only nodded. "Let me help."

Only a fool would hop through a broken window when he couldn't see what awaited on the other side. A wiser man might use the big oak door for cover—much like he and Grant were doing at present—and choose to lead a charge from that position. If he were lucky or ambitious enough, such a man might even blow the hinges and use the door as a shield all the way down the corridor.

Perhaps. If another man or two were present to help him carry it.

Gideon knew he was overthinking the situation, but Grant didn't say or do anything to suggest that the extra precaution wasn't warranted, so he considered himself correct and proceeded with the wiggling, shoving, and balancing of the upright clock. Finally it was in position, and between the two of them, they knocked it ajar, forcing it into a diagonal across the door.

"That'll hold it for now." Grant sounded pleased.

"It also gives us more cover at the windows. But only a little," Gideon frowned. The clock was very tall, but when slapped across the entry, it looked much shorter. Only by virtue of a decorative column did it remain in position at all; otherwise, it might've fallen right to the floor. "This wouldn't have been my first pick for a defensive position."

"Mine either, but we rarely get a chance to choose such things. We're usually stuck with what we get. Anyway," he added, surveying the area with a critical eye. "As I told Polly, I've worked with worse. Only three entrances on the first floor—in a building this size, that's a relief. It could be far more. And given the high ceilings . . . unless they bring a ladder, that's all we'll need to defend for now. Assuming all the curtains are drawn—and between you and Wellers, I trust that's the case."

Gideon nodded firmly. "And for all they know, we've got an armed man in every room."

"Oh, they know better than *that*. But they aren't dumb enough to risk it. Or, more likely, they don't have enough men to undertake an empirical study in the matter."

"So far."

"That's true: We must assume they've sent for help, but they can't assume we haven't done likewise. At least three or four men are out there, by my count, never mind the fellow on the stairs. You can bet they were able to spare someone to run off with a message, requesting reinforcements or instructions. They don't really know what to do," he said almost gleefully. "This isn't what they expected. Now they have to make a decision. A *big* one."

"Whether or not to kill us all, knowing that the president's inside. And Lincoln, and two women."

"They know about Polly, but they didn't see Mary. And, as you said, we could have another half-dozen servants inside—all armed, all ready to defend the place with their lives. Polly didn't let the man in—she closed the door and left him there. Neither he nor his friends saw anyone but her. They know almost nothing, and that's to our advantage."

"I'm happy for any advantage we can claim, no matter how small." And again, he considered the wiles of Polly, for whom his admiration grew by the moment.

"It's not small. On the battlefield, information is currency."

Gideon sighed grouchily. "But *we're* missing as much information as they are. We don't know how many men they have any more than they know the reverse."

"True, but we know what they want. We know they're near the house, but lurking in the shadows—which means they fear us. Otherwise they'd charge, storm the place, and call their mission a success. We know who sent them, or we can make a good enough guess to predict their future course of action."

"And what might that be?" Gideon asked. He was confident he wouldn't care for whatever came next, but he wanted to hear Grant's assessment.

"Violence, and plenty of it. Haymes will kill me if she thinks she needs to, and leave William to run the show from under her thumb—which is how she prefers things, you know. Everything would take place under her thumb if she got her way."

Gideon didn't know much about the vice president, so he didn't know how likely this was. "Can she do that? Is Wheeler so ethically flexible?"

Grant shrugged, a gesture Gideon barely saw through the gloom. "He has a reputation for trustworthiness, and I've trusted him this long. But he's a politician, and the more time I spend in Washington, the less I know about such men. I've trusted plenty who proved me a fool. Given the present situation, I'd rather rely on soldiers. And I have *good* soldiers tonight, don't I? You and Wellers, both smart men who know their way around guns. And since Wellers is a Pink, I know he has some experience with danger, despite what a frail-looking fellow he is. All height and no weight, do you know what I mean?"

Gideon nodded. He'd had the same thought himself.

"But you can't put anything past him, so I don't mind what he looks like. And what of *you*?" Grant wanted to know, as if it only just dawned on him that he ought to ask.

"What *of* me?" Gideon responded in the rhetorical. "Can I fight, you mean? I've never fought in battle, but I escaped the South, and I've survived more than one attempt on my life. I've protected my family and served my benefactors as I was able, to the point of violence if necessary."

"That's good enough for me. And you're no coward, which is worth more than any formal service, in my experience," he said politely.

Gideon was almost touched. He hid it well. "My father fought in the Mexican War—for Texas, as you might expect, if not approve. My grandfather served in the Revolution. He died before my father was born."

In the dark, he could barely see Grant's eyes, but he saw them flicker. "Is that his coat? The one you wear all the time?"

"Yes. Old-fashioned, I know. But it suits me. My father left it to me, and I . . . I prefer it."

"I recognized the old army cut," he said. "No business of mine, and so I never asked, but a man can be curious, can't he?"

Outside, the invaders tried again with their untrustworthy shouted compromises. "You send out Wellers, and we'll all go away! Call it a night!"

Grant and Gideon went to opposite windows and looked outside cautiously.

"This is good," Grant murmured. "They want to make a deal. Men who are confident of victory don't seek to make deals."

"Maybe they can't get reinforcements after all."

"That's possible. It's also possible that Haymes doesn't want the deaths of two presidents on her hands, and she's told them to withdraw. Don't forget: The advantage is ours, though we do not know its extent."

"Forgive me if I don't get too excited while they're out there holding us hostage."

"Absolutely." Grant lifted the quilt an inch farther, holding it away from the broken glass with the barrel of his '58. He raised his voice to project it, and hollered out into the night. "Forget it! Wellers is innocent!"

"You can't hide him forever!"

"We don't have to, and you know it!"

Gideon frowned. "What do you mean by that?" he whispered.

Grant whispered in return. "Confused? Good. They'll be confused too. Let 'em think we're up to something. Right now, they'll assume we mean to dig in our heels, but we could also have a plan to sneak him away, or call in reinforcements of our own. Lincoln has many friends, and someone will come calling eventually—or, for that matter, someone will notice that the president is missing."

"Good. If we can hold on until dawn, they may decide this is more dangerous than they'd prefer and try a different approach. But," Gideon warned, "they'll come again. For him. For *me*."

"Son," Grant said. It was precisely the sort of voice that usually felt like nails on a chalkboard to Gideon, but for some reason, he didn't mind it now. "All I can do is buy you time. But I doubt you need much more than that to think your way out of this."

"Your vote of confidence is . . . meaningful to me."

"You're welcome."

Someone outside disturbed the moment with a threat: "Don't make us set fire to the house!"

Gideon and Grant paused and looked at each other across the door—each one trying to read the other, and gauge what they thought about that. Grant shook his head first. "If they could, they'd have done it already," he said. "Haymes is a gambling woman, but she wouldn't push them that far."

"How do you know she's a gambler?"

"She spends all her time with politicians. Name me a bigger risk if you can."

"Are you going to answer them?"

Both men sat on the floor, watching from behind the swaying blankets. The wind had calmed, but only a bit. The night was still full of treacherous gusts, and threatening, broiling black clouds that hid all the stars.

"Yes, I'll answer them. Like *this*," Grant said. Then he shouted, "Light up a flare, and we'll shoot any man who holds it!"

Silence in response.

After a few seconds of what must have been conferral: "Our offer stands!"

Quietly, Grant said, "Oh does it, now? Well, good for them."

Nelson Wellers came tiptoeing around the corner, and announced himself by saying, "They'll do it, if they're Haymes's men. She's done worse than cook a family alive."

"Sit down, doctor."

"I can't let them harm the Lincolns. I won't have that on my conscience, not when I prevent it just by being less of a coward."

"Thinking beyond the first option isn't cowardice. If we beat this, you stay alive, and Gideon stays alive, his credibility intact. His editorial finishes taking the nation by storm—we all know the story is *well* on its way around the globe, so maybe, if we're very lucky, it takes the South by storm as well. The war ends. The walking dead are vanquished. Stepping stones, doctor. Stepping stones."

"Send him out, or we're coming in!"

Grant said, "See? They're backtracking. They aren't threatening to burn the place down anymore. First blood was ours, and the first retreat is theirs."

"Maybe they couldn't reach Haymes?" Wellers suggested, but he put a question mark on the end.

"That would make sense," Gideon mused. "They're rather marvelously disorganized out there."

The president peered out once more. "You could be right. And if you are, that's one more advantage. We're racking them up, over here!"

"Until they actually try to come inside." Polly stood at the edge of the foyer. She spoke from the shadows behind the staircase, where no one could see her very well. "*Then* what do we do, Mr. Grant?"

"Then, my dear, when they try to come inside, we forcibly keep them *out*. Wellers, now that we've gotten the house as secure as possible, it's time to ask: Does Abe have any other guns on the premises?"

"I'm sure he must."

Polly answered. "There's a cabinet in the cellar."

"There's a cellar?" Grant hesitated. "Oh that's right. And it opens to the outside?"

"Yes, sir, it does."

Gideon threw up a hand, volunteering himself. "Polly, take me to it. I'll secure the cellar and bring up guns for everyone."

Wellers was taken aback. "Mary, too?"

"Abe said she's a better shot than *he* is," Grant replied.

Gideon groaned. "I've seen her. She's not terrible, but close enough. Still, he's in that chair, and his hands barely work—so technically, he's right. Doesn't matter. We need every able body, and Mary's able enough. Polly, take me to the guns, and be quick about it."

"Good plan," Grant said, endorsing it. "Now, Wellers, I want you to stay here and man the front. This is where they've been trying to communicate from, up until now, but they'll be investigating the rest of the house, testing doors and trying their luck in other places. I'm going to do some reconnaissance. And as soon as Gideon gets back from his mission, I want him to relieve you."

"All right." Gideon agreed over his shoulder, one hand on Polly's arm so she could lead him through the darkness.

The president's instructions to Nelson Wellers followed behind him. "When he returns, you take the east wing. I'll patrol the west. Do your best not to answer them, except with bullets. They may know your voice. Let's keep them guessing about who's inside."

Polly drew Gideon into the large entryway, past the parlor and its unattended fireplace, burning low. Softly, she asked him, "Are you really going to give Mary a gun?"

"If she'll take one."

"So . . . that's a yes?"

"Yes," he affirmed. "She doesn't have to shoot well or wisely; we only need people who can shoot from inside, at various locations, giving the impression that the whole house is occupied . . . and there's not just the six of us to hold down the fort."

"So you'll give *me* a gun too?"

"Yes, and I'll expect you to use it."

"I don't know if I can," she whispered. "Watch out for that—yes, there. There's a step before the door."

He caught himself before he could fall, smacking one hand against the frame in order to steady his balance. "You can, and you *will* if you have to. This is the cellar? I've never been down here."

"There's not much to see," she said vaguely. "Some storage, is all. Canned things, preserves. No books, though."

"No books?"

She shook her head as she unlocked the door with a key from her apron pocket. "No. Mr. Lincoln says it's too damp, and he loves them all too much to keep them there."

"He doesn't love any of them so much that he won't build a wall with them, in the hope that it filters out any stray bullets."

Polly shrugged a little and opened the door. "It's different for him. He says books saved his life. I guess he figures books can go on saving his life, but he won't stash them someplace damp and let them rot. They don't do *anyone* any good that way. And, you have to admit, he has a point."

The cellar was utterly black, without the first hint of a light. "Polly, I can't see a thing," Gideon said as he felt his way down the steps with his toes, scraping them across each board in search of its end, and then lowering them blindly until they stopped against the next one.

"Don't worry. There's a lantern at the bottom in case the electric lights go out."

"Does that happen very often?"

"When there's weather like this, yes. The gas lamps are more reliable, but Mr. Lincoln says electricity is the future. He's having the old system replaced, a bit at a time, but he started in the cellar. He said he didn't want to put the technology anyplace important until it was tested."

"His love of novelty has always been at war with his innate sense of caution," Gideon mumbled. "Where's this lantern? And are there any windows down here?"

"Almost got it. And no, no windows, so no one will see it when we light it up."

She pulled farther ahead of him, and soon, from the bottom of the steps, a light came up so brightly that it nearly blinded him.

He winced and looked away until she carried it off and his eyes adjusted. Then he joined her in the cellar—a finished, clean space, but low of ceiling and somewhat cold compared to the rest of the house. From down there, the wind was much subdued, as there were no nooks or crannies, loose window panes, or fireplaces for it to scrape against. There was nothing at all to see but foundation stones and rough-hewn shelves holding canned goods, disused kitchen supplies, and seasonal items that would come upstairs when the calendar called for them.

And against the far wall, a nice pine cabinet.

Polly approached it and tugged the knob. It wasn't locked.

Upstairs, the temporary quiet was broken by more pops of gunfire, some from within, some from without. Gideon counted six shots from the Lincoln compound, and eight from outside it. Waste of bullets, all. A game of spending time and ammunition, seeing who had the most and who could least afford to lose it.

Polly also paused to hear out the shots upstairs. Their eyes met—hers wide and worried, his calculating and angry. The yellow glare of the lantern engulfed them, but not much beyond them; everything past the gun cabinet and the nearest wall of preserves remained cast in darkness. One more muffled bang—from inside, he thought—and then silence.

Whatever was going on, it wasn't going away. The men outside would find their way inside eventually.

He spied the cellar door, up a short set of stairs. He climbed them and made sure it was locked, then returned to the cabinet.

He nudged Polly aside and reached for the contents. Two rifles and three smaller handguns. At a glance, it looked like a lone Colt and a pair of Remingtons. No surprise there. Old military men often preferred them, and every president counts as military by default. Two boxes of ammunition of varying sizes lurked beneath the guns. He pointed them out to Polly. "Take those and follow me. We'll sort it out in the library, and get you ladies armed like men."

"I don't know if I can kill anybody," she objected, so softly that, had she been another foot away, he wouldn't have understood her.

"No one's asking you to kill anyone. I'm asking you to stand inside and shoot outside, into the darkness." He made for the stairs, and she tagged along behind him, bearing the boxes and the lantern. "Shoot into the trees, for all I care. Just *shoot,* and it will tell them we aren't alone, we won't let them have Nelson Wellers, and *none of us* are going quietly."

Upstairs in the library he divvied out the available weaponry, leaving out the rifles for the present, since the women had no experience with them, Lincoln didn't have the reach to fire them, and besides, there was less ammunition to fuel them.

Mary took the Colt. Polly took one of the Remingtons. Mary vowed to teach Polly how to shoot, a prospect that worried Gideon—hardly better than the blind leading the blind—but not so much that he tried to stop her. She understood the mechanics, even if she was a danger to herself and others when she employed them. That was fine. It'd *have* to be fine.

Back to the front door he went, to relieve Nelson Wellers.

"I'm running low," the doctor confessed.

"There are bullets in the library. Not a magnificent stash, but enough to keep us on the defensive for another few hours yet, at this pace."

"They won't give us another few hours."

Gideon swallowed, and tweaked the edge of the blanket to look outside. He saw nothing at first, and then motion. Two men, and then a third. Then he heard shots at the other end of the house—and more shots answering from within, from Grant. "They've found reinforcements."

"They've been free to go and get them. We haven't. If we can make it to dawn . . ."

"Then what?" Gideon asked. "Then they'll be able to see us if we try to sneak away. No. If we're going to make some great move, we ought to make it before the sun comes up. The president likes to go on about our copious 'advantages,' and we can't afford to squander one."

"Then what do you propose?" The worry on Wellers's face was digging in hard, setting lines there and drawing bags beneath his eyes.

"I propose to sit here and think about what to do next." Another shot, back in Grant's direction in the far hall. "Go see if he needs help. I'll stay here and watch the new fellows. If you run past the office, send me Mary."

"Mary?"

"She's a wild shot with an ax to grind. I may need to guard the east wing where her husband is."

"You think she'll leave him?"

"I think she might trust my aim more than hers. Go and see," he urged again. As Wellers left, he continued to eye the shadows outside. Yes, more men had definitely been rallied. If someone was shooting at the west wing, they'd added at least two—no, three, because here came another, scuttling through the darkness. It was looking like six to six, if Gideon were feeling optimistic. Even odds, except that it was three able-bodied men, two women, and a chairbound cripple versus six mercenaries.

Mary appeared beside him, her approach announced by the swish and sway of her skirts—and only then did Gideon notice that the wind was dying down. The makeshift curtains were not blowing quite so hard, and the chimneys were no longer being played like a set of organ pipes.

"All right, Gideon." She was brandishing her weapon in a way that made him nervous, so he gently aimed it toward the floor for now. "What do I do?"

"Mrs. Lincoln, I want you to sit here and keep an eye on the front door, right here—through the edge of this blanket, see? Stay low, and keep from moving any more than necessary. The curtain will move some, because of the wind, but that's all right; we just don't want them taking shots at your head."

She nodded grimly, her eyes narrowed. "All right. And if anyone approaches the house, I shoot!"

"No! Or, yes, you *should* shoot . . . but like this: If anyone approaches the front door here, I want you to fire a warning shot. Aim it anywhere: the sky, the ground, what have you. If it's a friend who's accidentally slipped through, coming to see about the ruckus, he'll identify himself. If it's a foe, he'll shoot back or start making demands. Either way, we'll hear you, and one of us will come to help. Is that all clear?"

"Crystal clear, yes." The old lady squeezed her gun with both hands, and sidled up to the wall beneath the window. "Now, go look after my husband."

He left her, and proceeded down the east wing hall, where the former president remained with Polly. He leaned his head around the corner, saw that all was well, and said, "Polly, I want you to come with me."

"And leave Mr. Lincoln?"

"Mr. Lincoln," Gideon addressed the man personally. "Do you have any objections?"

"None," he said firmly, holding one of the rifles across his lap, despite the previous decision to leave them for later. Gideon wasn't sure who'd given it to him, or if this was the best choice, given the man's lack of depth perception and limited use of his hands, but it looked impressive all the same. And, ah, yes: He still had the handgun ready, half concealed by the blankets.

Polly gazed at the man as if she'd do what she was told, but she wasn't prepared to like it much. "All right, Dr. Bardsley. What do I do?"

He led her out of the room and toward the foyer, to the stairs that led to the second story. "You go upstairs, and go back and forth between the windows. Draw all the curtains if they aren't drawn already, but do it carefully. Keep from being seen. I don't want anyone spying your shadow and taking a shot at you."

"Yes, sir. I'll do that."

"And I want you to watch for men who might be sneaking up on us from different sides. If you see such a man, fire a shot through a window in his general direction. Don't worry about hitting him, just let him know that you saw him."

"All right. I can do that."

"I know you can. And don't try to open a window—just shoot right through it. Glass isn't that expensive. You're worth more than the window, you hear me?"

She blushed, and even the dwindling firelight couldn't hide it. "Thank you, sir."

When she was gone, Gideon said to Lincoln through the still-open door, "I'm going to check the other end of the hall, then work my way back. If you have any trouble, fire a warning shot, but fire it into those books. Anywhere else, and it might bounce in this little room."

"I'm not an idiot, Gideon."

"I'm only thinking out loud," he assured him. In the quiet that followed, he really should've turned and left; but, like Polly, he found himself reluctant to leave Lincoln alone. "Is there . . . anything I can get you? Anything you need?"

"I need for my friends to believe I'm still a capable man," he said. "I will be *fine,* and so will the rest of you. With you and Grant defending the place, I'm confident that it will stand."

Gideon wished he hadn't said that, even if he agreed. "We'll do our best," he said, and he stalked off down the hall, praying their best would be enough.

 *Twenty*

"I thought we'd landed closer to the road than this," Maria grumbled, tripping over a tree root and scraping her already-raw hand against a trunk when she caught herself.

"So did I." Henry grimaced with pain, so often that it seemed his whole face was set that way in a permanent expression of discomfort. But a broken arm was plenty of excuse, to say nothing of the assorted scrapes, bumps, and bruises that plagued them both.

Maria ached in places she rarely thought of, and she bled from more injuries than she let on. Besides the cut on her head, under her coat she hid a hard puncture that had made it past her corset stays. She didn't know how deep it went, and she didn't know what had caused it. Part of the *Black Dove,* as they'd kicked free of its tumbling wreckage? A tree branch on the way down? Something else, when she'd landed?

The wound was under her rib cage, on the right side. It left a great stain on her dress, so she kept her coat fastened around herself, even tighter than before. Now it wasn't just the cold. She needed for Henry to believe that she was all right, because if he thought otherwise, he'd attempt to coddle them both and they'd never get anywhere.

Just this once, she was glad for the cold.

It kept her numb enough to keep walking, hiking between the trees and around them. She hoped they were headed in the right direction, but had no way of knowing for certain. She had no compass, only Henry's gut feeling; and she did her best not to second-guess him, because she had no idea herself.

Finally, they saw a line where the trees thinned. When they stumbled up out of the woods, they found themselves on a road. It amounted to little more than four sets of ruts in places, but the rain that season had been bad, and it was no secret that the Confederacy was low on money. Public works were suffering along with everything else.

No other vehicles or travelers were present, a fact that bothered Maria. She'd hoped to find carts—of the motorized or horse-drawn variety, she did not care which—and use her wiles to flag one down for a lift. She was exhausted and sore. Henry surely was in no better condition, though he also seemed to be hiding the worst of his pain.

So they trudged forward, southbound and surly, until a benevolent farmer heading in the right direction came along. Maria bribed him with sorrowful eyes, and Henry sealed the deal with the few Confederate coins from his pocket that hadn't rained across the Georgia countryside as he'd fallen to earth.

The ride was faster than walking, and it gave them time to rest, if not recover.

When the farmer took a turn for the west, he left them on the road and they continued on foot, thankful for the help but wishing for more assistance. It didn't come.

The day grew later, and the shadows grew longer. Maria didn't know what they'd do when night fell. They had almost nothing in the way of supplies, much less any source of light, and roaming along a road at night was a surefire way to get robbed or murdered . . . or so she'd always been told.

She squeezed the battered satchel that still hung around her neck, and yes, her gun was still there. But none of her bullets had survived the trip, so whatever was in the wheel was all she had left. Henry had done better for himself: His shoulder holster was under his coat, and therefore his firearm and supplies had survived the trip more completely.

She doubted their guns would be of much use against the Maynard device, but they made her feel better all the same.

Another hour passed, and her feet were blocks of ice. Her nose had lost all feeling, and her injuries hurt terribly. Henry was flagged as well: His ordinarily fair complexion had gone positively white, his glasses were long gone, and when he wiped at his nose with one torn sleeve, it left a damp, bloody streak on the back of his arm.

And then they heard voices, accompanied by the crush and roll of large wheels on uneven turf. Not far ahead, there were people. Carts. Horses.

And then the dome of the big black cargo dirigible came into view.

Henry stopped and took her arm. "Let's leave the road. Come around to the side."

"You want to sneak up on them?"

"I want to watch them before we try to engage. We might learn something. Spot a weak point. If we walk up to them now, they'll shoot us before we get close."

She wasn't so sure, but she didn't fight him when he led her off the tracks that passed for a highway and back into the trees. They circled quietly around, staying just beyond the clearly visible road, until they were within earshot.

The caravan had stopped. Only a few minutes of eavesdropping told them why.

"God*damn* this road! How does anyone ever move anything?"

"There's not much left to move," someone said wryly, but not loudly. "The state's bankrupt—the whole *country*'s bankrupt. Hell, I'm just I'm glad there's any road at all. We could be stuck hacking our way through the woods, and then what?"

"Then we'd be stuck in this hellhole forever," griped someone close. "How are we going to get this thing going again? Frank said we can't push the crawler's motor any harder, or we'll blow it."

"Then we won't push the crawler's motor any harder," said a new voice—someone who spoke with a commanding bent.

Maria strained to see him, but between the trees she saw nothing but a flash of gray uniform and a shock of hair beneath a cap that looked like it might be red. "There's the man in charge," she guessed aloud to Henry, who nodded.

The man in charge said, "We'll have to dig ourselves out."

"You're sure the ship can't lift us?"

"You saw us try it. Did it work? No? Then *yes,* I'm sure the ship can't lift us. We can't burn through its hydrogen, anyway. Not if we want a way home, when all's said and done."

"Sir, we're . . . we're fish in a barrel if we stay in the middle of this road."

"Heavily armed fish in a military convoy. Pull yourself together, and get a shovel."

"Do we have shovels?"

"Check with the ship; they might have some. If not, we'll improvise. We have axes, and we have a whole forest full of wood we can commandeer if we have to. Bring me Lieutenant Engel, and I'll see what exactly we have at our disposal."

Henry leaned over and whispered into Maria's ear. "Maybe we'll get lucky and he'll wander away from the caravan. We may have to swipe him, but we'll make him listen to us."

"We're a pitiful pair of kidnappers, you and I."

"We're armed. We don't have to overpower him, just surprise him."

"Is that our plan?" she asked.

"It's a possibility. Should we split up?"

She thought about it and said, "We could, but let's not. We'd just double our chances of getting caught."

He nodded. "All right. Let's go together, then."

Forward they crept, staying low and working toward the giant rolling-crawler—a Texian-made monstrosity that operated on floating axles, and was renowned for its ability to traverse uneven terrain. Apparently it wasn't quite advanced enough for Georgia roads, which made Maria smile ruefully until she drew near enough to really look at the thing. It was huge—bigger than any such contraption she'd ever seen before, in the North or South. Six wheels on three axles, and about as tall as a single-story building, except for the back portion, which was open like a cart.

This segment was occupied by something huge and—if the set of the wheels in the road was any gauge—quite heavy. The rear half was bogged down, oversized tires lodged into fresh ruts that had been made all the deeper by their spinning, digging, lunging efforts to free the thing.

"Can you see it?" Henry asked, craning his neck.

"They've covered it up with something. We'll have to get closer, though it may be dangerous."

"We might . . . not have much choice," he said slowly, turning his head sharply but carefully to the right.

Maria followed his new gaze, and was horrified to see a gray-dressed soldier with a large army-issue rifle. The rifle was long-barreled with its hardware in gleaming condition, and it was aimed directly at them.

He said, "Hello there. I'd ask what we have here, except I can make myself a guess."

"It's not what it looks like," she promised him.

"It's not two people spying on a military caravan?" he asked with a smirk.

Maria instantly disliked him, not that there was anything she could do about it. "No, it's *not* that. Not exactly."

Henry stood up straight from his crouch, and said, "I'm a U.S. Marshal, and I'm here to help. I'm going to get my badge out of my coat, see? I'm not drawing a gun."

"U.S. Marshal my ass. Don't you dare move." Over his shoulder he shouted, "Hey, Captain, I've got something over here!"

"What?"

"A couple of spies; come and see 'em," he called. "One says he's a marshal."

"A marshal?"

Seconds later the captain appeared—and, yes, it was the red-haired man they'd identified before, in a well-fitting uniform, as opposed to those of his subordinates. He was handsome in a way that red-haired men tended not to be, in Maria's experience—though there was always an exception to the rule, and here he was. His eyes were cool, intelligent, and very blue.

Another gray-uniformed man appeared with him, and now they were outnumbered.

"Captain," Henry said, not bothering to address anyone anymore, except the man who made the decisions. "My name is Henry Epperson and I'm with the U.S. Marshals Service. I was sent here by the president himself, with regards to Project Maynard."

Maria gave him a bit of side-eye. She wasn't sure she would've played it so on the nose, but between the pair of them, he was the one most likely to be listened to, so she chose to trust him. It was too late to do anything else, anyway.

"The president?" The captain huffed a small, incredulous laugh. "If you've got word from President Grant, then why are you sneaking up on us, hiding in the woods? And furthermore, let me see your badge."

"It's here in my coat pocket," he said again, fumbling for it with his good hand, and finding it this time. He tossed it to the captain.

While the captain examined it, Maria answered the rest. "We're sneaking up on your caravan because the big cargo ship you're traveling with shot us down a few miles back down the road. You'll have to forgive us if we weren't fully committed to approaching you openly—not while that thing docks overhead."

"Shot you down?" he frowned, and glanced back toward the road. "So that's what all the commotion was about. We heard it, but couldn't see it for the trees." Over the trees they could all see the craft's dome, bobbing slowly in the dying wind. "Why would they shoot you down? Why would . . ."

The man obviously had more questions, but maybe he had answers, too—and he didn't like them much. He tossed the badge back to Henry, who caught it with a fast jab of his hand. "What about you?" he asked. "You're not a marshal, are you, ma'am?"

"No, sir, I'm not. I'm a Pinkerton agent, hired by Abraham Lincoln. This marshal and I have been working together with regards to this project you're transporting to Atlanta—and I do note that you didn't contradict us, or argue, when Henry called it by its proper name. You're Union soldiers, the lot of you. Blue wearing gray, undertaking a top secret mission to deploy a terrible weapon in Atlanta. You know it. We know it. And the president knows it, too. He's trying to stop it."

"Ma'am," he said, adjusting his hat and shifting his weight. He lowered his voice, but not much. "This project is as top secret as they come, or so we're told. If you're Confederate spies, you're not very good ones—traveling alone and naming names, when you ought to play dumb and ask for help. But your badge looks like the real thing," he said to Henry, "and if you say the president sent you, then that's either the stupidest tall tale you could pull out of your ear on a moment's notice, or it's the truth."

Maria wanted to breathe a sigh of relief, but she didn't dare, not yet. "Captain, we came here to warn you. The project is more dangerous than you know: It's a suicide mission for you and your men, authorized through unofficial channels, and paid for by a warhawk tycoon with the help of the Secretary of State."

The captain's lovely eyes narrowed, and he crossed his arms. "Is that so?"

"Who gave you your orders? And don't answer me—I'm asking you to ask *yourself*. Did it come from the top? Or from some underling who professed to speak with presidential authority?"

"The Secretary of State is hardly an underling, really."

Maria stood to her full height and brushed scraps of forest floor off her battered dress. "He's an underling to the *president,* who is scrambling, sir—absolutely *scrambling*—to put a stop to this project. And if I were to wager a guess, I'd say that his wasn't the name on your orders. The cargo craft that accompanies you— I saw through their window with a spyglass. They're Baldwin-Felts agents, hired by this warhawk tycoon."

"But acting with the authority of . . ." His voice trailed off as he pondered the implications. The captain's two juniors exchanged a worried glance, but their officer didn't take his eyes off Maria, who refused to blink or retreat. "So you two . . . you're the ones tasked with the mission of reaching us? And giving us this message?"

Henry responded, "There were half a dozen potential deployment locations, and no one could—or would—say exactly where the weapon was headed. Washington, D.C., is in disarray, Captain. At this time, it stands as divided as the nation. The president wants to bring the war to an end, but he's being hampered and hindered on all sides by those who would profit from it."

Again the captain looked up at the cargo dirigible, deliberating. "The men in that ship—they're Baldwins, you're right about that. They're supposed to be our supply and evacuation team."

"They're trusting you to civilians?" Maria asked.

To which he replied pointedly, "Last I heard, Pinkertons were civilians as well, ma'am, and you profess to work on behalf of the District yourself. And I don't believe I caught your name, but I know your accent isn't any farther north than the line."

"Maria." Then she swallowed hard and said, "Maria Boyd. I come from Virginia, but I work from Chicago."

If he recognized her name, he didn't react to it. All he said was, "All right, then, Miss Boyd and Mr. Epperson. You know an awful lot about what we're doing."

"More than you do," she said urgently. "Please, you have to listen to us, Captain . . . Captain, I don't believe I caught your name, either."

"MacGruder," he told her. "I'm commanding officer for this operation, such as it is," he added unhappily, gazing toward the trapped rolling-crawler.

"Captain MacGruder," she said, turning the name over in her mouth, feeling the letters tumble together and thinking that it sounded familiar—very familiar—but she couldn't put her finger on it. Finally, she gave up and asked, "Do you know what the weapon does?"

He hesitated. Maria thought that it must not be that he didn't know, but that he wasn't sure how much to tell her. "It's a bomb. An advanced bomb that will do . . . untold damage." He said it like he was confessing to himself. "But it's a bomb that can end the war, like the president wants—and that is my mission. These are my orders."

"No, sir, that *isn't* your mission, and your orders were falsified. That weapon is a bomb, yes, and it will do far worse than untold damage—but it won't end the war, you can safely bet on that. Katharine Haymes is readying herself to make a fortune on a gamble that this bomb works well enough to become the talk of the town, but not well enough to end a goddamn *thing*."

"Haymes?" The captain looked startled. "That's a name I know."

Henry said, "You ought to. She killed hundreds of Union prisoners at a camp in Tennessee."

"With gas," he said thoughtfully. "She did it with gas; I heard about that. I tried to tell people, but they didn't want to hear it. . . ."

"Hear what?" Maria asked. "Tell people what?"

He shook his head. "I told my superiors that I'd seen that kind of devastation before. I'd reported it once already . . . not that anyone listened then, either. What she did, that weapon she tested. . . . But, wait, I thought she was a Confederate?"

Maria shook her head. "No, she claims no nation. She belongs to whichever side can pay her best, and we both know that means she's working for the Union now. That thing you accompany, it's a gas bomb of such a size that it could wipe out half of Atlanta, including whoever's nearby when it's released. You'll never escape it. There won't be time."

"But, the cargo ship . . ." The soldier with the rifle asked the captain, "The ship'll pull us out, won't it?"

"How?" Maria demanded, addressing him once more, rather than the handsome captain. "That thing isn't big enough to hold the lot of you, and someone would have to stay behind and set the bomb off, anyway."

The captain argued with her, but without much conviction. "We're going to shoot it from the air. It's a big enough target. But . . . I've wondered." Then he muttered, like he couldn't shake the significance, "If it's . . . a gas bomb . . ."

"And one that doesn't just *kill* . . ." Henry continued.

"It's the walking plague." The captain said the words softly, almost under his breath. "It's a bomb that gives people . . . that turns them into the living dead. That's what this is, isn't it? The walking plague is created by a *weapon*."

"Well, yes and no," Henry said. He might've said more—asking how the captain had drawn such a conclusion, correct though it might well be—but at that moment Maria had a revelation.

Two thoughts had been bouncing around in her brain, ever since the captain had identified himself: his name, and where she might've heard it before. Those two ideas finally collided, crashing together so that the sparks illuminated the truth. She blurted out, "You're the Captain MacGruder from the nurse's notes!"

Everyone froze, mostly from confusion. The captain asked her, "I'm sorry, nurse? What nurse?"

"On the train," she continued excitedly. "The *Dreadnought*—you were on the *Dreadnought*! I read about it!"

He recoiled, stunned. "Read about it? Where on earth could you have read about it? No one's written about it except for me—and what I wrote went 'missing,' according to anyone I asked," he said angrily. "I tried to tell them! The walking plague doesn't just walk among soldiers, and it isn't confined to the front."

"But it *is* you," Maria persisted. "*You* were the Union captain the nurse trusted, who survived what happened in Utah. Just admit it!"

"The nurse," he muttered, flailing to find the context she prodded him for. "There . . . there *was* a nurse, yes. Mercy, that was her name. She . . . she wrote a book? She's alive? I tried to find her, but the ranger, the nurse, the Rebs who made it out alive . . . everyone's gone. Reassigned, they told me," he recounted bitterly. "Secret missions. Secrets everywhere, no one talking, no one listening. No one left. All of them, gone."

"And you'll be gone, too, if you finish this mission. We all will."

The forest whistled and shook, as the wind gave one last gasp through the trees, scattering what was left of the leaves and tweaking the brittle branches. No one spoke while they watched the captain reflect, consider, think, and finally . . . conclude.

He gave a good, hard glare at the cargo ship through the trees and said, "Get me Frankum. I need to speak with him. You two—Miss Boyd, Marshal—come with me. Graham, Simmons, keep an eye on them."

Maria began to protest. "But we're—"

"I'm not taking any chances."

So, at gunpoint, they followed the captain up the side of the hill, onto the road, and into the middle of the caravan—where they were greeted with stares and gossipy whispers.

The captain announced, "Gentlemen, we have guests: a U.S. marshal and a Pinkerton agent, pulled from the woods like foundlings. They were left there courtesy of Captain Frankum, or so they tell me. So, where is our fine, upstanding dirigible pilot, eh?"

Something about his pronunciation of "fine" and "upstanding" implied a keen sense of irony.

Maria and Henry kept close to each other, nearly back-to-back. No one had taken their firearms, which might be construed as a lack of caution on Captain MacGruder's part, except that they had nowhere to go, and they weren't likely to stage a gun-blazing escape in their battered state.

"You two, over here," one of their guards told them, gesturing with the barrel of his gun. He guided them to the big rolling-crawler, and suggested they should stand against it and wait for further instructions. "Captain? Where are you going?"

"I'll be back in a minute," he answered vaguely, and stomped off to the far edge of the convoy, where Maria could no longer see him.

She didn't like it, and Henry didn't, either, but they did as they were told. They put their backs to the thing and tried not to think about what was inside it, now only inches from their bodies. Maria fancied that she could hear a hum, some strained, coursing sound from within. She could feel it better than she could hear it, as the vibrations rattled at her ribs. It was almost as if the bomb were a living thing, with pulse and respiration and a sense of urgency—an awful destiny that it wanted to fulfill.

Maria banished her imagination's wanderings and closed her eyes, exhausted. She wanted to sit down, but she couldn't bring herself to do so, not while so much danger remained . . . and she didn't know what form it was likely to take, or even where it might come from.

But she was so, so tired. And so very sore. And she so very badly wanted to sleep.

Eventually, Captain Frankum appeared in their midst, joined by two of his fellow airmen. The captain himself was a short, sturdy man without an ounce of fat on him, but a squared-off appearance that indicated a great deal of muscle. He was no more handsome or friendly looking up close than he had been in the clouds, nor were either of his men.

Captain MacGruder also returned from whatever errand he'd wandered off to. His face was set in a firm expression, all business and ready for conflict—an effect that was slightly undone, in Maria's opinion, by the pink flush across his nose, brought on by the cold.

"Frankum, there you are. I've got a question for you," he said.

At approximately that precise moment, Frankum noticed the newcomers. At first, his eyes glanced past them, but he did flash a quick second look at Maria. It could've meant anything: He might have recognized her from the sky, or maybe he was only confused at seeing a woman there.

"Who are *they*?" the Baldwin-Felts man asked.

Captain MacGruder feigned innocence. "You don't know?"

"No, I don't."

"Then why'd you shoot them down a few hours ago?"

"Why did I . . . ?"

"You heard me," MacGruder said, coming in closer. He leaned forward, craning over the shorter man and casting a shadow over him. "Why did you shoot them down? What we have here, *Captain*"—spitting out the word like it tasted bad—"is a U.S. Marshal and another agent, sent as messengers from the White House."

Maria appreciated that he'd left out the "Pinkerton" part, given how little love was lost between the two firms. It meant he was thoughtful for her safety, perhaps; or it meant that he was smart, and didn't feel like adding the extra trouble to the mix.

"A marshal? Why would the president send a marshal?" Frankum tried to redirect the inquiry, but he didn't do it smoothly—and before the crisis could be forced any further, he gave up the pretense of innocence. "I didn't have any way of knowing who they were. Besides, you have your orders, I have mine. Mine say to keep all crafts away from this convoy, and I was doing my job."

"Mr. Epperson," Captain MacGruder said to Henry, but kept his eyes on Frankum. "Were you flying in a federal craft? Did you make any attempt to identify yourself?"

"A federal craft in Confederate airspace? *No,* for Christ's sake. And we weren't given the opportunity to identify ourselves; we were attacked without warning upon approach."

Frankum flashed a quick glance at the sky. Then, as if it had just occurred to him, he asked, "Wait a minute. Where's Kramer?"

"Kramer?" Henry echoed.

"Captain Kramer," Frankum said crossly. "He was following us out, in his little supply ship. He stayed behind us; he was supposed to . . ."

"To what?" Maria demanded. "Kill us? Shoot us down? I hate to disappoint you—or, rather, I don't mind it in the slightest: We survived that encounter somewhat more cleanly than we survived our dustup with your craft. The ashes of that other ship are, at present, raining down softly over Georgia." She added a fluttering motion with her numb, bruised fingers for emphasis.

"You took it down? In your little two-seater?"

"She's a mighty good shot." Henry was exaggerating, but Maria was pleased nonetheless.

"Look, look, *look.*" Frankum held out his hands, both attempting to defend himself and shush everyone else. "What I want to know is, how do we know these two came from the District? And why are you so fast to assume they're telling the truth? You're just going to let them waltz out of the woods and derail this operation? This *very expensive* operation, months in the planning? I don't guess they had anything with the presidential seal on them?"

Henry said, "No, but—"

"So we take their words for it? Blow the whole mission, on the word of two spies?"

"We aren't—"

But MacGruder interrupted, "No, I'm not willing to blow the whole mission. But I am willing to delay it a bit. I don't even have much choice, given that we still have to extract this damn thing from the road," he said, scowling at the rolling-crawler. "Texian technology . . . you'd think it could handle a Southern road. *Jesus.* Anyway, since we've got a minute, I just now put Bradley on a fast horse to Atlanta, to the taps there."

"But the taps are down, all over the place," the air captain argued.

"Yes, but if they're up again anywhere, they'll be up in the city. We'll just take a break and ask the president ourselves what he wants us to do."

"But, but, that'll take hours!" Frankum sputtered. "And you can't just send the president a note and wait for orders—you already *have* orders!"

"And I'm following them, until I hear differently," MacGruder said coolly. "But it'll take an hour or more to get this damn cart dug out, and once we're back on the road—well, at our pace we're lucky if it's another four hours to the city. Bradley ought to catch us before we reach it, and we can reevaluate the matter depending on what he says."

Frankum stayed calm, but his men were getting antsy. Maria watched them fidget and exchange nervous glances, though their captain's expression was a fierce threat to maintain their composure. The man to his left lost it first. He asked, "Hours?"

The word was small, but it was almost too frightened to be heard.

"Hours," MacGruder nodded.

"We don't *have* hours."

"Shut up," Frankum said to his man. Then, to MacGruder, "Hours aren't in the plan, and you know it."

"Plans change."

"You're stalling."

"I am *stalled*," Captain MacGruder declared. "And what does it matter if we reach Atlanta come sundown? The city will go to hell as easily at dusk as midday."

Frankum shook his head, and his eyes darted back and forth between his crewmen. "We were supposed to be there by now. We should've been halfway back to the Mason-Dixon by now."

"Plans change. We adapt. Without flexibility, we're all doomed to fail."

"*I'm* not," Frankum insisted. "And I have obligations elsewhere. I don't have to hover with you fools while you get your act together." He snapped his fingers, and pointed at the cargo craft. "You two, get back in the ship. We're taking off."

"No, you're not," MacGruder said, flatly.

"We need more hydrogen; we've burned off too much sitting around waiting for your men to fix this. If we don't go get more, we won't have enough to pick you up and get us all clear of the blast."

"You're not leaving this caravan until everybody leaves it."

Maria saw an opportunity to deepen the wedge between them, and she seized it. "That was never part of the plan," she blurted out. All eyes turned to her, so she said it again. "It was never part of the plan for *any* of you to survive the trip."

MacGruder came forward, until he stood directly in front of her. "Out in the woods you said this was a suicide mission for me and my men."

"That's right. That's one reason the president rejected the program."

"There were others?"

"Once he learned what the weapon really does, yes. President Grant doesn't want to create a legion of walking dead men any more than you do."

As she spoke, Frankum and his men began a slow retreat, designed to keep from attracting too much attention.

It didn't work. MacGruder's men stopped them with rifles primed, promising violence if anyone tried to leave the area. The captain himself whirled around on one heel, stomped up to Frankum, and seized him by the collar. He dragged the pilot off his feet, pulling him forward, and slamming him up against the nearest cart.

Frankum's eyes bugged out, darting frantically back and forth. He sought his men but found only MacGruder's face wearing a very big frown.

"Is she telling the truth? Were you supposed to leave us here?"

"You don't understand . . ."

"So *help* me understand. She's telling the truth—she *is,* or you wouldn't be writhing like a worm on a hook. You're caught; now be a man and tell us what we'd be in for if we followed the orders that so conveniently rely on you and your company."

Frankum rallied a nasty laugh, choked off by MacGruder's hand against his throat. "Inconvenient fools, the lot of you."

"We're inconvenient? So we die with the mission?"

"Why do you think there are so many of you?" he spit. "How many men do you think are required to move that damn crawler and haul the fuel to keep it rolling? Not the thirty you've got. It could be done with a dozen."

"So this is a death sentence? For being inconvenient?" MacGruder squeezed harder at Frankum's throat, twisting his fingers in the fabric of the man's coat collar. "I know that they want me silenced, and I know *why;* but the rest of these men are innocent."

"And expendable."

Henry, gone pale with pain but still standing, cleared his throat. "They're part of the weapon. That's it, isn't it? They're supposed to be the first wave of the walking plague after they loose the gas upon the city."

Frankum nodded, insofar as he was able.

Captain MacGruder asked, "But then why are *you* here? Why send the ship along? To make sure we finish the job? To watch us die?"

"To set off the weapon. But you know that!"

"And why else? Why *else,* goddammit!"

"To *observe,*" Frankum squeaked. "To observe and report, and make sure that you do your jobs without . . . any . . ." His face was turning red, but he forced out the last word anyway. "Interference!"

"From people like them?" MacGruder waved a hand toward Maria and Henry.

"From . . . anyone . . ."

The captain released his grip. Frankum's knees folded, and he dropped to the ground, feeling at his throat as if to make certain he was still in one piece. MacGruder stalked back toward his nearest lieutenant and said, "We're stopping here. We wait for Bradley to come back with word from Washington, and then we'll reevaluate. And those three"—he pointed balefully at the cargo ship's crew and captain—"are staying right here with us. Tie them up and throw them into the crawler. If they want to watch the bomb that badly, they can sit on top of it."

"No!" Frankum objected, loudly and suddenly. "No, you can't do that!"

"Why's that?"

"Because . . . because . . ." He swore under his breath, yanked off his hat, and threw it at the ground in a gesture of protest. "Because the damn thing won't hold much longer."

"It'll hold, so long as no one blasts it from the air. None of our crew has anything big enough to set it off. We'll need your ship's turret gun for that."

"No, no, you won't. We're here with our ship to shoot the thing and set it off—that's true; I swear it's true," he said, hands aloft again, protesting innocence. "But we're running so late, and there's the failsafe built in . . ."

"Failsafe?"

He cleared his throat. "An accidental failsafe, really. The bomb is too hard to control—it isn't stable. Once it's set and armed, it has half a day before the gas corrodes the interior components." He was speaking quickly now. "Half a day, while the gas eats the metal like acid. If we don't detonate it as planned, it'll go off on its own."

"Half a day?"

"We haven't got another two hours to wait for your messenger," Frankum insisted. "We may not have *one*. If you want to follow orders, Captain MacGruder," he said, trying to keep a sour note out of his voice, and only succeeding because he sounded so afraid, "there's still time to get Maynard to . . . to the edge of Atlanta. The gas will settle, spread, and roam anyway; precision in this regard was never very important."

"Oh, God," the captain said, though how he meant it, Maria wasn't certain.

"Follow your orders. Finish the mission, and, and, and we'll fit all of you into our craft somehow. We'll get all of you out of here safe and sound, I swear it on my mother's grave. We can take you out of the blast range—which isn't far: the gas does the damage, not the detonation, and the gas is heavy. It'll stay low, and we'll go high. Just . . . you can't keep us *here*. None of us can stay here much longer, that's what I'm saying. And that's the truth— that's the God's honest truth, and I swear it."

MacGruder returned his attention to Maria and Henry—who

by now had slid down into a seated position. He'd recovered a little of his coloring, but still looked weak. "Do either of you know how far this gas can travel? How much space it can cover?"

Maria put her hand on Henry's shoulder. "No one knows. It'll roam like a cloud, killing everything it touches until it dissipates."

The captain looked mad enough to chew nails and spit tacks. But he couldn't afford to lose his temper in front of his men, not at a moment like this, when the nervous chatter was whispering its way to a crescendo of frightened soldiers, the rumor fleeing back and forth along the caravan to anyone who wasn't present to witness the exchange.

"All right," he said, his teeth grinding against the words. "Apparently we don't have time to fulfill our mission objective; we'll never make the air base in Atlanta with this cargo, not now. These guys," he said, with regards to Frankum and his crew, "aren't going anywhere without us. And *we're* not going anywhere without *them*. Evans," he said to a uniformed soldier standing by. "Get me that map from the front car. We've got to find someplace to dump this. Sanders—" He signaled someone else. "As per my original request, I want these three tied up and stuck in the crawler with the bomb."

"But Captain—"

"Not another word out of you. We don't have time to wait for Bradley, which means we're acting on faith. Now, the rest of you—in teams, as we talked about before—start digging. We need those wheels free in less time than it'd take you piss by the road, or else we're all dead men." He turned to Maria and Henry, then gave Henry a second, appraising gaze. "He's not looking so well. We don't have a doctor, but we can put him in a cart so he can rest."

Maria looked down at Henry, who indeed seemed on the very verge of fainting. "Henry, I think you'd better let them help you," she said wearily.

"No, I'm fine."

"No, you're not. Here, someone get him up," she pleaded, and MacGruder nodded toward one of his fellows. As Henry was lifted up and assisted to someplace more comfortable, Maria turned to the captain and said, "You're doing the right thing."

"At present, I'm only making a go of it."

"Do you have a plan?"

"No." Evans returned with a map roll. MacGruder took it and stretched it out across the back of a crate they'd pulled down off the crawler, hoping to lighten the load. He weighed down the paper with a rock on one side, and his fist on the other. It was a detailed production, with known farms, small towns, and topographical features all marked out. With his free hand, the captain traced out the particulars as he spoke. "We're right about *here,*" he told her—and Evans, too, who lingered at his side. "Still a good forty miles from Atlanta, but there are a few little towns between here and there. And behind us, too."

"What about . . . what about a lake?" Evans asked, pointing down at a wide, oval-shaped spot to the east. "We could drag it out to a lake, and toss it inside. Maybe the water would, I don't know . . . hold down the worst of the gas?"

The captain shook his head. "Not a bad idea, but that's six miles out, seven maybe. Through the trees, with no road to take us there."

"Not a lake, then . . ." Maria scanned the sheet, helping hold the corner near the captain's fist and accidentally leaving a smudge of blood on it. Her hands ached terribly, but what could she do? "What's this right here? Is that what it looks like? A cave?"

"A cave . . . yes, I think so. And it's close."

"Then let's pray it's deep, too. If so, then, captain . . . we may have our answer!"

He double-checked the location and let go of the map. Maria let go, too, and it curled shut around the rock. To Evans, the captain said, "Take the fastest horse we have left and go back to that little town a mile or two behind us. It was just a wide spot in the road, but they had a store."

"What am I getting, sir?"

"Dynamite. As much as they'll sell you."

"I don't have any money, sir."

"Then run up into the cargo ship and take whatever money you find. I doubt the Baldwin-Felts boys travel without any cash."

"Yes, sir," he said, and he was off.

MacGruder returned his attention to the crawler, which now had the three agents perched atop it, looking none too happy. "How's the digging?"

Without looking up, a soldier answered, "Another five minutes. Someone get inside and start the thing, would you?"

"Thomson, that's you. Crank it up. Davis, get me four or five crate lids. Pry them off and bring them over here. We're going to stick them under the wheels for traction." Then, to Maria, he said, "It's the cave or nothing at this point. We'll toss it down as far as it'll fall, and blow the top to keep it covered. I don't know if it'll hold all the gas," he confessed to her, more quietly than he'd said the rest. "But it'll buy us time, if nothing else."

She put a hand on his arm. "That'll do. When the war's over, the president can send the army engineers to take a look at it."

The great rolling-crawler rumbled to life behind them. Up in the cabin, Thomson wrestled with the gears, working the engine back and forth between first gear and reverse, trying to rock the thing free. On the sixth try it scooted. Its wheels caught on the crate lids and ground them to splinters . . . but under Thomson's expert handling, it skidded to the left a few feet, spewing smoke and chips of wood from the crate lids as it hauled itself up, out, and onto the road once more.

The men cheered, and the machine jerked to a stop once it

was clear. The road ahead was full of ruts, but the first hurdle was mastered, and it was time to proceed.

Over the engine, the captain shouted, "Move! Move everything—the carts, the horses, the other cars, everything! Get them out of the way; leave 'em on the side of the road if you have to. Now! This is all we're taking!" he announced.

"Captain!" Frankum cried. "I can feel it moving underneath us; it's going to blow! You have to get us down! Let us run so we have a fair chance!"

"Like the one you were going to give us? Forget it," he told them. "That's just the engine you feel. The bomb is fine for now."

"I can hear it," he insisted. "A hissing noise . . . a *hissing*. . . ."

"Shut your mouth, Frankum, or I'll shut it for you. Cross your fingers and say your prayers, and maybe you'll survive long enough for a court-martial. Thomson, Sanders, you're with me. Davis, when Evans gets back, tell him where we've gone," he said, then detailed the cave's location—not far down the road. "We'll turn off and try to work this damn thing between the trees—we'll knock a few down if we have to, and we *might*. The cave is only a few hundred yards off the road, if I read the map correctly."

"Don't forget about me," Maria said.

"Ma'am?"

"*Me.* I'm coming with you."

"There's room behind the driver. Get in."

She climbed on board, and as the crawler lurched forward—struggling with the road, but winning, this time—they passed the cart where Henry was resting. He waved as she went, his good hand offering a weak salute. She waved back, swallowing the lump in her throat and wondered if he'd make it back across the line. She didn't know how badly he was hurt. There might have been more wrong than she could see.

She put a hand to her torso, where the puncture wound had stopped bleeding, but was hurting fiercely all the same. It was one of the only places on her body where she was warm enough to feel anything at all.

Maria watched Frankum and his men over her shoulder as they bounced, slid, and finally rolled down to the cart's bottom. When they disappeared, she first thought they'd been thrown— but no, they were wedged firmly in place between the bomb and the rails that kept it on the cart.

She smiled.

MacGruder gave her a look that asked her what was worth smiling over. She pointed down into the cart to indicate that their foes weren't going anywhere. "Maybe we should toss them in with the bomb," he suggested.

"Maybe, but your court-martial idea was probably better. Our side isn't ruled by pirates or scoundrels, Captain. You have to play fair. On the bright side, maybe one of them will make a run for it, and you can shoot him."

Now he smiled back. "A man can dream."

The crawler heaved and hauled them up over the road's raggedy bits with a motion like a ship in terrible seas. Maria found it worse than flying, even in the stormy air they'd navigated thus far that day; but she clutched her seat and—as they traversed one particularly bad pothole—the captain who sat beside her.

"There!" he called out. At first Maria thought it was a strange reaction to being grabbed by a woman, but that wasn't his point at all. He was looking off to the right, where a dirt road passed between the trees.

The crawler shuddered to an idling stop. Thomson asked over his shoulder, "Sir, you think this is it?"

"It's about right, so far as the map goes. If it doesn't take us right to the spot, it'll get us close, and there will be fewer trees to mow down. Just take the turn, if we can make it."

"Oh, I can make the turn. I'm just not sure we can make that *road*. It's barely big enough for a pair of horses."

"Try it and see. We're out of plans, and we're running out of time," he said.

He was right, and Maria knew it. The Baldwin-Felts men might have been hysterical, but that didn't mean they were wrong. She could hear it, too, behind her: a different frequency of hum—an off-beat vibration that drummed up against her spine. The bomb's integrity was failing. The jostle of the rolling-crawler couldn't be helping matters, and it only grew worse when the vehicle turned right in a slow, perilous arc, then began its passage between the trees on a road even worse than the one it was leaving.

Maria thought it wasn't possible for the ride to get any rougher, but she'd been wrong before, and here was another fine example.

"Get your head down!" MacGruder ordered her—and perhaps the rest of the men, though she took it personally.

He was right to make the command, as the trees at the road's edge had sharp, low branches. Their limbs were bare and cold, and they whipped viciously against the crawler and its occupants. Maria huddled down low, ducking as far as she could behind Thomson, who valiantly held the thing steady and forced it forward, ever forward, in the lowest gear imaginable.

"Can't this thing go any faster?" Sanders shouted.

"It can barely go *this* fast!" Thomson replied, jerking the steering wheel as it reeled against him, the wheels having snapped against some dip that threatened to trap them. "But if we stop, we're damned! We'll never get it moving again!"

So they fought onward, their bones rattling with every turn of the wheels. With each foot the weapon behind them grew a little weaker, a little louder. A little harder to ignore.

"That must be it!" Thomson hollered, pointing at a pair of structures no bigger than shacks. He drew the crawler up close beside them, and let the motor rumble.

One of the shacks was barely a roof on timbers, a covering for a hole in the ground. The structure beside it had a sign out front that said, CUMBERLAND CAVERNS! ONE CENT PER PERSON! SEE THE WONDER! AT YOUR OWN RISK! SUPPLIES AVAILABLE!

"Someone's selling visits to the cave?" MacGruder wondered aloud.

"It's not uncommon," Maria informed him. "But it's deserted now," she said aloud, to herself more than anyone else. "It *must* be."

"Thomson, get the back of this thing as close to that hole as you can manage!"

"Yes, sir! You get out and guide me. I'll do my best!" he vowed.

MacGruder flung himself over the side and went to the rear, hollering instructions and giving whatever guidance he could—and finally the crawler was positioned with its back deck beneath the overhang, almost immediately above the open hole below.

"That's as close as you're going to get!" the captain called, and made a throat-cutting gesture that told Thomson to stop the motor.

When he did, the crawler fell silent, except for the pops and pings of the engine cooling almost immediately in the bitter air. But the forest wasn't perfectly quiet, even without its raucous growling. The crisp afternoon was interrupted by the slow hiss, sizzle, and creak of the Maynard bomb shifting in its housing.

"Captain . . ." begged Frankum. "You have to let us go!"

"And I *will*," MacGruder told them. He reached into his boot and pulled out a knife, then leaned into the compartment and cut the ropes that bound Frankum and his men. "Get out now. You're going to help us shove *this* goddamn thing into *that* goddamn hole."

The Baldwin-Felts men agreed to this immediately. They might as well. There was no time to run.

They climbed out of the rear and rubbed at the sore spots on their wrists as Sanders untied the ropes that held the tarp over the awful device.

When he was finished with the knots, he whipped the sheet

away, revealing the monstrous creation: a smooth, elongated box with round edges, banded with steel and rivets. Its nose was fixed with gleaming copper plate, and in its tail lurked a vast tangle of tubes, coils, and wires. Three tanks were mounted atop it, side by side like pig iron from the smelter. These tanks were the source of the hissing, the creaking, and other ominous sounds of something tight beginning to split under pressure.

It horrified Maria to her very core. This object could kill millions, if the weather was right. A terrific device, indeed, intimidating on the outside, even without ever releasing its deadly power. But compared to what it was capable of . . . it looked deceptively small. Nothing that could fit on the back of a crawler should be able to wipe out a city.

Frankum also stood staring, without speaking, until he said what Maria was already wondering. "I don't know if we can lift it, Captain—just us men, and *her*," he said. "We haven't the strength between us, not even if we had a team of horses!"

"You idiot, the back of this thing is on a hydraulic lift. It was built to carry and dump construction supplies," the captain said. He gave Thomson a signal, and a different motor kicked to life— something quieter and smoother, but still wildly loud in the otherwise silent woods. With painful slowness, the back compartment rose, tilting the bomb by tiny, incremental degrees. "We won't have to pick it up and carry it; we'll just have to climb in and give it a push, until it starts to roll."

As predicted, the crawler's bed wouldn't go high enough to let the bomb drop of its own accord, so all the men climbed in behind it. Maria stayed on the ground at their insistence—partly for all the usual thickheaded reasons, she was sure; but partly because space was limited, and there was only room for the strongest bodies.

The men braced themselves and pressed their feet against the bomb, and while Maria crossed her fingers and prayed, they shoved with all their might, rocking the big device back and forth like Thomson had rocked the crawler itself to get it moving.

They strained, swore, sweated, and pushed. The grade of the crawler's bed was so steep that Maria tried not to worry about what would happen if they just toppled right in after it.

Finally, Maynard wiggled.

It creaked back and forth, just moving by inches at first. Hardly noticeable at all. Then it rocked. Then it rolled, tumbled, dropped.

And fell.

Right into the cave, careening with the weight of a city's dead, crashing through the earth and settling down somewhere below, farther than any of them could see when they scrambled after it to stare into the hole.

"Where is it?" Frankum asked, leaning over so far that Maria was tempted, for one nasty second, to give him a shove. The pirate soul she harbored within her corset objected to her decency, but now was not the time or the place. Like she'd told the captain, they had to play fair. After all, they were not alone. Soon, the world would be watching. And someone had to save it.

The captain said, "No idea. Too dark. Anyone have a light?"

"Just the lantern on the crawler, and I can't pry that off without my tools," Thomson told them.

Echoing up from below, the sound of failing machinery grew louder as it bounced and rose off the rocks.

Behind them they heard the telltale clomp and clatter of a horse's hooves. Maria guessed that it was Evans with the dynamite, and it was indeed him, carrying a promising pack on his back.

"Hurry up with that!" the captain yelled, and Evans did his level best.

He yanked the horse to a sliding stop and dropped off the saddle to his feet, tossing the pack to the captain. "Wire it up, sir! I've got the line and pump in the saddlebags."

The captain went to work immediately, with Frankum lending a useful hand—for once in his life, Maria added disparagingly in her head. But it was his life, too; his, and theirs, and everyone else's. So he planted the sticks, threaded the wire, and ran with the rest of them back to the far side of the crawler—where Evans had already secured the horse, as far from the trouble as he could put the poor animal.

The captain paused while he checked the settings and connections on the pump, then set it on the ground.

Evans turned his nose to the air. "Sir . . . do you smell that?"

He did. He must be able to—Maria could smell it, even though her nose was so cold she couldn't feel it when she wiped it with the back of her scraped-up hands.

It was a toxic smell: rotten eggs and ruin, sharp death and troubled sleep. It stank of chemicals and poison, and it grew stronger while they sat there, mulling it over and wondering what could possibly smell that way?

The captain shook it off first, that numbing, stupefying creep of confusion and curiosity.

He shoved the plunger. A jolt went down the wire, along the ground, and into the hole.

And the earth exploded.

Twenty-one

The night ticked by in seconds, in minutes. In bullets, fired *one-two-three* from the woods and answered *one-two-three* from inside the house. It was not a stalemate, not exactly. From a second-floor window—the window almost directly above Abraham Lincoln in his library—Gideon watched the other men amass, and he knew that this relative peace could not hope to last the night. More men had joined the siege crew outside, and now they numbered fifteen by the scientist's count . . . though, given the gloom outside, it was always possible that he'd missed a couple.

He always built some wiggle room into all his assessments and plans—not because he didn't value precision, but because the universe was sometimes imprecise, and prone to hiding things.

He released the edge of the curtain and retreated to the hallway, pausing to duck into the Lincolns' bedroom and peer out through the window beside a tall wardrobe. Outside it was nearly as dark as inside. He thought he saw motion, maybe a flash of a man running quickly from cover to cover, or maybe only a shift of moonlight on something smaller below. The night was full of raccoons and rabbits, after all.

Knowing this did not prevent him from assuming the worst.

Leaving the window, he carefully walked back to the hallway, where there was almost no light to give him guidance. He worked from memory, from the map in his head of a house he'd visited dozens of times before, though he'd rarely seen these private chambers upstairs, where the aging couple spent their quieter days.

At the end of the hall was an oversized dumbwaiter—or that's what Gideon had jokingly called the thing when he and Wellers had installed it together last June. It was a closet with a floor built on a lift, an elevator large enough to hold Lincoln and his chair, and perhaps one other person. The structure of the house would permit nothing larger, unless Mary could have been persuaded to give up part of the kitchen pantry. And as it turned out, she could *not.*

The last room on the left before the elevator was the guest room. Gideon peered through the narrow slit in the curtains, but saw nothing he didn't already know. Men in the woods. Shadowed figures, distinguished mostly by their movement—and occasionally by a glimmer of brass buttons, the hardware on a gun, or the glint of a spyglass lens.

The hints of spyglass worried him.

He could not tell if the glass was only for observation, or if it was affixed to the barrel of a weapon. Gideon fervently hoped that none of the new recruits were sharpshooters, but he couldn't count on it; he couldn't count on *anything,* not tonight. So he remained wary of any seams in the cloak of darkness they'd forced upon the house. He'd turned off all the gaslights and electric lights, and forbidden any torches—electric or otherwise. Any light within would tell the men without where they were, and offer up a target. It might be a vague target, but it'd be a direction in which to shoot.

Two more rooms to check—and then he was done, and the second story was clear. Back down the stairs he traveled, announcing himself with incautious footsteps, and then calling softly, "Mr. Grant? The upstairs is as tight as I can make it."

"Good," came the reply by the front door. But it sounded distracted.

Gideon kept his back to the wall until he reached the president;

then he slid down into a sitting position beside him. "They're collecting more men."

"I know. And we're not."

"They know."

"It's only a matter of time, now," Grant said, low and quiet, "until they come inside."

"We can hold them off a while longer, put on a show for another hour or two."

Grant nodded, scratching his salt-and-pepper beard. "I don't suppose that big brain of yours has come up with any plans, has it?"

Only stalling tactics, but he offered them anyway. "We need to spread out. Put Polly and Mary upstairs, at opposite ends. Let them play sharpshooter, or at least make a lot of noise. By sound alone it's hard to tell a couple of shooters from half a dozen or more. With them taking the second story and us on the first, we can mount a satisfactory defense that may look like a much better one. And, besides, it gets the women upstairs, where they'll be marginally safer."

"Any thoughts how we might send a message?"

"A few. None of them good. We can't spare a runner right now, and even if we could, we'd be sending someone on a suicide mission . . . which is why you wouldn't let Polly go in the first place," he said, giving a voice to something he'd suspected. Grant didn't contradict him, so he continued. "Wellers is willing to make a dash for it, but he'd never make it. Mary would have the best chance; she's a little old lady, and a well-known one at that . . . but I don't suppose that's on the table."

"No, it isn't," Grant said fast. Then, after a pause, "She'd do it if we asked her, though. We'll work around it."

"The cellar is a fortifiable position of a kind, but it's a dangerous one. Only two ways in or out, but, once in, we'd never be able to mount any kind of response. It should be considered, but only as a last option. Not least of all because we'd have to carry Mr. Lincoln down those steps."

"Doesn't he have an elevator?"

"Yes, but it only goes between the first and second floors. Structural issues prevented us from sending it any lower or higher."

"Higher?" Grant's eyebrow lifted.

"There's an attic, but it won't be of any use to us. Just another place to get ourselves stuck. And the cellar is more defensible. I think."

"I think you're right." He sighed. "It's a damn shame we don't have that machine of yours here and handy, isn't it? We could just ask it what to do, and it'd tell us."

"That's not how it works."

"No?"

Since the president seemed genuinely curious, Gideon told him, in brief. "The Fiddlehead collects information, and sorts out the possible results into levels of probability. It can tell you what's likely to occur, but if you prefer a different outcome, it's your responsibility to find another path."

"Ah. Sounds complicated."

"Of course it's complicated. If it wasn't, you'd already have one in every parlor. But," Gideon added more warmly, afraid he'd been too cold, which wasn't called for, "it's a useful kind of complicated. Just not useful to us, personally, right now."

Outside, they heard men scrambling back and forth, their boots scraping the gravel or whispering through the grass. The wind that had hidden their movements before had all but died, and now the night was a quiet place, and the Lincoln house was listening.

Grant shifted his shoulders and scooted over to the other window, keeping his back to the door and his head below window level. "I think they need another good warning, don't you?"

Gideon checked his gun. It was fully loaded. "I've got enough bullets to say something loud."

"Good. On the count of three . . ."

They fired together, not in perfect time, and with less than perfect aim . . . but the scuttling noises of men coming closer retreated into a scramble of running and ducking as they went back toward the trees. Then, from the east wing, Nelson Wellers fired off a rapid series of four shots, one after the other, so fast that they must've been aimed at something.

Gideon stiffened and his knees locked, then he dropped down to the floor and retreated toward the stairs on hands and knees.

Two more shots, and then Nelson either had to reload or grab another gun. He'd taken a second gun—they all had—and now he was using that one, too; Gideon could hear its deafening patter from the other side of the house. It wasn't the sound of a man giving a warning, it was the violent bass of self-defense.

"Gideon!" Grant called with a sharp, quiet bark that penetrated the distance between them, but not by much.

Gideon paused long enough to look back at Grant, crouched beneath the window with one foot propped on the fallen clock and both hands holding his gun in a ready position: a general turned king, not done fighting even though he'd been told he didn't need to worry about guarding the castle he'd been given. A thin wash of watery light from the dying fireplace painted him gold and threw a smattering of shadows across his craggy face. He looked older than his years.

But not finished yet.

A louder blast rocked against the door, something harder and bigger than a handgun—something more like a shotgun, Gideon thought wildly. The door shuddered, and the clock that barred it rocked but did not fall. Then a second blast much like the first took out the window in the trestle above Grant's head. He ducked away from the falling glass as the blanket swung out—then settled again, full of holes.

"Buckshot, that's all it is!" the president said, waving Gideon away. "A big gun, though—sounds like a punt gun. Don't worry, I've got it. Go on, help Wellers. I'll take care of this!"

A third blast hit the door again, shattering the lock and shaking the whole portal as Grant slipped past it to the other window. From there, he peered through the edge of the curtain, and carefully— even slowly, thanks to the distraction—took aim and fired.

A loud grunt and a moan, and then the clamor of something heavy being dropped. Close. Very close. Closer than they'd realized. But Gideon knew about punt guns, and he knew you had to be close to make one count.

"Go!" Grant said again, and this time the scientist didn't argue.

He stood when he reached the hall and was safe from wandering bullets, only to run smack into Mary. He grabbed her by the shoulders, and before she could speak, he said, "Upstairs with you! I'll send Polly, too, and both of you should run from window to window, and fire at anything that moves. Don't let yourself be seen, understand?"

"Dr. Bardsley?" Polly squeaked from behind him.

"Did you hear that?" he asked.

"Yes . . ."

"Then *go,* both of you. Get up there and stay there, and don't come down until we give the all clear. Run!"

He released Mary's shoulders and tried not to worry at how frail they felt beneath his fingers, and how small a woman she really was.

Down the other hall he ran—away from Lincoln, which he didn't like, but he couldn't be everywhere at once. For now, no one was shooting down the corridor they were in, so he'd have to pick and choose.

Wellers was reloading. He *had* to be, for the inside defense had fallen silent. And, yes: As Gideon flung himself down beside his friend, he saw through the window's shattered edge that men were approaching.

"Gideon! For God's sake . . ." Wellers voice trailed off as his attention returned to his ammunition.

The interlopers wore scarves over their faces like ordinary burglars or bandits. For some reason the mundanity of it all offended Gideon. You'd think people would have the good grace to dress up for an assassination.

One man was nearly to the bushes. The fluffy things were half naked, courtesy of November, but they kept the house from being wholly open to the elements. Gideon flung the blanket aside and took aim, faster than Grant did, because he had less time: The man was right on him, close enough that he could see the fellow's breath puffing out around his face in a foggy aura.

He fired, and caught the man square in the chest.

Even Mary couldn't have missed him, he had come so near. Another man behind him swerved to avoid his compatriot's body and began a sideways retreat, or revisal of strategy—but Wellers was on his feet now, and he fired, too.

Gideon couldn't see what he hit, but the second man went down, and both the scientist and the doctor dropped back to cover. Now it was Wellers's turn to shoot while Gideon reloaded everything he had. When he was done, he covered his friend so he could do the same. It was a brutal give-and-take, a frantic cooperation that had to work for them both to stay alive.

"You good?" Gideon asked.

"Good as I'm going to get. You hear that?"

Yes, he heard shots from the front of the house, and from the far end behind him as well. "Lincoln," he murmured. "Stay here. I've got him."

"You're not the one being paid to protect him," Wellers objected, climbing to his feet and hugging the wall to make himself as small a target as possible.

Another loud blast, similar to the one at the front door, shattered the window and blew the curtains halfway across the room.

"More buckshot," Gideon griped, which once again meant that someone was close.

Wellers whipped his gun hand around to squeeze off three fast shots, two of which hit home.

He ducked back as fire was returned, but Gideon leaned out and shot again—mostly wanting to see what had happened. Yes, there was a dead man on the lawn right before the protective hedge. Yes, a shotgun with a snubbed, sawed-short nose was lying in the grass beside him, its hardware shimmering in the moonlight. The new mercenaries were better armed, or differently armed; it all depended on how you looked at it.

In the trees, something moved. Two somethings.

"Gideon, stay here—I *have* to reach Lincoln."

"Fine."

Gideon took out his frustration on the two men nearest, right as they stepped out of the woods. Faces covered. One with a handgun, one with another big fowling gun—a punt gun, Grant had called it, and Gideon had heard them called shotguns by cavalrymen. Whatever they were called, he knew they were a deadly mix of imprecision and power—bad enough at a distance, and terrifying at any nearer range.

Wellers retreated in a crouched position. His shoes slid on the wood floor until they found the rug in the hall, and then he dashed.

Gideon returned his attention to the window and saw . . . nothing this time.

Nothing and no one, except the dead man on the ground . . . and, over there, another dead man. He heard footsteps running around the side of the house, someone retreating, or falling back to regroup. Someone making a run for another location, where the pickings were easier.

"Goddammit!"

He leaped to his feet and ran to the hall, shutting the door behind himself and locking it. For all that it wouldn't stop a shot-gun or a determined enough kick, the noise would give them a bit more warning.

From upstairs, the ladies fired madly, wildly—too fast, Gideon thought. They'd burn through their ammunition too quickly at this rate. But there was nothing he could say to them now, noth-ing he could do to instruct or steady them; so he just listened to the violent bursts from the windows above him, and the sound of Polly's fast little feet running from room to room, window to win-dow, between exchanges.

Next, he ran for Lincoln's room.

Past the front door, and past Grant, who was using the door for cover—standing now, rather than sitting behind the window sills—and aiming with a measured, frightening accuracy. Wasting no bullets. Giving as good as he was getting, and he was getting it pretty good.

Gideon jumped as a vase on a table behind him shattered.

He dived back into the hall, leaving the president to his defen-sive measures, and kept scrambling over to the library, where Lin-coln had had just about enough of this. The old man wheeled out into the hall, his chair humming warmly, its wheels grinding against the expensive rugs like they meant business. The revolver in his hand underscored the threat nicely.

Gideon heard a crash from upstairs—or was it downstairs? Or behind him? There were too many explosions, too many things breaking at once for him to sort them all out.

Lincoln shouted, "Gideon!," and raised his handgun.

In return, Gideon cried, "Mr. Lincoln!," and raised his own.

They fired simultaneously, Gideon's shot taking down a man at the end of the hall—a man on the verge of running for the elderly leader. Lincoln's shot singed Gideon's ear like a firebrand, and as Gideon toppled to the side, ducking any further fire that might come, he saw a man reeling backwards behind him, stunned and bleeding.

Lincoln fired again, and the man went down.

"Sir!" Gideon ran to Lincoln's side. "We have to get you out of here."

"Where will we go? They're outside, aren't they? No—we defend *this* place. If I'm to have a last stand, let it be here!"

"No! No talk of last stands!" Gideon shouted at him, then dropped his voice. "We will live through this. *All of us.* And we will stop the war, and we will save the world." He grabbed the mechanical chair and tried to force Lincoln back into the library . . . but another man appeared in the hall, and Gideon swore like the sailor he'd never been. One of the big crashes must've been a breach in the study. Those sons of bitches. There was a hole in the fort, *goddammit.*

"Get this bastard out of the way!" Lincoln roared. Gideon was startled to hear his voice so strong, as he was so often softer spoken. But now he shouted, gesturing down at the man he'd shot. "Move him! Let me through!"

"Yes, sir." Gideon shook his head, but he bent down and grabbed the corpse under its arms. He dragged it to the foyer and tossed it in, freeing the hallway for Lincoln to pass, then barreled forward before he realized there was another armed man in front of him. Lincoln guided the chair away from the newcomer as Gideon opened fire. The man jerked aside, seeking cover, but finding none. He fell to the scientist's next round.

Upstairs Polly screamed, and it was like an ice pick to Gideon's soul.

"Help her!" Lincoln called without looking back. "Help the women upstairs, for the love of God!"

Upstairs, indeed—for, yes, it'd been his idea to put the women up there, and now Polly was screaming. He found the steps by the lingering firelight and tripped up them—he'd climbed them a thousand times, but the light was so dim and he was so hurried. Someone was still shooting up there, and his money was on Mary. He banged his knee on the top step, but that was fine, he needed to stay low anyway; so he used it as an excuse to fall down to all fours, then proceed in a low, awkward crouch toward Polly. Where was she? West wing, yes. He followed the sound of her voice until he could see her silhouetted in the hall light.

She wasn't alone. A man held her . . . from behind? From her side? It was hard to say—she was fighting him like the devil, wrestling this way and that, until both their shapes were one great knot of shadow. Gideon wasn't sure who was who, so he certainly couldn't shoot.

He shoved his gun into his coat pocket.

He ran forward and seized the pair of them, wrenching them apart and taking the man by his shirt, then flinging him against a wall where he smashed a great crack in the plaster. The man lunged back, but he launched straight into Gideon's fist, which caught him square in the stomach. He doubled over, catching the scientist's knee in his face as he did so. As he staggered backwards, he found no retreat except the wall. As he reached up seeking to steady himself, the man found an oil lamp, turned down to nothing but still full of fuel. He grabbed at it, slipping when the glass shattered, but eventually got hold and pulled himself back to his feet. He must've been bleeding from the glass, but Gideon couldn't see it. He saw nothing except for the fellow trying to step backwards, and a brighter shade behind him—someone wearing lighter clothing. Someone who swung an enormous stick and caught the intruder on the back of the head.

"Polly!"

"Got it from the broom closet," she panted and pointed. The man had fallen to his knees, on the ground in the oil and glass, so she hit him again. He went down and stayed down, sprawled out between the scientist and the maid.

"Give me your hand," Gideon commanded. She did, but she held on to the broom as she jumped over the unconscious figure on the floor. "Where's the attic? There must be a door in the ceiling; where is it?"

"Here," she said, leading him along the hallway, picking a spot, then changing her mind and going back a little farther. "I'm sorry, sir, it's over here. It's so hard to see, I can barely tell at all."

He held up his hand, feeling around for the rope pull that would bring the door down. It fluttered against his fingers. He missed it, tried again, missed once more. Finally, he caught it and gave it a yank, and a set of rolling stairs rumbled down. He caught them with his shoulder so he could lower them more quietly than was their wont. "Get up there," he ordered her. "This is getting out of hand. Just *go*. I'll get Mary."

"But, Gideon—"

"Do as I say!"

He left her, not knowing whether she'd obey or not, but knowing that Mary was not shooting anymore; she was shouting instead. He found her in the back bedroom, leaning out the window and shoving hard, then cackling like a witch as someone beyond hollered and fell heavily.

"Mrs. Lincoln!"

"Ladders!" she responded. "The bastards got themselves some ladders!"

"Didn't think they'd manage that so fast," he said under his breath, then went to her side. "You're out of ammunition?"

She nodded, and the silver in her hair caught what little light came from the sky. "Fresh out. But *they're* running out of *men*," she said optimistically.

He drew her back from the window. "You have to get up to

the attic now," he said. "Polly's already there; she'll pull the stairs up behind you."

"What about Abe?"

"He's down there with Grant and Wellers. They're watching him. The mercenaries are inside the house, now."

"They're inside my *house*?" she shrieked.

"Keep your voice down, ma'am—and yes, they're inside. I want you to go up to the attic and wait for us. We'll let you know when it's safe."

"When it's *safe*?"

"Yes, when it's—"

"This is my house! I'm not going anywhere! Give me another gun!"

"Oh for the love of . . . *no,* Mrs. Lincoln."

Downstairs it was heating up, getting louder. He heard footsteps coming up the stairs, running. He couldn't tell who they belonged to. He told her, "Stay here!" but she followed right behind him.

For a moment, he seriously considered tying her up and sticking her in a closet, if only to get her out of his way.

No. There wasn't time.

A large shadow loomed at the top of the stairs. Before he could demand that the shadow identify itself, a shot from below caught it in the back. It threw up its hands and fell backwards, tumbling down to the first floor like a rock down a fall.

"Wellers!" Gideon hollered.

"Right here," said a voice from below. "That was close, eh? How are the ladies?"

Mary yelled, "We are just fine. *Just fine,* do you hear me, Dr. Wellers?"

"Gideon," Wellers called, with a note of concern creeping into his voice. "It's getting hot down here."

"I know. I'm about to put her upstairs."

"You aren't putting me—"

Gideon grabbed Mary around the waist and threw her over his shoulder. "Ma'am, I do apologize, but you're getting out of the way if I have to toss you up in that attic *myself*."

"I'd like to see you try!" she yelled, beating her fists on his back.

"You are *watching* me try," he said, but when he reached the attic stairs, he collided with them, because he hadn't been able to detect them in the dark. "Polly," he called up. "You there?"

"Yes, Dr. Bardsley, sir."

"Incoming," he warned, and climbed up just far enough to push the wriggling Mrs. Lincoln up into the overhead space. Then he jumped down, grabbed the edge of the steps with his fingertips, and flung the door back up into place. Polly said something through the ceiling, but he didn't catch it, and he didn't have time to ask her to repeat it.

He banged his leg on an old sideboard, no doubt a priceless antique, then dragged the thing away from the wall to leave it blocking the top of the stairs. Wouldn't stop anyone, he knew, but it'd make a lot of noise and surprise the hell out of someone who happened onto it. Might even trip a body up. Maybe they'd get lucky and some damn fool would fall down and break his neck.

Gideon was of the very firm opinion that when men want to kill you, there's no such thing as fighting dirty.

Back down on the first floor, things were not improving.

He ran into Wellers, still lingering at the bottom of the stairs, his back to them—his gun aiming first at the front door, and then the west corridor, while Grant held down the spot at the front windows. Lincoln rolled out from the library, briefly confusing Gideon, who had last seen him leaving it.

Wellers explained before he could ask: "We've barricaded the east wing with a pair of cabinets. I couldn't have moved them on

my own, but that chair of his is tougher than it looks. I didn't realize we'd given him something with so much towing power."

"I'd forgotten. Never thought he'd use it."

"Now he's running ammunition back and forth, but we'll be
out of everything before long."

"At this rate, sooner than you think," Lincoln said, delivering
a box that looked frightfully empty. "This is the last of it. Where's
Mary? And Polly?"

"They're stowed in the attic. They ought to be safe, so long as
they stay quiet. They were out of bullets." Lincoln gave Gideon
a quiet stare he couldn't quite read in the darkness of the foyer,
even by the light of the last of the parlor embers. So he added, "It
was the best I could do, sir. Considering."

"Considering, yes. Let us pray it's enough. Though if we're
relying on Mary to stay quiet . . ."

From his position at the front of the house, Grant hissed, "They
can't have too many men left. I saw three go scampering into the
trees like frightened rabbits, and we've killed more than a handful. They've stopped making requests and demands, and now
they're only sneaking. We've held the fort, men."

"But how much longer can we hold it?"

"The rest of the night?" the president guessed. "Listen, do
you hear that? They've stopped shooting."

He was right, but no one relaxed. They clustered together, three
men standing and one sitting, listening for the next wave of peril.

"This is your last chance!" cried someone outside. "Give us
Nelson Wellers and the negro, or we're coming inside!"

Gideon scowled, partly because they'd figured out he was present, and partly because they hadn't even bothered with his name.

Grant shouted in return, "No, it's *your* last chance! You've
already tried to come inside, and what's it got you? Half a dozen
dead men and nowhere!"

For a full minute, no one responded from outside. Then, just when the men inside had begun to hope they wouldn't hear anything more: "We have more men on the way! You won't survive until dawn!"

At that point, it might have gotten strange. Tense conversations might've occurred within, as the men in the Lincoln compound admitted that the men outside were probably right.

But instead, a new voice entered the conversation.

A loud one, projected mechanically from somewhere above, higher than the roof and with greater force than anyone below it: "*On the contrary!*"

A brilliant white beam of light shot down into the front lawn, illuminating everything a hundred feet around with such blinding vividness that even the men inside averted their eyes.

Gideon's adjusted first. He held up his arm and squinted, coming closer to the broken windows covered by shredded blankets that barely served as any cover at all, anymore. He stood to the side and narrowed his eyes.

The column of light blasted down from something black and massive above the house—something that hovered with a rumble and the hiss of hydrogen. He saw no details, no refined lines of anything outside the ferocious column, which then began to move.

The light pivoted, swung, and swayed, strafing the tree line and revealing three men with their faces covered . . . and now their eyes covered, too, as they slunk away, seeking cover from the all-knowing beam. The light shifted again, passing over the lawn to reveal bodies, some unmoving and some still twitching. It ran the length of the drive and chased two more men into a ditch; they scrambled up the other side and fled.

And from the great light the voice came again. *"We can see you! We will shoot every last one of you sons of bitches, and we'll enjoy it! You have until the count of ten exactly to be clear of these premises—and then we open fire!"*

It was a big voice, even without the electrical amplification. Gideon could tell it belonged to a big man. But that wasn't what surprised him. What surprised him was the fact that the speaker was almost certainly another colored man—though this man's voice had slightly different inflections from his own, so he was probably not from Alabama. He wracked his working knowledge of Southern accents, trying to place it. Not Louisiana, not Mississippi. Not a river man, this one. Not Tennessee; he'd learned that one well.

"Ten! Nine! Eight!"

The light showed motion in the trees, men departing as quickly and gracelessly as fleas leaping off a dog.

"Seven! Six! Five!"

There was a ratcheting sound, the drop and shift of something heavy, as the voice continued.

"You know . . . I never was a very patient man."

And then, without a further countdown, something preposterously huge opened fire.

It sprayed the woods with bullets that pierced trees and shattered saplings, raining down broken limbs and splinters from all angles. It blew great holes in the lawn, blasted pits into the drive, and left nothing but a crater where the lamppost used to be.

And, above it all, they could hear the sound of a big man laughing.

When the yard seemed clear and the driving pulse of the enormous gun had ground to a halt, an immense armored dirigible lowered itself toward the remains of the Lincolns' yard. A side panel opened—and an oversized harpoon appeared and was fired directly at the ground, smashing an awful hole in the lawn that Mary would surely complain about in the morning. But there it stuck, as firmly as any ship's anchor.

Beneath the craft a hatch opened, and then a set of stairs extended, much like the ones that led up into the attic.

Grant, Wellers, and Lincoln joined Gideon at the front door.

Lincoln said, "Pardon me, men." And he opened that door, wheeling himself forward onto the stoop. The others followed close behind but lingered together, scarcely breathing as they watched a bulky colored man in a Union-blue coat descend, every step a stomp, and every shift of his shoulders like the rolling of river rocks in motion.

Bald as an onion, the man was not young—closer to fifty than forty, Gideon guessed; and he had a scar across his cheek that must have come from some grievous old wound. But right now he was smiling from ear to ear, crinkling the scar and his eyes alike.

He opened his arms toward them and cried, "Gentlemen! I am Captain Croggon Beauregard Hainey, and I bring you the services of my ship and crew."

Gideon was taken aback. "Hainey? Of the Macon Madmen?" Well, that accounted for the accent.

Captain Hainey performed a little bow. "At your service! Are you the renowned doctor, Gideon Bardsley?"

"I am."

"Then it's a pleasure!" He came forward, hand extended, and vigorously shook Gideon's hand. "From one old criminal to a young one: I've heard great things about you—great things indeed!"

President Grant came forward and gave the next handshake. "I've heard many tales of the Macon Madmen. You're the last of them, aren't you?"

"So far as I know," the captain confirmed. "I was innocent of all those crimes, but I've since committed plenty I could be convicted for more fairly. Perhaps I can talk a pardon out of you before the sun comes up."

"You've got one whenever you want one," the president assured him. "That was some amazing shooting. What sort of gun is it?"

"Oh, that?" he said casually. "That's the Rattler. It's a Gatling conversion. I'll show it to you, if you like. But first . . ." He turned his attention to Lincoln.

Lincoln sat serenely, a peaceful and knowing expression on his face. "Do I have Kirby Troost to thank for your intervention?" he asked.

"You know Troost: The man's a miracle, but he can't be every place at once. So, yes, you owe it in part to that strange little fellow, and in part to those strange little ladies." He jerked a thumb back over his shoulder, where Mary and Polly were descending the dirigible steps with caution.

"Wait . . . how?" Gideon began to ask, and then he shouted to the women, "You're supposed to be in the attic!"

To which the captain said, "I found them on the roof, which is close enough. They flagged me down, and good on 'em for doing so! I wasn't sure I could find the place; there's not a ray of light anywhere for a mile. The weather's done a number on the District, taking the power and taps alike—but your missus was up there with a lantern, waving it around on the widow's walk like . . . like a little maniac," he grinned.

Nelson Wellers gasped. "Mrs. Lincoln, you could've been shot!"

"But I *wasn't!*" she hollered back. Then, in an ordinary voice, she said, "Thank you, young man," as a tall, slender negro with long, braided hair took her elbow and helped her down the last step.

"That's my engineer," Hainey told them, as the man saluted. "And the first mate's inside. Mr. Lincoln, I want you to know: It was *your* name that brought me here. I would've done it for the scientist, here . . . but *you* were the reason we came so fast. It took us twenty hours of wild flying through storms and darkness, and I don't mind telling you we're just about spent . . . but you were the man who said the truth the loudest, and made it law: You were the man who reminded the world that we are *free*."

Twenty-two

LEAD DEVELOPING RE HAYMES IN MISSOURI STOP
DETAILS TO COME STOP MAY NEED TO ARRANGE
TRAVEL ON SHORT NOTICE STOP UNTIL THEN
REMAIN IN DC WITH WELLERS STOP APINK

COURIER PACKAGE RECEIVED STOP ARRANGING MY
OWN TRANSPORT STOP DO NOT ASK FOR DETAILS
AND I WILL NOT INVOICE YOU STOP I WILL WANT A
VERY NICE COAT STOP PERHAPS ALSO AN EXPENSE
ACCOUNT STOP MB

IF THE RIDE IS FREE THE COAT IS YOURS STOP APINK

Twenty-three

Three Weeks Later

The National Republican.

VOL. XXI.—NO. 3.   WASHINGTON, D. C. TUESDAY MORNING   FIFTY CENTS PER MONTH.

FINALLY

To the west of St. Louis, Missouri, was a small outlying town known to few who did not live there. Ballwin, it was called, and it boasted little of interest—no major industry remaining, no famous hometown sons or daughters, not even a site of former military action. The only thing worth mentioning at all was that it seemed to be the only city named Ballwin on the entire continent, a point of trivia that Maria Boyd found a little pitiful.

But Maria knew something about the town that few others did, even those who lived there—who'd spent their lives within a ten-mile radius of the place.

Which was: At the edge of this town on the edge of a city on the edge of a river was a large compound built of brick and stone. It had begun its career as a foundry; and when the foundry closed it'd become a storehouse; and now that the storehouse had packed up and moved on, it hosted a factory that made very dangerous things under the direction of a very dangerous woman, who had thus far altogether escaped the justice she so richly deserved.

Katharine Haymes still roamed freely, which surprised no one who had any idea how money worked. Haymes had more money than any other woman in the freshly reunited country, so far as Maria knew. She might well have been one of the richest people in the world.

HAYMES AND SONS INDUSTRIES, read the sign over the gate, and the office that bore Haymes's name was empty when Maria carefully peered inside, a gun in one hand and something more unusual in the other.

Croggon Hainey had given it to her before he'd set her down in the woods outside, with a promise to pick her up again at dusk. He'd said she was going to need it.

He'd asked if she wanted help, or company, but she'd told him no. He was supposed to be going straight. It was *her* turn to be the pirate.

Even though she knew that the factory had been shut down—at least, officially—she hadn't expected it to be so empty, populated only with massive machines that hadn't been fired up for weeks. She hadn't anticipated that there would be no exterior lights, no workers, no guard dogs to keep trespassers like herself away.

She had not expected to feel like a ghost, haunting a place she'd never been.

In the rooms without windows, the factor was dark as a tomb, but only half as silent. The place pinged with stray drips of oil and settled with the creaks and groans of old floors holding heavy things; and the rooms echoed every small sound into a bigger one that said someone, somewhere, might be home after all.

Allan Pinkerton had provided Maria with architectural drawings, including schematics of the basement, which had received a great deal of restoration following a flood six years ago. The restoration details had been filed with the county, as is the way of such things; they had been stamped and approved by someone, somewhere, and left in a cabinet for a man like Mr. Pinkerton to find, once Maria had thought to ask about it.

As soon as she'd seen the schematics, Maria had known where Katharine Haymes was hiding. Oh, but there was no one there!, the policemen told her. The factory had been investigated!

But she doubted they'd gotten to the underground level, the expansively renovated basement with the unmarked entrance strategically hidden by an industrial vat that looked too heavy and too rusted in place to have serve as a *door*. Surely that wasn't the case. That would be ridiculous.

No, ridiculous would've been hoping for the architect to note the entrance in pencil before filing the work order away.

Maria praised God for ridiculous men.

She examined the vat, running her hands along its rough contours, its rivets, bands, and bolts. To one side she saw a scuff on the floor that gave a hint in which direction it may have been moved. She got a good grip and leaned against it with her shoulder and thigh. It moved aside with only the faintest scrape, much more easily and quietly than she would've expected.

And descending below the vat, she discovered a narrow set of stairs. At their bottom a dim light glowed, from a source that was either feeble or quite far away. She readied her gun again and put Croggon Hainey's gift inside her skirt pocket. It barely fit, but it nestled against her leg in a comforting fashion. In a way, it was more comforting than the gun.

Down the steps she went, slowly and carefully, letting her eyes adjust to the lessened light. It was the color of muddy water, and it showed her mostly shapes and angles, but little detail. She had an electric torch in her bag, but such things were hot and unreliable, and would only call attention to her presence.

And she didn't need it yet.

She'd committed the schematics to memory, so she knew where she was. Under the old storage room floor. Proceeding toward an open area beneath the center of the factory, partitioned off into sealed rooms that locked from the outside.

She passed a huge door that looked ready to be shut in case of emergency, capping off the entire wing and trapping any threat in place. The sort of thing that might be a safeguard against fire, though Maria knew better than to think that the door—or *doors,* for here was another one—were installed to save the building or protect its inhabitants. These doors were a safeguard against the weapons themselves, the very products that were being developed in the cavernous, secret place below.

She heard a weird, unsettling buzz from down there, no louder than a whisper. A faint, mechanical drone on a frequency so low that her ears could barely detect it. The timbre made her shudder; it sent shivers up and down her arms, though the underground level was almost too warm for her preference.

A clatter. A shuffling thump.

Maria held very still and listened. It came again, uneven and slow, the stuttering motion of something mindless that wanders.

The corridor ended in a T, offering her the option of proceeding left or right. Left would lead to a series of chambers that might be offices. Right would send her to an open area without cover, an unmarked space that looked to be a testing center.

Maria went left.

The hazy murk of light grew stronger, and soon she knew why: along one side of the hall, there was a series of doors with small, square windows fixed at face height. The rooms were lit from within, and what spilled out into the corridor gave plenty of illumination, none of it reassuring.

The dull thumping sound grew louder; it came from the second door. She stood on tiptoe to peek inside, and at first she saw nothing—only a yellowish fog too thick to scry. The fog wavered, swirled, and settled, disturbed by the movement of something ponderous and grim. She finally spied a shape at the far end of the smallish room: a figure like a man, but it didn't move like anything human, like anything alive.

Transfixed, Maria watched as it ambled and roamed, stumbling forward, toppling back, but never falling. Always catching itself, as if the last systems still working were the ones that kept it upright.

Then it saw her.

It pivoted, almost smoothly—and without a pause, without a hesitation of recognition, without any mindful awareness, it ran toward the door. If it knew anything, it knew only that Maria was on the other side of it, and that she was alive.

And it knew that it was hungry.

It slammed against the wood, flinging itself again and again at the barrier, as if by pure persistence it might bash its way through.

Maria recoiled in horror. When she was confident that the thing could not reach her, she stepped back to the window and forced herself to watch it. She took it all in: the smashed, bloody face with yellowed skin; those bulbous, jellylike eyes that made no true contact with her own—no understanding, no moment of knowing. The creature was naked. Its skin was loose and sagging; here and there, it split like an overripe tomato, revealing grayish tissue and oozing gelatinous pus.

The thing was lifeless, and yet it lived.

She shuddered, gagged, and turned around, closing her eyes

and opening them again, wanting to wipe the image away. But in the next room was another shambling ruin of skin and bones; and in the next room down, another pair of them.

Her stomach lurched, and lurched again as she proceeded, and the dim, golden light took on a weird, offensive odor halfway between sour well water and a sun-bloated corpse.

She hugged the far wall as she walked, confident that the doors were secure, but still wanting as much distance from them as she could muster. She hurried along, knowing that the hall opened up before long—and it did, and then there was more light, and another emergency door.

Maria leaned against this door as she paused to catch her breath. She noticed that it was treated with some waxy or rubbery substance, and around its edges were flaps to complete the seal.

A big picture formed in her mind. It was *horrific.*

On the other side of the fire door and at the end of a corridor was a room that looked like a laboratory. When Maria found a way inside, her suspicion was confirmed. It was filled with recording equipment—advanced cameras and electrical printing devices not altogether unlike the one attached to the Fiddlehead, which Gideon Bardsley had been kind enough to show her before she'd left the District. Freshly restored and churning out its facts and figures, the machine was a marvel once more. Now it occupied a new position on the first floor of the Jefferson building—in a jumbled room full of fumes and noise, papers and equipment.

But this room was white and clean, and so was everything inside it. This was an observation room, designed to observe in a clinical fashion whatever occurred in that central space.

From what felt like a place of relative safety, Maria looked outside the laboratory and observed vents near the ceiling, connected to a system of fans, tubes, and unmarked tanks. She noted a collection of detritus in a corner that might've been a pile of bones, or might've only been trash. Dark stains spread across the floor. She did her best to imagine that they were oil, grease, dyes, or anything other than the most likely fluid, though the stain drooled in runny streaks toward a drain in the center of the room.

While she watched, a light came on, revealing that yes, the stain was an incriminating shade of brownish red.

This light had all the cold brilliance of a surgical lamp. She briefly winced against it, but there was no time to close her eyes. Along with the light came the sound of footsteps—the determined, hasty sort of someone who had someplace to be. It was not the pace of a dead thing, but that didn't mean it was friendly.

Maria went to the observation room door and shut it. She was relieved to see that it locked from within, unlike the cells she'd passed before. She was furthermore glad to observe that it was sealed like the emergency door, for the safety of its occupants.

She returned to the window just in time to see Katharine Haymes arrive, stop, and stand beneath the brilliant overhead light. Their eyes met through the glass, and locked.

Haymes carried a carpetbag and was dressed for travel, in a smart brown suit and gloves. The bag was unfastened, as if there was one more thing she needed to stuff inside it before she was on her way. One last item she simply couldn't leave without.

Maria broke eye contact first, but only to look down at the console before her. Lying beside it was a short stack of files. She looked up again, and this time she smiled.

Haymes glared murderously at Maria. "Open that door," she said. Maria couldn't hear her, but she could read the woman's lips clearly enough.

She shook her head in response, and in doing so, she saw a button out of the corner of her eye. It was labeled, "Control Room Communication." She pressed it, and a small panel slid open, revealing a round black screen.

"Open the door!" Katharine said again, and this time Maria heard her. The little circle of mesh transmitted her voice quite well, passing along the enraged tone with perfect clarity.

"Oh, no, I don't think so."

Haymes stood stiffly, ramrod straight, as if she were so filled with anger that the smallest movement would cause her to shatter on the spot. "You don't know what you're doing. You don't know what you're playing with."

"I have an idea, thanks to you. This is where you did the rest of your research? After Tennessee, I mean," Maria asked coolly, gliding her fingers over the assorted buttons and making some guesses about what they did and did not do. "After you killed all those prisoners."

"I know what you mean. And yes, this is . . . my laboratory."

"You say that like you're some kind of scientist."

"I *am* some kind of scientist," Haymes objected.

Maria disagreed. "You paid people to do your dirty work."

"Who doesn't?"

"*Real* scientists," she countered. "Did they even know what they were doing? Or did you lie to them?"

"Eventually they knew. Some secrets are hard to keep." Haymes's grip on the carpetbag's handle tensed.

"By then, I suppose, they were in too deep to leave even if they wanted to. I understand that's your preferred method for keeping people in line."

"One of several. Now, open that door. I won't ask again."

"Good. Though if you mean that you'll come and open it yourself, I doubt that very much. I see there's a spot for a key," she said, glancing over at the door to make sure. "But there's a handy-dandy dead bolt, too. Very secure, this room. Practically a tiny, clean castle."

"Get out of there."

"No." Maria sighed heavily, with great dramatic effect. "I really *am* tired of saying that. So why don't you tell me where you're going? Or where you think you're going?"

"I'm leaving. And there's not much you can do about it from in *there*," Haymes said smugly. "You can keep me out, but that's the sum of it. I want the last of the research notes, but I don't *need* them."

"You're arguing awfully hard for something you don't need."

"I paid for them. They're mine, and they should come with me."

Maria took her time responding, as if considering the possibility and then discarding it. "It's funny . . . You set me up to say something clever, there. I ought to have replied that all of it—you included—would be coming with me instead. But I don't want to take you with me. I don't have to. In fact, the warrants for your apprehension read 'dead or alive'—did you know that?"

"No warrant reads that way."

"Not the usual kind, no. You were tried in absentia and found guilty, and sentenced to death. You must know *that*."

"So this is your plan? Bring me back to Washington to see my sentence carried out?"

"That's someone's plan. Maybe when I left the District that was my plan, but it's not anymore. If you ride with pirates, you get *ideas*."

"Ideas?" Haymes asked, raising an eyebrow as if she sensed an opportunity.

She sensed wrong.

"You see, over the last few weeks I feel like I've really . . . gotten to know you. Uncomfortably well, if you want the truth. And if I take you back to face justice, you'll only writhe loose, or buy your way free of it."

"You have great faith in me."

"Faith? Of a sort. I have faith in your bank accounts and your wiles. I have faith that you will absolutely do the most awful things necessary to have your way. I don't know how you became such a monster, and to be frank, I do not care." Maria's hand settled on a checklist beside a lever.

"Then why are we still talking? You're awfully chatty for someone who doesn't want information or conversation."

"Oh, you know. Just killing time while I figure out this . . . system."

The checklist read:

• Activate overhead light source.
• Close control room communication vents.
• Seal observation door.
• Close emergency doors.
• Pull to release gas.

A second checklist beside it read:

• Before exiting, close off gas.
• Turn on fans.
• Wait for window to clear.

Maria didn't know what it meant about the window clearing, but she understood everything else well enough to proceed.

"What are you doing?" Haymes asked, as Maria closed the communication portal, cutting off the last word. She said something else, but Maria didn't hear it.

"They'd hang you," she muttered, staring down at the controls and making sure she knew what came next. "Or shoot you. Either way, it's better than you deserve. This is more fitting, I think." She looked over at the door and saw that yes, it was sealed. She couldn't close the emergency doors from within the control room, but she had a feeling it wouldn't matter.

Katharine Haymes dropped the bag and ran to the window, hitting it with her fists. She shouted, but Maria couldn't hear her;

the glass was uncommonly thick. She wondered if even a bullet would break it. It was almost like the windscreens of a big airship, and maybe that's what it was. Something very similar, at least.

Haymes had thought of almost everything.

Maria pulled the lever. She pulled hard, and it drew down slowly. She did not hear the hiss of gas spilling through the tubes and out of the tanks, but she could see it: a yellow jet of air, puffing, curling, and falling to the floor like syrup.

Katharine Haymes stopped pounding on the glass. She took a step back away from it, collecting her composure as the room began to fill. Stoically she stood as the gas pooled at her feet, hiding her boots and the hem of her skirt. She remained there without budging as it crawled up her thighs, and covered her to her waist, then her breasts. Her breathing faltered, but she stayed strong, holding back the coughing fit that her body begged for until the last moments, when the poisonous air flowed down her throat.

Maria could still see her through the murky air, a shadow of a well-dressed woman, standing stock-still save for clenching and unclenching her fists, until she fell to her knees, then to her hands and knees.

Then to the floor, where she writhed and twisted.

And then stopped moving altogether.

When Maria had asked the Fiddlehead how many people would die from the gas, and how many would turn into shambling fiends, the machine told her that 70 percent would die but keep walking. Maybe Haymes was in that fortunate 30 percent who'd stop for good. Maybe she'd poke her head up again momentarily, as the noxious fumes tugged at her nervous system and puppeted her into cannibalism.

Either way, Maria had a gun. Hainey said she should shoot for the head.

And she had a mask. She pulled it out of her pocket and drew it over her face, exactly the way Hainey had showed her, making sure it fit without any gaps or leaks. "When it hurts to breathe, you know it's on right," he'd assured her. He should know. He'd worn them in Seattle.

The air she drew through the filters tasted like mildew and charcoal, but that was better than sulfur and blood.

She glanced out the window one last time. The image of Katharine Haymes wavered and wobbled as if it were surrounded by rainbows—distorted by the window itself. Ah, so that's what the note had meant. The glass didn't just protect observers, it detected the gas as well. The whole thing must be polarized, which must've cost a fortune.

But Katharine Haymes had a fortune.

Maria seized the research files and stashed them in her bag. She readied her gun, tested the mask one last time . . . and opened the control room door.

Twenty-four

"'It did not happen immediately, but it happened quickly in the wake of Katharine Haymes's death: Word was out. Word went even farther the next morning, when all of us—Abraham, Gideon, Nelson, and myself—exhausted to the bone yet thrilled to be alive, scattered to the four winds. We took the news wherever we went, threw it as far as our aim could reach.

"In the ensuing weeks, we found others reaching out from across the Mason-Dixon—reaching across a barrier that had once seemed insurmountable. The diminutive Confederate officer Sally Louisa Tompkins regained her standing and her credibility by force of will, and her voice amplified our message. Maria Boyd's voice did likewise, for although she belongs to neither North nor South, she speaks to both with equal authority. So, too, Gideon Bardsley, no longer a slave but a citizen, both of Alabama and the District. Outcast and hero, the inventor and scientist who created the machine that might save us all with its warnings.'"

Julia shook her head. "Dearest, no one talks like that. Least of all *you*."

"No, but people *write* like this. This is the language that 'keeps' the best."

"I wish you wouldn't bother. Sounds a bit forced to me, if you don't mind me saying so."

"I don't mind," he said, not taking his eyes off the papers he'd so meticulously written out by hand. They'd taken five months to compose, and they went off to the printer tomorrow. This was his last chance to read it before he committed indefinitely to the saga. "But if I wrote it as it happened, with all the swearing and sweating, no one would want to read it."

"Oh, but you're wrong about that," his wife murmured with a sly smile. She lounged in an overstuffed chair beside a cooling fire. "If anything, I think the readership might *blossom.*"

"No one wants to read about men being bored on trains, or swearing every day when the post comes."

"Or threatening to punch telegraph operators."

"That only happened the once. You may rest assured, I've left that part out."

She grinned, and she was beautiful. "More's the pity. Honestly, I can't believe you've written so much so quickly. Anyway, go on."

"'Those who had been silenced were heard, and although forces conspired to silence them once more, the truth grew larger than the lies—large enough to rise above them, and stand its ground. The undead leprosy was a threat to all. It cared nothing for the color of a man's uniform, or the state of his purse. It disregarded politics, age, and virtue. It came for all alike.

"It came for *us.*'"

"Oh, very *dramatic,* dear."

"But it *has* come for us, hasn't it? You've seen the measures we've taken—the measures we've been *forced* to take." He meant the quarantined quarters. He meant the pits dug at the far side of town, and filled with the remnants of the writhing corpses, killed again and burned, then buried.

"The war is over, and that's cause for celebration, isn't it? We're living at the beginning of a brave new age—a new era of cooperation against a common foe. But here you go, writing your memoirs like you're already living the epilogue."

"It *is* an epilogue of a sort," he said defensively. "The end of the conflict—the reunification of the United States of America."

"The ink on the treaty is scarcely dry, and here you go spilling more of it. You've earned some time to rest, and I wish you'd take it."

He shook his head and bit his tongue, not saying aloud what he suspected at the bottom of his heart: He did not have as much time as she thought. Something was wrong; he felt it when he swallowed, when he woke in the night after nightmares of hands clenched around his throat. He sensed it in the weight he'd lost, and in the weakness he felt upon standing.

Julia would've called it old age, but it was something else, something he'd shared with no one but the physician Nelson Wellers— who now visited him weekly, for a chat and some brandy. And for an examination, after Julia went to bed.

Wellers saw it, too, and had offered prescriptions and suggestions, but not much in the way of diagnosis or hope.

Perhaps months, perhaps years. Perhaps it was nothing at all, for in some respects the human body was as foreign a frontier as the moon, or the bottom of the ocean. But in truth, Grant did not expect to find medical treatment. He only wished to tell someone in confidence that he knew he was dying, and to have that secret kept so long as it needed keeping.

He had withdrawn his bid for the presidency, and forfeited the November election, even though word in the papers and on the taps suggested he'd win in a landslide, after the tale of his exploits at the Lincoln compound became public news. He was a hero again, the upstanding general of legend rising one last time to prove his mettle against treason and treachery.

The public ate it up, and if anything, this feather in his cap did more to spread the Fiddlehead's message than he cared to admit. He did not want their cheers, because he did not deserve them. He'd come around in the eleventh hour, in time to control the damage, but not prevent it. The fault was his. Not the credit.

If he hadn't been the president, he might've even been able to take action sooner. His authority had never come from his figurehead position, but on the strength of his tactics and his "great brass balls" . . . as the air pirate—and now formally pardoned free man of color—Croggon Hainey had so eloquently put it.

Grant was glad the office was finally someone else's problem. Now the freshly rebuilt United States rested in the hands of Rutherford B. Hayes, a lawyer from Ohio. A good man, by Grant's estimation. Their disagreements were relatively few and minor. Grant had high hopes that the country's restoration might be managed well and wisely now that the battlefields had fallen silent, the casualties were buried, and everyone lived under the same flag once again.

"Well," Julia said, drowsy with the warmth and the lateness of the hour. "It's a very exciting story, however you tell it. You've kept the ladies in it, haven't you? I mean, I know you mentioned them in passing—but I hope you recounted their troubles. They were no less brave than you."

"How could I tell the tale without them? They helped us save the Union, from opposite sides of the line."

"And I hope you've left in the bit about the pirates."

"The crew of the *Free Crow,* to be certain, and its captain—the last of the Macon Madmen. I left that part in, too, for the sake of *spice.*"

"He must've been little more than a child when the jailbreak happened." Then, as if it'd only just occurred to her, she blurted out, "And they were going to hang a child? How *barbaric.*"

"Hang him, shoot him. The particulars are lost to time and memory," he said vaguely, of the notorious incident of thirty-five years previous. Nine colored men convicted of arson and murder

on spurious evidence and sentenced to die. In prison, they re-
volted, escaped, and scattered to the four corners of the earth.
Only two were ever recaptured. Grant had drawn the story out of
Hainey over whiskey one night; they had traded war tales and
dirty jokes, and somber silences wherein their eyes did not meet.

"Quite a character, that one," Julia summed it up. "I'm glad
you pardoned him. And what of Troost?"

Grant shook his head. "He's still refusing his own pardon. For
one thing, he says he's guilty of enough that he doesn't deserve it.
For another, he doesn't want it. He likes his reputation in its tar-
nished state, and wouldn't have it any other way."

"Odd little man."

"Truer words were never spoken. I ought to have him arrested,
I suppose, but we all know that won't happen. The world is too
complicated a place; it has room for men with good hearts and
bad hands."

"I like that. You should put that into the book."

"No, he asked me not to. He asked me to leave him out of it
altogether. He prefers his anonymity, he said. I'm choosing to respect it."

"How kind of you."

He shrugged. Was it kind? Or was it merely convenient?

Kirby Troost had murdered a representative and fled, taking
up with a pirate crew and contributing to the havoc of the unincorporated West. But he'd also moved heaven and earth to send
help when he couldn't be there himself. He'd saved two presidents, a scientist (as well as that scientist's kidnapped family), a
doctor, an old lady, and a serving girl. And countless colored men
and women through the years, smuggling them up the railroad
lines and into safety. He was a hero, but a dangerous one. And in
the back of Grant's mind, he felt that it was simply easier to let the
man have his way.

In cooperation with former Confederate States, we created a task force to manage the encroaching threat of the guttersnipe lepers, the wheezers, the cankers, the Hungry, the zombis. They had many names, for they had found a foothold in many places. But by their sheer unlikelihood they had successfully remained a fearsome bedtime story long enough to grow their numbers and expand their menace.

By the time the Fiddlehead was heeded, it was almost too late.

I watched Hayes and Stephens sign the papers, while Gideon Bardsley stood stiffly beside me, and Abraham Lincoln sat next to us, confined to his marvelous chair. Maria Boyd was there, too, standing by Croggon Hainey and the crew of the *Free Crow,* for apparently they were acquainted already. (I never did learn how that odd, unlikely friendship came to be.) The marshal Henry Epperson joined them, having been released from the Robertson hospital in Virginia, where his care was managed by the renowned Sally Thompson. And Robert Lee's son was in attendance, for the great man himself had passed away three years previously.

Likewise, Jefferson Davis was there, looking tired. He looked like a man watching other men finish something he'd started, and he was neither happy nor unhappy—he barely looked present.

Desmond Fowler was not in attendance. He was in a grave, beyond the edge of Arlington, for I would not see him buried with the heroes. According to the doctors who examined him, he committed suicide after his involvement in the treachery that nearly ended us all was discovered. There was a note. I was never privy to its contents, but I do not care what he had to say for himself, if in fact the note was even real. If in fact the gun in his mouth was put there by his own hand, and no one else's.

I have my doubts.

It is possible that he was heartbroken when his puppet-mistress abandoned him, leaving him to face trial alone for the war crimes they perpetrated together.

But even as those of us who remained stood there and signed, holding our breaths for this momentous occasion—this moment in history—we heard unsettling scrapes from outside, the sound of ragged breaths being drawn through shredded lungs.

The courthouse was evacuated, and we finished the ceremony in the Capitol, on the steps of Congress. The taps lit up around the globe.

The world was watching.

"Good night, dear."

"Good night," Grant replied, turning his cheek for her to kiss on her way to bed. "I'll be up before long."

"Do you promise?"

"One drink, and no more."

"And one pipe," she chided.

"And one pipe," he confessed. "I'm restless, that's all."

She nodded, and kissed the top of his head. "The new routines have been difficult for everyone."

"You've adjusted easily enough."

"You know me—I've always been able to sleep through anything."

"Must be nice," he mumbled, reaching for his glass, then rising to fill it. "Some of us are not so lucky. Still, I'll join you soon."

She retired upstairs.

He was as good as his word. He put the bottle away when he'd finished pouring, and once his pipe was stuffed and lit, he put the tobacco pouch away as well.

One more drink. One more smoke.

The tobacco comforted him in a way the drinks did not, anymore. Once he had been delighted for the blurry feeling of brandy, or the wobbly pleasantness of whiskey. Now he needed his faculties too much to dull them, much as the temptation remained. His memoirs were nearly finished, and that was a relief—one project accomplished before he reached the end.

As for the rest . . .

He walked to the window and looked out over the stretch of grass behind his house, bright with floodlights that would blind him if he gazed straight into them. They were electric, designed by Bardsley and installed with haste at the same time as the fence—which was also electric. A powerful current ran its length, created by the noisy diesel generator that ran day and night. Anyone who touched the fence would surely fry, and notices to that effect were posted round its length. The host of warnings declared: FENCE IS ELECTRIFIED FOR THE OCCUPANTS' SAFETY. DO NOT TOUCH. These warnings were underscored by the Secret Service agents who patrolled in full body armor, night and day. Grant was getting used to them. He was even beginning to learn their names.

At the fence's far left corner, a bright burst of sparks announced the sizzling demise of something human-shaped, but no longer human. It shuddered and jerked, and collapsed into a smoking pile of flesh.

He closed the curtains and finished his pipe.

Then he left the remainder of his drink on the sideboard, and joined his wife in bed.